continued . . .

Highlander in Her Dreams

"Scottish charm, humor, and . . . hot romance."
—Night Owl Romance

"Sexy . . . imaginative . . . a fascinating mix of exciting action and passionate romance."
—Romance Reader at Heart

"[A] pleasing blend of wit, passion, and the paranormal . . . a steamy romance that packs emotional punch."
—Romance Reviews Today

"A fabulous mixture of magic and romance. Allie Mackay has penned an enchanting romance of lovers from different times . . . a captivating paranormal romance and a wonderful addition to a book lover's library."   —Fresh Fiction

"Cleverly plotted and well-written . . . a fun, sexy story."
—*Romantic Times*

Highlander in Her Bed

"[A] randy paranormal romance. . . . The premise is charming and innovative. . . . This novel definitely delivers a blast of Scottish steam."   —*Publishers Weekly*

"A yummy paranormal romp."
—*USA Today* bestselling author Angela Knight

"A delightful paranormal romance. The writing is poetic, compelling, and fun, and the story features an imaginative premise, crisp dialogue, and sexy characters whose narrative voices are both believable and memorable. HOT."
—*Romantic Times*

"A superb paranormal romance." —*Midwest Book Review*

"A sexy, humor-filled romance with delightfully amusing characters. Artfully blending past and present, *Highlander in Her Bed* is an entertaining read. Well-written. Readers will enjoy this one!"   —Fresh Fiction

"Appealing and amusing. Sizzles with passion."
—Romance Reviews Today

"A whimsical read that will have you panting from start to finish! Mackay knows what a Scottish romance novel needs and socks it to you! Red-hot sizzling chemistry ignites from the moment Sir Alex materializes in front of feisty Mara . . . a sure-bet bestseller."   —A Romance Review

ALSO BY ALLIE MACKAY

Must Love Kilts
Some Like It Kilted
Tall, Dark, and Kilted
Highlander in Her Dreams
Highlander in Her Bed

Haunted Warrior

Allie Mackay

A SIGNET ECLIPSE BOOK

SIGNET ECLIPSE
Published by New American Library, a division of
Penguin Group (USA) Inc., 375 Hudson Street,
New York, New York 10014, USA
Penguin Group (Canada), 90 Eglinton Avenue East, Suite 700, Toronto,
Ontario M4P 2Y3, Canada (a division of Pearson Penguin Canada Inc.)
Penguin Books Ltd., 80 Strand, London WC2R 0RL, England
Penguin Ireland, 25 St. Stephen's Green, Dublin 2,
Ireland (a division of Penguin Books Ltd.)
Penguin Group (Australia), 250 Camberwell Road, Camberwell, Victoria 3124,
Australia (a division of Pearson Australia Group Pty. Ltd.)
Penguin Books India Pvt. Ltd., 11 Community Centre, Panchsheel Park,
New Delhi - 110 017, India
Penguin Group (NZ), 67 Apollo Drive, Rosedale, Auckland 0632,
New Zealand (a division of Pearson New Zealand Ltd.)
Penguin Books (South Africa) (Pty.) Ltd., 24 Sturdee Avenue,
Rosebank, Johannesburg 2196, South Africa

Penguin Books Ltd., Registered Offices:
80 Strand, London WC2R 0RL, England

First published by Signet Eclipse, an imprint of New American Library,
a division of Penguin Group (USA) Inc.

ISBN 978-1-61793-471-1

For Griff, a mini dachshund with the heart of a Great Dane, the bravery of a Highland warrior, and enough charisma to rival a romance novel hero. He was Lily's canine protector and soul mate, the love of his mommy's life, and very dear to me as well.

I couldn't have loved him more if he'd been my own. He left this world much too soon, leaving us unprepared to say good-bye. Like Jock in this book, Griff was extraspecial, making all who knew him love him just a bit more. I know he's smiling and wagging his tail at us still, eager to run into our arms again. As Graeme and Jock will agree, it's only a matter of time. Until then, Griff, you're in our hearts!

ACKNOWLEDGMENTS

My books are always inspired by my great passion for Scotland. Home of my ancestors and land of my dreams, Scotland calls to me as nowhere else, and I visit as often as I can. To me, every inch of Scotland is magical. There's enchantment in ancient rock, blowing mist, and wild, windswept moors. And who wouldn't find wonder in the quiet places, awe in the huge seas and soaring granite precipices? Each time I return, I'm reminded anew that Scotland truly is a place like no other. Yet some places there, and the memories made in them, wrap themselves just a bit more soundly around my heart. When that happens, stories are born.

Haunted Warrior is set in one of these special places, beginning at Balmedie Beach, where I've enjoyed walking on chill autumn afternoons as Kendra does in the book's opening, and ending with a tiny fishing village on Scotland's northeastern coast that's exactly as I've described Pennard. The real Pennard shall remain unnamed because, like Graeme and Kendra, I believe its charm would be dimmed if it were "discovered." Luckily, the cliff road, which really is harrowing, and the frequent thick sea mist (haar) that rolls in to cloak the shore, help the village remain a near-inaccessible hidden gem. I hope that never changes.

For the curious, I once did spot a lone man atop the high dunes at Balmedie. As Graeme is doing when Kendra first sees him, the man I saw was looking out to the North Sea. He was tall, striking, and kilted. And he had an air about him as if he owned the strand. The word "guardian" struck me as I watched him. And as I did, he vanished before my eyes. Balmedie is known to be haunted. And it is true that many ships have met their doom in the rough seas there. I'll never know whom I saw on the dunes. But it was an unforgettable incident and also inspired another book of mine, *Highlander in Her Dreams*.

Concerning ghosts, they've always fascinated me. So much so that I've spent years traveling the UK with two like-minded friends, exploring haunted locations and enjoying extraordinary experiences. Like Kendra, I believe spirits are just people, too. Whether they haunt a country manor house, a castle, a medieval battlefield, a pub, or a ruined abbey, they should always be treated with respect.

I'd like to add that driving on the left isn't as bad as I make it seem in my books. But it does have its moments. Even so, it's the best way to see Scotland.

Three special women helped me through this book's writing. Roberta Brown, superagent and my dearest friend. She's my champion always. Thanks to Kerry Donovan, my talented editor, for her input and direction. Thanks, too, to my copy editor, Robin Catalano, for her skill and sharp eye. She makes copyedits a pleasure. Ladies, I'm appreciative.

Much love and appreciation to my very handsome husband, Manfred. Keeper of my stronghold, he fends off all trouble, not letting anything darken my days. I'm eternally grateful. As ever, my little Jack Russell, Em. He's the whole of my world and my greatest love. I hope he knows how much I love him.

"The dead don't come back to life. They never stop living."

— Kendra Chase, spirit negotiator for
  Ghostcatchers International;
  landscape historian for
  the rest of the world

The Beginning

Balmedie Beach, Northeast Scotland
A chill autumn afternoon, present day

She wasn't alone.

Kendra Chase, hardworking American from Bucks County, Pennsylvania, and a woman much in need of some private downtime, knew the instant someone intruded on the solitude of the wild and rugged North Sea strand she'd been walking along for the last two hours.

In that time, she hadn't seen a soul.

Now her skin tingled and the fine hairs on her nape lifted. Awareness flooded her, her entire body responding to the changed nuance of the air. The atmosphere was charging, turning crystalline as her senses sharpened. Everything looked polished, colors intensifying before her eyes. The deep red-gold of the sand glowed, as did the steely gray of the sea and even the crimson sky. The brilliance was blinding, and the chills slipped down her spine, warning that the changes weren't just a trick of the light.

Something other than the sinking Scottish sun was responsible.

Kendra took a long, calming breath. So much for surrounding herself with white light to block unwanted intrusions from the Other Side, though . . .

No ghost was causing the back of her neck to prickle. As one of the top spirit negotiators employed by Ghostcatchers International, she always knew when she was in the presence of the disembodied.

This was different.

And although she'd been assured by the desk clerk at her hotel that Balmedie Beach, with its high, grass-grown dunes and long, broad strand, was a safe place to walk, the teeming city of Aberdeen was close enough for some wacko to have also chosen this afternoon for a jaunt on the strand.

She doubted there were many ax murderers in Scotland, but every urban area had its thugs.

Yet she didn't actually feel any sense of menace.

Just something unusual.

And thanks to her work, she knew that the world was filled with things that were out of the ordinary.

Most people just weren't aware of it.

She was, every day of her life.

Just now she wanted only to be left alone. So she pulled her jacket tighter against the wind and kept walking. If she pretended not to notice whatever powerful *something* was altering the peaceful afternoon, she hoped she'd be granted the quiet time she really did deserve.

But with each forward step, the urge to turn around grew stronger.

She needed to see the source of her neck prickles.

Don't do it, Chase, her inner self protested, her natural defenses buzzing on high alert. But the more her heart raced, the slower she walked. Her palms were dampening and she could hear the roar of her blood in her ears. There was no choice, really. She had to know who—or what—was on the strand with her, affecting her so strongly.

"Oh, man . . ." She puffed her bangs off her forehead and tried to brace herself for anything.

Then she turned.

She saw the man at once. And everything about him made her breath catch. She blinked in surprise and astonishment, and a thread of alarm rose in her throat.

For a peace-shattering interloper, the man was magnificent.

No other word could describe him.

He stood on the high dunes a good way behind her, his gaze focused on the sea. Even now, he didn't glance in her direction. Yet his presence was powerful, claiming the strand as if by right.

Tall, imposing, and well built, he was kilted and appeared to be wearing a cloak that blew in the wind. Even at a distance, Kendra could tell that he had dark good looks. And—she swallowed—there was an air of ancient pride and power about him. So much so that she could easily imagine a long sword at his side.

He looked like the sword-carrying type of man.

Limned as he was against the setting sun, he might have been cast of shadows. But there could be no doubt that he was solid and real.

He was a true, flesh-and-blood man, no specter.

Yet . . .

Kendra's pulse quickened, her attention riveted by his magnetism. She pressed a hand to her breast, her eyes wide as she stared at him. The same wind that tore at his cloak also tossed his hair. A dark, shoulder-length mane that gleamed in the lowering sun and that he wore unbound, giving him a wickedly sexy look. His stance was pure alpha male. Bold, fearless, and uncompromisingly masculine. He could've been an avenging angel or some kind of sentry.

Whoever he was, he seemed more interested in the sea than a work-weary, couldn't-stop-staring American female.

And that was probably just as well, because even if she'd hoped to enjoy her one night in Aberdeen, she wasn't in Scotland as a tourist.

She was working and couldn't risk involvement.

Not that such a hunky Scotsman would give her the time of day if he did notice her.

She had on her old, comfortable, but terribly worn walking shoes. Her waxed jacket had also seen better days, however warm it kept her. And the wind had made a rat's nest of her hair, blowing the strands every which way until she was sure she looked frightful.

It was then that she noticed the man on the dune *was* looking at her.

His gaze was deep, knowing, and intense, meeting hers in a way that made her heart pound. The air between them seemed to crackle, his stare almost a physical touch. Her nerves rippled and swirled; fluttery warmth spread through the lowest part of her belly. Decidedly pleasurable, the sensation reminded her how long it'd been since she'd slept with a man.

Embarrassed, she hoped he couldn't tell.

She didn't do one-night stands.

But she felt the man's perusal in such an intimate way—how his gaze slid over her, lingering in places that stirred a reaction. He made her *want*, his slow-roaming assessment sluicing her with desire.

She tried to glance aside, pretending she hadn't stopped walking to stare at him. But she couldn't look away. Her eyes were beginning to burn because she wasn't even blinking.

Retreat wasn't an option.

Her legs refused to stir. Some strange, invisible connection sizzled between them, then wound around her like a lover's arms, shocking and sensuous. The sensation dried her mouth and weakened her knees, making it impossible for her to move as he took in everything about her, from her tangled hair to her scuffed-toed shoes. His gaze returned to her chest, hovering there as if he knew her bulky, all-weather jacket hid breasts she considered her best asset.

Kendra stood perfectly still, her heart knocking against her ribs.

He was scrutinizing her, she knew. Perhaps he was trying to seduce her with a stare. He had the looks and sex appeal to tempt any woman, if that was his plan. Before she could decide how to react to him, the wind picked up, the chill gusts buffeting her roughly and whipping her hair across her eyes.

"Agh." She swiped the strands from her face, blinking against the sting of windblown sand.

When the wind settled and her vision cleared, the man was gone.

The high dunes were empty.

And—somehow this didn't surprise her—the afternoon's odd clarity also had vanished.

Sure, the strand still stretched as endless as before, the red-gold sand almost garnet-colored where the surf rushed in, dampening the beach. The sea looked as angry as ever, the tossing gray waves white-crested and huge. Their roar filled the air, loud and thunderous. And the western sky still blazed scarlet, as vivid as before. But the sense of seeing through cut glass had faded.

"Good grief." Kendra shivered. Setting a hand to her brow, she scanned the long line of grass-covered dunes. Then she turned in a circle, eyeing the strand. The beach was just as deserted as it'd been since she'd started her walk. Nothing broke the emptiness except the scattered World War II bunkers half buried in the sand up ahead of her. Built, she'd heard, so men could watch for German U-boats. Now they were part of the strand's attraction.

A little bit of history, there for those interested.

The bunkers were also a reason she'd shielded herself before setting foot on the strand. Ever cautious, she'd taken a deep breath and tapped into the protective energy that dwelt at the center of everyone's soul. Thanks to her inherited sensitivity and her work experience, she knew how to summon such power. White light and a firm word declaring her wish for privacy usually kept spirits at bay. If any long-dead soldiers felt a need to hover around their old guard post, she didn't want to attract them. She was off duty, after all.

And it was clear that the kiltie from the dune had taken off, as well.

He was nowhere to be seen.

He must've headed away from the strand, disappearing across the wide marshland behind the dunes. There'd be a road out there somewhere, a place where he could've parked a car. Or maybe he'd gone to a nearby farmhouse where he just happened to live. Something like that could be the only explanation. He definitely hadn't been a ghost.

Sure of it, Kendra pushed him from her mind and made for the bunkers. She'd eat her packed lunch there — late, but necessary sustenance — and then head back the way she'd come. Until then, a brief rest would do her good.

She did enjoy solitude.

And the bunkers looked like an ideal spot to be alone.

But as she neared the first one, she saw that someone else had the same idea. A tall, ponytailed man leaned against the bunker's thick gray wall. Dressed in faded jeans and a black leather jacket, he could've been a tourist. But Kendra sensed that he was local. Arms folded and ankles crossed, he also looked very comfortable, like he wasn't planning on going anywhere soon.

Kendra's heart sank.

She'd so wanted just one day of peace. Her only wish had been a walk along an empty strand, soaking in the tranquillity and recovering from weeks of grueling work counseling ghosts at the sites of lost medieval villages in England.

Her energy was drained. The prospect of quietude had beckoned like a beacon.

Now even a beach reputed to be among Britain's wildest and least disturbed proved crowded. The man at the bunker might not be a throng, but he had enough presence to fill a football field.

Kendra bit her lip, wondering if she could slip past him unnoticed and walk on to the other bunkers farther down the strand. Before she could make her move, he pushed away from the wall and turned toward her. As he did, she felt the blood drain from her face.

He was the man from the dunes.

And he was coming right up to her, his strides long and easy, his dark gaze locked on hers.

"This is no place for a woman to walk alone." His voice held all the deep richness of Scotland, proving she'd tipped right that he was local. "Sandstorms have buried these bunkers within a few hours of blowing wind. The seas here are aye heavy, the surf rough and—"

"Who are you?" Kendra frowned, not missing that his

dark good looks were even more stunning up close. It didn't matter that he now wore his hair pulled back with a leather tie. The blue-black strands still shone with the same gleam that had caught her eye earlier. "Didn't I just see you on the dunes? Back there"—she glanced over her shoulder at the long line of dunes running the length of the strand—"no more than ten minutes ago?"

"I'm often on the dunes." A corner of his mouth lifted as he avoided her question. "And you're an American." His sexy Scottish burr deepened, as if he knew the rich, buttery tones would make her pulse leap. "A tourist come to visit bonnie Scotland, what?"

"Yes." Kendra's chin came up. Hunky or not, he didn't need to know her business here.

No one did.

She *was* interested in his business. Only Superman could change clothes so quickly.

"Weren't you in a kilt just a while ago?" She kept her chin raised, making sure he saw that she wasn't afraid and wouldn't back down.

"A kilt?" His smile spread, a dimple flashing in his cheek. Then he held out his leather-clad arms, glanced down at his jeans. "I do have one, aye. But as you see, I'm no' wearing it now."

Kendra saw how he was dressed. She also noted that his jacket hugged his shoulders, emphasizing their width. How his shirt made no secret that his chest was rock hard and muscled. Her gaze slipped lower—she couldn't help it—and then even the tips of her ears heated. Because, of course, his well-fitting jeans revealed that a certain manly part of him was also superbly endowed.

She took a deep breath, hoping he hadn't seen that she'd noticed.

"You did have one on." If she didn't know better,

she'd swear he was trying to spell her. Use his hot good looks to fuzz her mind. "A kilt, I mean."

"You're mistaken, lass." He lowered his arms, fixing her with the same intent gaze as he'd done from the dunes. "I've been here at the bunkers awhile, listening to the wind and keeping my peace."

Kendra felt her brow knit. "I know I saw you."

He stepped closer, his smile gone. "You could've seen anyone. And that's why I'll tell you again, this is no fine place for a woman alone. Youths from the city come here this time of the evening." He flicked a glance at the bunker's narrow, eerily black window slits. "They dare each other to crawl inside and stay there till the moon rises. Such lads drink their courage. They turn bold and reckless. If a bonnie lassie then happened along—"

"I'm not a lassie." Kendra wished he wasn't standing so close. His broad shoulders blocked out the strand and the bunker, narrowing her world to him. His scent was fatal. Heady and addictive, it invaded her senses, filling her mind with images that weren't good for her.

There was something terribly intoxicating about the blend of leather, brisk, cold air, and man.

Any moment she was going to blush like a flame.

She could feel the heat gearing up to burst onto her cheeks. A problem that escalated each time her gaze lit on his hands. They were large, long-fingered, and beautifully made. She couldn't help but wonder how they'd feel gliding over her naked skin.

She wasn't about to look at his mouth. One glance at his wickedly sensuous lips had been enough. It'd been so long since she'd been properly kissed.

This man would kiss like the devil, she knew.

And no man had ever affected her so fast, or with a mere glance.

He towered over her, his big, powerful body inches from hers. She could feel his warm breath on her face, teasing and tempting her. His nearness made her tingle. And his rich Scottish accent was melting her, wiping out every ounce of her good sense.

She never mixed work and pleasure. Early tomorrow morning she'd embark on one of the most important assignments of her Ghostcatcher career. She'd require all her skill and sensitivity to settle the disgruntled spirits of a soon-to-be-refurbished fishing village.

Souls needed her.

And she needed her wits. A good night's sleep, spent alone and without complications.

"So, you're no' a lassie, eh?" The Scotsman gave her a look that made her entire body heat.

"I'm an American." The excuse sounded ridiculous. "We don't have lassies."

"Then beautiful women." He touched her face, tucking a strand of hair behind her ear.

Kendra's pulse beat harder. Tiny shivers spilled through her, delicious and unsettling. "There are lots of gorgeous women in the States. Smart women who—"

"I meant you." He stepped back, his withdrawal chilling the air. "Those other women aren't here and dinnae matter. For whatever reason, you've found your way to Balmedie. It'd be a shame if aught happened to you here on your holiday."

"I can take care of myself." She could still feel the warmth of his touch. The side of her face tingled, recalling his caress. "I'm not afraid of youths and their pranks." She couldn't believe her voice was so calm. "As you said, I'm American. Our big cities have places I'd bet even you wouldn't go."

"Rowdy lads aren't the only dangers hereabouts." He glanced at the sea and then the dunes. Already higher than any dunes she'd ever seen, they now also looked menacing. Deep shadows were beginning to creep down their red-sanded slopes, and the wind-tossed marram grass on their crests rustled almost ominously.

"There are ruins here and there." He turned back to her, holding her gaze. "Shells of ancient castles set about the marshlands beyond the dunes. Many locals believe some of those tumbled walls hold more than rubble and weeds. Ghosts are said to walk there and no' all of them are benign."

Kendra bit back a smile. "Ghosts don't scare me."

Ghosts were her business.

And the discontented ones were, after all, her specialty.

"Then perhaps you haven't yet met a Scottish ghost?" The man's voice was low and deep, perfectly earnest. "They can be daunting. You wouldn't want to happen across one on a night of cold mist and rain, certainly not here at Balmedie in such dark weather."

"It isn't raining." Kendra felt the first icy drop as soon as the words left her mouth.

"If you hurry, you'll make it back to wherever you're staying before the storm breaks." His glance went past her, back toward the Donmouth estuary where she'd entered the strand. "I'd offer to drive you, but my car is probably farther away than your hotel."

"I don't need a ride." She wasn't about to get in a car with him, even if he had one close.

He was dangerous.

And he was also right about the weather. Looking round to follow his gaze, Kendra saw the thick, black clouds rolling in from the west. Dark, scudding mist already blew along the tops of the dunes, and the air was suddenly much colder. Even in the short space of her backward glance, rain began hissing down on the sand and water.

She'd be drenched in minutes.

And that was all the encouragement she needed to leave the beach. Ghosts didn't bother her at all. But the last thing she wanted was to catch a cold. So she pulled up her jacket hood and then turned around to bid the too-sexy-for-his-own-good Scotsman adieu.

Unfortunately, she couldn't.

He was gone.

"Hey! That's not funny." She went to the bunker, scrambling over fallen chunks of masonry to peer into the long, vertical slit of its window. Blackness and a whiff of stale air greeted her.

Total, empty silence.

Wherever the man had gone, he wasn't inside the bunker.

And—Kendra's jaw slipped as she looked up and down the strand—he also hadn't left any footprints. Not even where they'd stood just moments before.

"I'll be damned." Her astonishment was great.

Generally, only spirits could move without a visible trace. Yet she knew he wasn't a ghost. She had seen enough to know the difference. He'd been real, solid, and definitely red-blooded.

So what was he?

Burning to figure it out, Kendra clutched her jacket tighter and hurried down the strand. Scotland certainly was proving to be interesting.

And in ways she'd never expected.

Chapter 1

Pennard, a Seaside Hamlet
Scotland's Rugged North Coast
The next day . . .

"My time has come." Kendra Chase gripped the steering wheel of her small rental car and knew her end would greet her swiftly if she dared take her foot off the brake. Nothing but empty space opened before her. Fog blurred the horizon, but here at the top of a great, rocky promontory, the mist was thin enough for her to spot several colorful fishing boats chugging in on the incoming tide. They were surely headed for Pennard's little marina, a harbor said to be just across from her hotel, the Laughing Gull Inn.

Supposedly the only hotel in the village, it was also hailed as quaint and cozy. She'd been looking forward to a quiet night of cheery warmth before launching into her work.

Now . . .

She puffed her bangs off her brow with a breath.

It was almost a given that she wouldn't survive to spend her evening in the Laughing Gull's renowned pub restaurant, enjoying North Sea ambience, a corner table with a harbor view, and a fine fish supper.

Even if her work constituted talking with ghosts, driving willy-nilly over cliff edges wasn't in her repertoire.

Driving on the left was madness enough.

Braving heavy city traffic in Aberdeen was a nightmare she wanted to forget. Finding her way out of those clogged and busy streets had used up much of her fortitude. The admittedly scenic drive along Scotland's cliff-riddled northern coast proved much less harrowing. In fact, the sweeping sea-and-landscape view had taken her breath away. But it'd still been a relief to finally spot the signpost for her destination, the tiny fishing village of Pennard.

A charming, picturesque place she might never see in person because, much to her horror, the long road leading out to Pennard ended at the edge of a sheer bluff. To be fair, the road didn't exactly stop. It simply nipped over the edge of the bluff as if vanishing into thin air. The village wasn't spread along the top of a headland as she'd imagined. She couldn't see it at all, which meant Pennard hugged the base of the frightfully steep cliff.

And the only way to get there appeared to be the thread-thin, perpendicular road that hairpinned straight down to the sea.

Something inside her tightened and clenched. Nerves prickled, and it wouldn't have surprised her if her knees started trembling. If anyone could see her, she was sure they'd say she'd gone chalk white.

Somewhere a dog barked. And a strong gust of wind shook the car, the wind's power making sure she remembered hearing of hill walkers and even well-pitched camping tents, complete with occupants, being swept off Scottish cliffs. Unfortunates whirled through the air and then hurtled into the sea, never to be seen again.

She shuddered just imagining it.

Another blast of wind rocked the car, this time rattling the windows. Headlines flashed across her mind: AMERICAN WOMAN'S RENTAL CAR BLOWN OFF THE CLIFFS AT PENNARD, TOURIST AND VEHICLE SINKING BENEATH THE WAVES.

Her stomach knotted.

Much of the day had been rainy and chilly, leaving the road's surface wet and slick. Her car was small, a light-bodied economy model.

She had to get out of here.

Her heart rate went up. Her palms began to sweat. And the stress spot between her shoulders tensed and throbbed. But she wasn't able to loosen her white-knuckled hold on the steering wheel.

She did close her eyes and take a long, deep breath.

She was a strong, modern-day woman.

Things that would send many grown men running to their mothers didn't faze her at all. Zachary Walker, owner of Ghostcatchers International, frequently praised her cool head and unflinching nerves, often giving her assignments no one else would tackle. More than once, she'd faced down dark spirits who defined nastiness. Some had even followed her home on occasion, invading her personal space and bedeviling her with all kinds of annoyances. Yet she always banished them with the same ease she used to cut off pesky telephone solicitors.

But everyone had their limits.

Pennard appeared to be hers.

She couldn't help but think that Scotland's Past, the

historical restoration group responsible for her visit, might just have to hire a different spirit negotiator. According to Zack, the organization was presently starting a refurbishment project of the popular seaside hamlet, made famous when a low-budget Scottish nostalgia film used the village as a setting. Aptly titled *The Herring Fisher*, the movie gained cultlike fame, putting Pennard on the tourist map.

The Herring Fisher's heyday was decades ago, but the village's notoriety never faded. Hence the eagerness of Scotland's Past to make Pennard into the crown jewel of their historic sites: an entire seaside fishing hamlet preserved as a living history museum.

The village would become a place where the days of yore could be observed and experienced, the old ways never dying, but upheld for prosperity.

Scotland's Past had high hopes for Project Pennard.

Only problem was that all the comings and goings were causing the village spirits to stir. And, according to Zack, the discarnates weren't happy about seeing the home they still loved turned into a tourist attraction.

But Pennard's ghosts could be helped by one of Kendra's colleagues.

There were others with her abilities.

Wrong-sided driving on a suicidal goat track of a downward-plunging road was beyond her capability.

And, regrettably, her special stress remedy of surrounding herself with calming white light wasn't working just now. Either the spirit guides who usually helped her in uneasy times were on holiday, or—and she suspected this was the reason—her dread of driving left down a sheer rock face simply packed a greater punch.

"Oh, man . . ." Beads of moisture formed on her forehead. A similar nuisance droplet trickled between her breasts, quickly followed by another one.

And despite the afternoon's chill, the inside of her rental car felt hotter and stickier than if she were driving without AC through the worst heat of a Florida summer. Any moment she would suffocate.

Going forward wasn't an option.

Backing up . . .

It was a possibility. A glance in the rearview mirror showed no other car in sight. The road stretched narrow and straight, leading across empty moorland of heather and high grasses, the whole swathed by mist and scattered with groupings of boulders.

She needed only to avoid the verge. High grass hid the road's edges, but after such a rainy morning, they'd surely be soft and squishy. This wasn't a place to risk a wheel sinking into peat muck.

A shivery prickling at her nape warned that might happen.

She had to take the chance.

As carefully as she could, she began reversing. At first she let the car creep backward by the inch, then— becoming more daring—she covered a few feet, followed by a good couple yards. Turning would be too precarious. But unless another vehicle appeared, she'd eventually reach the main coastal road. She'd find the first place to pull over safely. Then, thanks to the five-hour time difference in Bucks County, Pennsylvania, and Ghostcatchers International headquarters, she'd call Zack, catching him at the beginning of his work day, before the office became too hectic.

Ghosts were popular these days.

And Ghostcatchers' phone and e-mail hopped with as many hopeful ghost-catching wannabes as with people needing their services.

Kendra shouldn't have allowed those reminders of work to enter her mind because . . .

She'd just felt the back left wheel dip and lurch as she edged along the verge. Thankfully, she righted the car before it tilted too badly. But the almost mishap made her anxious all over again.

The prickles at her nape also returned. And this time, ripples of awareness washed over her, the sensation familiar enough for her to slow to a crawl and scan the seemingly endless moorland that stretched away on both sides of the ribbon-thin road.

As her aura glowed much brighter than most people's, it was possible Pennard's spirit residents sensed her approach and were coming to greet her. The like happened often enough, though she'd rather not meet anyone just now. Corporeal or incorporeal, it didn't matter.

But the only thing stirring was wind in the heather. And, nearer the cliff edge, a handful of seabirds wheeled on the air currents. Beyond, the sea gleamed like beaten pewter, winking with choppy, white-crested waves until rolling mist blotted the view.

The returning fishing boats must've already reached Pennard's tiny harbor.

Not a soul—quite literally—was anywhere in sight.

But then a dog barked again. And this time he sounded close enough for her to hit the brakes sharply. Dread slammed into her, horror squeezing her chest.

She'd survive the shame of refusing an assignment.

But she'd never forgive herself if she hurt an animal, especially a dog.

Fortunately, she spotted the dog at once and he wasn't anywhere near her rental car, though he was headed her way. A frisky border collie, he was bounding gleefully along a coastal path she hadn't yet noticed because of the high grass and heather.

She did notice the tall, ponytailed man strolling oh, so casually behind the dog.

He was the sexy Scotsman from Balmedie Beach.

Shock raced through Kendra as she recognized him. Her body turned alternately hot and cold, her heart jolting as man and dog drew closer.

Now, as at Balmedie, he wore faded jeans and a black leather jacket. And what watery sun there was glinted in his raven black hair. No ghost, although there was still something about him. He had an air of power and presence no modern man possessed. As if her eyes were playing tricks on her, she saw a quick overlay of him, resplendent in a kilt, plaid blowing in the wind, and a huge, wicked-looking sword belted low on his hip. The blade had a jeweled hilt that caught the light. Then the image vanished, gone as if it'd never been.

His incredible aura remained, potent and compelling.

Kendra blinked to clear her eyes.

She was sure even at this distance that he'd locked gazes with her. It was also evident he wasn't pleased to see her. His stride quickened, turning purposeful. Clearly he was a man who'd make any woman weak in the knees, but just now reproach showed in every line of his beautifully made male body. He came toward her like a predator, his mouth set in a hard, determined line. The air between them sizzled, his displeasure as tangible as her racing pulse.

Still, flutters of pure appreciation curled deep in her most sensitive regions. Tingly warmth spread, igniting feelings she needed to squelch.

Before she could try, his dog leapt forward and bolted for her car. Coming fast, he almost flew the last few feet, not stopping until his muddied paws smeared her window and his friendly black-and-white face peered in at her. All lolling tongue and bright eyes, he stole her heart in an instant, even making her laugh.

The nightmare of driving on the left side of the road

and her fear of sheer rock faces receded, chased by the rascally dog's eagerness to meet her.

Until his master sprinted up to the car and his frown dashed her much-needed levity.

"Jock, down." He spoke firmly, taking the dog by the collar and pulling him off the car when he refused to obey. Undaunted, Jock broke away and lunged again at the window, this time slurping the glass.

Kendra opened the car door, getting out. "It's okay. Please—"

"He's a ruffian." The man reached for him again, but the dog bounded aside, circling them. "I'll clean your window in the village. Jock shouldn't—"

"It doesn't matter." Kendra gripped the car door as the wind almost knocked her down. Cold, damp air that smelled of the sea—tangy, invigorating, and oddly beckoning—surrounded her. Almost as if the very air called to her, challenging her to breathe it and not be captivated.

An elixir she'd always yearn for if she left now.

A ridiculous notion she shoved aside as Jock bumped against her, nudging her hand and eyeing her hopefully as if she had treats.

She glanced at the smeared window and then at Jock's master, who still looked furious. "I don't mind the smudges. I love dogs."

"Sit, laddie, and be still." The man ignored her and motioned to his dog, giving him a look. This time Jock stayed away from her. But he remained standing, his tail wagging happily.

Obviously, Jock had obedience issues.

His master . . .

Kendra suspected his dog was the only soul able to get the better of him. A law unto himself, he wouldn't allow others' rules to sway him. He breathed strength, a roguish self-assurance that was incredibly appealing.

He liked dogs.

That pulled weight with her.

Jock barked as if he knew and was pleased. Then he dropped onto his haunches and bobbed his head, giving her an enthusiastic canine grin.

"Your dog is friendly." Kendra met the man's eyes, letting her own imply the rest.

"And I am not?" He took the bait. His dark gaze measured her, his frown firmly in place. "I did pull Jock off your car."

"Dogs never bother me." Kendra stood straighter, hoping the wind would cool her flushed face and hide the film of moisture on her brow.

His mention of the rental car brought her frustrations spiraling right back to her. They hit her like a fist in the chest, bringing embarrassment, because he'd surely seen her snail-like reversal from the cliff edge. Knowing she was American and thinking her a tourist, he'd no doubt guessed the reason for her flight.

Americans were known to dread UK driving.

As a matter of pride, Kendra tossed back her hair and lifted her chin. "What does bother me is wondering what you're doing here."

"Walking Jock." He glanced at the dog. "We take the coastal path every afternoon."

"Yesterday you were in Aberdeen, at Balmedie Beach." Kendra expected him to deny it.

"I had business there." His honesty surprised her. The way he narrowed his eyes, looking her up and down, annoyed her. "You didn't say you were headed for Pennard. Not many tourists come here these days."

Kendra knew why.

Zack had told her Scotland's Past's initial refurbishment work was negatively impacting tourism. Visitors didn't generally like construction noise.

But she kept that knowledge to herself.

She also narrowed her eyes, following his inquisitive lead. "Not many people walk on sand without leaving footprints."

"Then you didn't listen to a word I told you." He didn't miss a beat. "The winds at Balmedie Beach are fierce. Gusts so strong they blow away tracks before your foot even touches the ground."

Kendra didn't buy his excuse. "The wind wasn't that strong last night."

"I say it was." A faint smile touched his lips, causing the dimple in his cheek to almost deepen.

The air between them crackled again and—as if at his bidding—the chill wind whipped around her, pushing her toward him, teasing her with his scent. It was the same mix of leather; cold, clean air; and man that she'd found so heady the night before.

She still did, and that made her defensive.

He was much too attractive.

And his soft, buttery rich burr proved why so many American women melted at the first hint of a Scottish accent. No man should have a voice so wickedly seductive.

It was an unfair advantage.

So she let her gaze flick over him, trying to appear unimpressed.

"Do you always share your opinions with strangers?" She lifted her chin, waiting.

For a moment he looked surprised, but then he smiled again. This time his dimple did flash. "Right enough—I do. And as you just spoke of the wind, we're quit, aye?

Besides"—he took a step closer, his gaze not leaving her face—"we aren't strangers. We met last night."

"I don't even know your name." His nearness made her pulse leap.

"I'm Graeme MacGrath." His burr deepened on the *r*'s, softening as if he'd just said something much more intimate than his name. "I have a cottage at the end of Harbour Street—the Keel." He glanced out over the rough seas, then back at her. "It's a wee place, but suits me well. My family has lived there for centuries.

"And you"—he reached to steady the car door when the wind strengthened—"are Kendra Chase, come to stay at the Laughing Gull Inn."

Kendra blinked, instantly suspicious. "How do you know my name?"

"If you weren't a tourist, you'd know." A corner of his mouth lifted as he stepped even closer, shielding her from the wind. "There are no secrets in small Scottish villages. Iain Garry, who owns the inn, mentioned you last night. Everyone in Pennard now knows an American is coming to see the famous setting of *The Herring Fisher.*"

"The film does make you want to visit Pennard." Kendra didn't correct his assumption. "I don't know anyone who's seen it and not fallen in love with the area. They really did make the scenery look spectacular."

"This coast *is* spectacular." His tone held pride, his gaze flicking over the moors. "But it's no place to visit now, in the autumn when the seas are in a rage and the haar spoils the views. Haar is mist, if you didn't know. Thick and sleety at times, it sweeps in from the sea to pulse across the land. You wouldn't want to be caught by it."

"I like wild weather." She did.

"Is that why you were backing away from the cliff?" He raised one black brow.

"I . . ." Kendra tucked her hair behind an ear. It was hard to think with him so close, his arm bracing the car door, caging her.

She could feel his warmth. And his jacket sleeve touched her shoulder, the contact sending ripples of sensation spilling through her. His scent flooded her senses, making her heart race.

She was sure he knew.

"I wasn't trying to leave Pennard." She wasn't about to admit her dread of left-side driving and perpendicular roads. "I thought I'd taken the wrong turnoff and wanted to check the signpost."

"You'd do best to drive on to Banff." He didn't believe her. "The coast road onward isn't too harrowing, and you'll like Banff fine. There's a lot to see. Duff House, with its art gallery and tearoom—"

"I came here to see Pennard." It wasn't a lie.

And her words made Graeme MacGrath's mouth tighten into a hard line. "Pennard is filled with workmen these days. No place for tourists."

Kendra straightened. "I'm not just any tourist." That, too, was the truth. "And I spent much of my life in Philadelphia. I'm used to jackhammers, street traffic, and all kinds of other noise I'm sure is much worse than a few workmen in a Scottish seaside hamlet."

Graeme frowned. "Pennard isn't just any Scottish hamlet." He tossed her argument back at her. "There are other fishing villages—"

"Maybe I'll decide for myself." Kendra couldn't stand overbearing men.

Worse—because it meant she'd now have to drive down the cliff road—she wasn't about to let this one tell her what to do.

She'd doomed herself.

Her entire body prickled with annoyance. "If you'll just be on your way, I'll be on mine."

His scowl deepened. "You'll never make it down Cliff Road."

"Of course I will." The very idea turned her knees to jelly.

"If you try to drive —" On the word *drive*, Jock bolted between them, leaping into the car. "Jock! Get out of there!" Graeme bent, reaching in after him, but the dog jumped into the backseat.

And it was clear he wasn't budging.

"Damn you, Jock." Graeme straightened, glaring through the window at his dog.

Jock grinned back at him, triumphant.

Kendra smiled, too, unable to help herself. "I'll drop him off at your cottage. The Keel, right?"

She started to get into the car, sure adrenaline would see her safely down the horrid road, but a firm grasp to her arm stopped her.

"Aye, it's the Keel, but you'll no' be driving there." Steering her around to the left side of the car, he opened the passenger's door and urged her into the seat, buckling her in before she could protest.

"I'll see you safely to the Laughing Gull and then" — he shot an angry look at Jock as he quickly circled the car and slid behind the wheel — "I'll take your car back to my cottage and wash it for you, inside and out."

In the back, Jock barked and rested a muddy paw on the console.

Then, before Kendra had time to be afraid, Graeme started the engine and expertly drove them right over the cliff edge and onto the plunging, ribbonlike road that led down into the village.

It was all Kendra could do not to close her eyes.

Pride alone kept them open.

Impossibly tight, the road was even worse than she'd imagined, zigzagging steeply between the high stone walls of houses hewn right out of the bluff. A jumble of slate and red pan-tiled roofs rose like stepladders right to the water's edge, where a single row of whitewashed cottages looked across the road to a sliver of pebbled beach and the choppy, foam-crested waves of Pennard Bay.

The little harbor with its stone pier, sea defenses, and fishing boats dominated the east end of the hamlet. And high above the marina, as if keeping guard, a large white house claimed a perch halfway up the far bluff. Low mist drifted round the house's walls, but Kendra could see the glint of picture windows and the soft gleam of lights behind them. The house would have commanding views, and was clearly someone's pride. Smoke rose from its chimney, the blue of peat smoke standing out against the gray fog.

"Thon's the Spindrift, owned by one Gavin Ramsay." Graeme glanced at her as he drove slowly along the narrow waterfront road. "You'll no' be wanting to go up there. The road's private and the bluff footpath is steeper than the way we just came down."

Kendra leaned forward, craning her neck to get a better view of the house. Graeme's tone told her that his warning had more to do with Gavin Ramsay, the homeowner, than the way to his door.

"You don't like Ramsay?" She looked again at Graeme, not missing the tightness of his jaw.

"I didn't say that." His face turned even stonier.

From the backseat, Jock thrust his head between them, breaking the tension. When he tried to push forward, joining them in the front, Graeme took one hand off the wheel to thrust him back.

"Jock knows we're here." He pulled to the edge of the road, stopping the car near the marina.

Directly across from them, the two-story inn, white-washed like Pennard's cottages, waited, gable end to the street. Large black lettering above the black-painted door announced the building was the Laughing Gull Inn. The windows were also black rimmed, giving the hotel a distinctive look. Thin blue smoke rose from two pipe-stack chimneys, letting visitors know a lit fire waited within.

Several doors down, a cottage with vacant, curtain-less windows caught her eye. Scaffolding covered one side of the whitewashed house. An empty paint bucket stood on the door stoop. Kendra's nape prickled. Even in the car, she could sense stirrings there, a restless aura about the house. A dark energy lurked within the empty walls, perhaps a lesser entity, not even a human spirit.

Whatever it was, the energy knew she'd arrived. She could feel it watching her, waiting.

Not wanting Graeme to notice—she suspected he would if she looked too long at the deserted house—she reached for her shoulder bag and unlatched her seat belt.

The house would be her first stop on this assignment.

Just now, she was still a tourist.

As if he agreed, Jock squirmed, bumping the back of her seat.

"Jock likes the inn?" Kendra could see he did.

Graeme shot a glance at the excited canine. "Iain keeps dog treats behind the bar. All the dogs between Fraser-burgh and Macduff know Garry's a pushover. He's why I walk Jock so often. If I didn't, Iain would make him fat."

"If dogs are welcome, then I've picked a good place to stay." Kendra let herself out of the car before Graeme could open the door for her.

"It's the only place to stay." Graeme stepped in the way when Jock tried to jump from the car. "Our one hotel and, with your arrival, it's full up. Scotland's Past's work crews occupy every room and have also let what beds any enterprising locals deigned to offer them."

"Scotland's Past?" Kendra pretended not to have heard of the restoration trust.

"Aye, them and no other." Graeme's voice held scorn. "They're the lot responsible for such placards." He gestured to a red phone box near the marina where a homemade poster declared STOP PROJECT PENNARD in bold black letters. "They want to buy out the locals and turn the village into the eighteenth-century fishing hub of its heyday.

"People here aren't happy." He closed the passenger's door, ignoring Jock's unhappy face pressed against the window glass. "Money can't replace tradition. A new house somewhere else might be more spacious and have better plumbing and no crooked floors, but it wouldn't be the house where your father and grandfather and his father before him lived, worked, and breathed their last."

"Oh." A coil of guilt curled in Kendra's middle. Put that way, Scotland's Past lost sympathy with her. She glanced at the empty house's construction trappings, noting that whatever had been there was now gone. "I didn't realize that was going on here."

She hadn't.

She'd assumed the villagers were ecstatic about Scotland's Past's interest.

No one had told her people would lose homes.

"It's no' your problem." Graeme was already on the other side of the car, the driver's door open a crack. "Iain will see to you. And I'll return your car after I've rid it of Jock's mud tracks."

"Thank you, but I really didn't mind." She hadn't, and the truth was she wished he'd gone straight to his cottage so she could've helped clean the rental car and spent more time with him and his dog.

And that was the last thing she needed to be doing.

She was here to work.

Graeme MacGrath had the potential to be a huge distraction.

Thoughts of him—the kind of thoughts she shouldn't be having—already filled her mind, making her pulse quicken and her long-neglected sex drive waken with bells on. One glance from his dark, thick-lashed eyes sent sensation tripping along her nerves. His dimple was a deadly weapon, capable of undoing her composure in a single flashing smile. His presence was intense, charging the air and making her almost wish he'd kiss her.

No man had ever affected her so swiftly or so powerfully.

And that wasn't good.

Pennard's spirits needed her. Now more than ever, since she'd learned more about the village's troubles. Zack had mentioned only disgruntled souls upset about restoration work. Construction chaos often irritated those who preferred eternal peace. Yet she'd felt something more than a riled ghost in the empty house.

The spirits' annoyances could be drawing in darker, more dangerous energies.

If so, she'd soon have her hands full.

But Graeme couldn't know that. Every assignment she took on swore her to confidentiality. Getting involved with a local would not just lead to the inevitable heartbreak of a "holiday romance," but also imperil her job. So she forced a bright smile and lifted her hand to wave, only to lower it as quickly, because he'd already driven away. Somehow he'd turned the car and managed to get halfway down the harbor road before she'd realized he was gone.

Kendra frowned, looking after him as the car's red taillights disappeared into the mist.

There really was something about him....

And it had to do with more than his dark good looks and Scottish accent.

But before she could decide just what it was, she took a moment to see if she could sense any of Pennard's other residents—the disembodied ones who hadn't yet shown themselves, but would soon become aware of her presence and come looking for her.

A few locals *had* noticed her.

She saw the signs in her peripheral vision: lace curtains twitching at windows as curious eyes peered out at her as she stood beside the marina's stone slipway. And they looked even harder as she started across the road toward the Laughing Gull Inn's black-painted door.

Kendra knew the curtain twitching would stop if she returned the stares.

So she didn't, minding her business as she always did.

But with each step she took, she felt something that disturbed her. And it had nothing to do with village gossips or the poor, disembodied souls she soon hoped to meet.

It was Pennard.

A sense of darkness reflected on the sea and along the pebbly, wave-swept shore. Whatever it was, its shadow was etched in the stones here. Even the fine mist beading cottage windows held tinges of mystery. And strange echoes hid in the roar of the sea wind.

Something much more troubling than disgruntled discarnates was wrong here.

Kendra knew who'd have answers.

She just hoped questioning Graeme wouldn't stir up problems of a different sort. The way her blood quickened in anticipation of seeing him again warned that she was swimming in dangerous waters.

And the undertow was already pulling her in.

Chapter 2

"This is your fault, laddie."

Graeme MacGrath, lifelong resident of Pennard, scowled at his dog, Jock, as he bent to dip a sponge into a bucket of soapy water. His frown turned even blacker when a curtain of sea spray flew over the wall of a nearby breakwater, dousing him and the small blue rental car he was presently washing.

The spray didn't reach Jock, sprawled as he was on the Keel's door stoop.

And the dog's smug expression said he felt his master deserved the brine shower.

"If it weren't for you"—Graeme circled the sponge over the car's driver's-side window—"thon American lassie would be halfway to Banff by now. She'd spend the night in a posh tourist hotel and take tea at Duff House on the morrow. She wouldn't be here where her like has no business."

Jock shifted on the stoop, clearly settling down for a nap in the afternoon's cold sunlight.

It was a favorite trick—feigning sleep when he wished to wriggle out of an argument.

"She isn't an ordinary tourist." Graeme dipped his sponge in the bucket again, sure of his statement. He'd seen the sheen of her aura at Balmedie. It'd been what first caught his attention when he'd seen her from the dunes. And this afternoon, up on the bluff, the light halo surrounding her glowed like the sun, almost blinding him.

She was likely unaware.

Most people didn't even know they had auras.

Unfortunately, he wasn't the only soul in Pennard who understood such things. Feeling bile rise in his throat, Graeme shot a glare at the Spindrift, high above the far end of the village. If his nemesis, Gavin Ramsay, spotted her, he'd know in a beat that she was exceptional. Like Graeme, he'd recognize her as so much more than a sexy, desirable woman with a fetching American drawl.

And that meant . . .

"We'll have to look out for her, Jock." Graeme glanced again at his dog.

He wasn't surprised when the sneaky beast's lip lifted in Jock's version of a self-satisfied smile.

"Better yet"—Graeme returned to car washing—"we'll have to make sure she leaves Pennard quickly."

Jock rolled over, showing Graeme his back.

Fluting canine snores soon filled the air, joining the whistle of the wind and the splash of waves on the stone of the breakwater.

Graeme knew he'd lost a battle.

Jock always won.

Not that Graeme minded. Far from it; knowing the dog was happy was one of the high points of his life. He doubted he could tolerate certain things without Jock.

But Kendra Chase's arrival had soured his day. He just hoped Jock's badgering for a second afternoon cliff walk hadn't had anything to do with the lovely American.

If so . . .

He tightened his grip on the sponge and threw another glance at the dog.

Jock's snores grew louder.

Any further glares were pointless. Jock played the game well and wouldn't stir until hunger disturbed him. Now as always, Jock's appreciation of food would prove greater than his wish to irritate his master with make-believe slumber.

So Graeme pretended, as well, acting as if the snores didn't faze him.

He did look down the narrow street where rolling mist slid past the Laughing Gull. Thicker now, the sea haar drifted in from the bay, blotting the inn and other cottages from view. Wind brought the cold, damp smell of rain and the sun vanished again, slipping behind clouds to leave Pennard in the usual gray tones of autumn.

Graeme frowned and grabbed the hose, washing soap foam from Kendra Chase's hired car. A vehicle she clearly had no business trying to drive. Although her walking about Pennard in such dense, enveloping mist as was now gathering proved a much worse prospect.

So much in the tiny fishing hamlet wasn't as it seemed.

Pennard wasn't just a tightly knit community bound together by ages of raw weather, hardship, and the sea. Nor was the village's reality anything like the picture-postcard quaintness so loved in recent times by the hordes of camera-packing summer tourists eager for a taste of briny wind, fresh seafood, and a good dose of *Herring Fisher* nostalgia.

Such visitors enjoyed experiencing the feel of bygone eras without the modern world's hectic pace and stress.

Others came to trace their ancestral roots, their interest sparked by *Braveheart* and the popularity in America of certain Scottish actors.

They hoped to find a simpler time in Pennard.

But those days were gone.

The erstwhile herring fleet had long been usurped by a handful of small fishing craft and, in season, the pleasure boats hoping to take visitors to see seals, dolphins, and the still-impressive coastal views.

Other things also remained.

More than dark and mist curled around the stone cottages come nightfall. Just as foaming swells weren't all that crashed against the breakwaters. And curious old women weren't always responsible for the twitching edges of curtains when a stranger passed by.

Pennard held dangerous secrets.

And his was the most damning of all.

Scowling again, Graeme snatched a dry cloth and began polishing the driver's door of the car, scrubbing with a vengeance.

It scarce mattered that his burden was a noble one.

Keeping Pennard and its residents safe was a legacy his family had carried for centuries. Their status and title as Guardians of the Shadow Wand, a timeless relic entrusted to their care with all the honor's attendant requirements, had altered his life.

And duty alone was the reason he'd return the American lassie's car by parking it outside the Laughing Gull. He'd leave the key with Iain rather than inviting her for a walk along the shore, followed by an offer to cook dinner for her. He wouldn't regret not treating her to a romantic Scottish evening before his peat fire.

Women, as far as he could recall, enjoyed snuggling before the hearth on chill, damp nights when the mist pressed against the windows. The occasional call of a foghorn or the sound of the sea running out beyond the arm of the harbor didn't hurt, either.

Suchlike made a woman lean into a man, welcoming his strong embrace.

And Kendra Chase was a woman he wouldn't mind pulling into his arms. Lithe and shapely, she had the kind of well-made curves that would fill a man's arms nicely, warming him on the fiercest winter night. He liked her shining blond hair, cut at her chin. The first time she'd turned her gaze on him when he was on the dunes at Balmedie, her large blue eyes captivated him, instantly heating his blood.

But it was how those sparkling sapphire eyes had widened, then softened with understanding when he'd told her what Scotland's Past's plans would do to the locals, that sealed it for him.

She might be an outsider, a tourist from a world and culture he couldn't begin to comprehend and also didn't care to, but she clearly appreciated the importance of heritage and pride in one's birthplace.

Her spirit also drew him. She would've driven down Cliff Road simply to prove to him that she could, even though dread had been written all over her face.

Instinct told him she'd respond if he pursued her. He burned to do so. To bring her here to the Keel for just this one night. An indulgence he shouldn't allow himself, especially not with her, yet the prospect proved almost irresistible. Even the thought of standing behind her, holding her arms lightly and bending his head to give her a simple neck nuzzle, set his pulse to roaring.

If he restrained himself, it might be possible to just enjoy her company.

A few kisses and . . .

He cursed and tossed the drying towel onto the bench beside his cottage's blue-painted door.

If Kendra Chase came anywhere near him again, he'd want more than kisses from her.

He already did.

He also felt a chill sweep the back of his neck in the same moment that Jock sprang to his feet and leapt off the door stoop. Not feigning sleep now, the dog snarled, hackles rising. Then he shot around the corner, making for the shed at the back of the cottage.

"Jock, wait!" Graeme sprinted after him, wishing as so many times before that his dog was less bold.

Canine heroics led to heartache.

Running faster, Graeme raced down the muddy path alongside the house, nipping around Jock just before the dog could launch himself at the spike-haired youth who stood frozen before the shed door.

He was Ritchie Watt, local ne'er-do-well.

And he'd been trying to break into the shed.

Jock froze, as well. But he shook with menace, his growls reverberating low in his chest.

"Inside, Jock." Graeme jerked his head toward the front of the cottage, fixing the dog with a look he used only on rare occasions. "Away with you now, and dinnae be coming back out here."

Jock didn't meet his eye, his unblinking stare pinned on the white-faced youth. But when Graeme angled his head, putting all his will into a silent command, the dog gave one last snarl and then trotted back down the path, disappearing around the front corner.

Graeme released the breath he'd been holding.

Ritchie Watt was good with a gutting knife and he held one in his hand now. It was the blade he'd been using to try and pry open the shed door. And the glazed look in his dark-circled eyes left no doubt that if Jock had sprung on him, he would've used the knife.

"Drop your blade, lad." Graeme started toward him,

hoping the boy didn't do anything foolish. "You dinnae want me to take it from you."

"I'll drop it in a pig's eye." Ritchie made a dash for the rock face rising steeply behind the shed. The knife fell from his hand as he flung himself at the cliff, scrambling for a foothold.

"You're no' going anywhere." Graeme reached him in three easy strides. He plucked the ruffian off the rocks, thrusting him back against the shed. "And you wouldn't have made it into my shed if you tried for a hundred years. You know that, I'm thinking?"

Ritchie gave him a surly look rather than answer.

"There's naught but old salt barrels in there." The thought that Gavin Ramsay would send a lackey to invade his shed, prying into one of the few things he cherished as a semblance of normalcy in his life, stoked a fury Graeme didn't want to unleash on a misguided lad like Ritchie Watt. "They're from o'er two hundred years ago, when the herring fleets crowded this wee harbor.

"Thon barrels"—he leaned in, anger giving an edge to his voice—"were once packed with *silver darlings*, the herring that meant bread and living for Pennard and this whole coast in those days."

"I don't care about herring barrels." Ritchie's eyes glittered, his chin jutting defiantly.

"You should." Graeme glanced at the shed door and then at the youth. "I do, and my shed's full of them. Whole barrels, half barrels, and a few firkins, sweet little quarter barrels, if you've forgotten so much of this place's history, you dinnae ken what a firkin is.

"They're the salt barrels I restore and give out on loan to the Laughing Gull and anyone needing them for a ceilidh or other gathering." Graeme released the youth, letting a hard stare hold him in place.

"And there's nothing inside the barrels except air,

age, and a hint of brine." He stepped closer, bracing a fist against the shed wall next to Ritchie's head. "Tell that to Ramsay, and warn him that the next fool he sends to my house will suffer more than leaving here with his knife bent from prying into places it dinnae belong."

"My knife's not bent." Ritchie glared at him, his gaze flicking to the rock face where the herring knife had slipped from his fingers.

The muddy ground was empty.

Following his gaze, Graeme smiled. "Your blade's here." He held out the knife on his palm, watching the youth's eyes round as he snatched the bent-double weapon from Graeme's hand.

He suspected Ritchie knew he'd bent the blade.

Just as the lad now knew that the boundary spells Graeme kept around his property worked better than any dark magic Gavin Ramsay could conjure. It didn't matter that Ritchie and his like, or even the whole village, never dared voice such suspicions.

Worrying about his supposed powers was enough to keep them at bay.

At least, it had been until recently.

So he reached for the shed's door latch, lifting it with ease. "This shed is ne'er locked." It *was* sealed against evil. But that wasn't his point. "If e'er you feel a true interest in preserving old salt barrels, the door will open for you. I'll gladly teach you how to get the salt crust and grime off them and bring them back to their original beauty. Until that day comes . . ."

He let his voice trail away, piercing the youth with a look that said more than words.

"Off with you now." He gave the lad a light shove. "And tell Ramsay what I said. Then, if you've any sense, you'll say him good-bye."

His last words were lost, carried away by a quickening

wind as Ritchie tore down the path and disappeared onto Harbour Street. His running footsteps echoed through the evening as Graeme quietly closed the shed door. As always, he didn't lock it.

Nor was there a need.

The Shadow Wand wasn't kept inside Graeme's barrel shed. It was an unlikely reason for Ramsay to send the youth to peek about the shed. Ramsay wouldn't be so witless as to send a stripling like Watt to look for such a powerful relic.

More likely, Ramsay hoped to strike Graeme where it would hurt and must've ordered the lad to damage the salt barrels or roll a few of them into the sea.

Everyone knew Graeme loved the old barrels.

What they didn't know was that the cooper who'd made them had been a good friend of Graeme's.

But that was long ago.

Remembering made him start determinedly down his cottage's narrow side path. He'd been careless of late. Watching so diligently over Pennard and the coast, keeping out an eye for Ramsay's growing influence, caused him to lower his guard at the Keel.

Coming with ill intent, Ritchie shouldn't have been able to set foot onto Graeme's property. He should've been repelled at the street.

So Graeme did what he should have done weeks ago and collected a pail from beneath the blue-painted bench beside his door. Kept ready thanks to the moon-water that filled it—gathered rain regularly replenished and set out to catch the moon's silvery glow—the pail felt light in his hand.

Lightness that proved the moonwater still held a good measure of power.

Not enough to keep Watt off the property, but it'd surely helped to prevent him from opening the shed door.

Still . . .

Stronger measures were required. The strengthening of Graeme's protective shields around the Keel needed immediate attention. Preferably without the interference of a certain border collie.

"You stay here." Graeme gave his dog a look. "I'll no' have you shadowing me."

Jock, now sitting on the stoop, lowered his head solemnly, as if in agreement.

Not trusting him, Graeme indicated the door, slightly ajar. "Away in with you, laddie. You've a fine, warm plaid before the fire and I'm no' of a mind to have an audience just now."

Jock didn't budge.

And Graeme didn't have the heart to scold him further.

He did reach to rub the dog's ears. Then he emptied the pail of its moonwater before crossing the road in front of his cottage. Harbour Street ended at the Keel, bounded by the high bluff at its back. Just beyond, a small cave marked Pennard Bay's western edge.

Little more than a gash in the rock, the cave wasn't large enough to hold the picnic table on the pebbly strand before its entrance. A relic from the filming of *The Herring Fisher*, the table was popular with tourists because the cave offered shelter from wind and spray.

Above all, its black-glistening walls couldn't be penetrated by curious eyes.

The cave, Graeme suspected, had been used by his like for centuries.

He certainly appreciated its positioning.

As, he was sure, had every MacGrath Guardian before him.

He headed that way now, already focusing on the task before him. Without looking back at Jock—a single glance over his shoulder would have the dog running to him—he left the road's end and stepped onto the strip of beach skirting the cave.

Strong wind hit him at once, sharp and smelling of seaweed and brine. Cold, bracing air, thick with salt and seasoned with peat smoke, to Graeme it was a blend headier than wine. Wet stones shifted and crunched beneath his feet, and spray splashed against the larger rocks at the water's edge. This was his world, and he gloried in the surge and swell of the sea, the wind and mist that he loved so much.

Sadly, Pennard's balance was bruised.

And it fell to him to keep the damage from worsening.

It was a burden he shouldered gladly.

Even so, his jaw tightened when he couldn't keep his gaze from straying to the high crags at the far end of the bay. The haar was thickening, hanging low over the water and cloaking the cliffs. But pinpricks of yellow light glimmered through the mist where Ramsay's Spindrift claimed a prominent ledge, the big house taunting and tormenting him. Just as the bastard's forebears had bedeviled every MacGrath Guardian down the ages.

A self-proclaimed entrepreneur—windbag and arse, to Graeme's mind—Ramsay's seemingly endless funds supposedly came from his family's involvement in the Aberdeen oil boom of the previous century.

Graeme suspected other origins.

Not that it mattered.

What did matter was that Ramsay had always shown an aptitude for noticing the supernatural. And now, of all times, a fetching American with an overbright aura had to visit Pennard.

Graeme's gut clenched at the ramifications.

Ramsay would seek to charm her, believing he could

manipulate her natural energy to aid his grasping, power-hungry schemes.

Graeme set down his pail and rolled his shoulders. He also flexed his fingers, shaking off all negative thoughts. He'd deal with Ramsay later. So far, the oily bastard was all glare and bluster. And only when he suspected no one but Graeme saw.

If he touched the American ...

Graeme closed his eyes, willing the thought from his mind before it could create an image. He wouldn't be putting his hands on her, either, much as he'd like to. He would look out for her as long as she lingered in Pennard, a visit he hoped would be of short duration.

And if he meant to do that, he needed to keep his wits. He couldn't be distracted by Ramsay's hooligans skulking about his property.

So he took a deep, cleansing breath and turned to the open sea. Closing his eyes, he stood with his legs apart and ground his feet firmly into the loose stones. That done, he raised his arms above his head, opening himself to the elemental energies he needed to balance his powers.

He allowed his hands to stretch for the sky, his fingers already tingling, as if he touched the heavens. His feet warmed, welcoming the connection to Mother Earth's heart, beating so deep beneath him. Awareness poured into him, strong and potent, a river of molten heat sweeping his body as the distance between the manifest and unseen world began to close. Only then did he center himself.

His eyes still shut, he delved deep into the earth's inner core for the intense white-light energy he needed. He summoned the same power from high above him, hardly breathing until he felt both energy sources flow together, surging and fusing inside him.

At last, he opened his eyes, fixing his gaze on the dark, rolling sea as he lowered his arms. As he'd done so often, he let the energy gather in his hands and then flow from his fingers to fill the little cave and the curving strip of shore.

With all the knowledge he possessed, he willed the summoned power to cleanse and neutralize any negative energy around him and his home.

This tiny corner of Pennard that was so needful of his protection.

Would that he could expand his boundary shields all up and down the coast. But even good energy could turn bad if sent out without permission.

It had to be enough to guard these shores.

The Keel . . .

There he could expend his fullest powers.

So he retrieved his pail and went to the sea's edge, collecting a bucketful of the energy-charged water. Slippery, weed-draped rocks where the swell washed ashore and clumps of the glistening wrack also littered the tide line. This flotsam he also gathered. Though he took only what he could carry in one hand.

The Keel was a small cottage.

Glancing that way, he was relieved to see that Jock hadn't left the stoop. Though he must've gone inside the cottage at some point during Graeme's summoning, because the door now stood more than a little ajar. Jock was adept at opening doors, latched, knobbed, or otherwise, as long as the door wasn't locked.

He also had a penchant for sneaking treats from the kitchen cupboard when Graeme wasn't around. Jock's present air of exaggerated innocence warned that that particular habit was the reason for the half-opened door.

But Graeme would deal with Jock's overeating later.

Just now, he turned back to the sea, thanking the elements for the blessings they'd given him and releasing any excess energy back whence it'd come.

He kept only the charged water and sea tangle.

These he'd use to place a protective shield around his house and property, warding against the intrusion of anything negative or evil.

Hoping to take advantage of the evening quiet—Pennard residents were known for their curiosity, but most would now be gathered at the Laughing Gull—he left the little strand and crossed to the landward side of the road where the Keel awaited him.

He skirted Kendra Chase's car, not even glancing at it, lest thoughts of her rush into his mind. Her essence still clung to the vehicle, humming in the air. His heart thudded, proving how easily she'd captivated him.

She could make him forget time and duty.

Even now, he could imagine claiming her mouth with his, threading the fingers of one hand in her hair as he kissed her, and using his other hand to whip off her bulky, waxed jacket, revealing the woman beneath.

Graeme fought back a scowl, pushing her from his thoughts.

This was no time for such intrusions.

And that's exactly what she was.

Before he lost his concentration entirely, he walked back to the barrel shed and removed the withered bundle of seaweed tacked above the door, and replaced it with a few strands of the fresh sea wrack.

He also set down the pail and dipped his hand into the cold water, flicking droplets onto the shed's ancient, salt-crusted wood.

"By my will and the powers of all worlds, no darkness may tread here." He stepped around the shed, going sunwise, and spoke shielding words as he trailed a line of water along the foot of the cliff behind his house. "Only those I wish to see may cross this boundary. Blessed be this place and those welcome here." He circled around the cottage's far corner, replacing old seaweed with new and dabbing water along the windowsills. "Nothing evil can touch these walls and those within."

Almost finished, he reached the front of his house and stepped back onto the road. Setting down the pail beside his blue-painted bench, he scooped up a handful of the seawater and flung the droplets above and beneath the cottage's blue-rimmed windows.

"No harm will come to this good and blessed place." He took a breath, vowing not to let more than a month pass before he renewed the boundary ward.

To complete the blessing, he poured a thin line of water along the edge of the road, a necessity because Pennard's single row of seafront houses all opened directly onto Harbour Street's pavement.

"And I"—he'd almost emptied the pail—"will continue to guard this property to the best of my ability in all the days to come."

It was only when he returned to the front door, expecting to have to cajole Jock into moving aside so he could dash the remaining water at the door lintel, that he noticed the dog was gone.

Sure Jock had gone looking for another tasty, normally off-limits tidbit, Graeme finished the warding. He was just reaching to fix the last of the seaweed above the lintel when the dog popped his head around the door, peering out from the shadows of the entry.

It was a stealthy move.

And the cunning in Jock's eyes made Graeme instantly suspicious.

He flashed a look at the dog as he worked the sea wrack around the two hooks that held it in place. "What are you about, laddie?"

"What are *you* about?" Kendra Chase appeared in the doorway, ducking beneath his raised arm to step out onto the stoop.

Graeme blinked, furious to have been caught unawares.

"What are you doing here?" He tossed the question back at her. "How did you get into my house?"

He could well guess.

His dog, the traitorous beast, proved his guilt by slinking back into the cottage's darkened entry hall.

A place he hoped Kendra hadn't spent too much time.

"Why are you putting seaweed above your door?" She eyed the dripping strands of wrack.

"I asked what you're doing here." Graeme spoke more harshly than he'd intended.

But his hand seemed frozen where it was, his fingers hovering over the seaweed he'd just threaded around the lintel hooks.

He knew he looked ridiculous.

He also had the distinct impression she'd seen him cross the road from the little strand. That somehow she'd read his face when he'd passed her car, and picked up the thoughts that had rushed him.

Thoughts he had no business harboring about her.

"Well?" She flicked another glance at his hand, still raised above his head.

"It's an old Aberdeenshire tradition." Graeme thought fast. "Fisher folk believe that a bit o' tangle above the door keeps out the tidewater if a storm sends the seas surging up and o'er the road."

To his shame, her eyes lit. "O-o-oh, I love that."

"Humph." Graeme refused to deepen the lie by commenting.

He did lower his arm. He also stepped away from her,

not liking how her scent wafted beneath his nose, distracting and enchanting him.

Everything about her did things to him, much to his annoyance.

He turned to face the sea, hoping she wouldn't notice. "People hereabouts have many uses for seaweed. It's used for fertilizer, as food when times are hard, for healing, and in legend."

That was true enough.

"Folklore fascinates me." Her voice took on a tone of wonder, making him feel even worse for having just invented the wisdom. "It's such age-old beliefs that make Scotland so much more romantic than the States."

"You came for your car." It was the only plausible reason for her to be here. And yet—he shouldn't go down this road—despite everything, he wished she'd come to see him.

"I did, yes." She didn't deny it, her voice oddly businesslike now. "I wanted to stretch my legs after the drive, and there seemed no point in expecting you to bring the car to the inn.

"Not"—she tucked her hair behind an ear, her smile cutting straight to his heart—"when I was out walking right past here, anyway. Jock was on the stoop and—"

"He let you in." Graeme was sure of it.

"I did mean to knock." A becoming wash of pink bloomed on her cheeks. "I called out, but when you didn't answer, Jock nudged open the door and trotted inside as if I should follow him. He kept stopping and looking back, wagging his tail. Of course, I—"

"Were you in there long?" Graeme thanked the Powers that his dog hadn't yet discovered how to turn on lights.

"Only a moment." Kendra tightened her jacket against the wind.

"Aye, right, then." Relief swept Graeme. "Your car key is just inside the lounge. I'll fetch it, and you can be on your way."

Rude as it seemed, he didn't invite her in.

The reasons peered at him from an endless assortment of wall-mounted picture frames as he strode purposefully down the cottage's entry hall toward the door that opened into his lounge.

A motley collection, the frames were everything from age-worn wood to silver, some of those tarnished. And each held a different picture. Some were quite blurry, sepia prints dating as far back as 1857. Others were clearer, packing a greater emotional punch because the canines caught on film were easier to recognize.

The photographs lined both sides of the entry. Nearly every imaginable breed had a place. Scottish deerhounds; Great Danes; Irish wolfhounds; innumerable terriers of all sizes; dachshunds; Labs, black and golden; and far too many mongrels to count. Dogs of all ages who, if viewed by someone with their heart in the right place and a sharp sense of observance, appeared to have the same eyes.

Even more startling, a small brass plate fixed to the bottom of each picture frame revealed that every dog bore the name Jock.

Only *Jock* was missing.

And Graeme dreaded the day his good friend would join the others.

Though he knew such a parting wouldn't last long.

He also knew he didn't want Kendra Chase stepping into the entry hall and chancing to study the photographs. If—his gut twisted—she hadn't already done so.

She struck him as the sort who'd notice the dogs' eyes. And once she did . . .

Frowning, Graeme stepped into his lounge and

snatched her car keys off the lamp table by the door. Jock lay sprawled on his plaid before the hearth fire, feigning innocence as he did so well.

It was a talent he'd perfected.

He'd certainly had enough time to do so.

And thinking about *time* and its passing was one very good reason for Graeme to stop thinking about kissing the delectable American tourist waiting on his door stoop.

He also flashed an irritated glance at his dog. "Your false innocence doesn't fool me." He kept his voice low, not wanting Kendra to hear.

He knew Jock did because the dog's ear twitched.

"I dinnae need a woman in my life. And"—he paused before the lounge door—"your tricks to push thon lassie beneath my nose won't serve anything. She'll be gone in a few days, away to her America, where she belongs."

On his plaid before the hearth fire, Jock cracked one eye.

It was a look Graeme knew well.

And every time he'd seen it, Jock had won.

"No' this time, laddie." Graeme tightened his grip on the car keys and strode back down the entry hall, eager to place the keys in Kendra's hand.

The sooner she left here, the better.

Meantime, he would look out for her from afar.

But something told him it would be a very long time before he could forget Kendra Chase.

Worst of all, he didn't want to forget her.

Chapter 3

"Ah, there's yourself, lassie."

Iain Garry, owner and proprietor of the Laughing Gull Inn, smiled as he raised the flap of the bar and came over to Kendra the instant he spotted her on the threshold of the hotel's cozy pub restaurant.

"I've saved the best table for you." A portly man of middle years, his rosy cheeks and twinkling eyes marked him as an easygoing, amiable soul. "Though"—he beamed at her, his bald pate shining in the lamplight—"as you can see, the locals prefer crowding the bar to sitting at tables. Yours is in thon corner, by the far window."

Kendra looked to where he indicated, more than pleased. "That'll suit me fine."

Truth was, the entire pub restaurant delighted her. People did stand three deep at the long, polished bar. But even with such a crowd, she caught the gleam of old-fashioned brass ale pumps and the glint of sparkling glasses and bottles arrayed on wall shelves. Better yet—to her love of all things old—the stone-flagged floor and low oak-beamed ceiling lent an air of warmth and cheer that made her heart beat faster. As did the whitewashed walls, cluttered as they were with all manner of sea memorabilia, including a large, old-timey photograph of herring fishers. A caption scrawled in white ink across the bottom of the picture declared, with implied pride, that the men had been a WILD ROUGH LOT.

"They were that, aye." Iain followed her gaze as he steered her past the photo, dated to the late 1800s. "Men who make a living of the sea have to be tough, even nowadays. Though"—he led her around a half barrel filled with smooth, silvered driftwood—"their numbers decline each year. More the pity."

"I know—" Kendra broke off as a heavyset woman hurried past, carrying a large platter of fish and chips. The delicious smell made her mouth water.

The Laughing Gull Inn truly was her idea of heaven.

There was even a small hearth against the back wall, its glowing peat fire adding to the coziness.

Her table couldn't have been more perfect.

Tucked by the corner window, the small table looked out over the street and marina. Just now, thick sea haar pressed against the windowpanes, but the mist only made the view more atmospheric.

As if all time stood still within the quaint confines of the little pub.

She could stay here, too.

Surely, there were worse fates.

Especially with a resident hunk like Graeme Mac-Grath living just down the road. Even if the sexy Scotsman seemed more keen on seeing her leave Pennard than on having her hang around. He'd certainly hurried her from his house, closing the door in her face the instant he'd thrust the car keys into her hand. She hadn't even had a chance to say good-bye.

Kendra frowned, heat beginning to creep up her neck.

She wasn't that bad.

She wouldn't exactly call herself a head turner, but no man had ever given her such a brush-off. And wasn't it typical that, despite all, she still found him so damnably attractive. His accent so divine she'd almost be willing to beg him just to stand and talk to her for hours.

He could read her the telephone book or the impossibly thick instruction manual for her newest digital camera. It wouldn't matter.

Anything at all would do. As long as she could listen to his rich, buttery-soft burr washing over her like verbal silk, melting her.

Kendra touched a hand to her breast, trying not to think about him.

"Would you rather have a table by the fire?" Iain was looking at her, clearly mistaking her hesitancy for a wish to sit elsewhere.

"No, no . . ." Kendra quickly removed her heavy jacket and draped it onto the back of an empty chair before settling onto the window seat. "This is ideal." She glanced over her shoulder at the mist rolling down the street and the blurry yellow halos cast by lights from a few of the fishing boats in the marina.

"I was hoping for just such a table." She turned back to him, enchanted.

"Right, then." The innkeeper's smile returned. "I'll have Janet bring you a menu." He flicked a look after the bustling woman who'd delivered the tray of fish and chips to a nearby table. "We've fine sea bass on special tonight. Our pepper steak is also popular."

"I know what I want." Kendra reached to touch his arm when he turned to move away. "The fish and chips smelled so good going past just now. I'll have that."

"Fine choice." Iain Garry nodded, not looking surprised.

No doubt every American tourist ordered fish and chips.

And that was fine, considering she was supposed to be one. Besides, if the Scots—or any Brits, for that matter—didn't want tourists always asking for the tasty dish, they shouldn't make it so irresistible.

Still . . .

She was sure she'd caught a few of a locals smirk at her choice.

"And, Iain . . ." She sat up straighter, flashing her most confident smile. "I'll have a pint of Black Isle Brewery Hibernator stout."

She'd seen the almost-black ale on the neighboring table.

It looked potent enough to fell an elephant, and she could smell its richness from here. After the cliff road from hell and the force of nature that was Graeme Mac-Grath, she wouldn't mind something that packed a bit of a punch.

"That's strong ale, lass." Iain sounded skeptical.

But the locals who'd chuckled at her dinner choice had lost their smirks.

And for that reason alone, she'd drink the stout. She'd just be sure to temper its kick with several large glasses of water.

"I've heard Hibernator is excellent." Kendra smiled at the staring locals. "I'd like to try it."

"You might prefer a nice Stella lager?" Iain tried one last time to dissuade her.

A flurry of exchanged glances and elbow nudges at

the bar helped her stay firm. "No, thanks. I'm sure it's good, but ..." She sat back in her seat and shook her head. "I'm sticking with the strong ale."

Iain shot an annoyed look at the men at the bar, but nodded and left her.

It was then, once she was alone at the little corner table and the locals returned to their own business, that some of the pub's coziness retreated. It was no more than a ripple in the air, yet a new and disturbing current had entered the atmosphere, tingeing the feel of the crowded room.

Kendra's nape prickled, bringing back the ill ease she'd felt on first arriving in Pennard. An image of the empty house flashed across her mind, the strong aura of menace almost palpable again. The sensation had been fleeting, and had left her completely when she'd reached Graeme MacGrath's cottage. But that could've been because she'd raised her guards, allowing protective white-light energy to fill and surround her until she was ready to lower her shields so Pennard's unhappy discarnates could approach her.

Even then she'd been aware of something.

Yet upon entering the Laughing Gull moments ago, she'd almost believed she'd imagined her initial reaction to the fishing village.

Now ...

She tensed with a sense of keen awareness, her nerve endings alert to everything around her. *Breathe deep. Relax. This is your night off to unwind and enjoy. A well-deserved break. Inhale fully; exhale slow* ... She spoke the words in her mind, using the soft orange glow of the fire's peat bricks to focus on until she felt balanced again.

"Your Hibernator, miss." Janet, the serving woman, arrived with her pint of strong ale. Her expression said she didn't approve of women drinking stout.

"Thank you." Kendra took a deliberate sip, sure the

woman also didn't care for young American females visiting pubs on their own.

"Anything else?" The woman looked at her, her lips tightening even more when Kendra took a second swallow of the dark ale.

"A glass of water, please." Kendra regretted asking, but impressing the dour Scotswoman wasn't worth suffering a headache later. "I prefer still, if you have it—no fizzy water."

Fizzy water made her stomach ache.

Janet's sourness made it difficult to reclaim the mood of cheery warmth that had greeted her on entering the inn. The woman's disapproval hung in the air, even after she'd marched back to the bar.

Blot her from your mind. Kendra glanced again at the peat fire, wishing it wasn't half hidden by the legs of the nearby tables and chairs.

Even so, the soft glimmer of the peat was soothing. And the earthy-sweet smoke added just enough haze to the air to enhance the pub's old-fashioned, lamp-lit ambience.

Whatever had brought her here and the outcome of her stay, the Laughing Gull and the out-of-the-way village outside the inn's thick-set windows was a special place, caught in a time long past.

Almost inaccessible and sequestered, Pennard was just the kind of haven that should always remain serene and tranquil, a place apart from the rest of the world. Unaffected by the traffic-filled brashness of loud, teeming cities and suburbs, as existed elsewhere.

Kendra's heart clenched when a small man with a weather-beaten face caught her eye and gallantly tipped his cap to her as he hopped off his bar stool and headed for the door. Watching him as he stepped out into the cold, dark mist and disappeared into the whirling gray mass as easily as suited brokers strode down the streets of Manhattan drove home just how appealing she found little Pennard with its mini harbor, colorful fishing boats, and blue-painted benches.

She tightened her fingers on the pint glass, her gaze going again to the peat fire. Images of crowded sidewalks, exhaust fumes, and billboard-lined highways flashed across her mind, quickly followed by strip malls, huge supermarkets with even larger parking lots, and an endless stream of fast-food restaurants.

"Damn . . ." She circled the pint glass on the polished wood of the small table.

From the bar, she heard the soft music of Scottish voices. And through the window, she caught the wash of the sea against the harbor's breakwater. But other sounds claimed her mind's ear, reminding her of a place she knew well, a distant place where days often began with the rumble of garbage trucks, and leaf-blower serenades always seemed to kick in just when a person most needed silence.

She understood why Pennard's locals weren't happy about being forced from such a quiet and unobtrusive place.

She, too, loved quiet.

And for the first time ever, she felt an unpleasant pang at the thought of leaving an assignment and returning to her own world.

But if she did her work well here, she might be able to help ensure that Pennard held on to a good measure of its perennial charm. And that the disembodied residents, at least, would find peace again.

Hoping so, she took a tiny sip of Hibernator, her tension easing.

"I admire a brave woman." A deep Scottish voice caused her to almost choke on the ale.

Looking up, she met the appreciative gaze of one the locals. He stood directly before her, managing to appear worldly-wise despite his casual fisherman's garb of jeans, work boots, and a bulky Aran sweater. Tall, broad shouldered, and blessed with a shock of gleaming black hair and clear blue eyes, he was also devilishly handsome.

But in a smooth way that made her scoot back against the window bench, instinctively putting distance between them.

"Brave?" It was all she could think to say.

She did turn her head slightly, not liking how his cologne invaded her space. Heavy with musk and citrus, it spoiled the hint of peat smoke and fish and chips she'd been enjoying.

"Courageous you are, aye." He stepped even closer, his smile deepening. "It's clear you're not liking your pint of Hibernator."

"I love it." Kendra took an overlarge gulp, hoping the lie wouldn't circle back and make her gag.

The dark ale *was* too much for her.

But she'd rather choke it down than admit it.

"I'm Gavin Ramsay. My house, Spindrift, is the one up on the bluff, beyond the east end of the village." He thrust out a hand, leaving her little choice but to take it unless she wished to appear rude.

She remembered the name, how Graeme MacGrath's jaw had tightened as he'd spoken of Ramsay.

Now here was the man, smiling down at her, his hand extended.

And every local at the bar—including Iain Garry and pinch-faced Janet—were turned their way, craning necks to watch them.

"Kendra Chase." She accepted the handshake, not surprised to find that though strong and warm, his hands weren't at all calloused. They were smooth as a banker's and nothing like one might expect of a man so ruggedly dashing and dressed in fisherman's garb.

"I'm American, here on holiday." She withdrew her hand, leaving it at that. He didn't need to know she hailed from Bucks County, Pennsylvania.

He looked at her very intently. "Och, I ken you're from the States. No other country produces such glamorous blondes. We don't see many sleek, long-legged beauties hereabouts." He lowered himself into the chair opposite her, stretching his long legs to the fire. "That you're here . . ."

He didn't finish the sentence, his gaze flicking to her pint of strong ale. "I've ordered a fine welcome dram for you." His voice turned intimate. "A wonderful single malt from Royal Brackla, one of the few distilleries privileged to carry the word *royal* in its name."

His *r*s rolled beautifully, his burr rich and smooth—as if practiced to perfection.

Kendra suspected it was.

She also understood why Graeme didn't care for the man.

She didn't, either.

"I don't drink whisky." She glanced at her watch and started to get to her feet. If she didn't leave now, she'd also tell him she couldn't abide Romeos, Scottish or otherwise. "It's late and—"

"You'd miss something very fine." He smiled, apparently certain his charm would dissuade her. "Scottish whisky is water of life. *Uisge beatha*, in the Gaelic. You can't visit Scotland without— Ah, here's Janet with the drams."

He glanced up at the tight-lipped woman, his smile not wavering as she set down the two small glasses. The whisky neat, save one ice cube in each dram.

"Aye, a ray o' sunshine, you are, Janet." He watched her march off, waiting until she disappeared into the kitchen before he turned back to Kendra. "You see why you're a breath of fresh air."

Kendra glanced at the closed kitchen door. "I saw a woman who must've gotten up on the wrong side of the bed this morning—nothing more."

She didn't add that she suspected Janet did so every day.

Or that she couldn't stand smooth talkers. Dressed as she was in her sturdy walking boots and warm and comfortable pants and pullover, she knew well that she looked anything but glamorous.

She didn't even like glamour.

And she wouldn't be a sleek beauty if she was wearing a string bikini.

She might be tall and her legs therefore long. But there all resemblance to such females ended. And the truth was, she didn't mind her extra few pounds. She also appreciated shoes and clothes that were comfortable.

No one would catch her in heeled, strappy sandals. And she wouldn't don a filmy wisp of a cling-to-every-curve dress even if she could.

She did sit up as straight as possible and pushed the little dram glass away from her. "My dinner should be here soon." She kept her tone cordial, pride making flight impossible.

So she tipped her head toward the bar, hoping her unwanted table guest would take the hint. "I don't want to keep you from your friends."

To her dismay, he sat back, getting comfortable in his chair. "I like a challenge." His blue eyes met hers, his smile roguish.

"And you"—he glanced to a nearby table where an older couple were eating fish and chips—"would've done better to order Iain's lamb shank." When he turned back to her, he looked her over, letting his gaze skim her breasts. "The flesh is tender and succulent—"

"Kendra, lass!" Graeme MacGrath's deep voice filled

the room, the outside door banging shut as he approached the table with long, purposeful strides. "Sorry to keep you waiting. I hope you haven't been troubled."

"Graeme ..." Kendra blinked, never more glad to see anyone in her life. He was almost at her side, his dog trotting right beside him.

Anyone who saw the look on his face had to think he was madly in love with her.

And that if he could tear his gaze off her long enough to do so, he'd knock Ramsay flat for daring to have glanced her way. Sitting at her table, speaking to her, and buying her a dram might well prove fatal.

That was the air he had about him.

Kendra's heart raced, her pulse leaping to see his dark eyes blazing with such intensity.

Apparently noticing, Gavin Ramsay stood. "I didn't know you knew our seal man." He spoke to Kendra, but his gaze was on Graeme, his blue eyes hard now. His smiles and innuendoes vanished.

"She's here to visit me." Graeme didn't even glance at Ramsay.

Instead, he shouldered past him and looked down at Kendra, his mouth set in a tight, determined line. His eyes narrowed into the expression a man might wear before jumping into an abyss.

"Come here, you." He circled an arm around her shoulders, pulling her to him in a swift, bone-crushing hug that took her breath.

Pressed against him, Kendra felt delicious heat sweep her even before he lowered his head to nuzzle the sensitive spot beneath her ear. His hair, still ponytailed, swung forward to brush her neck, unleashing swirls of pleasurable tingles throughout her. "Graeme —"

"Shhh ..." He nipped her neck, his beard stubble grazing her skin. His scent flooded her senses, melting her with its sexy blend of woodsmoke and the sea. The wool of his sweater caressed her cheek, the rough weave cold from the night's chill. "I'm sorry, lass . . ."

The words, spoken against her ear, dashed the sensual spell he'd cast over her. Genuine regret sounded in his voice, letting her know his sudden and fierce embrace wasn't something he'd wanted.

Kendra stiffened, and caught Gavin Ramsay flash a scathing look at Graeme. "This isn't over, seal man," she thought she heard Ramsay snarl beneath his breath just before he strode for the door.

She wasn't sure because in that same moment, Graeme tightened his arms around her and claimed her mouth with his, kissing her long and hard. It was a savage kiss, bold, brazen, and so heated that Kendra's heart began to hammer loud enough to block out everything except the thunder of her own pulse in her ears.

Everything else vanished. The world spun away, leaving only silence filled with the roar of her blood. And— she couldn't believe it, considering where they were—a slow, insistent burn deep inside her, liquid flame sluicing intimate places, melting and arousing her.

Kendra closed her eyes, surrendering to the embrace.

She brought her hands up between them, gripping the rough wool of his sweater. She could feel his heart thumping beneath her fingers, the warm, solid strength of his chest. She doubted any man had ever held her so tightly, kissed her with such fierce possession.

When he took her face in his hands, thrusting his fingers into her hair as he deepened the kiss, she didn't care who saw them.

Nothing else mattered.

Until someone—a woman—cleared her throat right behind them.

Kendra froze in embarrassment. Her eyes snapped

open, her mortification complete at finding stout, sour-faced Janet looking right at her. The older woman's lips were set in a thin, tight line and her eyes were cold, twin shards of judgment.

If she could, Kendra would've sunk into the floor.

She was so not into displays of public affection.

Yet . . .

She couldn't have resisted Graeme's kiss if her life depended on it. Already he fascinated her. And even though it wasn't an excuse, he had taken her fully by surprise. What red-blooded woman could keep her head when a sexy Scotsman with a knock-your-socks-off burr grabbed her, pulled her into his arms, and gave her the kiss of the century?

She certainly couldn't.

Stay unaffected, that was.

So she did the best she could and summoned a smile, flashing it in the general direction of the goggle-eyed locals at the bar.

She didn't look again at Janet.

Graeme was still holding her crushed against him and showed no sign of letting her go. It was just a shame that her overly sharp intuition warned her that his kiss and his embrace had nothing to do with a fierce and sudden affection for her. His reasons were elsewhere.

And that stung more than it should.

She could easily fall for Graeme MacGrath.

Worse than that, she suspected she already had.

Chapter 4

Kendra felt her nerves fraying, torn one by one under the steady gazes of every patron in the Laughing Gull Inn. An unpleasant hush spread through the room, an awkward silence broken only by the swell of the sea slapping against the harbor's breakwater outside. Although perhaps that sound—muffled, rhythmic pounding—was the roar of her blood. She could feel the hard beat of her pulse, the heat staining her face. Her cheeks were surely crimson.

She didn't wear embarrassment gladly.

Could there be a more conspicuous place in the world for such a kiss?

She highly doubted it.

Graeme didn't seem at all troubled. He even looked pleased with himself. And his devil-may-care attitude only made her feel all the more self-conscious.

Whatever the kiss was about, it suited him well.

"Ah, my . . ." He glanced around the crowded room, somehow managing to look charmingly sheepish. "I didn't notice how many o' you were here."

Some of the locals chuckled and turned back to the bar. Most kept staring. Their interest revealed that such spectacles didn't often happen in Pennard. The publican, Iain Garry, attempted to draw their attention by setting aside the pint glass he'd been polishing and offering to refill everyone's ale on the house.

Unfortunately, Graeme holding Kendra so tightly in his arms proved more exciting than free beer.

"People are staring." Kendra didn't bother to whisper.

"So they are, aye." Graeme didn't seem to mind.

He did release her, but slowly and with apparent reluctance. Straightening, he smiled at Janet, who'd brought Kendra's fish and chips. She huffed a greeting, the words too rushed to make much sense.

"A fine e'en to you as well, Janet." Graeme winked good-naturedly, his charm already working on the older Scotswoman. No longer quite so pinch-faced, she placed Kendra's plate on the table.

"Your lass's supper." She spoke to Graeme, not looking at Kendra.

"She is that, aye." He slid his arm loosely around Kendra's shoulder, underscoring the claim. He glanced at her, leaning in to lightly kiss her brow.

"I haven't seen her in a while." He spoke the lie loud enough so not only Janet, but also the entire, gawping crowd at the bar also heard his explanation. "Everyone knows how busy I've been of late."

"They know you've never brought a lassie here." Janet eyed him suspiciously.

"Now I have." Still smiling, he took the seat Gavin Ramsay had vacated. He glanced at Kendra's fish and chips, then back at Janet. "I'll also have one of Iain's special cream cheese and hot smoked salmon sandwiches. And a pint of whatever Kendra's drinking."

"It's Black Isle Hibernator." Janet flicked a look at the still-full glass.

Graeme raised a brow at Kendra, but nodded to the older woman. "Hibernator it is, then."

Janet bustled off, leaving them alone. The locals at the bar didn't seem as inclined until Graeme, apparently feeling their stares, turned around in his chair.

"Any man"—he called to them, his tone pleasant—"who wouldn't be as happy to meet with his lady after a long separation can keep on staring. The rest o' you loons..."

He didn't need to finish.

Every man sitting or standing at the long, polished bar swiftly turned away, once again giving his attention to his drink and his companions.

Kendra still felt dizzy from Graeme's kiss, her heart pounding madly. He twisted back around to look at her across the table.

"What was that all about?" She met his gaze, not caring if she looked angry.

"That was a nettle grasp." He reached to take her hand, kissing her fingertips.

"A what?" She blinked.

"It's an old saying. 'Grasping the nettle' means to do something you must, however unpleasant." He had the decency to look embarrassed.

Kendra understood why. "I see."

She did. And hearing what he thought of something she'd viewed as the kiss of the century sent hot color rushing to her cheeks again.

"No, you don't." He waited when Janet appeared with his sandwich and ale. "I didn't mean kissing you wasn't nice. It was—I'll no' deny." He gave her a slow smile that quickly faded when she didn't return it. "But I'd ne'er have done such a thing here, in front of everyone, if it hadn't been the only way to get Ramsay away from you.

"Save tossing him out on the street, which I would've done if he hadn't left." He leaned across the table, taking her hand again, squeezing her palm firmly. "I hope you can forgive me? Jock will disown me if you can't."

"Your dog has nothing to do with it." Kendra looked to where the dog had flopped down in the middle of the room. He lay sprawled on one side, his legs sticking straight out. His black-and-white face wore a look of bliss, as if he enjoyed blocking the pub's busiest footpath.

Kendra turned back to Graeme. "Jock is innocent. Don't bring him into it. Just tell me why you kissed me. The whole village will think we're a pair."

His smile returned, and with it his charm. "Is that so bad?"

"That's not the point." She held his gaze, frowning.

What was bad was that the notion struck her as wildly appealing.

She didn't do holiday love affairs. And even if she wanted to, letting herself in for a bit of romance with Graeme MacGrath would leave her scorched when their time together ended. She also had more to do here than allow herself to be swept off her feet by a roguish, dog-loving Scotsman.

Kendra exhaled slowly. Her work mattered.

Besides her integrity—she really was an old-fashioned sort of girl—she hadn't been born with a silver spoon in her mouth. She came from good middle-class stock. Her father was a self-employed cabinetmaker, and her mother worked as a medical-records clerk in a hospital.

In her family, luxury was knowing the monthly bills were paid, not flashy cars, designer clothes, or frequenting the latest chic restaurant.

Homemade chicken and dumplings or her mother's secret-recipe meat loaf ranked higher than a teeny portion of some impossible-to-pronounce gourmet fare. And no one left the Chase table hungry. Large servings and second helpings were part of the enjoyment of an evening meal.

Hard work made that possible.

Kendra's values hadn't changed.

She couldn't risk her job.

"If you keep frowning, you'll attract attention again." Graeme's soft Scottish voice brought her back to the present. "Would it help to know I didn't come here to kiss you? I saw Ramsay through the window. When I came inside and caught his innuendos—"

"What matters is why you did it. Kiss me, I mean." Kendra took a bite of her batter-fried haddock. It was delicious, the fish white, tender, and moist, the batter beyond perfection. But it was hard to enjoy her dinner's scrumptiousness when he'd just turned her world upside down.

Maybe all Scotsmen were great kissers, but she rather suspected it was him. She knew no one had ever kissed her like that before.

He'd knocked her socks off, plain and simple.

Yet he'd not just done so publicly, but for reasons that ruined the pleasure.

"I know you don't like Gavin." She set down her fork and reached for her pint glass and took a sip. "But why should you care if he joined me?"

"You didn't look too pleased by his company." His dark eyes took on a shuttered look, his whole expression hardening. "Ramsay is a known scoundrel. No woman, especially a tourist, is safe from him. He'd take you up to Spindrift, have you for his supper, and then he'd spit out your bones for the gulls to pick."

"And you wouldn't?" Kendra lifted a brow. "Ramsay didn't kiss me. You did."

He couldn't argue with that.

But his face went a tad stonier.

"I kissed you with good reason." He leaned forward, lowering his voice. "Word spreads quickly in tiny Scottish villages. Before the sun rises tomorrow, everyone will have heard what happened tonight. And"—he gave the locals a quick sideways look—"if all of Pennard thinks you're mine, Ramsay won't touch you. He knows better." His tone held satisfaction.

"I wouldn't let him near me anyway." Kendra tucked her hair behind her ear. "I don't care for such men."

A slow, sexy smile started at the corner of Graeme's mouth and he sat back in his chair, looking pleased. "I'm glad to hear it."

"You aren't my type, either." Her words took the burgeoning grin off his face.

"That's no' a bad thing." His answer stung more than it should. "But"—he picked up his sandwich, watching her rather than taking a bite—"so long as you're here, it's for the best if folk think you've come to see me. We'll spend some time together."

Great.

He couldn't have said anything that would make her more uncomfortable. Much as she was attracted to him, she did have work to do. She'd planned to get busy in the morning. And her field wasn't the kind where an audience was appreciated. Having Graeme look on while she communed with ghosts was a prospect that could give her indigestion.

Only Zack and others like her understood.

Graeme would think her nuts.

And even if she wasn't into casual relationships, his kiss had finished what his burr started. She was strongly attracted to him and didn't want to make things worse by having him see her in action, as it were.

So rather than go anywhere near his comment about spending time together, she changed the subject. "Why did Gavin call you a seal man?"

"No' because I'm a selkie—dinnae you worry." He took a sip of his ale. "Ramsay calls me that because I use my boat, the *Sea Wyfe*, to take tourists to see the seals. This coast is home to common harbour seals and grey seals. They're everywhere, though their number has diminished in recent years. I study them, too, monitoring their whereabouts and behavior for the University of Aberdeen."

He set down his pint and glanced at the night-darkened window. Drifting sea haar still blurred the view, but the half moon could just be made out behind a line of fast-moving clouds.

"The seal research keeps me busy." He turned back to her, his expression serious. "It's one of the reasons I was in Aberdeen. And"—he lowered his voice again—"on the beach at Balmedie."

"I didn't see any seals in the surf there." Kendra speared another bite of haddock, trying hard not to notice how wickedly handsome Graeme was. Soft light from a beaten-copper wall lamp fell across his face, emphasizing his proud cheekbones and the sheen of his long black hair, sleekly knotted at his nape. But it was the dark stubble on his jaw that tempted her most, making her want to reach across the table and touch his face. She'd love to trace the contours of his chin, those lips. . . .

She tore her gaze away, not wanting to stare.

Although he really was the embodiment of her dream man.

Not that her work permitted her to indulge in such fantasies often. Being a ghostcatcher did put certain limitations on one's private life.

She looked back at him, hoping her face didn't reveal that just sitting so close to him made her heart leap. "Were you hoping to spot seals at Balmedie?"

"I was there to walk the dunes." He took another sip of stout, watching her over the rim. "It's a fine place for that. I stop by Balmedie Beach whenever I'm in Aberdeen. The seals now . . ."

Trailing off, he stood, motioning her to stay seated before he picked up her almost-full glass of stout and headed for the bar. When he returned, he set a half-pint of lager next to her plate.

"I mind the stout is too strong for you." He winked, his gaze flicking to the half-pint. "Thon's more or less local. Macbeth from Deeside Brewery; it's a fine pale ale guaranteed to please."

"Thank you." Kendra tried the golden brew as Graeme carried Ramsay's two untouched drams back to the bar. The lager was perfect, delicious and crisp.

"I like to see a lady happy." He came back quickly, reaching to clink his stout glass to her half-pint as he reclaimed his chair. "The seals, now," he began again. "Most of them are at Peterhead these days. That's to the east of here, around the coast at Fraserburgh and then south. All the big commercial fishing is there, and the harbour seals, especially, are clever opportunists.

"They swarm the Peterhead harbor, waiting for the fishing boats to come in." He glanced at the window again, then back at her. "The seals pounce on any fish the boats lose overboard and" — he smiled — "whatever bits kindhearted fishermen pitch to them.

"Myself" — he smiled again — "I pay most heed to the seals hereabouts, counting and monitoring them through their natural annual cycle. When and where they prefer to haul out, for example—"

"Haul out?" Kendra blinked.

"Haul ashore, aye." His smile deepened, dimple flashing. "The time they spend on land. Learning why they go ashore where and when they do and how long they stay there is crucial to determining which areas need to be deemed SACs, special areas of conservation.

"For instance"—he leaned forward, his passion for the seals making him all the more sympathetic—"we know they're less likely to haul out on days of strong winds and rain. So the sites they most favor are usually the wind-protected sides of skerries or sandbars. Also rocky ledges that offer the best vantages at low tide. And—"

He broke off, sitting back again. "I'm boring you."

"No, not at all." Kendra reached out to touch his arm. Even that innocent connection stirred a strong response in her and set her pulse racing.

She withdrew her hand at once, hoping he couldn't tell.

"It must be fascinating work." She looked to where Jock was now snoring loudly in the middle of the pub's stone-flagged floor. "I'd enjoy such research. I love animals and believe in protecting them."

"Is that what you do?" He was watching her intently, as if her answer really mattered to him. "Have you a career in veterinary medicine or perhaps animal rescue? When you're not holidaying in Scotland?"

Kendra shook her head. "I'm a landscape historian." The half-truth, spoken so often, came easily. "A plain, working-class girl from a Philadelphia suburb who just happened to develop a penchant for medieval history and archaeology—that's me. I'm self-taught but somehow manage to land freelance work helping heritage organizations throughout Britain locate sites of lost medieval villages. At least, such sites are my specialty." That much was true.

"And how do you do that?" Graeme's voice softened, his accent getting to her again.

"Many are the ways." Kendra glanced at the window. The sea haar was thinning now, the moon casting the harbor in an eerie silver light. "It's mostly done by fieldwork, hours and days spent looking for traces of earthworks that mark forgotten village roads and home sites. You also need to watch for grassy mounds and other such lumps that are often remains of medieval walls.

"People like me are called in to assess the land before an excavation team moves in." She looked back at him, suddenly embarrassed.

More than once, Brits outside her working perimeters scoffed at an American being so presumptuous as to claim the ability of finding their medieval remains.

But Graeme was *Scottish*—which Scots always put first, before calling themselves British—and he was neither laughing nor looking superior.

He did look good.

So much so that she almost forgot what she'd meant to say. "Most of the sites I've worked on were abandoned in the fifteenth century. They're usually located in England. I was down there, working, before I came up here. Pennard"—she looked out the window again, not wanting to fudge while facing him—"is a much-needed break before I fly home."

"So you aren't just any tourist. I didn't think so." His words made her feel worse, even though she was contractually bound to withhold the few critical details she hadn't shared with him.

"I'm a tourist here." Now she really *had* lied to him.

Certain her deceit was stamped on her forehead, she

kept her gaze on the harbor, which was still hazed by mist but had a soft glow in the moonlight.

"Pennard isn't showing you its best side." His tone hardened, and she knew he meant Scotland's Past and Gavin Ramsay. "You would've done better to drive on to Banff."

"I like Pennard." She did.

At least, she liked the Laughing Gull Inn. She could imagine staying here, enjoying its cheery warmth. Any place with heavy-beamed ceilings, stone-flagged floors, and mist curling past the windows suited her fine. The peat fire and huge portion of fish and chips for supper didn't hurt, either. Dogs welcome was a bonus.

"Pennard has a lot going for it." Kendra warmed to the topic, feeling a need to defend the little fishing village. "Where else can you enjoy the freshest possible haddock even as the fishing boats come in on the tide?"

Turning back to the window, she watched their approach, glad that the mist had thinned enough to allow her such a gripping, age-old sight.

And the fleet's arrival was something to see.

The harbor lights glimmered through the haze and shone on the water, smooth and black now, glassy as a mirror. Far out to sea, beyond the harbor's breakwater, the lights of the fishing fleet twinkled through the darkness.

"I'm surprised there are so many. There must be at least a hundred boats. . . ." Kendra let the words trail away when she glanced back at Graeme and saw the expression on his face.

Not just that. The entire room had gone silent.

All eyes were on her.

And everyone wore the same look as Graeme: a sort of stunned perplexity, marked by either widened eyes and raised brows or angled heads and frowns.

"What is it?" She ignored the others and focused on Graeme.

"It's nothing, lass." His tone wasn't encouraging. "That's the problem, see you?" He leaned forward, placing his hand on her arm. "There isn't a fishing fleet at Pennard. The nearest fleets are at Peterhead and Fraserburgh, and those boats wouldn't be heading in here. There's no one out there." He sounded worried, a frown creasing his brow. "Not a single boat on the water, save the few already moored."

"But I saw them." Kendra twisted back around on the window bench, this time cupping her face as she peered through the cold glass.

Drifting mist and an almost-empty marina greeted her.

Pennard Bay lay deserted, not a single craft on its night-stilled waters. Beyond, the open sea proved equally lonesome. Nothing there except the silvery path of the moon, leading out to the horizon.

Kendra blinked and looked again.

When nothing changed, she knew what had happened.

Her shields hadn't worked properly.

More likely, they'd protected her fine until her powerful attraction to Graeme undermined her focus, causing her barriers to fall.

Whatever the reason, Pennard's first ghosts were coming to find her.

And, not surprisingly, they were fishermen.

Chapter 5

"Kendra, are you unwell?"

Kendra turned away from the window to find Graeme looking down at her, one dark brow raised in concern. He'd left his chair and now stood very close to her. So near that the room suddenly felt smaller than it was, as if the seafaring-memorabilia-decked walls had drawn in around them, forcing an intimacy that charged the air.

"Sorry?" Blinking, she peered up at him, her mind's eye still seeing the fleet of herring boats coming in on the tide, their riding lights glittering like diamonds on the night-blackened water.

They had been there.

She knew what she'd seen.

And that meant the fleet could reappear any moment. Years of experience with those of the Otherworld had taught her that when the departed wished an audience, they could be as determined as any mortal who sported a flesh-and-blood body. In some cases, ghosts were even more persistent.

Anything was possible.

Now just wasn't a good time to be confronted by an angry group of crusty, eighteenth-century herring fishermen. Much as she felt for them. So she forced an air of calm, hoping the fleet's arrival was only a bit of spectral theatrics. That, too, wasn't uncommon.

She'd seen ghosts in all shapes and sizes, and every kind of manifestation from barely-there shadows to full-bodied apparitions only discernible as spirits because she caught ripples of the glow surrounding them. Some didn't even have that telltale signature. Ghosts were as varied as living people's personalities. Their antics equally so. Nothing surprised her.

Except, perhaps, how few people saw them.

Everyone was capable of it, if only they weren't conditioned from childhood to see and believe only what they could accept as real.

She knew better.

And sometimes, when others were caught off guard and did glimpse a ghost, they became believers, too.

"You've gone pale." Graeme looked at her in a way that made her want to squirm.

"I'm fine." She could see he didn't believe her.

He stepped closer, placed a hand on her shoulder. "You could use some fresh air." He glanced across the pub to the door, then back to her. "A walk along the waterfront will do you good."

"I haven't finished my dinner." She wasn't about to go out into the cold, dark night with him.

The cold, she didn't mind.

Darkness was a different matter entirely.

The softly gleaming harbor lights, the wash of the sea and all that drifting, half-luminous mist could work on the psyche, planting romantic notions and bringing a man and a woman closer together.

One kiss was enough.

"You've only two bites of haddock left on your plate." Graeme squeezed her shoulder, torpedoing her excuse.

"I . . ." She couldn't finish.

Graeme saw to that, giving her a seductive smile that slid right past her defenses. "Just a short walk, lass. No more." But even as he spoke, he curled his hand around her nape, sliding his fingers beneath her hair, caressing her gently. "Jock needs to stretch his legs."

The dog was still sprawled on the stone floor, his snores louder than ever.

Kendra's chin came up. "He looks comfortable to me."

The dog cracked one eye, proving he was listening.

"It's all show, as you'll soon see." Graeme pulled a few pound notes from his pocket, anchoring them on the table with his ale glass.

Jock sprang to his feet, beside them in a flash.

"My dog loves his walks." Graeme reached down to rub Jock's ears. Looking back to Kendra, he lifted a brow. "You'll not want to disappoint him, what?"

Kendra glanced at the dog, knowing she was outmaneuvered.

Sensing her capitulation, Graeme grinned and reached for her hand, pulling her to her feet. He helped her into her jacket and then led her to the door, holding it open as Jock shot outside before them.

Kendra braced herself as Graeme pulled her over the threshold, pausing only briefly to close the inn door. He still gripped her wrist and—she didn't even want to think it—if any men from the herring boats meant to seek her out, they'd have an audience of two.

Three, if she included Jock.

Everyone knew dogs could see ghosts.

But nothing stirred anywhere except the small, decidedly modern fishing craft bobbing at their moorings in the harbor. The night had turned colder, and a chill mist drifted down the empty street. Deserted, it was, except for a big, gruff-faced man in gum boots and a yellow oilskin, apparently a present-day fisher. He was leaning against the red phone box across the road from the inn, his gaze on the Laughing Gull's cozily lit windows.

Kendra's nape prickled on seeing him.

He was solid and didn't have a tinge of spectral glow edging him as ghosts so often did.

Still . . .

She'd encountered more than one ghost who looked as flesh-and-blood real as anyone's next door neighbor. One never knew, and she often had to bite her lip to keep from telling skeptics that they might have seen plenty of ghosts and just not realized it at the time.

So the fisherman's solidity wasn't a guarantee that he was a living man.

She also heard a slight, high-pitched ringing in her ears that often signaled a spirit's presence. But Graeme was hurrying her across the street in the opposite direction. Her powerful attraction to him and the way his strong, warm fingers held her wrist sent ripples of awareness through her entire body, making it difficult to focus on the older man lounging against the phone box.

He did look their way then, bending to pat Jock as the dog trotted by him. Jock was clearly more interested in sniffing along the marina walk than stopping to greet someone who didn't have a treat at hand. The pavement smells and the cold night air, flavored with hints of brine, proved a greater temptation.

When the man straightened, smiling after the dog, Kendra decided she'd erred.

The man's attention was on the Laughing Gull Inn, not her.

Even so, she slowed her feet, glancing back at him.

It was then that Graeme stopped before a small alleyway between two tiny cottages on the seaward side of the street. Small enough to be dollhouses, the low, thick-walled cottages had doors and windows that were tightly boarded and gave off the resigned air of houses so long abandoned that they'd forgotten what it was like to have someone walk inside and greet the place as a home.

The tight space between the cottages ran straight to the water's edge. And except at the far end, where one of the harbor lights cast a reflection on the nearby water, the narrow alleyway was dark and filled with dank, briny air.

"Come, you." Graeme pulled her into those shadows, leading her down the alleyway to where a broken bench sagged against the wall. "We can speak here."

"I thought that's what we were doing in the pub." Kendra wasn't keen on speaking with him here, in the cold dark of a narrow space between two centuries-old cottages that positively reeked of sorrow.

She looked past him to where Jock paced at the seaward end of the alleyway, his ears pricked as he stared into the water, seemingly fascinated by the reflection of the harbor lights.

"Talking and"—she turned back to Graeme, not missing that the grin he'd worn in the pub was gone— "a few other things I'm still digesting."

"I won't kiss you again, if that's worrying you." He let his gaze drop briefly to her mouth. She could tell even in the dimness. When he met her eyes again, he was all seriousness. "I needed to get you out of the Laughing Gull, somewhere we wouldn't be overheard."

"I can't imagine why." That he could brush off such a kiss so easily made her testy.

He angled his head, studying her. "I would've thought you'd understand."

Kendra crossed her arms against the cold and stepped away from him. "You're a very unpredictable man, Graeme MacGrath. How can I begin to understand the motives for anything you choose to do?"

"Because"—he was right in front of her again, towering over her—"when you were gazing out the inn window, you looked like you'd seen a ghost. Or perhaps a fleet of ghost ships, as that's what you claimed."

"I said no such thing." His words made her throat go dry.

"You didn't have to." He took her chin, turning her face back to him when she tried to glance away. "You said you saw the herring boats coming in on the tide. Everyone in the pub heard you."

"So?" She jerked free of his grasp and flicked her hair behind an ear. "I saw the path of the moon glittering on the water. The boats I fancied I saw out there were an illusion, nothing more."

She hoped he'd believe her.

The look he gave her said he didn't. "Whether you saw a few moon sparkles on the water or whate'er, the problem is that Scots are a superstitious lot. This might be an age of air travel and instant Internet gratification, but if you scratch the surface of any Scot's psyche, you'll find someone who believes in second sight, the evil eye, and all manner of other things our ancestors knew lurked in the mist, including haints. We call them bogles hereabouts— ghosts to you."

"I don't believe in ghosts." Kendra spoke the lie with the ease of long practice.

Ghostcatchers International drilled their staff to always be discreet. Zack's favorite credo was never to draw attention to oneself on duty. The business had been built on trust, not sensationalism.

Kendra's assignments, in particular, were highly sensitive ones.

Most historic societies didn't want the slightest hint of a haunting to tinge a site's reputation.

So she didn't turn a hair when Graeme narrowed his eyes at her, his gaze dark and piercing. "This isn't your America, lass. And Pennard, this whole stretch of coast, is a powerfully uncanny place."

"You've said that before."

"So I have, aye." He glanced down the alleyway, toward the night-blackened water. "There's aye a grain o' truth in old folklore and tradition."

"So you believe in such things?"

"Let's say I've lived long enough to accept that this world holds more than the eye can see." He looked at her a bit challengingly then, as if he expected her to argue the point with him.

She wasn't about to disagree.

She knew better than most that sometimes things weren't as they appeared on the surface. And that mist often held more than air currents.

But she held her tongue. She didn't trust herself to speak rationally to him.

He'd pronounced *world* as *warld*, his soft, deep voice pouring through her, his sexy Scottish burr getting the better of her.

She tucked her hair behind an ear, trying to keep her gaze steady on his, her expression neutral so he wouldn't guess that even now, just listening to him speak was enough to melt her resistance.

It was true.

And each word he spoke, every lilting syllable, set off curls of warmth low in her belly. Now, at last, she understood why so many American women swooned over Scottish men. It wasn't the long, proud history and heritage, all the flashing plaid and swagger. Nor was it the swinging kilts and the age-old mystery of what was or wasn't beneath them.

Above all else, it was the accent.

Such an accent employed by Graeme MacGrath was beyond distracting.

His dark good looks didn't hurt, either. Tall and broad-shouldered was always good, but his long black hair and thick eyelashes made him all the more irresistible. The harbor lights glinted in his ponytail, making the sleek strands gleam like ebony silk.

That she noticed, now especially, really irritated her.

But she couldn't help it.

Graeme wasn't just a man. He was a force of nature. No one had ever affected her so swiftly. She doubted anyone ever would again. And she couldn't believe that up until just a short time ago, she would've said, if pressed, that an English accent was the world's sexiest.

Little did she know . . .

She took a deep breath, straightening her shoulders. "I don't see what my comment about lights at sea has to do with all this." It was the only thing she could think to say. "Surely anyone who heard would have known I was mistaken. As you said at the time, there was nothing out there."

"Aye, there wasn't." He slid his fingers over her cheek, clearly meaning to underscore his words, but serving only to send delicious shivers across her nerves. "Even so, your talk of ghostly ships could stir trouble. I'd warn you no' to mention the like again."

"I didn't say anything about spectral ships," Kendra reminded him. "Are the locals so frightened of bogles, as you call them, that one slip of the tongue by a tourist could upset them so badly?"

"So it is, aye." He was deadly serious. "Mainly because the boats as you described seeing them exactly matched the ghostly herring fleet said to sail these waters. The tales arise now and again, though most folk credit the sightings to phosphorescence in the water. Thing is"—he leaned forward, his handsome face mere inches from hers—"there have been a few odd happenings here lately. Some folk are worried that the fishermen of yore are returning and creating havoc to show their displeasure with Scotland's Past's plans to turn the village into a living history museum."

He stepped back, gesturing to a lamppost at the seaward end of the alleyway. Even through the mist, enough light fell across the poster tied to the lamppost for the large black words to be legible.

SAVE PENNARD. STOP SCOTLAND'S PAST.

Kendra read the sign twice, guilt pinching her. No, the big hand-painted letters felt more like a solid kick in the gut, a blow executed with steel-tipped boots.

"What kind of havoc has been going on?" She looked back at Graeme, seeing his anger in the hard set of his jaw, the glint in his eyes.

"Little things at first, they were." He took her arm, leading her to the end of the alley and out onto the marina walk. Jock had moved off and was now shifting about near the stone slipway, sniffing seaweed and a large, wet pile of fish netting. "Old Widow Wallace, who has the last cottage on the opposite end of the village from mine, found all her washing off the line and down in the burn beneath her back garden. At the time, she thought it was the wind, but a week later a large stone quern she keeps propped against the wall beside her door went missing.

"It was found in the same place." Graeme glanced at

her. "Such a grinding quern is so big"—he extended his arms, showing her the width—"and so heavy a single man couldn't lift one."

"I doubt a ghost could, either." Kendra knew well that spirits *could* move things. But even she doubted that their capabilities could match the weight of a large, superheavy stone quern of earlier centuries. She'd seen them often enough and was sure of it.

"Sounds like teenage pranksters to me." That she could believe. "But"—this bothered her because she'd always thought of Scotland as a place apart, a world unto itself, and exempt from such troubles as Graeme described—"why would anyone target a helpless old woman?"

His lips twitched. "Widow Wallace might be on the far side of eighty, but she'd bristle if she heard you call her helpless. She's as feisty as they come and proud of the vinegar in her veins, as she calls it.

"Could be she was harassed because she was the first local to say she'd consider Scotland's Past's offer for her cottage." Graeme shrugged and then called a quick "No" to Jock, who'd started pawing at the fish nets. "She doesn't like her daughter-in-law, and thought she'd outfox her family by taking the money and living the high life for what years she has remaining. Her son and his wife, whom the widow speaks of as the shrew, wouldn't inherit her home."

"If her daughter-in-law is a pill, more power to her." Kendra liked the old woman, sight unseen. "Has anything else happened?"

"Not to Widow Wallace, and that's as well because the trouble escalated soon after the incident with her quern." Graeme glanced to where her cottage must be, at the far end of the small fishing village. High above, on its ledge halfway up the bluff, the lights of Gavin Ramsay's Spindrift glimmered through the mist. "You may have noticed the blue-painted benches everywhere in Pennard?"

He turned back to Kendra, and her heart raced at his nearness, making it hard to concentrate. "I have, and they're lovely."

She looked toward the nearest one, set directly before the water some yards beyond the slipway. With wood-slatted seats and backs but swirled, wrought-iron sides painted royal blue, the benches appeared to be a hallmark of the small fishing village. They were placed at regular intervals along the waterfront and also stood beside several cottage doors, such as at Graeme's home, the Keel.

The benches were just one of the notes of quaintness that made Pennard special. The haar obscured all the benches except the one by the slipway, but that same mist shimmered along the rocky foreshore like curtains of luminous silk, softening edges and giving a quiet, wistful feel to the tiny fishing hamlet. Kendra pushed back her hair and took a deep, calming breath, trying to remain unaffected. Just as she avoided getting involved with locals on assignment, she strove not to fall in love with a work site.

Yet . . .

Despite the dark undertones and bits of desolation like the two empty cottages framing the alleyway they'd just left, Pennard did have the kind of charm that she could so easily allow to wrap around her, catching hold and stealing her heart before she knew what had happened. And then it would be even harder to leave.

A warning flickered across her mind, cautioning her that Pennard and its local *seal man* might prove more than she could handle.

In the space of a very short time, Graeme had ripped away her usual restraint. He'd excited and fascinated her, challenged her, and even closed his door in her face. Yet he'd rescued her twice, once at the top of the cliff road and again in the Laughing Gull when Gavin Ramsay had come on to her. With one look from his compelling, dark eyes and the single flash of a dimpled smile, he'd swept her off her feet. He'd made her desire him, surprised her with a kiss she'd never forget, and, worst of all, he made her feel and want things that just weren't good for her.

She could drive away in the morning. Her bag wasn't even unpacked. There was still time to phone Zack and ask him to put someone else on the Pennard assignment. Leaving was an option and probably her best and most sensible plan. No work went well when the heart became involved, the mind distracted. And yet if she left now, she knew that more than Pennard's ghosts would haunt her.

She glanced again at the bench by the slipway, her heart thundering.

"Don't be fooled by the pretty blue paint." Graeme's rich Scottish voice came from right beside her. "Thon bonnie benches began the worst terror we've seen in these parts in many long years."

Glancing at him, Kendra met his gorgeous, dark eyes and knew she wasn't going anywhere. Not even if he declared that the benches turned into Pictish warriors at midnight and went on bloodthirsty killing rampages while the innocent villagers slept.

"Benches can't hurt anyone." Kendra turned her gaze back on the water, not wanting him to see her face and guess how strongly she was attracted to him. "I think"— she clasped her hands behind her back, striking a casual pose—"you're just trying another tactic to scare me away.

"If so, it won't work." She kicked a pebble into the water and then glanced at him. "I don't frighten easily."

"Except"—he smoothed strands of hair from her face—"when challenged by a plunging Scottish road?"

"That's different." She resisted the urge to close her

eyes and lean into his touch, for he kept his hand on her face, his fingers lightly stroking her cheekbone.

Any moment, she would melt into a puddle at his feet.

Instead, she collected herself, purposefully ignoring the sensations stirred by his caress. "So, what's with the benches? Why should I worry about them?"

"You shouldn't." He lowered his hand, his face serious again. "The benches were instruments only. Someone—"

"They all landed in the burn behind Widow Wallace's cottage?"

"Nae, but you're close." He paused when Jock trotted up to them, nudging Graeme's jacket pocket until he retrieved a bit of dried meat and gave it to the dog. "Someone threw all the village's benches into the bay from the end of the marina's longest pier. One of the benches"—he dusted his hands, looking back at her—"had a dummy chained to it, the words *Scotland's Past* painted in black across the mannequin's forehead. The inference was plain."

"That Scotland's Past's representatives would meet a similar fate?" Kendra couldn't repress a shudder.

"So it was believed, aye." Graeme's voice was low and calm, but his anger was evident. "Not long thereafter, once the benches had all been retrieved, repaired, and returned to their places, one of the historic society's workmen reported a missing compressor.

"It, too, was found in the sea." He reached down to stroke Jock's head when the dog leaned into him. "I found it at low tide not far from a wee cave at my end of the village. The thing was around the bluff from the cave, half hidden in the rocks. Whoever threw it there did so with enough might to put some good-sized dents into the machine."

Kendra frowned. "That doesn't sound possible. I've

seen plenty of compressors back home." Her apartment complex had undergone a horrid and lengthy refurbishment during the past year, and she'd grown to hate the boxy, infernally loud compressors used by the construction workers. "I can't imagine anyone being able to throw such a thing with enough force to dent it."

"Aye, well . . ." Graeme leaned toward her, his gaze intent. "Some would say that would depend on who or what did the throwing."

"Don't tell me the locals think ghosts from an eighteenth-century fishing fleet did it." Kendra imagined they did believe just that.

"Some do, aye." Graeme confirmed her guess. "But then . . ."

He paused to drag a hand down over his chin. "Then," he continued, "other things started happening, and to locals who have been especially vocal in their protests against the Pennard Project. Cow manure was poured down the chimney of Agnes Leith's cottage, the woman who makes the anti–Scotland's Past posters tacked about the village. And tar and feathers were smeared all over the new double-paned windows another protestor had just had installed at his cottage.

"The man was Seth Walker, and he'd used his just-received retirement bonus to pay for the windows." A muscle jerked in Graeme's jaw. "We all pitched in to replace the windows and helped clean up the mess. But the goings-on have unsettled folk. With the like happening to those supporting Scotland's Past and also those against the project, it's hard to say who's responsible."

"So people think it's supernatural?" Kendra glanced at him to see his response.

"That's why I had to get you out of the Laughing Gull." He slid an arm around her, pulling her close when the wind renewed its gusts, blasting them with chill, salt-laden air. "Tempers are frayed enough without the in-nocent quip of a tourist setting them all off again."

"I understand." Kendra tried to pull away, but he only tightened his hold on her. "We're not in the pub now. You don't have to pretend—"

He still didn't let go. "Once you've been here a while, you'll know why I just reached for you. And"—his lips quirked in a brief smile—"that all Scots have eyes in the backs o' their heads."

"Pardon?" Kendra's pulse raced to feel his strong, solid warmth pressed against her.

"The lace curtains of at least two cottages across the road twitched just now." He glanced at her, clearly be-mused. "We're under observation, lass."

"Oh." Kendra's heart dipped. She'd thought he was being gallant because of the wind.

Or that he just might be attracted to her.

As it was, he just wanted it to look that way.

"I hope you're not going to kiss me again." She wished he would.

"No worries. I promised you I wouldn't." He made it sound as if she should be glad.

"Of course. I'd forgotten." Kendra swallowed her dis-appointment.

"Then I hope I've reassured you?" He lifted a brow.

Kendra could've groaned.

"You have." She gave him her brightest smile.

"Good. Then you won't have any qualms about going out with me on the *Sea Wyfe* tomorrow." He gave her a wink and hurried her across the road, back toward the inn. "I'll call for you after breakfast, around nine, as Iain serves early."

"Wait . . ." Kendra pulled back, stopping just before he could open the inn door for her. "Isn't the *Sea Wyfe* your boat?"

"Aye, she is." He smiled and pulled her close, lowering his head as if to kiss her. Instead, he just rested his head against her hair, speaking in her ear. "Folk will wonder if we've just been reunited and I don't take you out on the water with me tomorrow.

"Consider it a free boat outing to see some really special seals." He straightened, seeming pleased with himself. And—Kendra just looked at him—as if the matter was all set and arranged.

"Nine sharp, America." He squeezed her shoulder and then turned on his heel, disappearing into the mist before she could argue.

And it was as she stared after him that she saw the big, gruff-faced fisherman again. As before, he was leaning against the red phone box across from the Laughing Gull. Still wearing his yellow waterproof jacket and gum boots, he was once again staring fixedly at the inn's windows.

There was only one difference.

This time, Kendra could see right through him.

Chapter 6

Kendra froze, her fingers gripping the door latch of the Laughing Gull Inn. Across the road, Pennard's first phantom resident to appear to her continued to lean against the red phone box. His jacket and boots glittered with beads of water, as if he'd just come from a place where it had rained. More likely, the droplets were sea spray.

His gruff face was fierce, despite its shimmering translucency. And as before, he didn't look at Kendra. His piercing blue gaze remained on the windows of the inn's pub restaurant.

Someone, most likely the innkeeper, had propped a large, hand-painted Project Pennard protest sign inside the window nearest the door. It was this poster that seemed to earn the specter's wrath.

His bearded jaw was tightly set and he'd lowered his bushy gray brows so they appeared as a thick, fearsome line across his brow.

Kendra studied him, not yet trusting herself to move. Instead she took a series of deep, calming breaths. As always when confronted with a discarnate she wished to communicate with, she relaxed her shields, allowing her aura's energy to warm and shine their brightest.

The ghost didn't react.

He kept his vigil at the phone box, where the soft light from a nearby lamppost illuminated his broad face. Kendra could tell that at some point in his earthly life, he'd broken his large, bulbous nose.

His contemporary clothing and the flash of a watch on his wrist revealed more, showing that he'd been a fisherman of fairly recent times.

The longer she watched him, the more the air filled with the unmistakable tang of herring and brine, the strong fishy smell underscoring the ghost's lifelong association with the sea.

He was clearly a man of Pennard.

And something here was making him unhappy.

Kendra had a good notion what. Darkness circled him like an impenetrable wall, letting her also know that his grievance went deep. Distress fueled by strong energy and emotions from the past.

The kind of ghost who'd loved his home so much in life that even death couldn't make him leave.

Such souls refused to settle into dust.

For them, the old days never faded away, but lived on just as they did. When they saw their world threatened, some tried to intervene. Sadly, they rarely achieved more than giving the odd chill to a few receptive people and making themselves miserable.

The ghost's unhappiness pulsed in the thin haze of darkness surrounding him.

Kendra's compassion welled, her heart clenching as always when she had to gaze on a spirit's suffering.

She had to reach him.

Wishing such an encounter could've happened elsewhere, she glanced up and down the narrow street. The hour had grown late, and no one moved anywhere on the waterfront. But muffled rock music escaped the grimy windows of a tiny pub she'd noticed at the opposite end of the village from Graeme's cottage. Called the Mermaid, the place looked more like a bar or tavern than a pub.

It had a seedy, rough-around-the-edges air even from a distance. And the low beat of some indistinguishable heavy metal tune underscored her negative impression. Kendra loved Beethoven and Mozart, Celtic rock, and mystical New Age tunes. The discordant strains from the Mermaid jarred the nighttime calm.

Suppressing a shudder, she tore her gaze from that direction before the bar's dubious atmosphere could tinge her perception.

Everywhere else along Harbour Street appeared quiet. Even the empty house she'd noticed on arrival seemed still now, its earlier menace gone. Cold mist hung over the marina, and thick clouds covered the moon. Lampposts glimmered, each one a loving replica of an old-timey gas lantern. Their soft glow spilled across the street's glistening pavement. And although she could hear the murmur of voices and the clink of glasses and cutlery from within the Laughing Gull's thick whitewashed walls, the noise wasn't disruptive.

Kendra just had to hope no one came outside.

She also stole a moment for a long glance down Harbour Street toward the Keel. She didn't need to be reminded of Graeme. Her entire body and all her senses went into overdrive just thinking about him. And this wasn't a good time for such an indulgence.

Not with an unhappy ghost right across the road, needing her undivided attention.

So she took another deep, cleansing breath, grateful that the night's darkness and drifting mist strengthened the illusion of being alone.

With the aid of long practice, she blotted the noise from the Mermaid from her mind, closing her ears—her world—to the beat of the music and the sounds of the rowdy crowd inside the bar.

She also raised a mental wall between herself and the Laughing Gull, willing the invisible barrier to hold off the buzz of conversation and other sounds slipping out into the street from within the cozy inn. The noise wasn't jarring like the heavy metal music from the Mermaid, but she raised her protective shields all the same. Any distraction could shatter her concentration.

Then she focused, delving deep so that her aura would glow even brighter. She asked the powerful white-light energy to cleanse and bless a sacred circle of space around her.

Such a purification rite was necessary to banish negative psychic imprints that may have been left behind by any number of occurrences. A couple arguing, someone's depression, or even the sadness of a homeless animal could all impact the atmosphere. There was always the possibility of dark, low-level energies hovering near if even a trace of negativity stained a place.

And once she opened herself fully, making contact with the unseen realm, Kendra knew she was vulnerable to attack from such entities.

So she never greeted a ghost without first practicing psychic self-defense.

It was a ritual she'd done so often, she needed only a few seconds before the protective energy rose, flowing through and around her.

Only then did she return her attention to the phone-box ghost, allowing her consciousness to slip into her most receptive state. The spirit still hadn't looked her way, his fierce gaze remaining fixed on the inn's front windows. But the dark haze around him wavered a bit now, as if his own deepest subconscious was becoming aware of her.

Encouraged, she focused harder, sending him a mental greeting. Using the words of power she always employed, she offered him respect and asked him to acknowledge her. She also assured him he could trust her.

As it harms none—she silently repeated the words of power, ensuring that no one nearby, corporeal or otherwise, would be endangered by her attempt to contact the spirit—*by your free will, speak to me.*

The ghost's eyes flickered, blinking as if coming out of a daze. Straightening, he pushed away from the phone box, turning at once to stare at Kendra.

Fool woman. The slur reached her as clearly as if the spirit stood beside her and had spoken into her ear. His voice was deep and gravelly, full of the sea, and very Scottish. He also sounded angry.

Ne'er ken what's good for you, aye? He started forward, drifting across the road toward Kendra. His eyes glinted and the sharp smell of fish and brine in the air intensified, growing so strong that her eyes began to burn as he reached the middle of the street. *Thick-skulled your like is, unable to see aught but—*

He jerked to a halt when two houses down from the Laughing Gull, a door opened and a small man with a weather-beaten face stepped out onto the pavement, a tiny tricolor terrier bouncing at his heels. The dog was energetic, circling the man's feet and barking excitedly as the two headed right toward Kendra and the ghost.

Kendra recognized the man as the same one who'd

tipped his cap to her when he'd left the pub restaurant earlier. He was wearing the same cap now. And his eyes, when they lit on her, again showed friendliness.

But he couldn't have chosen a worse time to take his dog for his evening constitutional.

The phone-box ghost's already-translucent form was fast fading. And the darkness around him was swiftly turning into ordinary night blackness. There was a cloaking smudge that would be visible only to Kendra and that curled slowly about him as he dissipated into nothing.

Then he was gone.

And the jaunty little fisherman and his dog were upon her.

"Fine night, aye, lass?" Again, the cheery man touched his cap, nodding respectfully.

His dog leapt at Kendra's legs, his small black nose nudging her knees.

"Charlie, get you down! Be a good lad." The man snapped his fingers at the dog, his face apologetic when Charlie only jumped higher, resting his paws on Kendra's legs, his stubby little tail wagging.

"It's okay." Kendra reached to pet the terrier, aware that Charlie hadn't seemed frightened by the ghost who'd been floating across the road just as he and his master had left their cottage.

She was sure the dog must've seen the spirit.

Animals, especially dogs, always saw ghosts.

"I love dogs." Kendra straightened, relying on years of experience with similar interruptions to keep from showing how untimely their arrival proved. She really did love dogs. But she would've preferred meeting Charlie some other time.

"He didn't bother me." She glanced after the little

terrier, who'd run ahead, sniffing the pavement with great enthusiasm.

Farther down Harbour Street another door burst open, and this time several pale-skinned, black-jacketed youths lurched out into the road. Loud and clearly full of ale, they leaned into one another as they swayed along the street in the opposite direction. Their gel-spiked hair glistened in the lamplight, and before they'd turned away, Kendra was sure she'd caught the flash of studs in their nostrils. She knew they were staggering drunk. The reek of stale beer carried on the wind, making her wrinkle her nose.

Charlie growled.

"He knows bad business when he sees it." The friendly man once more looked apologetic, though not because of his pet. His gaze was on the rowdies, now beginning to weave their way up the cliff path toward Gavin Ramsay's Spindrift. "Didn't used to see suchlike in Pennard."

Shaking his head, he turned back to Kendra. "You'd best be inside the inn, miss. Thon lads won't it make where they're headed. The way's too steep. They'll be stumbling back into the village anon, looking for trouble."

"I was just going in, anyway." She was—now.

"I'm Archie Dee." He thrust out a hand, his calloused grip firm and warm. "Salt Barrel Cottage is mine, two doors down from the Laughing Gull, if e'er you be needing aught. I'm aye home unless I'm away at the fishing, at the inn, or out walking with wee Charlie."

Kendra started to thank him, but he'd moved on, hurrying after Charlie, who'd bolted across the road, making for the two empty cottages and the little alleyway where Graeme had taken her earlier.

She felt a pang of loss as dog and man nipped into the

shadows, out of sight. Not because of Archie Dee and Charlie the terrier, but for the twinge of regret that Graeme hadn't kissed her in the darkness between the tiny cottages. Instead, he'd sworn not to touch her again. His vow still whispered in her mind.

I won't kiss you, if that's worrying you.

His gaze had dropped to her lips as he'd said the words. But even in the night's dimness, she'd been able to tell that it'd been only a perfunctory, instinctive glance. No warmth or desire had kindled in his eyes. Yet she'd been weak in the knees just standing so close to him. No more than a breath separated them, and she'd burned to step nearer, letting their bodies touch. She'd felt the heat rising inside her, the memory of his kiss making her tingle.

Kendra frowned, pushing him from her mind.

She'd never run after men who didn't want her. And she wasn't going to start now.

Duty also called.

So she glanced up and down Harbour Street one more time, making sure no one else was about. Then she reached down, using the pretense of adjusting her boot laces to lightly touch the flats of her hands to the cold, damp ground. She'd stirred a flurry of energy when trying to communicate with the phone-box ghost. That energy still shimmered in the air, broken by the disruption. Potentially dangerous if not returned from whence it'd come.

Excess energy needed grounding, especially in a place like Pennard.

Only when she was sure that the last remnants of summoned white light had flowed from her hands and were absorbed back into the earth did she straighten and allow herself another long, cleansing breath.

The night felt ordinary once more.

If a cold Scottish night on the moon-silvered North Sea coast could be called anything but magical.

Kendra didn't think so.

Pennard *was* special.

The night darkness only enhanced the fishing village's charm. The harbor lights danced on the glassy water, while the old-fashioned lampposts cast yellow pools of light on the rain-dampened pavement. Long tendrils of mist still trailed across the bay, and torn clouds drifted past the moon. High above, stars glimmered brightly, their brilliance rivaling any she'd ever seen.

Closer by, lights twinkled in a few of the cottages, and threads of bluish peat smoke rose from chimneys. The rhythmic wash of the sea against the harbor breakwater struck her as the most soothing sound she'd heard in a long while. Then her heart squeezed when a foghorn echoed, muffled as if from a great distance.

Pennard wore quiet well.

She could get used to such peace and tranquillity. Just as she could to feeling Graeme's strong arms sliding around her, his hands gripping her face as he dipped his head to kiss her. He'd taken her breath, whisking her into another world. A place where nothing mattered except the moment and how wonderful it had felt to be held fast against him.

Stop right now.

Her good sense shouted the words. And she knew better than to ignore them. So she inhaled deeply and lifted her chin, steeling herself to breeze back inside the Laughing Gull. She'd look carefree, as if nothing was on her mind except heading up the stairs to her room for the sound night's sleep awaiting her there.

Unfortunately, when she opened the inn door and stepped inside, she nearly collided with Janet, who was sweeping the entry.

"On your own now, are you?" The older woman clutched her broom, not budging. Instead, she lifted a brow, peering sharply at Kendra.

"I did book a single room." Kendra kept her poise in place.

Janet leaned forward. "So you did, aye." Her tone didn't warm at all. "And the room's ready for you, it is. I was just up there to turn down the bed and leave a wee dram on the night table."

"Thanks. But that wasn't necessary." Kendra tried to step past her.

"It's tradition." Janet straightened, her chest puffing on the words. "The Laughing Gull is an ancient inn. We still do things the old way. A turned-down bed and a night dram are courtesies we uphold."

"I understand." Kendra just wanted to sleep.

"Humph." Janet surveyed her, one brow inching upward again, as if to imply she doubted any tourist could grasp the desire to cling to heritage and culture. "Pride of place matters here, even if there be some who've forgotten the like." She bristled, two spots of red blooming on her cheeks. "Poxy souls they are, wanting to make Pennard a theme park."

Kendra started to speak — she really did sympathize — but Janet had already turned away, resuming her broom attack on the stone-flagged floor.

Starting to nip around her, Kendra paused when a door marked PRIVATE banged open and a young, wild-haired girl swept into view.

Janet stopped sweeping the floor at once, some of the sternness leaving her face.

Seeing the older woman, the girl flashed a smile.

Twenty at most, she had the whitest skin Kendra had ever seen. And the kohl around her eyes was as black as her long, curling hair. A tiny gold ring winked from the end of her left eyebrow and—Kendra blinked—a ruby-red stud glittered beneath the girl's bottom lip.

Plump but well made, she was what Zack liked to call a handful of woman. She also looked slightly out of time in her long, flowing, peasant-style dress. Wine red, the gown could've been a relic from the sixties and was low-cut to show off her bosom. At least what could be seen of it beneath the torn denim jacket she was pulling on even as she'd burst into the entry hall.

She reminded Kendra of a gypsy, and was pretty in an earthy, untamed way.

She also wasn't a stranger at the Laughing Gull, because she went right up to Janet, kissing the older woman noisily on the cheek.

"Thanks, auntie!" She patted the pocket of her jacket. "You've saved us again. Roan will pay you back as soon as the regulars—"

"Never you mind, lassie." Janet took the girl's elbow and steered her along the narrow passage. "Though"—she opened the outside door, letting in cold air—"I'll not be helping him again if he ..." The wind picked up then and Kendra didn't catch the rest of her words.

"My niece, Maili." Janet glanced at Kendra as she shut the door behind the girl. "She's a good lass." She started sweeping again, a bit more vigorously than before. "Pity is her boyfriend, Roan Wylie, who owns the Mermaid, a wee pub up the road, is aye letting his friends drink without paying for their ale."

She frowned, jabbing the edge of her broom at a corner. "Now the lad is telling everyone he's selling the Mermaid to Scotland's Past. Foolish loon thinks they'll pay him a fortune." She darted another look at Kendra. "He wants to open a new pub in Glasgow, right on Sauchiehall Street, saying it'll be the biggest and finest—"

She broke off, flushing as if she'd just realized she'd been pouring out family gossip to a stranger. "Aye, well!" She went to the other corner, employing her broom with a vengeance. "There be lots of folk hereabouts thinking the like. They're blinded by dreams of grandeur."

"Many people are." Kendra needed only to recall the scores of hopeful ghostcatchers who constantly called Zack or flooded the Ghostcatchers headquarters in Bucks County. People who mistakenly believed the organization would get them on national television, making them celebrities.

Once they learned Zack Walker ran his business on a lower-than-low profile, most would-be recruits took a fast track to the door.

They wanted fame.

Not hard work they couldn't even discuss in public.

And if she was going to get any work done, she needed a good night's rest.

Janet had other plans.

"Humph." The older woman's face darkened as she swept along the edge of the wall, her bulk and her fast-moving broom blocking Kendra's path to the stairs. "Think they can all be legends, they do. Poor Maili"— she arced the broom in a half circle around Kendra's feet—"has the voice of an angel, that girl. Thought she'd enter a talent show up Inverness way, sure she'd win and become a star.

"Do you ken what happened?" She stopped, clutching her broom in a white-knuckled grip. "The only *win* she pulled in was an offer to spend the night with one of the event's sponsors. Roan Wylie heard the man hassling her and slid his arm around her, claiming he was her boyfriend. Now he is and"—she took an agitated breath— "Maili spends her days serving up pub grub and pints at the Mermaid."

"She's young." Kendra didn't know what else to say. "She'll find her way."

Janet sniffed. "Not if she doesn't learn that a handful of pebbles from the shore outside thon windows is worth more than all fame's gold. Fool's gold, the like is, good for naught but sorrow and bother.

"Why else would all the townies up from Scotland's Central Belt and the Londoners aye be moving to the Highlands and hereabout?" She set her hand on her hip, her chin jutting fiercely. "Sooner or later, they ken what really matters and want a piece of it. The tartan dream calls to them, beckoning with images of heathery moors, fresh air, deep glens, and misty hills."

Kendra took a breath, unable to argue.

If she could, she'd move to Pennard in a heartbeat. No regrets.

But Janet was still looking huffy, her piercing stare underscoring her opinion of incomers. "I'm surprised your beau hasn't—"

"My beau?" Kendra spoke before she could catch herself.

"The MacGrath." Janet eyed her suspiciously, now standing before the door marked PRIVATE. "He knows better than most how eager some are to get their hands on good property up here." She shook her head, opening the door to release a waft of delicious cooking smells and the clatter of plates and the bustle of a working kitchen into the entry.

"Hard to believe he's said nothing." She flashed Kendra one last look before stepping through the door, taking her broom with her.

Kendra blinked at the closed door, the neat little sign warning away trespassers.

Laughing Gull's kitchen was off-limits to her.

As was Pennard, even if she was loathe to leave after her work stint ended. She wasn't like the Central Belt Scots or Londoners seeking a quiet life away from the crowds and hectic of the city. Nor did she have the good fortune of her neighbors to the north, the Canadians. They had the advantage of birthright and could pack up and move to Pennard or anywhere else in Scotland that they wished to go.

She was American.

She couldn't pop across the Big Pond and claim a piece of a tiny Scottish community just because the place appealed to her.

She also had no business allowing her whole world to be upturned by a sexy, dark-eyed Scotsman. Yet she couldn't stop thinking about him. He fascinated her. And now that he'd held her, even kissed her, she wanted more.

Being crushed against him hadn't just excited her; it'd felt right. True, his strong arms around her had sent delicious shivers rippling through her. But a flood tide of warmth had swept her, as well. And it'd been a heady kind of warmth, as if they belonged together.

She'd also seen the desire in his eyes.

And—she touched a hand to her breast—she was sure he'd recognized how powerfully she'd reacted to him. She could melt recalling how he'd gripped her face, his fingers sliding through her hair as he'd kissed her, claiming her mouth with his, tasting her with his tongue.

She wanted such a kiss from him again, preferably more than one. Long, hard kisses that took her breath and electrified her, making her forget he was the one man she couldn't allow herself to want so badly.

Unfortunately, she did.

And—she blinked, stopping just before the steep and

narrow stairs to her room—it didn't help to see his handsome face staring at her from a framed photograph on the entry wall.

Or so she thought, until she went over to the picture and took a closer look.

Part of a collection of wood-framed photographs grouped on the wall near the kitchen door, the pictures were from the previous century. Some even dated back to the mid-1800s, according to the tiny brass plaques on the bottom of the frames.

One grainy photo showed six fisher girls in their Sunday-best clothes. Also known as herring girls, named after their work of gutting and cleaning the fish caught each day, they looked proud to be dressed in style. Three girls sat with another three standing behind, each resting a hand on the shoulder of the girl sitting before her. Their high-buttoned, white-aproned dresses marked them as Victorian, as did their stilted poses and frozen-faced expressions.

Another photo was captioned PENNARD 1890 and captured a few of the village's low, whitewashed cottages. Several women sat outside their homes, knitting or baiting fishing lines while a stern-faced, bearded man looked on, smoking his pipe as the women toiled.

A photo of the herring fleet leaving Pennard gave Kendra chills. She stepped closer, examining the little stone marina and the numerous boats sailing out of the harbor. The fleet stretched the length of the horizon and filled the vast expanse of water between. Just as the lights from the spectral fleet had indicated a countless number of herring boats on the night-darkened sea.

Kendra rubbed her arms, suddenly cold.

Now more than ever, she was sure of what she'd seen.

But it was the blurry photograph of the crew of a

trawler that really caught her eye, punching her like a blow to the chest.

The boat, named *Josephine*, according to the picture frame, was at anchor in Pennard Bay. Her crewmen stood or sat near the harbor wall, each man wearing light trousers, a dark vest, and a seaman's cap. Their faces appeared well-scrubbed, their hair neatly combed, as if each man hoped to look his best for the photographer.

One man stood out from the rest.

And not because a large white dog with one black eye and ear sat beside him, its gaze full of adoration as he looked up at his master.

Beneath the old-fashioned clothes and hairstyle, the man could've been Graeme MacGrath.

And unlike his fellow fishermen, he was smiling. Although his smile was for the dog by his side and not aimed at the camera.

Kendra's brow knit as she stepped closer to the wall, leaning in to peer hard through the picture glass. The likeness was astounding. She angled her head, reading the inscription twice.

There could be no mistake.

The little plate on the frame stated the men were the crew of the trawler *Josephine*, and dated the photo to the long-ago year of 1875.

Still . . .

Something didn't seem right to Kendra. She could feel the fine hairs lifting on her nape and sensed stirrings of doubt that prickled her skin.

"Looks just like him, eh?"

She jumped, wheeling about to find Iain Garry standing directly behind her.

"It's amazing, yes." She saw no point in pretending not to know what he meant.

"Graeme aye laughs about it." The innkeeper rocked back on his heels, his gaze flicking to the photograph. "Thon trawlerman is your lad's great-great-grandfather. His name was also Graeme."

Kendra bit her lip, remembering her gaffe with Janet.

She understood Graeme's reasons for wanting people to think they were a pair. She wouldn't break his trust by telling the innkeeper Graeme wasn't her lad. In truth, she wished that he was.

She also glanced away from Iain to look again at the crew of the *Josephine*. Even to her inexpert eyes, she could tell the photograph was genuine. It appeared as old as the little brass plate on the bottom of the frame said.

And it wasn't just the family resemblance that jumped out at her.

It was more.

It was the strong bond between Graeme the trawlerman and his dog, a deep love that even hundreds of years and grainy, faded paper couldn't diminish. With her heightened sensitivity, Kendra could feel their connection even through the cold glass of the picture frame.

Their love was so strong, it hit her like a blast of energy. Her heart raced, heat pumping through her.

Iain Garry didn't seem to notice.

He did reach to tap the picture glass. "Your Graeme and his great-great-grandpappy have more in common than looks and a name. All the men in that family love dogs. Graeme's no different with his Jock, aye? You ne'er see one without the other." He smiled, lowering his hand.

"That's true." Kendra decided to play it safe.

Her mind was racing.

Something told her she shouldn't wonder too deeply why Graeme's resemblance to his forebear bothered her so much. But it did. And the chills slipping up and down her spine let her know she needed answers.

She just hoped she could handle them. She was already at a disadvantage.

Graeme and his dog were winning her heart.

Chapter 7

"Have you known Graeme long?"

Iain showed no sign of returning to his inn-keeping duties. Far from it, he folded his arms and looked at Kendra, waiting expectantly. And the friendly expression on his red-cheeked face made it impossible for her to brush off his question.

Too bad she didn't know how to answer him.

So she hedged, tucking her hair behind an ear and pretending to examine the photograph of the *Josephine* trawlermen and the other old pictures. They crowded the entry hall, grouped in collections. And they offered a viable excuse for her to peer at the wall.

With luck, the innkeeper would take the subtle hint and return to his public room and the lovely, polished bar awaiting him there.

"Did you and Graeme just meet, then?" He proved

what she'd always heard about Highland Scots being exceptionally curious people.

Pennard wasn't anywhere near the Highlands, but Iain's soft, musical voice gave away his heritage. Like Graeme, rich Highland blood flowed through his veins, giving him the oh-so-typical burr.

Kendra inhaled and looked away from the photographs, turning to face Iain. Instinct told her he wouldn't go away until she answered him.

"I've known Graeme a while." She just didn't say how short that while had been. "But this is my first time to visit Pennard."

That was true.

And it seemed to please the innkeeper, because he beamed.

"Then you'll know Graeme's family has been here for centuries." There was pride in his voice. "They once ruled these parts, the MacGraths. Graeme keeps to himself and doesn't speak much of his illustrious forebears. But"—he paused, looking back at the closed outside door—"he's surely told you about Castle Grath?"

"Of course," Kendra opted for a white lie.

She also gave him her most confident smile.

But her mind filled with the image of Graeme on the high dunes at Balmedie Beach. His stance had struck her as almost territorial. There'd been something possessive about his attitude, as if he owned every grain of sand on the broad, sweeping strand. A man who believed each blade of grass on the dunes should bend to his will. Such thoughts were fanciful, but they'd come to her at the time.

And hadn't Janet called him the MacGrath?

Kendra took another deep breath, trying to still her racing mind. If Graeme was some kind of laird or chieftain, he hadn't said a word. Nor had he mentioned anything about an ancestral castle.

Not that it was any of her business.

But Iain was looking at her as if it was. "There's a photo of Grath by the door." He headed that way, leaving her little choice but to follow. "Here she is, in all her fallen glory," he announced, looking at a large, framed black-and-white picture of a gaunt, ruined tower. "No one has lived there since medieval times. The MacGraths aye seemed to fight on the wrong side of battles in those days, and they made a lot of powerful enemies because of it."

"They were rough times, I know." Kendra's mind flashed again to Balmedie. When she'd first glimpsed Graeme on the dunes, for a beat she'd been sure he was wearing a plaid, much like the Highland chieftains of old. She also would've sworn he'd had a long sword strapped to his side.

Such a weapon would suit him.

The image made her pulse race. He would've been a magnificent medieval warrior. Proud, bold, and fearless in battle.

Iain tapped the picture glass, indicating Grath's ruined tower. "Some say it was Alexander Stewart, son of Robert II and known as the Wolf of Badenoch, who did the most damage to Grath, leaving the castle uninhabitable. That would've been round about"—he rubbed his chin, thinking—"the late 1300s.

"Thon Stewart was a right troublemaker, rampaging far and wide if the mood took him." He paused, nodding and smiling at two locals who'd chosen that moment to leave the pub restaurant and walk past on their way to the door. "Whoever slighted Grath"—Iain turned back to Kendra—"left a romantic ruin, wouldn't you say?"

"It is that." She stepped closer to the photograph, agreeing completely.

Who wouldn't?

Little more than a shell, the tower stood etched against a stormy sky. Once circular, only a crescent of age-worn stone remained. Three tall windows, lined vertically, showed the tower had boasted at least four floors. Traces of a winding stair could be seen near the top window, the shallow steps leading to nowhere.

"Where is it?" She traced the barely recognizable stair with a finger. "I didn't see a ruin anything like this on the drive from Aberdeen."

"You wouldn't have." Iain was looking just as intently at the photograph as she was. "Castle Grath is farther along the coast, a bit beyond the headland to west of here. The high bluff hides the tower. You'd have seen it if you'd driven on past Pennard."

"I'm sure Graeme will take me there." It didn't seem likely, but she couldn't help hoping he would.

The ruin was just her cuppa.

Half-standing walls, one holding the outline of a long-disused fireplace, stretched away from either side of the crumbling tower, proving Castle Grath must've been impressive in its day.

Above all, the ruin was spectacularly situated on the edge of a cliff, high above the crashing sea. And whoever had taken the photograph had used an artist's eye to capture the moody setting at its most magnificent. The dark sky boiled with low, angry clouds, while the rough sea gleamed, each long breaker bearing a crest of white. Somewhere the sun must've pierced a cloud because the castle's silhouette appeared limned by eerie silver light.

The play of shadows and darkness and the strange luminosity gave the picture a sense of the surreal. The longer Kendra studied it, the more she expected to see the motion of the sea. She could also imagine the clouds moving, drifting past the tower toward the distant horizon.

"Wow." It was all she could think to say.

The innkeeper didn't look surprised. "Aye, so say many folk seeing Grath for the first time. Wait till Graeme takes you there. It has an even greater impact when you see the ruin up close.

"There's more to the site than the photo shows." He smiled, nodding again to another local just leaving the pub restaurant. "If you know what to look for, there are piles of grass-grown rubble that were once the earthwork defenses of an earlier fortress."

"Really?" Kendra lifted her brows, hoping he wouldn't guess she'd instantly recognize the grassy lumps and weed-grown mounds at such a site. He clearly believed he was introducing her to things she didn't know. She didn't want to lessen his pleasure in the telling.

"Och, aye." Iain bobbed his head. "The castle was protected by the promontory on three sides, but there's a semicircular ditch that might've once been a moat. And the well is easy to spot even though it's been filled with rocks and debris over the years. The ruins of kitchens, storerooms, and other outbuildings are also scattered about, some quite well preserved. Most exciting of all"—he leaned toward her—"is a stretch of wall with a few pillared archways. Graeme once told me he thinks they must've been part of a covered walk to Grath's medieval chapel."

Kendra was sure that was true.

As the cliff-top ruin's site exposed it to the fierceness of the elements, long-ago MacGraths would've appreciated shelter from wind and rain when they made the journey from the keep to their chapel.

Kendra flashed another glance at the picture, imagining Graeme striding out from the tower door on just such a stormy afternoon as when the photo had been taken. He wouldn't have been troubled by the day's wild weather, she was sure. In fact, she suspected he'd love the rush of the wind, the heavy smell of rain in the air.

He'd embrace the wildness.

She knew that as surely as she could still taste his kiss.

Her pulse quickened on the admission, a sudden wash of heat blooming on her cheeks. But it was true. His kiss had branded her, doing so much more than saving her from Gavin Ramsay's oily come-on.

Even now, speaking about something as innocent as a cliff-top castle ruin with a talkative but kindly Scottish innkeeper, she could hardly think of anything except how badly she wanted Graeme to kiss her again.

Actually, she wanted more.

And that threw her completely. She'd always kept a good grip on her emotions. Her love life—she managed not to wince—had been anything but wondrous in recent years. She just didn't have the time and energy for a relationship, her interests always elsewhere.

Until now . . .

When she found herself attracted to a Scotsman and in a situation where so many barriers stood between them that she doubted she could tear them down even if she had Herculean strength.

She made it a rule not to break her word.

Zack and Ghostcatchers had her solemn oath never to reveal her assignments. Doing so could cost them thousands in lost contracts. Worse, any disruptions in her work could risk the much-needed solace for the disgruntled spirits she sought to help.

A romance with Graeme was out of the question.

Hoping Iain wouldn't see her discomfiture, she assumed her most carefree expression. Then she tucked her hair behind an ear in an annoying habit she'd often tried to curb, failing every time.

"Did Graeme take the picture?" She could tell the photo held passion. Whoever the photographer was, he was more than just talented. She could pick up the deep emotion captured in the photo.

"Nae, he didn't snap it." Iain shook his head. "Janet Murray made that picture. You've met her." He glanced at the kitchen door, the one with the PRIVATE sign. "It was about ten years ago, I'm thinking. She used to dabble in photography back then."

"Janet?" Kendra's eyes rounded.

"Aye, herself and no other." Again, a note of pride threaded the innkeeper's words. "She was a bold lass in those days, afraid of nothing. You can see she was up there on a dark, windy day. Gales can rise then, blowing a body right off the cliffs before you even know what hit you." He nodded sagely. "And the cliff path is dangerous in any weathers, steep and slippery as it is. Yet Janet went every day."

Kendra listened with interest. "She must like hill walking."

"She loved her husband." Iain shot another glance at the kitchen door.

Kendra blinked, not missing the past tense. "Was he a MacGrath?"

"Nae, Dod Murray didn't have a whit to do with the MacGraths or their castle." Iain lowered his voice, this time glancing at the open door to the inn's public room. The buzz of many male voices proved the Laughing Gull was still enjoying a full house. "Dod was a fisherman." Iain returned his attention to her. "A right good man he was, too. Hardworking, few words, but a big heart, salt-of-the-earth type, if you know what I mean."

"I do." Kendra smiled. He could've just described her

father. "But I don't understand the connection to the Grath ruin. Or"—she spoke quietly—"is Janet's husband buried there?"

It didn't seem likely.

"Ach, nae, he's not up there." Iain shook his head. "Dod's part of the North Sea now, God rest him. His ashes were strewn on the waves. Janet hasn't been up to Grath since he died. She used to go so she could see his boat coming in on the tide.

"Janet's father went down with a herring boat not long after she married Dod." Iain's face grew serious. "She ne'er forgot that. It put the fear on her, it did. Dod tried to talk sense into her, but she wouldn't have any of it, insisting she enjoyed the climb and that was all. Folk hereabouts knew better, of course."

"What a tragic story." Kendra had a terrible thought. "I hope her husband didn't die at sea."

To her relief, Iain shook his head. "He suffered a heart attack. And"—he straightened then, once again the cheery innkeeper—"I shouldn't be filling your head with sad tales when you're just arrived and surely wanting nothing more than your bed.

"I don't want Graeme fashed with me because I kept you from your beauty sleep." He winked, already starting for the door into the public room. "Not that a lass as bonnie as you needs the like."

Kendra looked after him, feeling her face color.

Above all, she felt bad for thinking of Janet as so soured. From what she'd heard, the older woman had reason to be less than jovial. Her devotion to her husband and the emotion evident in her photograph of the ruin proved that she'd once been a woman of passion.

Kendra's heart clenched for Janet, a shiver slipping down her spine as she looked out the window beside the Laughing Gull's entry door.

Moonlight filtered through the clouds, silvering the narrow road and the marina just beyond. It was another world out there and one that beckoned to her strongly, just as the strange and mysterious had done all her life.

And—she glanced at her wristwatch—at a very early hour, Graeme would be calling for her, beckoning her in an entirely different way.

Her heart raced at the thought.

Good sense told her that when he arrived, the last thing she wanted was to greet him with puffy eyes. She didn't wear morning well. She also hoped to use the time before breakfast to take a look at the deserted cottage a few doors down from the inn. Experience had taught her to visit such sites only when well rested.

So she tossed one last glance toward the open door to the public room and then the closed kitchen door before she hurried from the entry hall. She took the narrow stairs just as swiftly, glad that the carpet runner dampened her footsteps. It wasn't likely that another guest would hear her passage and put his head round the door, but she'd traveled often enough to know better than to push her luck.

Some people just loved to talk.

She wasn't in the mood for such conviviality.

And as she let herself into her small-but-tasteful room, she wanted only to shower and then dive into her bed, pulling the duvet over her head. Her wishes vanished like a pricked balloon when the room's atmosphere hit her. Wary, she closed the door, chills coming over her.

Something wasn't right.

The bed had been neatly turned down, as Janet had said. And the promised night dram waited on the bedside table, the tiny bottle and spotlessly clean glass surely a treat for those who enjoyed whisky. There was also a small packet of shortbread, which was much more to her liking. Her suitcase still stood beside the blue plaid chair by the window. And someone, most likely Janet, had thoughtfully lit the night lamp in the room's teeny bathroom.

Her toiletries stood on the mirrored dresser, exactly where she'd placed them.

The hospitality tray also hadn't been touched. The electric teakettle, tea packets, and extra packets of shortbread—all looked as they had when she'd first entered the room. Even the tray's jar of hot chocolate mix remained where she'd left it after making herself a cup earlier.

Yet she felt a presence.

Whoever it was, the energy was strong, lifting the fine hairs on her nape. And—this surprised her—the longer she looked about, the more certain she became that the entity wasn't in the room with her.

The vibrations came from outside, meaning the source was exceptionally powerful.

Knowing she wouldn't sleep unless she knew who was causing such a rift in the atmosphere, she went to the window and pulled back the drapes.

She saw nothing.

She'd expected to see the spectral herring fleet, the boats crowding Pennard's tiny harbor. At the least, she'd tipped on the phone-box ghost. It wouldn't have surprised her if he'd crossed the road and manifested beneath her window.

But Harbour Street was empty, its asphalt shimmering with nothing more ominous than the sheen of a light drizzle.

The few boats in the marina were equally quiet, their crews nowhere in sight.

Pennard was still, nary a ghost anywhere.

But there was a white minivan turning slowly onto

Harbour Street from Cliff Road, the steep and harrowing nightmare-of-a-ribbon road that plunged down Pennard's sheltering bluff.

Curious, she stepped closer to the window. At once, a flash of chills rushed up her neck. When the multipassenger van drew to a halt near the stone slipway, parking behind her car, shivers also rippled down her spine. Whoever drove the vehicle was the source of the strong vibes she'd felt upon entering her room.

There could be no doubt.

With her heightened senses, she could see energy pulsing around the minivan's exterior.

The strange luminosity was brightest where bold lettering adorned the van's right-hand driver's door. But the light rain and mist blowing along the road made it difficult to read the advertisement's words.

Taking care to stay behind the curtain, she pressed her forehead to the window glass and cupped her hands around her eyes. But the only word she could make out was *Heritage*.

The rest was blurred by rain and mist. And just when she scrunched her eyes, trying harder to read the sign, the driver's door opened and a tall, heavyset man climbed out.

Kendra blinked, certain he must be six and a half feet tall, at least six-four. He wasn't a hunk. His loose black trousers did show off his long legs. But the effect was spoiled because his white shirt, long sleeves rolled, revealed a good-sized paunch. His thinning hair—red, Kendra guessed, but unable to tell for sure in the dark, wet night—also didn't enhance his appearance.

Most notable of all, besides his height, were cheeks that shone like polished apples, making him look like an oversized teddy bear.

For a beat, Kendra doubted herself.

Surely such an innocuous-looking man hadn't been responsible for the heavy air in her room. There had to be another source for the chills that swept her.

But she couldn't deny the strange shimmer circling his van.

When he set his hands on his hips and looked up and down Harbour Street, surveying the village in a proprietary manner, Kendra knew why the Otherworld was marking him so clearly for her.

He had something to do with the Pennard Project.

But before she could focus strongly enough for one of her spirit guides—or a talkative Pennard ghost—to respond to her and reveal the connection, the man returned to his van and drove away.

Kendra's chills vanished at once.

She rubbed the back of her neck, glad she hadn't summoned Raziel, her main spirit guide in the Otherworld. A powerful entity who'd never had a human existence, his messages were often cryptic. Raziel believed she should find her own way. He held disdain for Kendra's other supernatural contacts, Saami and Ordo, who'd once walked the earth and were more inclined to divulge information when called upon.

Unfortunately, Saami and Ordo enjoyed spirit guiding so much, they spread themselves thin. As a onetime flower child of the 1960s, Saami believed in sharing her love. Ordo, famed in the Viking Age as a far-traveling Norse trader, simply enjoyed keeping busy. They helped many sensitives like Kendra and so they weren't always available when she needed them.

Raziel, intimidating as he could be, remained her last resort.

So she scanned the street again, making certain the energy she'd felt truly had vanished with the departure of the man and his minivan.

Unfortunately, her skin pricked anew when her gaze lit on the shadowed alley between the two cottages where Graeme had taken her earlier.

The mist drifting along the waterfront wasn't thick enough to hide the man standing there.

He was Gavin Ramsay, staring after the departing minivan with venom in his gaze.

Kendra's breath caught, her pulse quickening, ratcheting with edginess.

Worse, looking at him turned her blood cold and filled her with creeping ill ease. He wasn't just an oily Romeo. He had an agenda. And whatever it hinged on, the in-between time when the veil separating the Otherworld and the mortal one was at its thinnest.

Kendra sensed his menace as surely as she knew the remaining hours of the night would fly by at light speed, ensuring she'd waken without enough rest. She'd be doomed to greet Graeme with puffy eyes and a fuzzy mind.

She handled mornings so poorly.

And even as she watched Gavin Ramsay saunter down Harbour Street, making for the cliff path to his house, she knew that she'd need all her wits when the morning sun peeked above the horizon.

She just wondered if Graeme knew the strength of his foe.

Somewhere deep inside her, a strong voice warned that she must alert him.

But how could she explain knowing?

Much later, in the small hours of the night, Graeme stood at the front window of his cottage and watched moonlight glimmer on the bay. He could hear the incoming tide washing over rocks on the shore and the soft *chink* of boats rocking at their moorings. A light rain continued to fall. Harbour Street appeared quiet, though a few lights twinkled here and there, proving that some villagers hadn't yet sought their beds.

Jock was also restless.

Well tuned to Graeme's moods, Jock had enjoyed enough lifetimes at Graeme's side to read him. Just now, the dog's perked ears and his pacing was a sure sign that he knew Graeme was planning to do something important.

Jock insisted on participating in vital matters.

It was tradition.

One they'd kept for centuries.

"We're almost ready, lad." Graeme looked to where the dog fretted on the far side of the lounge.

Small and tidy, it was the Keel's best room, as Highlanders called such rarely used sitting rooms. And with so few visitors as came to Graeme's door, he saw no point in not enjoying the lounge's comforts. A peat fire always glowed in the hearth, and the armchair beside the fireplace was worn, welcoming, and never off-limits to Jock.

Instead of claiming a seat on the less-cozy sofa, Graeme left the lounge and went down the dark entry hall to the cottage's front door. Jock stayed behind, dropping onto his haunches and assuming his most grieved expression. It was an old trick, as well used as feigning sleep and employed in the hope that Graeme would swiftly return and man and dog could enjoy a few hours together before the hearth fire.

Jock's strategy failed.

Admitting defeat, he padded down the hall, joining Graeme at the door.

"One look, old boy. That's all." Graeme reached to pat the dog's head before he opened the door and stepped out onto the stoop. "I can't risk doing what we must if there's even a hint of Ramsay in the air."

Unfortunately, there was.

Graeme caught his foe's scent the instant he turned his face into the wind. The smell was faint but unmistakable: a trace of musk and citrus, the costly cologne tainted by an edge of sulfur only Graeme would detect.

Luckily, he could also tell that the whiff of scent was residue.

Wherever Ramsay had been on Harbour Street, he'd left now.

Even so, it didn't hurt to make certain.

Graeme stepped from the stoop into the street, ignoring the drizzle. He looked across the road, opening his senses as he focused on the bay's dark, glassy water. All appeared calm, with only a light chop stirring the sea. Moonlight silvered the road and the narrow stretch of shingle beyond. Otherwise, the village was still.

Not yet satisfied, he tipped back his head, clearing his mind. He inhaled deep, probing the night. The air smelled of the sea, cold rain, and peat smoke.

They were familiar smells and made his heart clench.

The essence of this whole coast, the scents reminded him of why he did what he did. They brought home the importance of keeping Pennard safe, preserving village dignity and the pride of a place so deeply ingrained in every inch of this magnificent stretch of shoreline.

Graeme took one more deep breath, letting his senses search for his enemy.

Gavin Ramsay's taint was barely discernible now.

"Ramsay's no longer about, no' now." Graeme glanced at Jock, not surprised to see the dog tilt back his head and sniff the mist rolling down the street. Jock loved mimicking Graeme's postures.

He growled on hearing Ramsay's name.

The dog would keep excellent watch when they went into the Keel's kitchen and Graeme retrieved his Book of Shadows, the ancient Grimoire—a tome of meticulous records—kept by his family ever since they'd been named Guardians centuries ago.

Guardians of the Shadow Wand, that was.

Graeme fisted his hands, wondering, as so often, why his clan had to have such a dubious honor placed upon their broad, plaid-draped shoulders.

But he knew why.

In times of old, honor and integrity meant something.

Great and selfless acts done for the greater good were noted and rewarded unnumbered years ago when Scotland was yet young.

And all the railing against the past and the heroic deeds of his forebears wouldn't change anything.

So he gave Jock's ears one more rub and then started down the narrow path beside his house. The rock face behind his barrel shed needed checking. It was there, deep inside the cliff's stone, that the Shadow Wand rested, not far from where young Ritchie Watt had flung himself in his haste to escape Graeme earlier.

To Graeme's relief, the small area behind his cottage and, more importantly, the bluff itself, felt clean. There was no trace of any visitors. All he sensed was the low pulsing of the Shadow Wand.

He frowned, not surprised when Jock bolted in front of him, his hackles rising as he snarled at the wet stone of the cliff face.

"Thon relic cannae harm us, laddie." Graeme wished that was true.

It would be true as long as the wand remained where it was.

The Shadow Wand was a highly polished relic of jet and amber, its spiraled length banded by narrow rings of clear, shining crystal. Once the most dreaded weapon of a dark druid named Morcant, the Shadow Wand earned its name for its terrifying ability to draw out a man's soul if the wand was thrust into a victim's shadow. The person was left hollowed and died, while the wand fed off the soul's energy, gaining power for its wielder.

In time, Morcant fed the wand so many souls that a single victim no longer slaked the wand's hunger.

Morcant soon learned that if he stabbed the wand into the shadow of a tower or stronghold, the souls of everyone within would be consumed by the wand.

When the dark druid's thirst for power brought about his own demise at the gates of Castle Grath, Graeme's ancestors took possession of the dangerous wand. The clan's fate was then sealed, their path forever altered. The Old Gods, preferring not to delve too deeply into the lives of mortal men, gave the MacGrath chief a span of seven days to decide the Shadow Wand's fate.

After much debate, clan elders wisely decided to bury the wand deep in the stone of a nearby cliff. There, it would never again see the light of day. Even so, the MacGraths vowed to guard and protect the secret site from anyone who would attempt to make use of the wand and its terrifying powers.

Pleased because the MacGrath chief wasn't tempted to seize the wand's power for himself, the Old Gods smiled on Clan MacGrath, naming them Guardians of the Wand. They were also entrusted with watching over the whole, formidable coast. And, not entirely to the chief's liking, they were given the magical powers to do so.

From that time onward, every MacGrath chief possessed strong ancient magic and the knowledge to wield it for good.

It was a responsibility Graeme could've done without.

But it was also a duty he honored.

The consequences of shirking such a legacy were unthinkable. Even if Graeme occasionally did contemplate walking away, damning heritage and liability, Gavin Ramsay's odious presence made any such relinquishing of his obligations an impossibility.

Ramsay was a direct descendent of Morcant.

And he'd inherited his ancestor's penchant for causing trouble and his boundless quest for power. In recent years, he also seemed to be gaining Morcant's talent for spellcasting and other witchery.

Graeme was certain of that.

He was also fairly sure that Ramsay had guessed Graeme's most hedged secret.

That like his father before him and his father before him, Graeme had also been granted a lifespan of seven hundred years and a day.

His time ran out in seventy-five years.

He was the last MacGrath.

And he'd take his legacy with him, leaving no future Guardians to suffer his fate. Before he went, he'd fulfill one final duty, even if it wasn't exactly what his responsibilities demanded of him.

He'd destroy the Shadow Wand.

The relic would never fall into Ramsay's hands.

Graeme glanced at Jock and went back inside his cottage. He needed to study the Grimoire. A crack had sprung in the cliff face behind the Keel and it was only a matter of time until the break widened, exposing the Shadow Wand's centuries-old hiding place.

Most alarming of all, he hadn't caused the crack.

It was the work of someone else.

And that meant trouble.

He'd been studying the Grimoire for ages, poring over its brittle pages and scrutinizing near-indecipherable text penned in old, faded ink, in search of a way to destroy the relic. Many of the tome's strange symbols and illustrations were even harder to grasp than the ancient words. So far, he hadn't found the answer he needed. He had hoped to have time to keep looking.

He'd have to search faster if Ramsay, or some potent energy drawn by his darkness, was responsible for the split in the cliff's stone.

Too bad haste wasn't known for improving matters.

Chapter 8

"Dinnae look at me that way."

Graeme slid an annoyed glance at Jock, almost wishing the dog had retired to his cozy armchair beside the fire when they'd come back inside the Keel. That was well over an hour ago, and Jock had been treating Graeme to his you-dinnae-ken-what-you're-doing stare ever since. It was a look the dog gave him every time he lifted a certain slab from the kitchen's stone-flagged floor and retrieved the ancient tome known simply as the Book of Shadows.

His family's most prized possession, the book was leather bound, heavy, and so old Graeme often worried it would turn to dust in his hands.

But somewhere within the Grimoire's cracked binding and inked on brittle parchment stood the key to destroying the Shadow Wand.

At least Graeme hoped so.

He'd been studying the book for centuries. Sadly, to no avail.

And each time he tried to glean the tome's secrets, Jock looked on with his unblinking canine stare. Until, at last, he grew bored watching Graeme turn the fragile pages. Then, as if washing his paws of his master's foolishness, he'd sit by the kitchen door, waiting for Graeme to take him for their late-night walk along the shore.

"I'm not done here." Graeme peered harder at the Book of Shadows, trying to decipher the strange words and symbols. Encoded secrets, conjurations, charms, and rituals that imparted mystical knowledge, allowing those adept to gain love, power, and riches. There were also instructions on how to punish enemies, avert evil, and divine the future. The tome was even rumored to offer an invisibility spell. The easiest-to-read notations covered natural magic, giving descriptions of medicinal herbs and enchanted gemstones. Sprawled in faded ink across the Grimoire's yellowed pages, the shrift belonged to a distant time.

An age before even Graeme's great-great-grandfather had walked the hills.

Yet some of those forebears had managed to unravel the meaning of a few words and symbols. Their helpful notes were penned in the margins, giving Graeme his only clues to what he sought.

In nearly seven hundred years, he hadn't come close to his ancestors' successes in cracking the maddeningly illegible writing and weird sketches. He'd made progress, but not enough. It seemed that time was starting to run out.

Yet the answers he sought eluded him.

He bit back a curse as he turned another page.

Swearing in the presence of a book so magic laden wasn't a mistake he'd make. The air in the kitchen hummed with the tome's power. And the pages warmed beneath his fingers, as if the parchment lived and breathed. Only absolute reverence was acceptable when handing the Grimoire.

Graeme treated the book with care.

Behind him, Jock showed less respect by whining.

But when Graeme shot him a look, the dog flopped down on the floor and wagged his tail. His expression turned hopeful, full of barely repressed excitement.

"No walk yet." Graeme straightened and rolled his shoulders. He'd placed the Book of Shadows on the kitchen's sturdy oak table, and bending over the tome for the past hour had made his back ache.

His head hurt, too.

And the trace of sausage, bacon, and eggs that lingered in the air—a reminder of his midnight snack—was making him hungry again.

Frowning, he reached to rub the back of his neck. Outside the rain had stopped and the night was still. All he heard now was the sound of the sea and the swish of Jock's tail across the kitchen floor.

Or so he thought, until he caught the unmistakable crunch of footsteps on pebbled rock.

Someone was walking the shore.

And the prickles on his nape warned that it wasn't anyone who should be there.

Jock's low growl said the same.

"You will stay here." Graeme flashed a stern look at his friend as he carefully closed the Grimoire and returned the tome to its hiding place.

If one of Ramsay's followers was looking for trouble— he could tell from the vibrations in the air that it wasn't Gavin himself—the last thing he wanted was to be worrying about Jock when he confronted the intruder.

"There's no time to say a sealing spell o'er the flagstone," Graeme spoke as he worked the stone into place over the cavity in the floor. His words would soothe Jock's pride. "You'll need to guard the book's hiding place until I return."

Jock gave another low rumble in his chest.

But he did leave his post by the kitchen door to dutifully sit beside the stone flag. And much to Graeme's relief, the dog held his head high, assuming a look that showed he felt important.

"This won't take long." Graeme rubbed Jock's ears and then took a well-honed dirk from the drawer set into the oak table.

It was a drawer that even the most curious eyes wouldn't notice and that only opened to his touch.

"Dinnae leave that spot, laddie." Graeme tucked the dirk beneath his belt. The blade was just as unique as the secret drawer, and he hoped he wouldn't need to make use of its capabilities.

He stepped out into the night, not bothering to will his footsteps into silence as he strode along the side of his cottage toward the road.

Whoever was on the shore knew he'd join them.

As soon as he reached Harbour Street, he could feel the eagerness to greet him. Two heartbeats rippled the air, and the men's aggression was dark and palpable, staining the night's peace.

Graeme's jaw set as he crossed the road, scanning the empty foreshore. The bay was calmer now, the water lapping gently on the pebbled strand. A glance to the far end of the village showed low clouds drifting over the cliffs and a few stars high above. Pennard slept, the tiny fishing hamlet seeming so far removed from the hectic pace of the outside world.

The tranquillity was an illusion.

Two dark shadows near the cave at the bay's edge

spoiled the image. They didn't move and could've been night-blackened fissures in the cliff. But Graeme knew better, and closed in on them with long, sure strides.

He recognized them as the Fleming brothers, Roddie and Patrick.

Dressed entirely in black, they were his equal in size. They were also Ramsay's best fighters, though they should know from their last encounter with Graeme that they'd made a grave error in coming to challenge him again. Their weapons, two-foot lengths of steel pipe, wouldn't help them. They were fools to think so.

Graeme let his gaze flick to the pipes, not bothering to hide his disdain. The Fleming brothers could be glad this wasn't an age when a man's foes could be killed with a single sword swipe.

They did tempt him.

"Didn't learn your lesson last time?" Graeme went to stand right in front of them. "Can it be"—he pulled the leather tie from his ponytail, freeing his shoulder-length hair—"you want your faces bloodied again? Or is it broken bones you're after now?

"I'll give you both, gladly." He shook his head, letting his hair swing menacingly.

Vikings and many medieval Highland warriors had enjoyed fighting with unbound hair. In his time in that world, it was a tradition Graeme had kept.

The Flemings narrowed their eyes at him, almost as if they knew.

Graeme flexed his fingers, eager to lash into them. "You're brave men, coming here."

"We're walking the strand." Roddie, the larger of the two, hefted his pipe, slapping the makeshift weapon against his palm. "The Keel is yours, last I heard. You have no claim on the foreshore."

Graeme stepped closer, ignoring the pipe. "I have

more than that, as you and your master know. Do yourself a favor and go back to the Spindrift and tell him to keep his goons out of my sight."

"He'll gut you, MacGrath." Roddie spat onto the ground.

"And you two"—Graeme looked from one to the other—"are still bearing the scars from our last fight. Are you really up for another?"

"Arrogant bastard!" Patrick lunged, swinging his pipe at Graeme's head.

Graeme ducked and spun, bringing up his arm to seize Patrick's wrist in a fierce grip. The pipe fell from his fingers, clattering onto the shingle. Graeme kicked the pipe into the surf, then thrust Patrick aside, hauling back to smash Roddie in the nose when he roared and leapt forward to defend his brother.

"Yeowww!" Roddie staggered backward, his pipe also slipping from his grasp as he dropped to his knees at the water's edge. "You'll pay for this, MacGrath!" He glared at Graeme from hate-filled eyes, one hand clutched to his nose, blood streaming through his fingers.

Recovered, Patrick scrambled for his brother's length of pipe. Cursing, he bent to grab the weapon, but Graeme was on him in a beat, yanking him up by the back of his jacket collar. He stiffened when Graeme whipped him around, defiance rolling off him.

"You'll no' be rid o' us so easy, seal man." Patrick jerked free, tugging his jacket in place. "Next time you'll no' see or hear us. We'll—"

"You'll fail every time you come for me." Graeme stepped back, allowing his magic to give his foes a glimpse of how he'd once been: a weapon-hung medieval warrior, tough, battle hardened, and terrifying. "Doubt me at your peril. I've no' enjoyed a true fight in a while."

Taking his dirk from beneath his belt, he aimed it at

Patrick's belly, his lip curling when the blade lengthened into the razor-sharp long sword it truly was. By the time its tip touched the other's man gut, the brand shone like blue fire, and Graeme was smiling.

But it was a mirthless smile.

The kind that chilled a man to the marrow—if he lived long enough to feel the cold.

Patrick blanched, his eyes going round. He backed away, raising his hands. "What are you, MacGrath?"

"Nothing you want to mess with." Graeme flicked his wrist and the glowing brand was no more. But he still held the dirk in his hand.

And the two brothers' faces showed they'd had enough for this night.

"I'll credit you both for not running." Graeme nodded in grim acknowledgment as Roddie lurched over to them, still clutching his bloodied nose. "A man willing to face his enemy and fight, even when he's misguided, is a man who aye deserves respect."

His words were met by sullen stares.

Neither man budged.

But Graeme clasped his hands behind his back and walked a slow circle around them, knowing nonchalance would irritate them more than aggression.

His steps also left an impassable barrier, trapping them if they tried to flee before he was done with them. He hoped no further use of his magical skills would be required. Despite Ramsay's presence, Pennard was peopled by good, salt-of-the-earth folk who didn't need to learn about worlds and powers far beyond their daily lives.

"You both ken you cannae beat me." Graeme stopped before them, folding his arms. "So tell me what brought you here tonight."

Angry silence answered him as Patrick flattened his

mouth into a hard, tight line. His brother glowered at Graeme from above his red-dripping fingers, his eyes glinting with resentment.

Graeme shrugged. "Speak or you'll be here a while."

He didn't warn them of the guarding circle, knowing Ramsay would've informed them of such interferences.

The look they exchanged proved him right.

"Your ma's a good woman." Graeme flashed a glance down the waterfront, letting his gaze light on one of Pennard's more modest cottages. "Do you really want her waking to see her lads standing naked on the foreshore?"

He lifted a brow on the word *naked*, letting them know he could arrange the like.

Willing it so was all that was necessary.

And as he'd guessed, manly pride won out over stubbornness.

"Ramsay sent us." Roddie broke first, his words garbled behind his bloody fingers.

"That I know." Graeme lifted a hand, pretending to examine his knuckles.

When neither brother spoke again, he sent another look down the silent row of Pennard's houses. This time he focused on a red-doored cottage where light still flickered behind neat lace curtains.

Then he looked away again, fixing his attention on Patrick. "I hear you've been seeing Lorna Gillespie. She's a fine lass—bonnie, honest, and hardworking. What would she think to see you out here, shivering in the dawn and no' wearing a stitch?"

Graeme would never allow Lorna or Mrs. Fleming to see such a sight.

But Roddie and Patrick didn't need to know that.

"You're a bastard, seal man." Patrick was seething.

Graeme smiled. "So some have said. Now tell me why Ramsay sent you here. Once you do, I'll let you go."

The brothers exchanged glances again.

Patrick spoke. "It's the American." His answer didn't surprise Graeme. "Gavin doesn't believe you're a pair. He saw her go into the Laughing Gull alone tonight. And"—he glanced over at Graeme's lit cottage—"he wanted us to see if she'd joined you later."

"That's no one's business." Anger kicked up inside Graeme, heating his blood. But he kept his face impassive. "Where Kendra sleeps is not Ramsay's concern. You can tell him she's mine, for she is."

Now, more than ever, he was determined to protect her.

Another, deeper part of him, sought to make her his in truth. But he ignored that strong yearning and focused his mind on the Fleming brothers, releasing the binding circle he'd cast around them.

"Tell him"—he went toe-to-toe against them both, fisting his hands in their shirtfronts—"that if he so much as glances at Kendra, I'll tear him into so many pieces, even the gulls won't find enough to fill their bellies with him."

Before either man could respond, Graeme spun them around and pressed his forearms against their throats. "Do that now"—he tightened his grip, making them splutter—"or you'll meet a fate as fine as Ramsay's. I wouldn't mind seeing you choking on your own blood...."

He didn't finish; just took his arms from their necks and then gave each a hard shove. "Now be gone and dinnae forget my words."

They reeled, stumbling before they righted themselves. Then, without a backward glance, they bolted from the strand and tore off down Harbour Street, their hurrying footsteps echoing along the waterfront.

Graeme stayed where he was, looking after them. Only when the night stilled again did he cross the road and go back inside the Keel.

Unfortunately, he wouldn't be staying there long.

Roddie and Patrick posed no further threat that night. But Ramsay would be furious. His temper might even send him straight to the Laughing Gull. It was a possibility Graeme couldn't allow.

He'd have to go there first.

And if he didn't want to frighten Kendra at this late hour, there was only one way to do it.

And so a very short while later, Graeme found himself back inside the best room of his cottage. He sat exceptionally still on his not-too-comfortable sofa, trying to ignore Jock's contented snores. Of course, the dog slept curled on the worn and welcoming armchair beside the hearth fire. Jock's black-and-white body took up the cozy chair's entire soft-cushioned seat.

Graeme didn't mind.

His dog deserved a good life.

Each time Jock returned to him, he made certain their new round together topped the one before. Knowing his friend was happy was one of Graeme's few pleasures in his own oft-times trying, seven-hundred-years-and-a day lifetime. Banning Jock from the armchair was the last thing he'd do.

Thwarting Gavin Ramsay, on the other hand, was a desire that burned in his blood.

The craven's face flashed before his mind's eye and he fisted his hands, forgetting he'd been trying to keep them relaxed at his sides.

Ramsay did get to him.

He was an enemy who took what he wanted, when he wanted it, and always with total disregard to the consequences. And now he'd set his sights on Kendra. The thought curdled Graeme's liver. It also made him again wish he and Ramsay could've clashed in days when they'd have faced each other in a medieval shield wall.

Graeme would've had done with his foe quickly, using a short ax to hook away his shield and then ramming a stabbing sword right into the bastard's throat.

As things stood . . .

There were still ways to get the better of a fiend like Ramsay.

And as far as Graeme knew, the other man hadn't yet mastered the fine and magical art of astral projection. Graeme excelled at sending his conscious mind elsewhere when need arose. He was skilled in several highly effective techniques. His favorite was a method of dual consciousness that allowed him to visit other places while never leaving his sitting room.

It was how he most often kept an eye on his ancestral home, Castle Grath.

Physically walking around the ruin was a painful experience, as being there reminded him too strongly of those he'd loved and lost over the centuries.

Tonight he'd use the awakened dreaming state, as dual consciousness was sometimes called, to visit Kendra's room at the Laughing Gull. Such a projection was too intrusive for his liking, but necessary under the circumstances. At least she wouldn't know he was there.

Yet if Ramsay or one of his henchmen harangued her, he would see and could be there in minutes.

And then . . .

Memories of long-ago shield walls flooded his mind. For a beat, he could almost feel the straps of a shield on his left forearm, the leather-wrapped hilt of a short stabbing sword gripped in his right hand. But he cleared the images from his thoughts and focused instead on the softly glowing slabs of peat piled on his hearth grate.

He also took several deep breaths, willing himself to completely relax.

Years of experience had taught him that he'd need to concentrate on the fire for at least a quarter of an hour before his mind would clear and slow enough for him to enter the required state of deep consciousness. Once there, he'd mentally walk himself out of his cottage. He'd move along the waterfront, slip inside the Laughing Gull Inn, and then head up the stairs to Kendra's room.

He didn't need to know the room number.

He'd scent her instantly. His senses sharpened when he astral projected, and her signature fragrance would draw him even before he reached the guest floor at the inn. Her overbright aura would also guide him.

All he had to do was make the journey there.

Then he was.

And as so often with his astral wanderings, arriving seemed almost effortless. He'd only had to visualize the path and he was transported instantly. Though he knew the whole magical process took at least a half hour, his prep work and focus time considered.

Not that it mattered.

What did was that Kendra slept in the nude.

Graeme frowned. Seeing her naked was not why he'd come here.

Sure, it'd been a risk. Sending a goodly portion of his conscious mind into her room at the Laughing Gull in the quietest hours of the night left little doubt that he'd find her slumbering.

He just hadn't expected his first glimpse of her to be the sweet curve of her bottom.

What he'd been prepared to discover was Ramsay or one of his goons lurking in the inn's upstairs hallway, watching Kendra's door. He wouldn't have been surprised to see the bastards inside her room. It wouldn't be the first time Ramsay forced himself on a woman, though he always managed to wriggle out of any legal ramifications.

But his nemesis wasn't here.

And he was just glad Kendra wasn't sleeping on her back. The view was tempting enough. She must've had a restless night, because the bed sheets had slipped down, only covering her to midthigh. In another time, another world, he'd have whipped the bedding right off her. He'd have savored every tantalizing inch of her, smoothing his hands along each sleek line and luscious curve of her body, kissing her all the while and making love to her until the sun rose. Even then he'd want more, he was sure.

He was getting hard just looking at her.

And he'd fisted his hands so tightly, his knuckles hurt.

Turning abruptly, he went to the window, keeping his back to her bed. It was not the time for such complications. Never in all his nearly seven hundred years of living had he done anything as foolhardy as come here tonight. Yet he had felt compelled to check on her. He was sure Ramsay had noted her beaconlike aura. If he'd caught wind of her mentioning the ghostly herring fleet in the pub—and Graeme was certain Ramsay had—he'd believe he could use her special talents.

Graeme knew she possessed a supernatural gift.

Frowning, he shoved a hand through his hair. He stepped closer to the window, looking down at the harbor just across the road from the inn. The tide was running swift, a light chop letting the boats rock at their moorings. Black, glassy water splashed over exposed rocks, glinting darkly in the moonlight. It was still a peaceful night. But the atmosphere in the room behind him crackled, the air picking up the turbulence of his thoughts.

He shouldn't have allowed his anger at Ramsay to accompany him. And he sure as hell was out of bounds letting one look at Kendra's delectable bottom fire such burning need inside him. Curvy and well made, she was the kind of woman no man could gaze upon and not want to possess thoroughly. He could easily imagine her soft, warm body beneath him, and the pleasure of losing himself deep inside her.

What he should do was leave.

He had only to retrace the mental path he'd followed to get here.

If he did, he'd be back on his sofa in quick time. He'd be alone in the Keel, no longer in danger of doing something he'd regret. He'd be free to get the sleep he needed, his night's rest serenaded by Jock's fluting snores.

But he couldn't make himself leave her.

Kendra's scent filled the room and—his scowl deepened—whatever it was bewitched him. Clean, light, and perhaps lily of the valley, the fragrance teased his senses. It also held him here as soundly as if he'd cast one of his own powerful binding spells.

Surely there wasn't anything wrong in relishing a few deep breaths of her soft, womanly scent?

Once more, and he'd leave on the exhale.

He couldn't remember the last time he'd had such a pleasure. It'd been even longer since a woman had stirred him so greatly.

And that was why he needed to go.

But just when he started to close his senses to her scent in preparation for his return journey to the Keel, he made the grave error of letting his gaze fall on the blue plaid chair beside the window.

Kendra's lingerie was on the chair.

He needed only one look at her lacy black panties and bra to run hard as granite.

"Damnation." He growled the word, fisting his hands again as his entire body tightened.

On the bed, Kendra stirred, rolling onto her back so that her full, round breasts were fully exposed, their lushness adding to his misery.

He refused to look lower.

There were some things beyond a man's endurance. And he had invaded her privacy enough for one night.

He did strike an immediate retreat, willing his conscious mind to drift back across the room, past her bed, and toward the waiting door.

Her eyes popped open and she sat up just as he was reaching for the doorknob.

"Graeme . . ." She looked right at him, impossible as it was.

He stared at her breasts, unable not to. "I'm no' really here, lass. You're only dreaming, seeing things that aren't there."

"I don't think so." She blinked and rubbed her eyes. The movement made her breasts sway, upping his torment.

"It's true." He willed her to believe.

Regret pierced him that he couldn't go to her, pulling her into his arms and kissing her. Only this time he knew he could never stop at a kiss. He'd cup and squeeze her breasts, rolling her nipples beneath his thumbs, and then . . .

He couldn't finish the thought.

Moonlight fell across the whole of her lush, feminine body, a benediction in light and shadow, all smooth, creamy skin and temptation.

Anger and frustration punched him like an iron fist in the chest.

Kendra settled back on her elbows, a slight frown now creasing her brow. Her lovely blue eyes looked heavy, the lids slowly lowering. His craft hadn't failed him, despite his inner turmoil. She'd bought his mental suggestion and accepted him as a dream.

Already, her fair head was sinking onto the pillow, true sleep upon her.

"You're an arse, MacGrath." He cursed himself softly, his hand still on the doorknob.

Then, when he could stand the agony no longer, he did what he should have done immediately upon finding her safe and alone in her room.

He slipped out the door and sent himself back along the waterfront to his cottage.

He just hoped that when he took her out on the *Sea Wyfe* later that morning, he'd be able to look at her without thinking of her naked breasts.

Somehow he doubted it.

Chapter 9

Early the next morning, Kendra slipped from the Laughing Gull Inn as unobtrusively as possible. She closed the door with even greater caution, keenly aware of the clatter of pots and pans coming from the inn's kitchen. Iain, and most likely Janet, as well, was clearly readying for the breakfast rush. The last thing she needed was for either of them to hear her and come asking why she was stepping outside at such an ungodly hour.

She could say she'd slept poorly and wanted a walk before breakfast.

That was even true.

She'd had the strangest dream. A vivid one in which Graeme had approached her bed, looking down at her with such desire, only to vanish into thin air even as his appreciative gaze moved along the length of her body. He'd been so real, her own longings had fluttered inside her, her heart beating wildly long after he'd gone.

She'd been unable to reclaim the dream.

But the impact of his devilish good looks had stayed with her, haunting her. Remembering the heat in his eyes, she could feel a flush spreading across her cheeks. How sure she'd been that she could've reached out and touched his arm, the rest of him. She'd wanted him, her body catching fire. She still burned for him now.

But she pushed him from her mind, summoning the focus her career required of her. Her assignment was the real reason she stood outside the inn, scanning the road and waterfront before more than a faint hint of gray edged the horizon. Pennard at this hour was dark, cold, and silent.

And she was about to go to work.

So she took a deep breath and lifted her head, closing her eyes as she drew on the powerful white-light energy that would shield her from any lesser energies she might encounter at the empty house she wished to explore. She opened her eyes only when the familiar, tingly warmth of her psychic defenses rose around her.

She never faced spirits, or other supernatural beings, without such a safeguard. Those unseen could cause her great harm.

Although, as she made her way down Harbour Street toward the derelict house and its scaffold-covered walls, her instincts told her that whatever Otherworldly vibrations she'd noticed there had all but dissipated. Only a trace remained, rippling the air with its dark, unknown energy when she stopped at the cottage door.

She sensed a presence, too. The spirit's anger and resentment felt steeped in the walls, as if the ghost and the cottage were inseparable.

Glancing around, she expected the spirit to appear any moment. But the only thing that moved was the large DO NOT TRESPASS — PROJECT PENNARD sign taped to the door. One corner of the sign had come loose, the edges lifting in the brisk morning wind.

Nothing else stirred.

And she was going inside. As a quasi–Scotland's Past employee, she surely wasn't bending the rules too badly by ignoring the no-entry sign. Besides, if the preservation society was so bent on keeping out intruders, they'd have locked the door. A quick jiggle of the latch proved anyone who wished could enter.

So she did.

And stepping inside the house felt like pushing through a thick cloud of negative energy, the antagonism almost a palpable force in the cottage's empty front room. Dim light was beginning to filter through the windows, revealing the mold growing up the walls. And the stone-flagged floor was cracked and dirty, giving the house an air of resentful reproach. Only a hint of residual menace remained, confirming her guess that the lesser entity she'd felt here on arrival had left. The spirit she'd sensed on approaching the house also seemed to have vanished, leaving only an echo of his or her anger.

Kendra frowned and moved deeper into the house, edging around a pile of empty buckets, broken boards, and tarpaulin. The ghost and the lesser energy might have fled, but her gift's heightened awareness warned her that something else was here, or approaching.

And it felt strong, very intense.

Its sense of positive force was also more than a little familiar.

Kendra took a deep breath, readying herself to deal with the powerful entity she knew would manifest any moment. She seldom reached out to him. The fact that he now showed proved the severity of Pennard's problems.

"Raziel." She turned to face a whirling vortex forming in a darkened corner. "I'd hoped I wouldn't need your help."

"So appreciative?" A tall man stepped out of the shimmering light column, his flowing blue robe and long, silvery hair shining with the same brilliance as his vortex. "You offend my heart, though I applaud your courage. No, you do not need me. Instinct will guide you, as always. Even so"—he came forward on a swirl of energy— "you should know the danger here comes from above and below."

"Gee, thanks." Kendra tucked her hair behind an ear, doing her best not to flinch beneath her main spirit guide's piercing gaze. "I suppose you mean this village is troubled by hellish and heavenly beings?"

Raziel folded his arms, saying no more.

He did lift a brow, letting her know she'd given the wrong answer.

"Must you always be so cryptic?"

"Stretching your mind to find the answers deepens your wisdom."

"You're my spirit guide. That means you're supposed to guide, not confuse me."

"I watch over you." His deep voice filled the little room. "*Spirit guide* is your term. I never called myself anything but my name. I am Raziel."

Kendra drew a breath, knowing the pointlessness of arguing with him.

Striking in a strange, otherworldly way, Raziel had the bluest eyes she'd ever seen. They reminded her of living sapphires, at turns looking like frosted chips of Arctic ice, and other times snapping with such blue fire she'd swear he could scorch with a glance.

Just now the glimmer of a smile lurked in his eyes, showing he knew he'd gotten the best of her.

"Okay, I'll think on your message." She let a slow smile spread across her own face. "Anything else you might want to relate?"

Raziel turned his head, sending a meaningful look at the darkened entry to a hallway. "You might ask her about books," he said, the energy around him turning brighter.

Kendra blinked—his aura could be blinding at times—and then he was gone, nothing but a few dazzling sparkles remaining. Then they vanished, as well, fizzing slowly from sight. But a movement caught her attention and she turned, not surprised to see Saami watching her from the shadowed corridor.

Her only female spirit guide, Saami stood right where Raziel had just cast his glance. Dressed as flamboyantly sixtyish as always in a colorful gypsy skirt and low-cut peasant blouse, Saami wore her curling dark hair hidden beneath an intricately knotted red scarf and had hooked large golden rings in her ears. Though short and plump in stature, the style suited her, matching her pretty face and flashing black eyes. She also smelled strongly of patchouli.

Kendra angled her head, studying her.

Saami favored citrus scents. She switched between orange blossom and lemon, depending on her mood.

As Kendra stared, the spirit guide set her hands on her hips. "You can see me."

Kendra stopped short. The voice wasn't Saami's. The entity wasn't Saami, she saw now, though the resemblance was startling.

"Yes, I can." Kendra stepped closer to the ghost and found herself looking into a face pinched with distrust. Now she knew the source of the house's anger. Its stones were saturated by this woman's spleen. "And I understand why you're upset." Kendra looked around, letting her gaze flit over the workmen's clutter. "It's hard to see other people move into a place you love."

"I hate this house." The ghost's sharp tone belied her words.

The brightness of her eyes said more.

"They're tearing down the walls." The spirit shimmered, whooshing into the room. "Every day they come, scraping and hammering, ripping away my shelves"— she glanced at the broken boards on the floor—"just like he always threatened to do, the two-timing bastard."

"Your husband?" Kendra knew she'd tipped right when the ghost's hands curled into fists.

"Who else?" The ghost leaned in, her eyes narrowing. "He hated my books, threatened to toss them into the sea if I didn't stop reading so much. But"—she straightened, her aura red with her grievances—"what was I supposed to do when he aye ignored me, going off to Aberdeen to carry on with the girls there?

"When he *ruined* one, he left me to marry her!" She spoke in a rush, the air around her crackling, ripping with the strength of her fury. "When I found out, I . . ." She clamped her lips, the unspoken words darkening her aura.

"She drove off in a rage." A soft voice whispered the explanation in Kendra's ear. She didn't need to catch the whiff of orange blossom to know the real Saami stood at her shoulder, shielding herself so the spirit wouldn't see her. "She had an accident, her car flipping when she swerved to avoid a deer. Her name is Lora Finney.

"She was a great beauty before bitterness marked her." An increase in the scent of orange blossoms showed Saami's empathy. "This village celebrated her as a hobby baker. She often won local scone-baking competitions. Now"—Saami lowered her voice—"she's spending her time terrorizing the work crews. Yesterday she sent a ladder dancing across the floor, and she's planning to toss that tarpaulin over their heads when they return this afternoon. Several of the men have quit, refusing to come back again."

"Lora, the men here are cleaning mold off your walls." Kendra used her gentlest voice and the best logic she could think to employ. "They aren't here to tear down your home. They're fixing it."

It wasn't the whole truth. But soothing the spirit's upset mattered more.

"Fixing it for whom?" Lora Finney jammed her hands against her hips again. "The rat"—Kendra assumed she meant her husband—"married his Australian student lover and moved halfway around the world."

"I'm not sure." Kendra didn't lie. But she did cast a glance over her shoulder, hoping Saami would volunteer a suggestion.

Unfortunately, the citrus-free air greeting her indicated her friend had gone.

But inspiration struck as she turned back to the angry ghost. "Did you know it's said that success is the best revenge? What would you say if I can arrange for your house to be made into a library? A special place where locals can read the books you loved? And"—she hoped she could swing this—"perhaps there could even be a few corner tables so tea and scones made to your recipes could be served each afternoon. It could be called after you, Lora's Literary Café."

Lora Finney stared at her.

Kendra felt a bead of sweat trickle between her breasts. She'd never made such an outrageous, difficult-to-keep promise to a ghost before.

But Lora's fate touched her.

"You do have a special recipe book somewhere here, don't you?" Kendra's instinct urged her to ask. When she caught a glimpse of Raziel and Saami watching her from across the room, each spirit guide nodding approval, she knew she was on the right track.

"I do." Lora's chin came up, the pride in her voice proving Kendra's guess. "It's in an old box in the kitchen. The workmen have buried the box under empty pails and tarpaulin, but it's clearly marked BOOKS. My recipe book has a red leather cover and my name on the inside."

"Then I'll see it's found—I promise." Kendra wasn't worried about locating the book. She did fret about her assurance that the house would be transformed into a reading and scone-serving refuge.

"You will do that?" Lora blinked, her stance relaxing as the last of her belligerence faded. "And see my bookshelves rebuilt? Do everything you've promised?"

"I will, and gladly." Kendra hoped she could. Her influence with Scotland's Past wasn't great enough to work miracles.

But she meant to try.

The lightening of the atmosphere in the empty house encouraged her. And the barely there "thank you" that Lora Finney gave her as she faded back into the shadows made her determined to succeed.

A short while later, Kendra sat again at the corner table by the window in the pub restaurant of the Laughing Gull Inn and decided that a "full Scottish breakfast" ranked almost as high as a Scottish accent on her fast-growing list of everything to love about Scotland.

A person could get by all day on such a feast.

Everything tasted so good.

It was just a shame that her visit to Lora Finney's house and her wish to enjoy the Laughing Gull's delicious breakfast offerings meant rising at an ungodly hour when she usually slept her deepest. Of course, her nine o'clock date with Graeme also came at a time she preferred burrowing beneath the covers.

Not that she'd minded crawling out of bed to help a needy ghost. The chance to spend the day with Graeme was also worth getting up early.

She'd done so gladly.

She just couldn't deny the powerful attraction she felt for him.

Now that her work had gone so well, her mind snapped back to the dream she'd had of Graeme in the night. Too bad the heated dream had been so brief, ending almost before it'd started. She could still see him in the shadows of her room, his dark gaze locked on hers as he started toward her. She'd sat up in bed, the covers slipping down to reveal her naked breasts. He noticed at once, lowering his gaze, his expression turning darker, so charged with desire, as he looked at her.

In the dream, she knew he was going to reach for her, pulling her into his arms, and then . . .

It was over.

Her heart began to race, a whirl of emotion flaring inside her.

Even if it was a dream, no man had ever looked at her so hungrily. Graeme wasn't just devastatingly attractive, able to captivate a woman with one look from his compelling gaze; he also loved dogs.

That meant something to her.

She toyed with her napkin, biting back a smile. It would surely strain her face muscles if she attempted levity before she'd had her second cup of coffee. And taking another sip of the weak instant brew reminded her to try the Scottish Breakfast tea the next morning.

Apparently, Scots couldn't make good coffee.

Grimacing, she set down her cup.

An older couple—West Highlanders on a touring holiday, from their conversation—had claimed the table next to hers, and just listening to their soft, lilting accents made suffering bad coffee as insignificant as a dust mote. A country that spoke so beautifully could be allowed the minor failing of less-than-palatable java.

Not wanting to be caught eavesdropping, Kendra pretended to study the breakfast menu.

Porridge
Cereal
Homemade muesli with fresh fruit and yogurt
*

Grilled kippers
Smoked salmon with poached or scrambled eggs
Sausage, bacon, and eggs
Haggis and eggs
Grilled tomatoes, mushrooms, and pan-fried potatoes
*

Toast, scones, soda farls, and homemade preserves
Tea, coffee, and fruit juice

Setting aside the tartan-edged menu card, she eyed her almost-empty plate. She'd chosen a large soda farl, which she'd learned was a huge and thick home-baked scone served toasted and filled with lots of crispy bacon and a poached egg. Rarely had she eaten anything more delicious.

She could get used to breakfast in Scotland.

And she was about to fork her last bit of bacon when a shadow fell across her table. Looking up, she met Graeme's smiling eyes, and her heart nearly threatened to burst from her chest.

"Iain serves up the best breakfast on the coast." His deep, buttery-rich burr quickened her pulse, pouring over her like molten honey.

The look in his eyes made her prickle with aware-ness.

She blinked, sure her face was heating. "Yes, he does." It was all she could think to say. He looked so good in his jeans and cream-colored, cable-knit Aran sweater. "I've never had a better breakfast."

That was true.

Her words deepened his smile. The attractive way his eyes crinkled did dangerous things to her emotions. She could so easily fall in love with this man. She feared she was already halfway there.

"It is a lot of food. . . ." She put down her fork, hoping to hide her feelings by looking at her plate. "I'm not sure I can finish."

"You'll hurt Iain's feelings if you don't." He set a hand on her shoulder, squeezing lightly. His touch sent delicious shivers along her nerves. "Dinnae worry your-self. Even if you're feeling full now, you'll be glad for the energy when we're out on the open water. A good Scot-tish breakfast will keep you warm."

Kendra almost laughed.

If her personal heat index rose any higher, Scotland would feel as balmy as Florida.

And not because of a soda farl stuffed with egg and bacon.

It was Graeme.

He affected her as no man had ever done. And she was pretty sure that agreeing to go seal watching with him had been a bad decision.

He looked more than pleased to see her.

"The *Sea Wyfe* is ready for us." His tone proved he

was also eager. "It's a fine morning." He glanced at the window behind her, his dimple flashing when he smiled again. "There's only a light mist and the water's mirror calm. The swells might get a bit choppy later, but—"

"Where's Jock?" Kendra didn't see Graeme's companion anywhere.

"Och, he's home sleeping on his hearth rug." Graeme stepped back, making room for her as she got to her feet. "Jock doesn't like the water. He aye finds excuses not to accompany me on the *Sea Wyfe*. This time he played his favorite trick: pretending not to hear me leave."

"He's a clever boy." Kendra reached for her jacket, her breath catching when, just in that moment, the phone-box ghost appeared in the middle of the road. She blinked, looking out the window at the ghost, but he vanished again almost as quickly as he'd manifested.

Kendra straightened, letting Graeme help her into her jacket.

Guilt sluiced her.

She had no business going out for a sightseeing boat ride when one of Pennard's disgruntled spirits wanted to make contact with her.

Although if this particular ghost kept vanishing rather than speaking to her, there wasn't much she could do to help him. Spirits, like living people, had their own free will. Nor was it her policy to press her attentions on discarnates who didn't want to communicate.

Manners counted in the Otherworld, as anywhere.

But she did risk another quick glance at the street. Not surprisingly, it was empty. And nothing moved near the red phone box except a seagull pecking at something on the pavement.

Kendra frowned, sensing the ghost's essence lingering in the road.

"Are you unwell, lass?" Graeme was already opening

the inn door for her, guiding her out into the brisk morning air. "Maybe you did eat too much? Iain's soda farls can be a bit heavy in the stomach."

"No, no." Kendra shook her head, her heart flipping when he tucked her arm into his as they crossed the road, heading for the marina. "I'm fine, really. I'm only a bit nervous about going out on a boat."

She'd improvised the excuse, but it wasn't wholly untrue.

Pennard Bay did look still as glass, just as Graeme had said. But far out to sea, she could see the long North Sea swells rolling steadily toward them. Huge and white-crested from here, she was sure they'd appear even larger once Graeme took them out of Pennard's sheltered bay. The waves already looked much more daunting than the light chop Graeme had so casually suggested.

But it was too late to back out now.

He'd stopped beside the little stone slipway and rested his hands on her shoulders. "I could handle the *Sea Wyfe* in my sleep, lass." He leaned in, dropped a kiss on her brow. "You've no reason to worry."

But she did.

Especially when his face hardened as he straightened. "I'll no' let anything happen to you."

"I know that." She did, just as she knew something else was bothering him.

Before she could ask, he tightened his grip on her and lowered his head again, this time kissing her full on the lips. It was a slow, deep kiss, shockingly intimate. And so potent she felt a flush rising through her entire body. Without thinking, she slipped her arms around him, leaning into the hard, strong length of him.

"I thought you weren't going to kiss me again," she pressed him the instant he released her. "You swore —"

"Keeping you safe matters more than a wee kiss." His words dashed her giddiness.

Along with the wild burst of totally unfounded hope that she meant something to him.

"I wouldn't call that a wee kiss." She tried to jerk free, but he'd slid an arm around her, holding her in a viselike grip.

"It wasn't meant to be." He looked past her again, and this time she followed his gaze.

"Oh." She saw at once why he'd broken his vow not to kiss her again.

Gavin Ramsay stood outside his house, looking right down at them. And even though the Spindrift sat on a ledge halfway up the cliff, the distance wasn't great enough to hide his narrow-eyed stare.

He was majorly annoyed.

Kendra could see the sparks of angry green and black glimmering in his aura. She looked back to Graeme, not liking the vibes coming down the bluff from the Spindrift. "You kissed me because he's watching, right?"

"Aye, well . . ." He looked uncomfortable. "That is what we're about, see you. The kiss in the Laughing Gull last night, this boat trip—everything. No woman is safe from Ramsay, and I'm only trying to—"

"Protect me," Kendra finished for him.

"That was my plan."

"I'm a big girl, you know."

"So you are." He touched her face, smoothing a few strands of hair from her cheek. "You're bonnie, too. And that's all the more reason Ramsay can't be allowed to get his grasping hands on you."

"Are Scots always so territorial?" Kendra's nerves still trembled from his kiss, and a flush was blooming on her face, warming her. "American women are independent. We're not used to men fighting over us."

"I've told you why I watch Ramsay." A breeze lifted Graeme's dark hair, the morning sun highlighting his proud, chiseled features.

He was so handsome.

But just now she could feel his annoyance, the force of his anger at the other man.

And the look in his eye when he shot another glance at his rival revealed that his reasons for disliking Ramsay went deeper than keeping pretty tourists out of reach of the local Romeo. Bad blood simmered between the two men, and she determined to find out why.

"He's already going back inside." She could feel the air lighten with his departure.

"He'll only be searching for binoculars." Graeme released her and turned to face the Spindrift. "Thon bastard doesn't give up easily. He'll keep an eye on us until we round Pennard Head."

Kendra started to press him, remembering the look she'd seen on Ramsay's face when he'd stood in the shadows of the alley between the two tiny cottages. His gaze had been directed at the Keel, she'd been certain. And enough anger had blazed in his eyes to set the entire village on fire. She'd known then she had to warn Graeme.

Although . . .

She glanced at him, not missing his fisted hands as he stared after Gavin Ramsay. Graeme was definitely aware of the animosity between them. And it mattered enough for him to cast aside promises and kiss her in full view of anyone looking on. The kiss hadn't meant anything to him, but it had taken her breath and unleashed a wave of yearning deep inside her.

Something told her there would be no turning back now.

Yet that was what she should do.

But before she could make up an excuse and head back to the inn, Graeme took her hand and led her away from the slipway and toward the marina's curving stone jetty. He strode almost to the end, taking her past a few small leisure craft and several fishing boats. One of the fishing vessels had just pulled in and was piled high with crates of prawns and bulging sacks of mussels. Seabirds wheeled and screeched above the boat, hoping for an easy meal.

Alongside the fishing boat, named *Gannet*, according to the black lettering on her side, men worked the lines and shouted greetings to another craft just chugging into the marina.

The second boat looked to have had as much success as the *Gannet*.

Even more gulls swooped in with the arrival of the new vessel. The cold morning air filled with the strong scent of fish and brine, a bracing mix laced with a good dose of salt, seaweed, and oily tar.

Kendra took a deep breath, appreciative. She'd never smelled anything so invigorating.

Sure, she knew women back in Bucks County who'd roll their eyes at her for finding such a smell heady. They were the kind of immaculately groomed, super-polished females who forked over a small fortune on expensive perfumes and cosmetics. She knew some who seemed to spend more on makeup than she did on rent. Point was, she knew many people wouldn't get the appeal of brine-filled air, the sharp bite of dripping bags of scallops, or the seaweedy tang of fishnets drying by the harbor wall.

She did get it.

She loved such places. And she couldn't imagine the world without them. A notion that pinched her heart when her gaze fell on a NO PENNARD PROJECT poster affixed to the base of one of the pier lights.

The fishing village was perfect as is.

And the mist-chilled morning, the busy marina, and the way Harbour Street glistened from the night's rain filled her with a sense of longing such as she'd never known. There was something about wet stone and threads of blue peat smoke rising from Pennard's row of whitewashed cottages that captivated her. Her heart thumped, her chest tightening. Closing her eyes, she took another appreciative breath. She released it slowly, savoring a world she knew she'd always carry in her heart, even long after she'd left.

No other place had ever affected her so strongly.

She felt a powerful pull, definitely.

And Graeme was looking at her as if he knew.

Kendra gave herself a shake, hoping the ache to stay here would fade away.

It didn't.

Graeme smiled. "You like it here, aye?"

She flicked at her jacket, embarrassed. "I do find the village special. The whole coast, really."

"There's nowhere else like it." His tone held pride. "Pennard is another world, and we owe it to coming generations to keep it that way." His face hardened, his gaze flicking again to Ramsay's Spindrift. "Scotland's Past and their fool plans must be stopped."

Guilt hit Kendra like a kick to the shins.

Scotland's Past was almost her employer. She was here at their behest.

"I've heard a lot of dissent from the locals." She had, and she did sympathize.

She waited for Graeme to agree.

"There's no' enough." His rich Scottish accent deepened, and he stopped for a moment. "See thon man sweeping the pavement before the Mermaid?" He tipped his head toward the seen-better-days pub, silent now in the early morning.

Kendra looked across the water, her gaze going right to the bar. Without the low beat of hard-rock music pouring from its door and no spike-haired, black-jacketed youths lurching in the street outside, the Mermaid looked only slightly neglected and tons sad.

The man Graeme meant was now attacking the door stoop with his broom. He had a thick, somewhat wild-looking mane of red-brown hair that caught the morning sun and was pulled back in a ponytail much like Graeme's. Tall and broad-shouldered, he wore jeans well, though he couldn't compare with Graeme. He'd tied a butcher's apron around his waist, showing he belonged to the Mermaid, so Kendra assumed he was the boyfriend of Janet's niece, Maili.

"He's Roan Wylie, the bar's owner." Graeme followed her gaze, confirming her guess. "He's a nice enough mate, but he's also one of the locals keen to let Scotland's Past grease his palm. The Mermaid hasn't fared too well in recent years and he's let their blether get to him. He thinks he'll make a fortune, selling out.

"Truth is"—he glanced at her—"he wouldn't be relieving himself of a bar that's fallen on rough times. He'd be selling his soul. He just doesn't realize it."

Kendra looked away, guilt pinching her again.

Indirectly, she was aiding the desecration Graeme hoped to avert.

"Heritage doesn't have a price, does it?" It was all she could think to say.

She did mean it.

And the way her throat thickened at the thought of

Pennard being turned into a theme park let her know she was already in deeper than was wise.

She cared too much this time.

And not allowing sentiment to creep into the work was another of Zack's and Ghostcatchers International's never-to-be-broken rules.

Yet . . .

How could anyone come here and not care?

She couldn't.

Especially when Graeme took hold of her hands, lacing their fingers, as he looked down into her eyes. "You're a fine lass, Kendra." He leaned close, kissing her brow lightly. "If it weren't for your American accent, I'd think you'd been born and bred in Pennard."

Kendra wished she had been.

She'd make the village's fight her own.

Most of all, she'd do something about the way Graeme made her knees go weak and her heart pound madly. If she were local, the path would've been clear. But whoever said life was fair? She knew from her work that it was often just the opposite. And trying to wrench things in one's own favor often ended in disaster.

But she could dream.

She wouldn't wish.

She knew too well how frequently one's words came out wrong, giving the cosmos a free hand to create havoc. She cast a yearning look along Pennard's waterfront. The soft morning light could only be called magical and luminous. Even Pennard's cliffs glowed, and the horrid, thread-thin road snaking down the bluff shone like a ribbon of gold. It was a scene wrapped in romantic seclusion. And anything that shattered such tranquillity and peace was a travesty.

Meeting Graeme's gaze, she vowed to do everything

in her power to help him avoid such a tragedy. Keeping her promise to Lora Finney was a start.

As for the rest ...

She bit her lip. His hands grasping hers so firmly and the intense look in his eyes made her pulse race and her heart beat faster.

Perhaps she could do a tiny bit of carefully formulated wishing.

Sometimes miracles did happen.

Chapter 10

"Come, lass." Graeme tugged on her hand, bringing her back from dreams and wishes, a world so perfect it wasn't surprising dark ripples strove to mar the surface. "I'll no' have us linger so long here that Ramsay thinks to fetch his own boat and follow us."

Kendra started, once again aware of the marina's bustle, the air full of yelling seabirds and the chatter of the fishing-boat crews shouting and laughing as they unloaded the morning's catch.

"What would he gain by doing that?" She looked at Graeme, not liking the answer she read on his face.

"Accidents happen at sea." His tone said he was serious. "No one in these parts blinks when they do. The sea takes and gives. It's an accepted part of life here. In olden times, folk even hesitated to rescue drowning men, believing the sea had claimed such men for her own and a worse fate would befall any who intervened."

Kendra had heard of such things.

In her work along England's coast and other places, she'd encountered more than one shipwreck victim who'd told her a similar tale.

But Graeme's words dashed the tartan gloss, reminding her that Pennard was a place in turmoil, despite the village's air of nostalgia and cozy quaintness.

He knew better than she what kind of secrets lurked behind the cottages' colorfully painted doors and neat lace-curtained windows.

She swallowed, hurrying to keep pace with him. "You don't think Gavin would—"

"I'd trust him to do anything." He quickened his pace as they neared a small white motorboat. Morning sun shone on the boat's clean, well-kept sides, while slanting blue letters declared that the sturdy craft was Graeme's seal-watching boat, the *Sea Wyfe*.

Kendra blinked. She hadn't realized they'd come so far down the jetty.

"Ramsay is a bad-tempered devil." Graeme stopped beside the boat, releasing her hand. "He'll no' let anything stand in his way. If someone disagrees with him, they won't for long. He knows how to persuade."

"I thought you were going to say *threaten*."

"I could have done."

"Scots are known for having strong minds." Kendra spoke hers. "I wouldn't think villagers would allow themselves to be bullied."

"They don't if they're aware of it." He bent to free the *Sea Wyfe*'s lines. "Ramsay is smooth and can charm when he wishes."

"I wasn't impressed." Kendra remembered how he'd come on to her.

"You're not a lonely old widow whose only excitement is looking forward to a winter of cold and solitude." He straightened, nodding a greeting when a man in a handmade sweater and a knitted cap walked past. "Or imagine a ne'er married fisherman past his prime and with no son to leave his boat and hard-earned savings. Such folk are easily fooled when someone shows them even a breath of kindness.

"And"—his voice held an edge—"Ramsay knows how to use timing. He finds the vulnerable and moves in when they're most likely to accept whatever nonsense he spins for them. Folk hereabouts aren't themselves these days. Many are up in arms, not wanting to see their village turned into an amusement park for tourists. Though there are a few exceptions, as I've told you.

"Misguided fools, thinking they'll benefit from the project. Then there are others with their own agenda." He glanced back across the water, toward the Spindrift. Ramsay wasn't in sight, but a sense of menace seemed to color the air around the house, making the atmosphere appear darker there than anywhere else along the cliffs.

Kendra wondered if Graeme noticed, but he'd already hopped onto his boat. She looked away from the house, turning back to Graeme.

"You mean Ramsay, with an agenda." She already knew he did.

"I do." He reached to help her climb down onto the *Sea Wyfe*. "That one has aye had his own plans. And"— his voice hardened again—"he doesn't stop at anything to see them put into place."

"You really don't like him." Kendra clambered aboard, gripping his arm when the boat swayed beneath her. "I do think the feeling is mutual."

"It is."

"I've seen how he looks at you." That was as close as she'd go for the moment. She couldn't mention auras and feelings, or the dark haze around Ramsay's house.

Such comments would spark questions she shouldn't answer.

She did let Graeme help her onto a seat near the front of the boat. As soon as she was settled, he untied the remaining lines, started the motor, and eased the *Sea Wyfe* away from the jetty.

"Ramsay and his ilk have aye been good at glaring." Graeme glanced at her as they left the mouth of the harbor and entered the bay. "I don't mind returning his scowls. Bad blood has run between our families for centuries. And"—he guided them past a cluster of black-glistening tidal rocks—"if you didn't know, grudges are forever in these parts. Once an enemy, aye an enemy, even long after no one remembers what began the feud."

"But you do know," Kendra guessed.

The look he flashed her said she'd gotten it right. "Och, aye. I know every grievance that ever fell between the MacGraths and Ramsays. Gavin is a direct descendant of a man named Morcant. He started the trouble in days back when time wasn't yet measured. Ever since, every man of Morcant's blood has kept the tradition.

"Gavin is trying to take the legacy to new levels. I don't let him." His dark eyes sparked pure male satisfaction when he glanced at her.

"So I've seen." Kendra shifted on the seat, for they were just leaving the bay and moving into open water. The long North Sea swells she'd watched from the shore were rolling right at them.

She wasn't ready to make their acquaintance.

So she touched her lips instead, sure they still tingled from Graeme's kiss. "You are going to great measures to convince him we're a pair."

"That I am, aye." His jaw was set, the smile she'd expected nowhere forthcoming.

"He must really annoy you." Kendra knew she

sounded peeved, but she couldn't help it. Recalling his kisses played havoc with her senses and her emotions.

He made them sound like a hardship.

Hoping he couldn't tell how much that bothered her, she gripped the edge of her seat, her gaze on the first roller's steady approach.

"Ramsay doesn't irritate me." The tense set of Graeme's shoulders said that wasn't true. "He just needs to be stopped. And"—he glanced at her—"to discover that this is no longer a world where plunder and glory can be had just because one wants the like. Raids, rape, and pillage went out of style centuries ago."

"You make it sound as if he's one of his forebears."

"He's worse. As one of their descendants, he carries the foul traits of them all."

Kendra started to ask for specifics, but just then her stomach tightened as the *Sea Wyfe* rose and fell over the white-crested swell she'd been dreading. The encounter wasn't as bad as she'd expected.

But she wouldn't call it pleasant.

Not like looking at Graeme.

It was more than the fact he was drop-dead gorgeous. It was nice to feel sensual shivers racing over her skin each time she glanced at him. But being with him went beyond appreciating his dark good looks and his sexy Scottish burr. He made her feel safe. As if he'd bend gravity or stop the earth's turning if such measures were required to protect someone he cared about.

She could see him thrusting her behind him with one arm and brandishing a sword with the other, challenging anyone who'd harm her.

He had that kind of air about him. He could have been a Highland warrior.

And she could look at him forever.

But as he needed to concentrate on maneuvering the

boat across the next onslaught of long, even larger-looking rollers, she opted to keep quiet and enjoy the view until they reached calmer water.

Large, glassy waves hissed past the bow, and the neat row of Pennard's whitewashed houses and the marina receded as they neared the jutting bulk of Pennard Head, the massive bluff that formed and protected the western end of the village. Rollers crashed against the rocks there, each breaking swell sending up fans of spray. The noise was deafening, elemental, and stirring. More seabirds than Kendra had ever seen jostled for room on the black, many-ledged cliff face and others soared and nose-dived everywhere, their constant flight making the crag seem alive.

The birds' cries, coupled with the roar of the sea and the rushing wind, filled Kendra's senses until she felt more alive, more exhilarated, than ever before in her life. It was a heady sensation, incredibly wonderful and yet almost painful in its intensity.

She could almost believe that nowhere else in the world existed.

As if nothing mattered except her and Graeme, alone in his boat, and the wild and beautiful sea and landscape surrounding them.

Glancing at him now, she felt a deep sense of longing, both for him and the land that seemed so much a part of him. With his profile limned against the sea and his long, dark hair blowing in the wind, he reminded her of their first meeting at Balmedie Beach and how he'd looked up on the high dunes, watching the horizon.

She would've sworn he was some kind of guardian.

That was the impression he'd given her that night.

If she was honest, the electricity crackling between them now had been strong even then. He'd taken her breath away at Balmedie. And even if she'd tried to ignore the attraction, it was real.

It was also more powerful than anything she'd ever felt in her life.

As if he agreed, he flashed a look at her that made her heart soar. Hoping he wouldn't guess, she smiled over at the seabirds cartwheeling up and down the cliffs they were just passing.

"This is incredible." She meant that. "I've never seen anything like it."

"Not many people have, lest they bother to take out a boat and come along this way." He glanced toward Pennard Head, then back at her. "There is a cliff path. But its zigzagging climb is slippery and dangerous. So, aye"—his voice took on a note of pride—"you're one of the few from out of town to enjoy this view of the bluff."

Kendra lifted a hand to shield her eyes from flying spray and tried to make out the track he'd described. She couldn't see anything except glistening black rock, screaming seabirds, and—her pulse jumped—a cute little seal sunning on a ledge just out of reach of the tide. Gripping the edge of the boat, she leaned forward, hoping to get a better look at the seal.

"O-o-oh, see there!" She pointed, her gaze locked on the seal's doglike face, sure he was looking right back at her. "Is he one of yours?"

"Seals belong to no man, lass. They answer only to their own good selves. Long may it be so." He smiled on the words, his fondness for the creatures apparent. "But, aye, thon wee one is from the seals I monitor. I recognize him by his markings and the shape of his head. Anyone who spends time around seals soon discovers they're as individual as we are.

"His friends will be a bit farther along the cliffs." He indicated a point up ahead where Kendra could just make out the flash of white breakers. "That's where their haul-out site is. I've told you"—he glanced at her—

"that's a place where they pull themselves ashore. They favor the protected sides of tidal rocks, ledges, and sandbanks. And they're greatest in number two hours before and after low tide. We'll be there soon and you'll see them."

"I can't wait." Kendra looked back at the seal. He'd slipped into the water, his dark, dome-shaped head bobbing in the waves as he stared after them.

Graeme was right.

This was a special place. Wonder surged inside her, warming her heart. The little seal rolled onto his back, lifting a flipper as if waving farewell as the boat moved steadily on.

"Are they all so playful?" She watched the seal until he dove beneath the water, disappearing.

"They are, aye. You can help me look for Bart." Graeme's voice held affection. "He wasn't there last time and I've been worried about him. Bart's an older bull seal. He's massive and thickly whiskered, but friendly as a dog. If you see him, you'll know he's Bart."

"Aren't seals tagged or something?"

"Aye, some. But their annual molt wasn't too long ago, in September. The transmitters are attached to their fur by epoxy." He paused as the *Sea Wyfe* arced over another roller and then plunged down the other side. "When seals molt, the transmitters often fall off. I suspect Bart has other ways of losing his. He's quite a character."

Kendra nodded, her gaze focused on the cliffs.

It was then that she remembered Iain had said Graeme's ancestral ruin, Castle Grath, was on a bluff just beyond Pennard Head.

She took a breath, knowing she had to ask about his family's home. "Isn't Pennard Head where—"

"Aye, it's where Ramsay can no longer keep us in his sights." Graeme was slowing the boat, moving carefully past a cluster of jagged-edged tidal rocks He'd clearly misunderstood her. "As soon as we're past these sker-ries, we're out of his reach.

"Although . . ." He didn't finish, his jaw clenching as he circled around the last jutting rock.

"What?" Kendra was burning to know.

Graeme didn't look at her.

His face closed even more. Then he drew a long breath, and she knew he was about to break, revealing something he normally wouldn't.

He shoved back his hair and the sight of his strong arm flexing made her forget about seals and even his oily foe. Only a short while ago, he'd slid his arm around her, pulling her hard against him.

She wanted more such embraces. She yearned for his kisses and the way he looked at her with his dark, intense gaze. She remembered her dream, how he'd approached her bed, his attention riveted on her naked breasts. . . .

Kendra drew a breath as a rush of desire washed through her. She shifted on her seat, growing restless. He was just too devilishly sexy, his appeal made lethal by his Scottish accent and dimples.

It was a potent combination.

Fortunately, the look on his face helped squash sen-sual thoughts and yearnings.

He was angry, though not at her.

"Ramsay"—he spoke the name as if it soured his tongue—"might not be able to see us from the Spindrift any longer, but he once tried to stretch his tentacles this far, the conniving bastard."

"I don't understand." She had an idea, but wanted him to tell her.

"There's a ruinous old castle up on the cliffs above my seal-watching place." He had to be speaking of Cas-tle Grath. But to Kendra's disappointment, he didn't

show any sign of admitting a connection to the stronghold. "Ramsay wanted to buy the ruin and sell one-
square-foot 'lots' to any Scotland-loving fools eager to
call themselves a laird. He hoped to finance the purchase that way and, of course, to make a tidy sum from
gullible American tourists."

Kendra blinked. "I've heard of such schemes."

She'd expected something worse.

"Aye, it's a common moneymaking ploy here." He
looked at her, his expression measuring, as if he were
debating what to tell her.

"That's surely not why you dislike him so much." She
knew there was more.

He cut the motor, letting the *Sea Wyfe* rock in the current. "There are many reasons Ramsay and I aren't
friends." His tone was somber, his dark gaze locked on
hers. "The land he wanted was my own. He sought to get
his hands on my family's ancestral seat, the crumbling
shell of Castle Grath.

"Selling deeds to Americans was only a front." His
voice turned cold, his disdain palpable. "Ramsay had no
intention of ever allowing Diaspora Scots to run over
the property, waving titles and maps and looking for
their little piece of the Auld Hameland.

"What he wanted"—he pushed back his hair again—
"was free rein to tear up the ruin and dig the land."

"He was hoping to find buried treasure?" Kendra was
again surprised.

Searching for treasure was the pastime of many.

But it didn't make people evil.

The look on Graeme's face said it did. "Not really
treasure, nae." He shook his head, watching her as he
spoke. "Ramsay hoped to find a relic he believed might
be secreted at Grath."

Kendra's interest quickened. "A relic?"

"Of sorts, aye."

"Of sorts?" Kendra repeated his words.

He looked sorry he'd let them slip. "An *instrument of destruction* is a better term."

Kendra felt her eyes round. "I don't understand."

"Be glad you don't." He glanced at the clouds gathering on the horizon and frowned. "Ramsay hoped to locate the Shadow Wand, a fabled length of jet and amber once said to have been in my family's possession. Anyone who wielded the relic held untold power." He looked at her as if he expected her to laugh.

She didn't.

"There's more, I can tell," she pressed, sensing in the air stirrings that the Shadow Wand was of much greater significance than a mere myth. She tucked her hair behind an ear, kept her voice neutral. "I'd love to hear why he wanted such a thing. Most people wouldn't—"

"Gavin Ramsay isn't like anyone you've ever met." He paused less than a second. "I told you he carries the taint of his ancestors."

"I remember."

"Their blood has influenced him." Graeme's face was deadly earnest.

"So?" Kendra hoped she didn't sound flippant. But she didn't want to show too much interest and risk him going silent.

"It's simple." He spoke matter-of-factly. "Gavin Ramsay's forebear, Morcant, was a dark druid. He was also the original owner of the Shadow Wand. When his greed and thirst for power made him even more corrupt, the wand fell into the hands of my ancestors.

"Or so clan legend claims." He turned back to the boat's wheel, as if the subject were closed.

Kendra was only getting started. "And now Gavin wants the relic back."

"That he does." Graeme restarted the motor. "And I am here to thwart him."

Kendra grabbed her seat as the *Sea Wyfe* surged forward, cutting straight through a swell, the spray pluming down the boat's sides.

And I am here to thwart him. Graeme's words echoed in her mind, something telling her there was much more to their rivalry than him keeping his foe from finding a legendary relic that might not even be real.

Graeme *was* real.

And seeing him so determined and fierce only made him all the more attractive to her. He'd wrapped himself around her heart now. It was only a matter of time before he noticed her feelings.

She was doing the one thing she'd vowed never to do: fall in love on the job.

Chapter 11

Graeme looked at the cliffs towering above the *Sea Wyfe* and knew he'd gone too far. Not distance-wise, but in sharing such confidences with Kendra.

He should not have spoken of the Shadow Wand to her.

He'd been equally foolish to show the depth of his animosity toward Ramsay. Kendra couldn't begin to understand the danger posed by the bastard.

And he wanted to keep it that way.

There were times when ignorance really was bliss.

This was one of them.

Sliding a glance at Kendra now, he saw that such a shield of innocence might just be possible. She leaned forward with her gaze on the cliffs, her eyes lit with wonder. He knew the look. It was the misty-eyed, oooh-this-is-the-land-of-my-ancestors sense of affinity most often seen on the faces of Scotland-loving Americans whenever they encountered anything even remotely resembling their sentimental ideals of *Braveheart* or *Brigadoon*.

Many of them wore that expression for the entire two-week duration of their Scotland holiday, telling anyone who'd listen that this is where they belonged. Even those without Scottish roots declared often and enthusiastically that they'd always dreamed of the Highlands.

Heather ran in their veins, they'd swear. Only half-jokingly, they'd claim that if you cut them, they'd bleed tartan. They were also quick to assert that bottled peat smoke would fly off the shelves in the States, proving irresistible to a public hungry for all things Scottish. Tins of Highland mist would do even better. As for kilts and the famed accent, the comments didn't bear recalling. Or that every castle, glen, or hill was some tourist's ancestral home, calling them back to Scotland. The pull, as they called such yearning, gripped them powerfully, giving them no peace until they bought a plane ticket and flew to Glasgow.

When they did, they felt complete.

Graeme stifled a snort of annoyance.

Like his fellow countrymen, he'd heard such proclamations often enough.

Loving Scotland was epidemic and those suffering the ailment were incurable. They also knew countless ways to express their passion. Any moment he expected Kendra to join their ranks, perhaps pressing a hand to her breast or gasping a few oohs and ahs.

Not that she struck him as a hopeless Scotophile on the usual coming-home pilgrimage.

But she did appreciate Pennard.

He blew out a breath, glad for the cold sea wind in his face.

Kendra's interest in the spectacular coastline let him

hope that she hadn't paid too much attention to his talk and complaints about Ramsay. Or the dread relic he wished didn't exist.

He'd spoken as if it was bit of fabled fluff, good for a fireside tale on a cold and dark winter night, but nothing real enough to impact the modern world.

Too bad it wasn't so.

What mattered was that a strong swell was running and a brisk wind blew from the west. In a few moments, they'd round the thickest bulk of Grath Point, and Kendra would see his seals. The creatures he monitored and protected. Looking out for them gave his many-yeared existence meaning. And—he shot another hopefully casual look at Kendra as they left the wider waters and headed closer to shore—soon she'd also spot the dark silhouette of Castle Grath etched against the scudding clouds, just appearing above the crags.

Somewhere deep inside him, something pinched and squeezed, an old pain he usually kept at bay. Not this morning. Now the ache stabbed with a vengeance, cruelly reminding him of what once was and could never again be.

He frowned, took a deep, steadying breath.

How he would've loved to show Kendra his home in another time and place.

Back in the days when Grath's walls were whole and strong, the roofs intact, and roaring hearth fires, tapestried rooms, and good food and ale ensured the comfort of all within. Years when every stone would've been clean, well swept, and polished, rather than how they were now—crumbling to dust and covered with grass and nettles.

Grath was now an empty, windswept place full of echoes and shadows.

And—Graeme tightened his hands on the boat's

wheel—he wished he'd taken Kendra to see the seals at Fraserburgh Harbor rather than risk bringing her anywhere near Grath Point and his memories.

He was vulnerable here.

It wasn't a state he enjoyed.

His blood pumped, but not in a good way. The past leapt on him from every tide-washed rock, each dark, wet-glistening fissure in the crag seeming to watch him with reproachful eyes. Everything here reminded him of those who'd gone before him and whom he wouldn't see again until his own seven hundred years and a day had passed.

Though if all went to plan—his plan, no one else's—he wouldn't meet his loved ones then, either. He didn't intend to leave the required heir. His obstinacy would damn him, but he didn't care. To his way of looking at things, he was cursed already.

So he'd vanish quietly, taking his legacy with him.

He'd be the last MacGrath.

That was the epitaph he desired.

And he had another seventy-five years to wait until the words could be carved into his headstone. So he pushed the thought from his mind and glanced again at his fetching passenger, surprised to see that she'd turned away from the cliffs.

They were deeply indented now, a steep, dark shoreline full of caves, narrow entrances to hidden coves, and secret glimpses of pristine, inaccessible beaches. Huge seas and white water made approaching the coast here a tricky endeavor, but he knew every rock and channel. Even when rain and darkness thickened the air, he could find a way ashore. And this day was glorious, with clear autumn light shining on the water and letting the spray sparkle.

It was a sight to stir the blood.

Yet . . .

He frowned. An uneasy sensation at the back of his neck warned that something wasn't right.

Kendra's gaze remained fixed on the horizon. Long lines of huge rollers could be seen there, their crests flashing white in the morning sun. They seemed to fascinate her.

"The North Sea aye has such rollers." Graeme watched her carefully. "You'd be hard-pressed to find rougher seas anywhere. These are unpredictably violent waters, the currents fatal if you're no' careful."

"M'hmmm." She didn't even blink.

And the look on her face was the same as at the Laughing Gull when she'd thought she'd glimpsed a ghostly fleet of herring boats.

Graeme shoved back his hair, ran a hand across his nape. Instinct told him he wouldn't like her answer if he asked what had caught her eye.

He didn't think it was the breakers.

Looking away from her, he shot a glance at the cliffs. Broad, flat ledges of glistening black rock garnished the foot of the bluff and sheltered them from the worst of the wind.

They were almost at Grath Point.

Being here was sheer torment, yet he returned again and again.

"I can see these waters are treacherous. Wild seas, full of danger, exacting a high toll on those who seek to know her." Kendra turned to face him then, her face clear again, her eyes bright. "Yet you love it here, the fine, deep harbor and the immense blue of the sea. Whether glassy and calm or sullen gray and rough, you live to be out here."

"Aye, I do." Graeme had never spoken more true words. Grath, Pennard, Balmedie—this entire coast was his life, literally.

"You'll soon see one of the reasons." He slowed the boat, wondering if she'd notice the colorful sea tangle waving in the current, the gleaming rock pools winking at them from along the proud, curving edge of Grath Point. "My seals' main haul-out site is just ahead."

Her gaze went upward instead of forward. The shell of Grath's ruinous tower was just coming into view, and it was there she'd focused her attention.

When she looked back at him, her blue eyes shone. "You didn't tell me you were a laird."

She might as well have kicked him in the gut.

"I'm not." His denial was a half-truth. As the last of his line, he didn't laird it over anyone.

He did hold the title.

She peered up again at the crumbling tower, the empty windows now coming into better view, each horrid opening like black, sightless eyes.

Graeme tried not to shudder.

She looked enchanted.

"I know you are." Her tone left no room for argument. "A laird, I mean." She angled her head, studying him. "Iain showed me the photo of the ruin last night. He also told me about Janet."

"Iain talks too much." Graeme made a silent note to tell the innkeeper to mind his own business. "And poor Janet should never have climbed up to Grath every day, and so doggedly." He purposely didn't comment on Kendra's remark about the old picture at the inn. "No good came of her vigils. Her husband didn't even die at sea. She wasted time and energy, putting herself in peril just to watch his boat return each e'en. It was all for naught. Poor Dod suffered a heart attack right in front of her workplace."

If he'd hoped to shock her, he'd failed. To his annoyance, she looked intrigued, even leaning forward to hang on his every word.

Not that he felt like divulging anything else.

"Was it near the red phone box?" Her question took him by surprise.

It was the last thing he'd expected.

He frowned, rubbed the back of his neck. He could almost feel the collar of his sweater tightening.

She pressed, getting that odd look on her face again. "Is that where her husband died?"

"No' quite." Graeme remembered the night well. "Dod died in the road. He'd meant to collect Janet, for they aye enjoyed a stroll along the waterfront after she finished work. Dod keeled over before he made it half-way across the road. He was beyond help, dead instantly."

"I see . . ." She nodded, reached to smooth her hair off her face. "Janet's had a rough time."

"She's no' been the same since, that's true." Graeme slanted a look down at the dancing tangle, not wanting to speak of death.

"That's understandable." She looked sympathetic.

"She needs to get on with her life."

"Sometimes it isn't that easy."

"Nothing ever has been in these parts." Graeme knew that well.

For centuries, here little had changed. Men went to sea, seeking their well-guarded fishing grounds and spending their time on land baiting lines, filling trawl tubs, or preparing lobster traps, all for the next day's haul. Their wives worked even harder, raising large families, darning socks and knitting sweaters, baking bread and cooking meals. In their spare time, they picked berries or dug clams. And throughout their toil, they kept one eye on the sea, always worrying, hoping their men would return safely.

In more recent years, the good fisher folk of Pennard also fretted about tourists. Since the success of the cult film *The Herring Fisher*, they arrived each summer with the regularity of herring shoals. They'd crowd the tiny village as they went about snapping pictures, paying for boat trips, booking rooms at the inn, and filling the salt air with their twangy American accents.

Pennard needed them.

Too bad their affection for the little fishing village also brought its doom. Scotland's Past wouldn't have glanced at Pennard if they didn't see its popularity as a milkable cash cow.

Graeme frowned, his jaw setting so tight he wondered he didn't crack a tooth.

He also didn't care to discuss Dod's passing. He'd liked the man. Just as he'd got on well with Dod's parents and grandparents and their parents before them. That they were no longer here reminded him of how fragile such relationships are. How unwise he'd been to bring Kendra to a place with the power to strip his defenses.

Yet there was no turning back now.

A large, curving tumble of rocks under the cliffs marked the deep, steep-sided cove that was the seals' haul-out site. On such a fine day, they'd be all over the stony little beach. Graeme just hoped Kendra wouldn't notice the inlet's other notable attraction.

Not many people would.

And he was so smitten with her—and eager to spend the day in her company—that he'd overlooked what she'd told him about her occupation.

As a landscape historian, she might well spot the hand-cut shape of some of the broken rocks piled at one end of the tiny cove. Or notice that the unobtrusive half arch set high into the bluff on that side of the beach wasn't a natural part of the cliff, but the remains of a gatehouse that once guarded Graeme's home.

She already knew Castle Grath loomed above them.

With luck, she wouldn't realize how easily they could reach the ruins.

If one was willing to climb and didn't suffer a fear of heights. As long as one kept a good toehold on the right rocks and possessed a secure and firm hand grip, it was possible. A willingness to get wet and dirty didn't hurt, either. Kendra's profession indicated she'd scramble up the broken, weather-worn steps with enthusiasm.

So Graeme had only one hope.

That she'd find the seals so enchanting, she wouldn't see anything else.

Not too far from Graeme's *Sea Wyfe*, but at a carefully calculated distance behind the shoulder of the crags, a smaller boat bobbed and pitched in the strong-running swell. Dark blue in color and bearing the stenciled name *Fenris* in white letters on her bow and again across her stern, the boat was outfitted with a powerful engine. Her speed and stealth made up for her lack in size.

Such things mattered to the man at the tiller.

The boat was called after the Viking god Fenris the wolf, believed to be the son of Loki the trickster. Like his better-known father, Fenris the wolf boasted a reputation as a troublemaker in Asgard, the Norse heaven. The *Fenris* served a similar purpose: stirring mayhem.

Sometimes worse.

If someone needed to find themselves wedged between limpet-crusted rocks beneath a little-visited, inaccessible cliff, their naked body battered by the tide, *Fenris* the boat escorted them there.

Whenever such dark deeds were necessary, Gavin Ramsay knew the fast little boat would do him well. The hurling seas did the rest, always dependable. As were the lobsters and seabirds, ever ready to disperse of what remained after a good slamming and crashing by the waves.

Gavin scarce needed to exert himself. And that was as well, because he was a vain man. He much preferred using his darker talents to dirtying his hands and risking scars if a foe put up a struggle.

He also enjoyed the stunned realization on their faces when they grasped that they couldn't escape their fate. He reveled in their shock and horror.

This morn was such a time.

MacGrath, the seal-loving bastard, had played right into his hands. It scarce mattered if the American was his long-lost girlfriend or not. And Gavin had his doubts that she was. No man, not even MacGrath, would let a woman he loved stray far from his arms.

And if that man knew—as he was sure MacGrath did—that she possessed strong psychic powers, her energy field almost blinding to those able to see such things, such a man would deserve to lose her.

Yet MacGrath, who regrettably wielded his own brand of magic, didn't seem troubled enough to keep her secure at his own cottage.

He let her sleep at the Laughing Gull.

And that told Gavin all he needed to know.

Their bond, whatever it was, could be broken. And once he had the chit in his own arms, she'd forget the seal man. Gavin shoved back his hair, dashing water from his face when the *Fenris* took a bow full of spray. Ever a man to embrace danger, he didn't mind the rough seas.

Soon he'd enjoy a very different challenge.

A shapely, easily besotted one he meant to have naked in his bed and writhing beneath him before this day's sun sank behind the hills.

A smile tugged at the corner of his mouth and he felt a most enjoyable twitching at his loins, as well. An insistent stirring he looked forward to indulging later this evening. He knew how to pleasure women.

American women were especially easy to please.

They melted at a flash of plaid, a hot-eyed wink and a smile, or a wee hint that one was descended from Robert the Bruce.

Gavin's lips twitched again at the thought of *his* forebears.

Not quite in the Bruce's league, they were far more powerful in their own right.

Even so, he'd stick with his charm and Scottish accent to seduce the American.

Graeme MacGrath wasn't the only Scot able to turn on a burr. Nor—Gavin ran his fingers through his hair again—was the seal man as good-looking as he was. Kendra Chase wouldn't be able to resist him.

And if his other skills were as sharp as he believed, she'd soon welcome his attentions. At the very least, she'd need comforting.

After that . . .

Gavin braced himself as the *Fenris* plunged into another steep trough, dousing him anew. He didn't care about getting wet, only even.

Destroying MacGrath was his plan.

Once he'd accomplished that, everything else would fall into place.

"You'd best hold tight now." Graeme's tone made Kendra's senses sharpen. "The currents are tricky here and it'll be a bit rough before we're around the rocks and into the shelter of the cove."

"I can tell." Kendra did as he suggested, gripping the side of the boat with one hand and using her other to hold on to the seat.

A bit rough was an understatement.

Submerged rocks fringed the cove's narrow opening and the sea churned there, the waves breaking up and swirling in all directions after crashing into the jagged skerries. Kendra looked about in excitement, her blood pumping as the *Sea Wyfe* pitched and tossed. She didn't doubt the boat's sea worthiness, or Graeme's skill at handling her.

She could feel the air around them come alive.

This was more than a popular gathering spot for seals. Grath Point held a vital pulse she could almost hear humming inside the sheer rock cliffs. The place possessed an intense power. Everything was sharply defined, clear, and vibrant. The sea, wind, and sky struck her as almost crystalline.

It could've been a dream landscape.

The quality was similar.

She flashed a glance at Graeme. Surreal vista or not, she wasn't going to think about dreams right now. Not after the one she'd had of Graeme in her room the night before. Just remembering sent a sensual warmth rushing through her entire body, even now.

And it'd only been a dream.

Yet . . .

The sensations it had stirred in her were as real as if he had actually been in her room.

In an attempt to distract herself, she thought back to the spectral herring fleet. She would swear she'd also seen the ghostly ships out near the horizon only a short while ago. Their sails had caught her eye, flashing white in the morning sun. But then she'd squinted while Graeme had been talking to her about the huge seas, and when she looked again, that was just what she saw: long, white-crested rollers moving slowly toward the shore.

Nothing else stirred except the spray hissing down the sides of Graeme's *Sea Wyfe* and the seabirds circling above the boat.

Even so, she'd allowed herself a moment to summon a protective shield of white-light energy, letting its power surround her, cleansing and blessing a sacred circle of space around her.

Psychic self-defense, once learned and practiced, was as simple as brushing teeth.

It didn't mean she wasn't willing to let ghosts approach her. They still could if they desired. Her talent was an inherited gift, passed down through the women in her family. No one knew when it began or who'd be the last so blessed. What did stand out was that it jumped generations indiscriminately, following no given pattern. For whatever reason it occurred, it was a legacy meant to be used and accessed. So she kept herself open to discarnate visits, encouraging and welcoming such encounters.

She was just selective.

Ghosts didn't lose their personalities simply because they'd moved on to dwell on another plane. Zack had a favorite caution: once an ax murderer, always an ax murderer.

There were also braggarts, liars, and connivers in the spirit world.

She'd also encountered more than one lothario. Ethereal men who'd been more than willing to leave the place—and the earthly women—they'd been haunting, only to reappear in Kendra's apartment on her return home, usually surprising her in her bedroom or bathroom.

Some ghosts were just plain mean.

It paid to be prudent.

But she was curious about the fleet. Hopefully she'd soon know what they wanted from her. She'd also love to see the phone-box ghost again, now certain that the big, gruff-faced fisherman was none other than Janet Murray's late husband. She was always careful not to press discarnates to speak to her, but she did have ideas when it was necessary to make a connection easier for them.

Something told her Dod Murray needed such a nudge.

Dod was a troubled soul, reliving his passing each time he left the call box and ventured into Harbour Street.

At least that was her interpretation.

"Have you no' seen them yet?" Graeme's voice startled her.

"Them?" Kendra's eyes flashed open. Her pulse leapt as she whipped around, for a moment thinking he'd guessed her secret: that she was one of the rare people able to see and speak with ghosts.

"The seals." He gave her a smile that made her forget all about spirits. "We're here. This is where I come to watch and record their behavior."

"I don't see any." She didn't. She saw only rocks and surging water, the glitter of flying spray.

"You will in a beat." He sounded amused. "They're aye glad for company. Like pet dogs they are, I say you."

"I've heard that." She glanced at him again, and his dimple flashed when he looked at her. She wished he didn't have one. It only added to his appeal. Worse, his burr was working its usual magic, his soft, lilting words making her heart beat faster.

His looks didn't help.

His sleek black hair whipped about his face, and although it was still morning, a sexy trace of beard stubble already shadowed his chin. His dark eyes seemed to look deep inside her, peering into her soul. . . .

She tore her gaze away, not wanting to go down that road.

She *was* going ashore with him.

While she'd been thinking about Dod Murray, Graeme had slowed the boat to a putter. They were only a few feet from the dark bulk of Grath Point. And dead ahead, a curving sweep of jumbled rock formed a sheltered, deep-sided cove.

They'd arrived.

Kendra felt instinctively that she'd know Graeme much better when they left.

Sure of it, she blew out a long breath. There was only one problem with getting closer to him: he'd also learn more about her.

And that's what she was supposed to avoid.

What a pity having to say good-bye to him felt like the greater hardship.

Chapter 12

"My seals"—Graeme's voice held pride and affection—
"they're there. You can see them through the opening in
the rocks." He was pointing ahead, with a broad smile
splitting his face.

Kendra followed his gaze, the arm he held outstretched to help her know where to look.

"Oh, my. You're right!" Kendra shaded her eyes, her
worries of the moment before fading at the sight in front
of her.

Morning sun glittered on the water. And beyond the
secret inlet's narrow entrance, a crescent of stony beach
beckoned at the cove's rear. Kendra leaned forward,
squinting to see across the bright-glinting waves to the
rock-strewn beach. Seals were there, more than she
could count. The strand sloped gently and it was clear
that Graeme meant to run the *Sea Wyfe* up onto the
shingle.

As if the seals recognized him and knew, they made room, wriggling aside or sliding down into the surf so that a landing place opened for the boat.

Kendra's breath caught watching them. "They know you."

"They should." Graeme's dimple winked again. "We've been friends for many long years."

Something in his tone made her skin prickle. But when she glanced at him, she couldn't see any reason for the ripple of chills.

He'd turned his attention on the seal-free strip of shoreline looming so close now, and she couldn't help but notice the flex of his arm muscles as he ran the boat deeper into the cove. Wind blew his hair about his neck and shoulders, making him look like a pagan Celtic prince or a dashing medieval warlord.

She could go for either.

Mostly she just wanted him.

She ached for him, her whole body needing and desiring him in ways she'd never wanted any other man. She felt a powerful attraction to him. She wanted him to kiss her, long and deep, and not because someone was watching and he wanted to give credence to their sham relationship. It wasn't just his sexy Scottish accent and dark good looks that attracted her.

It was him.

There was something maddeningly irresistible about a man who wasn't just drop-dead gorgeous and had a voice like a verbal orgasm, but also clearly cared deeply about the land and sea that was his heritage. So much so that he was fighting to hold on to tradition. His views and attitude spoke straight from her own heart, resonating with her on levels that went far deeper than mere physical attraction.

He loved dogs.

She couldn't get away from that—a love of animals, especially dogs, was right up there with old-fashioned honor and a good sense of humor. He met all those qualifications and then some.

And that made him an ideal candidate to break her heart.

Especially since—unlike her UK-based colleagues with Ghostcatchers International—she couldn't just up and relocate to the wilds of northeastern Scotland.

Life didn't work that way.

At least it didn't for Americans keen to transplant themselves across an ocean.

Like it or not, when her work was done, she'd be winging it back to Newark.

Kendra frowned, not wanting to think of her return.

She had today, this outing. . . .

"The seals are greeting you." Graeme shot a look at her. He smiled and then nodded at the curving strand. "Do you hear their singing? They save such a chorus for special guests."

Kendra followed his gaze, feeling better already.

The strip of rocky beach teemed with seals of all shades and sizes. They did seem to serenade her, the sound a cross between a dog's bark and the haunting cry of geese. Many were dark gray, some almost slate blue. A few small ones sported rich, chocolate brown coats, while others appeared mottled. All seemed playful and friendly, watching the boat's approach with round, curious eyes.

Kendra blinked, dashing salt spray from her own eyes. Though deep inside, with the backs of her lids stinging hotly, she knew that flying spume wasn't the reason her vision suddenly blurred.

She did love animals.

And she never thought to see such an incredible sight.

The seals were everywhere now, their domelike heads popping up in the water. Unafraid, they swam near, diving beneath the waves only to bob up again, their welcoming gazes never leaving her and Graeme.

"I knew you'd enjoy seeing them." Graeme smiled over at her again, his voice betraying his affection for the seals. "The wee ones are harbour or common seals. They've been diminishing in number in recent years. No one knows why." He turned back to the wheel, letting the boat glide gently onto the pebbly strand. "I have my own ideas, but no one wants to hear them, and any who did would deny it."

"What do you mean?" Kendra didn't like his tone, or the crease that had marred his brow for just a second.

"Ach, it's just a notion." He didn't look at her as they came to a smooth, scrunching halt. "People along this coast are of the sea. Even today, many of them depend on these waters for their livelihood. A fisherman needs a good haul to pay for his boat and his house, feed a wife and children. Seals eat fish. They're a natural competitor."

Kendra felt her eyes rounding. "Surely you're not saying—"

"Visit any isle in the Hebrides and folk aren't so secretive about it." Graeme grabbed a line and slung it around a huge iron anchor protruding upward from a mound of broken rocks. "Hereabouts, such things aren't admitted. If it happens, and I cannae say it does, any mate who talked would lose his work, ne'er to be hired again.

"And"—he knotted the line—"if he bought his own boat, he'd soon find himself run off the best fishing grounds. If he tried his luck elsewhere, he'd only discover his buoys cut. If that didn't send him on his way, he'd start losing gear or suffer an accident that would leave his boat in flames. Worst case, he'd end up as crab bait.

"So no one speaks of such things." He gripped the anchor stem, looking at her.

"You just did."

"And I'll keep on." A thread of steel entered his voice. "My family fished, too. Such cruelty isn't necessary. Hard work and long hours fill a day's quota just as well as eliminating fish eaters."

"Aren't you afraid of—"

"Ending up as a crab's dinner?" He tossed back his hair, smiling again. "Nae, I'm no' worried. I irritate a lot of people around here, but there aren't many who'd dare do anything about it."

Kendra bit her lip to keep from mentioning Gavin Ramsay.

Instead, she looked at the anchor, not wanting Graeme to see that his smile affected her. Or that the way his long black hair shone in the sunlight made her forget everything except her wish to touch the gleaming strands.

Besides, the anchor was interesting.

Badly rusted, a thick growth of wet, slippery weed covered its length, making it almost indistinguishable. It was the largest anchor she'd ever seen, and only half of it raged out of rocks.

Graeme caught her staring. "The anchor's from an old whaling ship that went aground here centuries ago. It holds the *Sea Wyfe* secure in all weathers." He patted the anchor's seaweed-draped stem. "I like to think it's glad to still be of use to someone."

"I'm sure that's true." Kendra's heart squeezed, listening to him.

In this special place, she could believe such whimsy.

And she doubted she'd find a single man back home in Bucks County who'd harbor such a sentiment.

She'd probably have difficulty locating such a man in all Pennsylvania. Americans weren't raised on legend and lore. They didn't hear lonesome pipers playing on eerie, mist-draped medieval battlefields. Or give names of meaning to stones and believe that a red-berried rowan tree holds special powers. They didn't know the heady elixir of peat smoke on a chill autumn wind.

Even Zack, who definitely believed in ghosts and other things that went bump in the night, would draw the line at giving feelings to a rusty old anchor. That Graeme did, allowing the anchor its dignity and pride, only made him more attractive to her.

"Are you coming, then?" He already stood on the shore, his hands extended to help her from the boat. The seals were all around him, clamoring for attention. Many perched on rocks, others surged forward, their round dark eyes inquisitive. The air rang with their doglike barks and soft gurgling. "They won't hurt you." He glanced at one seal that was rolling in the surf just a few feet from the beached *Sea Wyfe.* "They're only curious."

"I know. They don't frighten me." They didn't. But she did try hard not to notice the jolt of sensation that whipped through her when Graeme caught her by her waist and lifted her out of the boat. He set her gently onto the smooth-pebbled beach, forgetting her again as soon as he'd seen her safely on solid ground.

At least, that's the impression he gave her.

Yet she would've sworn he'd felt the physical charge between them. She could still feel the imprint of his hands on her body, the warmth spilling through her, tingling and delicious. Powerful sensations that caught at her heart and made her ache inside.

His smile deepened, wholly oblivious. "So what do you think of my seals?"

She looked around and did not need to feign interest. She understood his fascination with them. "They're wonderful, truly. I've never seen any this close."

They were coming nearer now, craning their necks to peer at her, their welcome giving her an excellent excuse to focus on something other than Graeme. How easily she could fall in love with him. How apparent it was that despite his kisses, he wasn't interested in her.

He lived for his seals.

Even Gavin Ramsay had called him *seal man.*

Apparently, he didn't do two-legged relationships. And that should be a warning not to get any further involved with him. The more she opened her heart, the greater pain he'd inflict on her, however unknowingly.

But for now they were here, and although she knew it'd been a mistake to accept his invitation, she had little choice but to get through the day.

Hopefully, she'd be able to do so with her feelings intact, her emotions buffered by her usual reserve.

Unfortunately, his proximity made that unlikely.

And he was looking at her in a way that set her heart to racing. His smile was warm, intimate, and so sexy that she almost forgot to breathe. He was good-looking in Pennard and he'd really knocked her socks off on the beach at Balmedie. But here, in this wild place that was so clearly his element, he made her think of a god.

She swallowed, sure her knees were trembling. "We don't have to stay here long," she offered, grasping the only excuse she could think of to speed them on their way. "I doubt your breakfast was as filling as the one I had at Iain's. You must be starving by now."

"I've brought a packed lunch." He vaulted into the boat, returning a moment later with a backpack and folded length of plaid. "Not a bad one, either. There's smoked salmon sandwiches, some aged Stilton, and mackerel pate with oatcakes. For a sweet, chocolate biscuits, which are"—he paused, winking at her—"*cookies* to you. And to wash it all down, a thermos of strong tea."

Kendra just looked at him. "That's a feast."

She was still bursting from breakfast at the Laughing Gull.

"Aye, so it is." He shrugged into the backpack all the same.

Kendra smiled, her mouth watering despite how her waistband bit into her. "Didn't you say something at the Laughing Gull about a good Scottish breakfast lasting the whole day?" She couldn't keep a teasing note out of her voice. "I do believe you did."

He held up his hands. "I would've insulted Iain and Janet if I'd not brought along the food. They prepared it for us, thinking this was a romantic outing."

Kendra wished it was.

"Why were they so surprised to hear you have a girl-friend?" She had no business asking, but the words just popped out. He fascinated her. "I mean"—she could feel herself coloring—"I know we're not really a couple. But surely they've seen you with your real girlfriends?"

"Folk in small Scottish communities see everything." He glanced aside, looking at a seal tumbling in the surf. "There are no secrets. If someone sneezes on one side of Pennard, you can be sure someone on the other end of the village will say, 'Bless you.'"

Kendra couldn't argue.

She did pretend to follow his gaze. But rather than watching the frolicking seal, she noted the emotions playing across his face.

Her question didn't sit well with him. And he'd avoided answering her.

That left one conclusion.

"Did you recently break up with someone?" The thought pinched her heart. It was an unmerited reaction, but one she felt strongly. "Is that why Iain and Janet were so stunned when you said I was here to see you?"

"Nae to both." He tilted his head back, looking up at the clouds. "I haven't split with anyone, leastways not in a very long while. The truth is" — he turned to face her — "I've been too busy in recent years to think of getting involved with a woman.

"Everyone here knows that." He took her arm and led her past the seals, guiding her with long, sure strides toward the far side of the cove. "They've also heard me declare myself a die-hard bachelor. I've been to more weddings than I can count and never leave one without someone cornering me and getting the same answer: that I've no time for a woman in my life, settling down, and all that.

"Now . . ." He glanced at her as they skirted a large, well-muscled seal. "They're wondering what happened to make me change my mind. They'll be curious about you, watching everything we do together. I wouldn't be surprised if they spread a rumor that you're a selkie. It wouldn't be a stretch for some to believe such a tale. They'll think you turned my head and are keeping me under an enchantment after I found you with my seals, like as not here."

Kendra smiled. "That's ridiculous."

He shrugged one shoulder, not turning a hair. "This is Scotland."

"I know, but—"

"We're weaned on all sorts of stories told around the fire on dark winter nights." He stopped, flicking out the plaid he'd been carrying, and spreading it on a broad rock ledge too high for seal intrusion. "There isn't a Scot

born, especially a Highland Scot, who'd deny the existence of second sight or the evil eye.

"Go to the Western Isles and you'll find countless
families who'll swear they have a selkie ancestor or an-
cestress." He smoothed the plaid and then turned to face
her. "You'd be wise not to doubt them. Scots know
there's more to the world than meets the eye.

"An underworld of dark just as real as thon rolling
sea." He glanced at the horizon, the long, white-crested
breakers flashing in the sun. "The seal people and the
tales about them are only one small part of that realm."

Kendra rubbed her arms against the wind, a sudden
shiver skating down her spine.

He'd spoken as if he really believed in such things.

"Did you know seals shed tears?" He was still watching the sea. "When they're sad, their moans are often
mistaken for human crying. They can pine for years,
never forgetting a lost mate or pup."

"I think you're trying to change the subject." Kendra
had seen his face close when she'd asked about girlfriends.

"Not at all." He angled his head, studying her. "What
about you? You're a bonnie lass." He stepped closer and
reached to trail his knuckles down the curve of her
cheek. His touch warmed her skin and sent ripples of
sensation along her nerves. "Is there a special someone
waiting for you back in the States? I'm thinking"—he
looked her up and down, appraising—"there must be."

"There isn't." She blurted the truth before she could
catch herself.

Pretending she had a significant other would've made
it easier to resist him.

Now . . .

She lifted her chin, hoping to appear strong, modern,
and confident. "Like you, my work keeps me too occu-

pied to get involved with anyone. I'm always on the road and pretty tired when I'm home."

That was true.

Equally so was that Graeme made her want to forget every excuse she'd given him. With his dark gaze locked on hers and a freshening wind riffling his glossy black hair, all she could do was take a deep breath and hope he couldn't read her mind. She'd never been the sort of woman to hop in bed with men she barely knew.

One-night stands and holiday affairs weren't her cuppa.

Yet just standing so close to Graeme—especially in this windswept cove with the sea crashing all around them—was so heady that she wished just once she could be more daring, even reckless, and cast aside her usual restraint.

But she was certain he could never be a mere holiday fling, enjoyed for his dark good looks and sexy accent.

And she was kidding no one if she denied wanting more.

She did keep her chin raised, her gaze steady on his. "You don't really think there are selkies, do you?" This time she changed the subject. "I can see someone in the Outer Hebrides still believing in seal people. But here, so close to a big modern city like Aberdeen—"

"Aberdeen is an ancient place with deep ties to the sea." He touched her face again, smoothing back her hair. "Myself . . ." He paused, resting his hand on her shoulder, as if it belonged there. "I will say I've ne'er seen a selkie. But"—his eyes lit—"I wouldn't be surprised if I did."

"So you do believe in them."

"I didn't say that."

"You didn't have to." Kendra stepped away from him, breaking the physical contact. It was dangerous to let him touch any part of her, even so innocently. Her legs already felt weak beneath her, her stomach all fluttery. She had to remember to breathe.

She did glance about the rocky beach, opting to study his seals rather than risk looking at him. Her heart raced, and something told her he knew.

His aura was warming, reaching out to her as if offering an embrace. She knew from her work and her gift that a person's energy didn't lie and couldn't be concealed from those able to read such things. Somewhere deep inside himself, he was interested in her. She was sure of it. The knowledge made her pulse quicken.

And even though she'd looked elsewhere, his gaze hadn't left her.

That, too, she felt.

But before she could figure out how to get through their time here without revealing her own feelings—something that could be fatal, she was sure—a huge, mottle-skinned seal caught her eye. Clearly a bull, he was lumbering out of the surf on the far side of the cove, where Graeme had tied the *Sea Wyfe* to a rusty old anchor.

"Oh, look!" She pointed at the powerfully muscled beast. "That must be Bart."

"Aye, that's him." Graeme sounded relieved. "He'll have been out foraging, looking as well as he does. Could be he knew I'd be bringing you with me today." He glanced at her, winking. "Bart likes the ladies."

As if to prove it, Bart turned his thickly whiskered head to look at Kendra once he'd hauled himself out of the water. His eyes were huge, liquid pools, his expression that of a trusting dog.

"He'll stop at the boat." Graeme started forward, making for his friend. "He knows I always carry a pail of herring for special treats."

But Bart barked and pulled himself past the *Sea Wyfe*, ignoring Graeme's approach and heading for a tumble of weed-draped rocks beneath an arch in the far end of the cove's sheltering cliff.

Kendra shaded her eyes, her attention snapping from the seal to the formation in the bluff. It was an incomplete arch, one half broken away, the pile of rocks at its base washed by the sea.

It wasn't a natural arch.

She saw that clearly. And the sudden darkening of Graeme's face showed that he'd seen that she knew and wasn't happy.

His frown deepened when Bart lunged onto a low, flat-topped rock beneath the arch. When the seal lifted his head, fixing them with a steady, determined-looking stare, Graeme swore beneath his breath.

"Bluidy beast." He quickened his pace, skirting the other seals.

Bart seemed pleased, barking noisily.

"He's in the remains of a sea gate, isn't he?" Kendra hurried to catch up with Graeme, sure she guessed right. She saw now that many of the rocks on the little beach were hand cut, their squared faces unmistakable despite the draping of seaweed or crusting of limpets.

The rocks were fallen rubble from what once would've been an impressive guardhouse. Tumbled stone walls now so easily identified. Each crevice, bump, and hollow in the half arch told a story. Even the shadows held secrets waiting to be discovered, especially by someone who made a living studying the past.

Yet she'd not have noticed if Bart hadn't gone there.

Graeme was too much of a distraction.

"The arch is part of your ancestral home, isn't it?" She stopped, bending to retie her bootlace. "I know Castle Grath is right above us."

"Aye, there was a sea gate here." Graeme sounded reluctant to answer. "It fell centuries ago and—"

A deep rumbling cut him off, shaking the ground. All the seals but Bart plunged into the sea. Graeme whipped around, looking up just as a boulder came hurtling over the cliff.

"Run!" He flew at Kendra, shoving her aside as the rock sped past, sending up a great plume of water as it slammed into the surf.

Catching her balance, Kendra dragged her sleeve across her face, wiping the moisture from her eyes. When they cleared, her heart stopped.

The boulder hadn't just crashed into the sea.

Graeme was lying facedown on the beach, a smear of red staining his right temple and the stones beneath his head. The rock had struck him.

And he wasn't moving.

"Dear God!" Kendra raced over to him, immediately seeing something worse. Graeme wasn't just stunned, lying unnaturally still.

He didn't appear to be breathing.

Her fears were confirmed when she dropped to her knees beside him and slipped her fingers beneath his collar to check his pulse.

She couldn't find one. She swore her own heart stopped. She hadn't performed CPR in ages. She sucked in a deep breath, hoping she'd do it right. Above her, something stirred, catching her eye.

A green-black haze glittering in triumph along the top of the cliff.

Chapter 13

"Graeme—wake up, speak to me!" Kendra felt the air change around her, icing the wind and frosting the wet rocks jabbing her knees. A worse cold swept in from the sea, tingeing the cove with the same green-black shimmer she'd seen edging the bluff. Leaning closer to Graeme, she smoothed back his hair, trying not to wince when his blood reddened her fingers.

She also ignored the eerie haze, not wanting to acknowledge that she recognized it as the glaze of death, which always appeared to taint atmosphere darkened by violent passings.

Instead she unbuttoned Graeme's shirt and slipped her hand beneath his bulky fisherman's sweater. "Oh, please . . ."

Begging didn't help.

His chest didn't rise and fall.

Kendra closed her eyes and tried not to think anything negative. She knew that painting devils on the wall was the best way to summon them. And Graeme's skin was vitally warm, the dusting of hair across his chest too alluring for him to be anything but strong and alive. Even so, her mind tugged her in unwanted directions, causing her worries to rise and making it almost impossible to keep calm.

He couldn't be dead.

Summoning all her composure, she took a deep breath and rested her hand against his cheek, willing him to draw on her life force and waken, whole and unharmed. But the day only turned darker, the chill air so unnaturally frigid she imagined frost forming on the rock-strewn beach and icy mist filling the cove.

And still Graeme didn't move.

She felt as if she'd been stabbed in the gut.

It was a battering that would've been much worse if her protective shields weren't in place. Even so, sharp, edgy dread slipped through to creep beneath her skin as the dark cold pressed against her defenses. Her chest tightened, making each breath a struggle.

Graeme's skin was turning pale, his lips gone blue. The gash at his temple gleamed red, the stain on the beach stones almost garish now.

"I don't believe this is happening." She smoothed back his hair, her mind rushing to recall everything she knew about emergency procedures and basic CPR. Worry and guilt made it hard to remember. If she'd not come here, he'd be with his dog at the Keel, or they'd be walking the shore, the high moors. Perhaps they'd even be at Balmedie, up on the dunes again.

But Jock was alone at the cottage, waiting for a master who'd never return.

And Graeme . . .

"Dear God, just breathe," she begged and interlaced

her fingers and braced her hands against his chest, pumping hard and fast. "Come on . . . Please be okay!" She tipped back his head, lifting his chin and pinching his nose as she leaned down to cover his mouth with hers and blow air into his lungs.

If he knew, he gave no sign.

Her stomach lurched and her heart raced as she reared up, once more pushing on his chest. Intended or not, this was her fault. The knowledge twisted inside her, bitter and agonizing. If she could, she'd reverse time or stop the world's turning. Anything to undo this.

But even though certain members of her family enjoyed—or carried the burden of?—a slew of super- and semi-supernatural powers, halting time wasn't one of them. Nor could they reverse death.

Even the Cosmos looked on benignly as mortals met their fates.

She took another deep breath, fighting her chills and the hot bile in her throat. Bending forward, she blew again into his mouth, willing him to respond.

As if from a great distance, she heard the splashing and gurgling of the seals as they clambered out of the surf, back onto the little beach. Bart still barked from the flat rock beneath the broken gate arch, his clamor echoing around the high-walled cove.

But the icy wind was louder now, shrieking as if in glee to have felled Graeme.

It was an unholy wind, she knew. The fine hairs lifting on her nape told her that. She also sensed a dark energy, ravenous for a vulnerable soul.

The carrion of the Underworld, circling in anticipation.

"No-o-o, you can't have him." She pumped Graeme's chest harder, not quite sure whom from such dark realms she was addressing, but adamant all the same.

It didn't matter, anyway.

She had other concerns. Graeme's life, for one. She didn't need to worry for herself. As long as her own time wasn't at hand, her shields would protect her. But the grasping energy from such bottom-feeders and other fiends could make her feel sick.

And she did.

Her mouth was dry, her insides roiled, and dizziness threatened, already blurring the outer edges of her vision. Everything around her swam and shifted as she worked on Graeme. She didn't need to feel bad now. Yet she felt worse than the one and only time a long-ago boyfriend had pulled her unwillingly onto a death-defying roller coaster at the Pennsylvania State Fair.

She pushed her hair back off her face, ignoring the queasiness.

"Please . . ." She inhaled deeply again, filling her lungs with the cold salt air, half afraid she was about to faint. She might talk to dead people, but she didn't do well with blood. Especially when the red stuff was spilling out of someone she was falling in love with.

No, someone she *had* fallen in love with.

Heat swept her, but not the good kind. And a small, annoying voice somewhere deep inside her chided that if she'd kept walking at Balmedie, never stopping to stare at Graeme on the dunes or to speak to him beside the abandoned WWII bunkers there, this wouldn't have happened. At the very least, she should've had the nerve to drive her own rental car down Pennard's Cliff Road, rather than sitting behind the wheel, too frozen by dread to take her foot off the brake pedal. If she'd been bolder, more daring . . .

Her throat began to close but she worked harder over Graeme, ignoring the heat stinging her eyes, blurring her vision.

"Damn." She couldn't remember the last time she'd cried. "Oh, God, I can't bear it. . . ." She pressed her fist against her mouth, not surprised to find that her hand trembled violently.

She didn't even taste the blood on her fingers.

She did tilt back her head, peering up at the sky. The clouds were thickening, dulling the brightness of the low Scottish sun. And the cold air smelled of coming rain, the sea and brine, the seaweedy musk of seals, and so much wet stone. Even so, her eyes burned as if she'd been torched by flames. She took a long breath, blinking against the searing heat. Wishing she could turn back the clock and decline this ill-fated excursion.

But it was too late.

She'd crossed a perilous boundary and—she knew— there was no going back. Things had happened, her emotions were involved, and this was one of those times when a mere moment changed life forever.

For now, she had to do something.

Her cell phone was in her bag on the boat. She had Iain's number at the Laughing Gull. He could send help. She didn't expect they would arrive in time, but it seemed the only thing she could try. She could never get Graeme over and around the rocks, then up into the *Sea Wyfe* on her own. Even if she managed that, she doubted she could get the boat out of the cove and along the rough waters of the coast, back to Pennard and the little stone harbor she wished they'd never left.

She blew out a breath, feeling hollow, her arms and legs rubbery. Her pulse pounded in her ears, the roar worsening her light-headedness. She wasn't sure she could stand, much less scramble the half length of the beach to the boat, dodging rocks and seals to get there.

Could she leave Graeme alone that long?

She feared she had to.

And that was when she felt the air shift again. Before she could push to her feet, the deep chill left the wind and its terrible shrieking lessened, dwindling to an ordinary-sounding whistle.

"Oh, God . . ." Her heart sank.

She knew what that meant.

Whatever energy had rushed into the cove had claimed its prize and was leaving, Graeme's soul in its greedy clutches. A glance at the cliffs proved her right. The awful, lightly sulfuric-smelling tinge of green-black haze was also dissipating. The faint glow faded into the brisk morning air until nothing remained to prove it'd been there.

She shuddered and started shrugging out of her jacket, thinking to bundle its bulk beneath Graeme's head before she dashed to the boat for her phone.

"Now isn't the time to get comfortable, sweet." Graeme's hand closed around her wrist, startling her so badly, she nearly choked on her gasp. "You're well enough, I trust?"

He bounded to his feet, pulling her up with him. "No hurt bones or bruises? I didn't push you too hard?"

"I . . ." Kendra could only stare at him, her eyes rounding. She shook her head, relief and amazement sluicing her. "You weren't breathing. I checked, did CPR—"

"So you did, and I thank you." He smoothed back her hair, his fingers warm and vital against her brow. His dark eyes were clear, without a trace of pain. "I was only stunned, lass." He looked at her, a slight curve at the corner of his mouth. "I'm fine, as you can see."

Stepping back, he held out his arms and turned in a slow circle. "You're the one looking shaken."

"Of course I am." Kendra eyed him up and down, seeing no sign that a rock had just conked him on the head, knocking him flat, taking his breath. . . .

She'd been so sure he was going to die.

The death glaze she'd seen on the cliff had been real. She'd recognized it from her work.

She also knew it from home, having first seen it as a child only moments before her grandfather had started lopping tree branches at his Pennsylvania farm. He'd fallen from the ladder, breaking his neck. The incident terrified her. As her first brush with the supernatural, it'd also introduced her to her special skills.

There *had* been something on the bluff.

Unless she'd erred, the Chase legacy tripping her up as it did now and then.

Chase women often had unusual gifts, inherited from a distant ancestor none of them could now trace. They used their talents for the greater good whenever possible. At times, things didn't work out as they should, despite their best intentions.

And sometimes, they simply made mistakes.

Graeme wasn't bleeding, after all. Nor was there any blood on her. She frowned, her pulse starting to quicken again. Had she imagined everything?

Was this a new trick? One she hadn't yet encountered?

She took a few steps away from Graeme, ran a hand through her hair. "I saw the rock hit you. It struck you on the head, knocking you down just before it crashed into the water." She spoke in a rush. "There was a gash on your forehead—" Her voice faltered, chills sweeping her. "It was bad, so much blood on your face, all over the stones—" She broke off again, went back to him. "Now there's nothing. I don't understand. . . ."

"It happened fast." He took her hands, gripping tight, rubbing her wrists with his thumbs. "And there is something, I vow." He shook back his hair, revealing a bluish mark on his temple, a slight swelling. "The rock clipped me, true enough. But it's only a graze. Ne'er you worry. I was stunned, no more. The breath knocked out of me, that's all."

"But . . ." Kendra frowned, her gaze going to where he'd lain so still.

There wasn't a drop of red on the stones.

"I was sure you were going to die." She couldn't wrap her mind around what she'd just seen—or hadn't. And the alternative to questioning him was grabbing his face and kissing him like a wild woman. She was that relieved.

"You can see I'm not dead." He released her hands, the truth of the words undeniable. "MacGraths cannae be killed so easily, sweet. It would take more than an errant rock to have done with me." He took her by the shoulders, looking down at her in a way that made her want to slide her arms around his back and just cling to him.

She was sure she'd seen blood. She knew she hadn't felt a pulse. Yet he had no reason to lie to her. Did he have the wind knocked out of him, and she'd overreacted? She'd certainly been worried enough to see things her mind expected.

Shock did that to people.

Still . . .

"Are you sure you're okay?" She resisted the urge to lean her head against his chest and check the strength of his heartbeat.

She did narrow her eyes, studying him carefully. "I've never seen anyone recover so swiftly." She reached to smooth back his hair, her fingers grazing lightly over his bruised temple. "If you had been seriously hurt"—she lowered her hand, still frowning—"medics could never have reached us in time. I shudder to think—"

"You needn't." He touched his fingers to her lips. "All is well, as you see," he assured, one corner of his mouth lifting in the tiniest smile. "Scots have a high tolerance of pain. That's been so for centuries and it is no less true today."

Kendra wasn't so sure. But she couldn't argue his point. He *had* leapt to his feet, looking no worse for wear. A few eye blinks and a dusting of his jeans, and he'd been good as new, as if nothing had happened.

So she summoned a smile, sure she'd overreacted.

"Does that happen often here?" It was the only thing she could think to say. "Big rocks flying off the cliffs, just like that?"

"Nae, it doesn't." He glanced up at the bluff's edge, then back at her. His expression darkened, his tone changing. "Not like that, anyway."

Kendra's gut clenched. "You don't think someone pushed the rock, do you?"

"I do, aye." He spoke bluntly. "That's another reason I'm so glad you're okay." He slid his fingers into her hair, gliding them through the strands. "I'm going to climb up there and have a look around. And I think you should come with me. I don't want to leave you alone."

Kendra swallowed. "I don't know. . . ." Her legs still felt like jelly and her heart hadn't stopped racing. "I'm usually a good climber. And I'm not afraid of heights. Any other time, I'd love—"

"You cannae stay here on your own." He looked to where Bart stared back at them from the bottom of the broken arch. The bull seal was quiet now, his dark, liquid eyes fixed right on them. "There are steps cut into the cliff. They're ancient and a bit narrow and slippery, but I'll not let you fall. I promise."

"Well . . ." Kendra bit her lip. She understood his need to get up there. Half of her burned to see the ruins, but the other half worried about what they'd find once they reached the cliff top.

Obviously, whatever trickster in her family's past was responsible for the Chase legacy's occasional gaffes had pulled a big one today.

The *death glaze* hadn't been a harbinger of doom.

There were other reasons for good air to go bad, turning green-black as the atmosphere about the bluff and in the cove had done.

Terrible things such as the otherworldly unmentionables her youngest sister, Melanie, refused to name or describe whenever someone pressed her about what she stumbled on each time she discovered a portal.

Kendra glanced at the water, Melanie's face rising in her mind. Melanie was still at college and—so far—more horrified than grateful for the gift she'd inherited as part of the Chase legacy. Unlike Kendra and their middle sister, Carolyn, who was clairaudient, Melanie's talents were broader and far more interesting because she possessed a penchant for happening on portals.

If an entry to centuries past was anywhere around her, Melanie would stumble into it, each time terrified she wouldn't find her way out again. Sometimes such portals opened into places other than the innocent past. When that happened, Melanie was given glimpses of dark, mysterious worlds she never spoke of to anyone, except to say she hoped the creatures she saw there never followed her back into the real world, as much as any of the Chase sisters could consider their day-to-day surroundings ordinary.

So much more existed, after all.

Most people just didn't know what lurked beneath the surface, or around corners they couldn't see. Kendra and her sisters—and one or two aunts and distant cousins—were very much aware.

Lesser entities weren't a fable.

If something like that had caused the weird greenish-black haze she'd seen and if that something still lurked on the bluff, skulking about the tumbled walls of Castle Grath . . .

Kendra wrapped her arms around herself, not wanting to follow such a thought.

Graeme had no idea.

He couldn't guess what he might be running into up there.

And he had it all wrong. If that was the way of it, she wasn't the one needing protection. Her shields were still up and humming. It was Graeme who shouldn't go climbing up a cliff stair on his own and then haplessly striding into something horrible.

She couldn't let him face such danger alone.

She started to say so, worded tactfully, of course, when a motion to her right startled her. Wary, she glanced toward the water's edge.

A whirl of bluish mist spun there, the outline of a huge, burly man at the vortex's center letting her know that, Ordo, her third spirit guide, was about to pay her a call.

And as so often, the once-famed Viking trader had chosen a bad time to appear. Having enjoyed life as a wildly popular man, Ordo still believed no visit was inopportune. Gregarious and bold, he was of a mind that he'd be greeted gladly wherever and whenever he chose to go.

Kendra frowned, shot a glance at Graeme, who didn't seem aware of Ordo's arrival.

At the water's edge, the whirling mist cleared and the big Viking stepped from his vortex, his mail and Viking war ax shining like the sun. His smile was just as bright, and his blue eyes twinkled. "You needn't fear scaling the cliff, girl." He threw a look at the half arch, the worn steps cut into the rock there. "I'll be behind you every step," he vowed, his chest swelling on the words.

A promise she heard in her mind, clear as if his boom-ing voice was as real as Graeme's or her own.

"I've followed worse tracks than that in my day, mind." His bearded chin jutted, pride rippling the air around him. "You can trust me to see you safely to the top."

I know. Kendra let out a sigh, aware Ordo would hear the silent words it carried. He clearly thought she was afraid to climb the bluff. Or, as she knew him, he simply wanted an opportunity to feel needed.

Ordo enjoyed playing hero.

It would crimp his ego to know she wasn't worried about the climb. How could she be, with Graeme guid-ing her every step of the way? She trusted him implicitly.

But Ordo was a born gallant. He'd worn the role well in his earth life and had trouble shaking it off now. And she didn't have the heart to let him guess that, quite of-ten, his help wasn't needed.

It *was* appreciated.

So she inclined her head infinitesimally, sending him her heartfelt thanks.

She knew better than to ask him about the green-black haze and its possible origins. Ordo wouldn't have seen it, choosing to spend his spirit-guiding afterlife in the same positive mind-set as he'd lived with his earthly days.

Negativity didn't exist for the Viking.

And Kendra loved him for it, his bluster and good heart often bringing much-needed levity into her work and her private life.

You're a fine man, Ordo. She smiled when he nodded acknowledgment of the praise.

"Just let him think it's him helping you." He flicked a glance at Graeme. "A man likes to feel needed," he boomed, stepping back into his vortex.

And then he was gone, though Kendra knew he'd keep his word and follow her up the cliff stair. An act of gallantry that meant she now had to climb the bluff whether she wished to or not. Refusing Ordo's well-meant assistance would only line the spirit guide's brow with furrows. She much preferred his smiles. She loved Graeme's, too.

He was giving her one now, a soft smile that turned her into mush. "You're not afraid to climb the steps with me, are you?" He leaned in, dropped a light kiss on her brow. "I'd ne'er suggest you go with me if there was any danger of you falling."

"I'm not worried." She wasn't. "I know you won't let me slip."

At the crumbling arch, Bart barked and flapped one flipper against his weedy rock, apparently agreeing. His friends and cousins, once again crowding the crescent-shaped strand, joined in.

Graeme ignored them all, his gaze steady on hers. "I've ne'er taken anyone up there." He took her face in his hands, something in his tone making her heart thump hard against her chest. "I wouldn't ask you if I weren't sure you're safer with me."

"I know." She did.

But she also felt a stab of frustration. His last words weren't what she'd expected him to say. She'd thought he'd tell her that every other woman he'd ever known hadn't meant enough to him to merit a visit to Grath. That only she had earned that honor.

When he'd caught her face, looking down at her so earnestly, she'd thought he was about to kiss her. Not a quick, barely there peck on her brow like he'd just given her, but long, deep kisses. The kind that would've erased the shock they'd just been through—such things were known to bring people closer, after all.

Not so with Graeme, sadly.

He'd shown her again that she was just a tourist to him.

Someone he'd taken under his wing and felt obliged to look after, thanks to circumstance.

Too bad she felt differently.

She wasn't a tourist in need.

She was head over heels in love.

Chapter 14

"You think Ramsay's up there, don't you?" Kendra watched Graeme's jaw tighten on the suggestion, seeing at once that she'd guessed right.

It was also apparent that he hadn't the foggiest about how her heart still raced from their encounter with the flying rock. His swift recovery had been startling. Ordo's appearance hadn't helped to settle her nerves. And now she was further flustered because she'd mistakenly thought Graeme had wanted to kiss her. While his mere proximity was enough to make her forget just about anything else, he appeared much better at keeping his focus.

Where that focus centered was obvious.

"I think he was there, aye. Ramsay or one of his goons." He spoke at last, not denying her suspicions. "No one else would do such a thing. I promise you that rock didn't sail on its own. Ramsay's wanted me gone for a long time. He saw his chance today and took it.

"He'll be gone now, running like a rat jumping a sinking ship. But he was at the ruin, I'm sure." His tone was terse. "Likely with his usual pack of fools and lackeys."

Kendra lifted a brow. "And if they're still around?"

"Then they'll regret they didn't leave when they had the chance." His hand went to the dagger at his hip—a Scottish dirk that now looked more wicked than earlier.

She'd asked him why he'd worn it and believed him when he'd said he always carried a knife when on the boat, not knowing if one would be needed.

Now she suspected his reasons went deeper.

She swallowed, pushed her hair back off her face. "You wouldn't use that on Ramsay, would you?"

"The blade's for cutting tangled lines and whatnot." He stepped closer and put his hands on her shoulders, squeezing lightly. "If I wanted to harm Ramsay, my fists will serve well enough."

Kendra wasn't sure she believed him.

She did cast another glance at the cliff. The steps winding up from the broken arch looked more treacherous than ever. One falsely placed foot or a wrong handgrip and they'd plummet onto the rocks.

Ordo might make the climb right behind her, but if she slipped and caused them to fall, they'd plunge right through him. Ordo might have a big heart, but he wasn't very substantial.

She knew Graeme would protect her. But she worried her feet might have a mind of their own.

Turning back to him, she drew a breath.

"Are you really up to the climb?" She still didn't like the idea, even knowing how sure-footed he was. "You did take a nasty bash. That path is steep, the steps old and slippery." She lifted a hand, lightly touching the bump at his temple. "Maybe we should just leave? Go back to Pennard and—"

"Everything around here is old, slippery"—he nudged a bit of seaweed—"or crumbling. Long may it be so. I'll not allow Ramsay, Scotland's Past, or anyone to destroy what makes this coast unique."

"I'm beginning to think you're obsessed with Ramsay." Kendra couldn't keep the edge from her voice.

"I am." He didn't blink. "I can't think of the bastard without catching the reek of sulfur or tasting cold, rancid ash at the back of my throat. I still bear the scars from when he tried to bring Grath into his clutches. Now with Pennard and after this today,"—he tossed back his hair, his gaze not leaving hers—"he'll be the wounded one."

Kendra shot a quick glance to the dirk at his hip. "You said you wouldn't hurt him."

"I said my fists would serve."

Kendra frowned. "Violence never helped any—"

"A few inches, and that rock would've hit you." Graeme's voice hardened, his glance flashing to the cliff top. "I can't ignore such a threat. Whoe'er was responsible went too far. A few benches and a compressor in the water is one thing. Hurtling rocks at innocent tourists is something else entirely and needs addressing."

"Why would he do such a thing?"

"For the same reasons most scoundrels do things: money, greed, and power." He made the words sound dirty, distaste all over him. "Ramsay's behind the trouble in the village and he's playing it both ways. He's hoping the locals will take a fright and sell their houses cheap, to him, of course. If that fails and they sell out to Scotland's Past, he's betting on the historians growing tired of all the upset and making a deal with him. He'd drive a shrewd bargain, aiming to get the whole village for nothing."

"He didn't get Lora Finney's cottage." Kendra seized

the chance to help the unhappy spirit. "I noticed the house is under renovation and asked Iain about it. He said Scotland's Past bought it from the Finney estate."

Graeme's face darkened. "They snapped it up from Lora's ex-husband's sister in Inverness. She didn't want it because the place is said to be haunted. Scotland's Past outbid Ramsay's offer. He was livid."

"Maybe he'd be even angrier if something really special was done with the house?" Kendra gave him a quick smile, feeling bold. She ignored his comment about the cottage having a ghost. "It's said the best revenge is success. Iain told me Lora Finney loved books and had quite a collection. I also heard she often won scone-baking competitions. Perhaps"—she glance at the seals, then back to Graeme—"her house could be turned into a lending library for Pennard's locals. I can picture a cozy place, full of bookshelves, driftwood, and watercolors of the sea. A few corner tables where people could enjoy tea and scones."

"That's not a bad idea." The glimmer of a smile flickered in Graeme's eyes. "Lora would've loved that," he said, but then the warmth faded from his face. "It's just a shame Scotland's Past plans to keep the cottage gutted, using it for storage only."

"Maybe someone can change their mind?" Kendra meant to try.

Graeme snorted. "If so, it'll only be Ramsay coming up with a scheme to get his hands on the house. I'm sure he's behind the cottage's 'haunting.' It wouldn't surprise me if he cooks up even more mischief there, even something that would injure a workman."

Kendra drew a long breath, considering. "All that to search unhindered for your family's Shadow Wand?"

"Mainly, though he'd no doubt also try to parcel off the village online in one-foot-square lots to unsuspecting Scotland lovers, as he'd once hoped to do with Grath." Graeme sounded sure of it. "That bastard is all about whatever lines his pockets and fuels his power."

"It sure sounds like it, put that way." Kendra bit her lip to keep from saying she still didn't think Ramsay had anything to do with the rock.

Her thoughts kept returning to the green-black haze she'd seen on the cliffs and which she still believed bode ill.

So she tried one last time to dissuade Graeme. If she could keep him talking long enough, he might give up wanting to scale the cliff. Shading her eyes, she glanced above them, letting her gaze scan the bluff's edge. "It looks pretty quiet up there now. I agree that if someone did push the rock, they're surely gone by now."

"I still want to look around up there." He took her arm, leading her toward the half arch. "Whoever it was, their presence will have soured the air, leaving traces. In another age, I'd be sharpening a boar spear." He glanced at her, deadly serious. "Such an end would suit the swine responsible. As is, he'll meet my fists if he's still up there.

"If not . . ." He didn't finish, but the frown between his brows and the tight line of his jaw warned that he wouldn't let the matter go.

"You do look ready to grab a boar spear." Kendra had to repress a shiver.

"I am." His tone held pride. "My hand itches to wield one right now. And it wouldn't be a four-legged pig who'd feel the stabbing spearhead."

"You sound like you've used such a weapon."

"Perhaps I have." He didn't elaborate, stopping instead beside the *Sea Wyfe* to retrieve the pail of herring he'd mentioned.

Kendra didn't tell him that there were beings who could snap a medieval boar spear with a glance. Something told her such knowledge wouldn't bother him. His face was grim now, hard-set and fierce. His stride was more than purposeful. And his grip on the handle of the herring pail was so firm, his knuckles shone white.

He didn't look like a man who'd be deterred.

But the tautness left his face when they neared the half arch and Bart stretched his great head, his whiskered nose twitching as his huge eyes focused on the fish-filled pail in Graeme's hand.

"I don't want him to sense my anger." Graeme's features relaxed further as he tossed a herring to the seal and then tipped out a trail of the remaining fish from the bucket. He smiled, nodding encouragement when Bart slid off the ledge and went for the herring. "If a bull seal becomes agitated, every other seal in the cove will react, especially the females. They're safe here. If something unnerved them, they'd flee elsewhere."

There was a flurry of movement and barking as the other seals on the beach hurried forward, each one hoping to nab a herring. Kendra looked at Graeme, for a moment forgetting everything else. His expression as he watched the seals said so much more than words.

"You really care about them, don't you?" She could tell he did.

"I always have." He caught her arm and drew her aside when one of the seals would've bumped into her.

"They're no' as important to me as Jock, but they're right special, aye." Their eyes met, his dark gaze holding hers in a way that made her forget to breathe. "Seals are remarkable creatures. I've been looking after this herd for a while now, more years than I can count."

"Something tells me they watch out for you, too."

"Who knows?" He rubbed the back of his neck, not looking at her. "Legend gives them enough ties to mankind and even more supernatural affinities. They're said to offer men aid and sympathy, just as they're believed to wreak terrible vengeance when wronged. Some older folk will tell you they can divine the future by listening to the seals' cry or watching which direction they swim in the sea. In parts such as these, the tales don't fade easily."

"That's one of the things I find so fascinating here."

"Dinnae be too fascinated."

"How can anyone not be?" Kendra looked out across the narrow cove to the rolling sea beyond, the long, white-crested rollers once more glittering in the morning sun.

"No one can remain unaffected." Wind tossed Graeme's hair, making him look untamed and so compelling. "My Hebridean cousins would argue the point, but northeast Scotland also holds magic. The veil separating the supernatural realm and the modern-day world is thin here. In some places or at certain times"—he looked at her, his eyes unreadable—"there's no distinction at all."

"Why do I think you believe that?" Kendra tried not to squirm.

"Because I do." He smiled, dimple flashing.

"I've always heard there's a storyteller inside each Scotsman."

"And so there is. Just dinnae forget that behind every tall tale is a grain of truth."

"Agreed." Kendra glanced at the now-empty ledge beneath the half arch. Bart had claimed the rock shelf so purposely. Yet Graeme had said the seal always went to the *Sea Wyfe*, waiting there for herring.

Today he'd gone straight to the half arch, pulling himself up onto the rock shelf and then making a ruckus until Graeme hastened toward him, missing the worst impact of the hurtling boulder.

Many would say the big seal had saved Graeme's life. Kendra believed so.

Bart was only doing what she was sure Graeme did every day for the bull seal and his herd: protecting a friend.

She just wished . . .

Uncomfortable truths played out across her mind.

She might've prevented the rock from clipping Graeme if she'd paid more attention to her own instincts. Maybe said something when she'd spotted the ghostly herring fleet out near the horizon.

They'd been there just an eye blink, flashes on the horizon and a shimmer of mist only she could see. As spirits of local fishermen, the boats' crews could've appeared as a warning to Graeme, a son of this coast. It was possible they had nothing to do with the recent troubles in Pennard and simply sought to protect one of their own.

They'd be aware of his long-running feud with Ramsay.

Ghosts often seemed to know what would transpire before it happened.

"Are you ready?" Graeme stepped onto the rock ledge vacated by Bart. He extended his hand. "We shouldn't wait any longer. I don't want the wind to blow away any signs of the trespassers."

"I know. . . ." Kendra glanced at the huge bluff rising above them. A sheer rock face, it seemed to go up forever. From the top, it would plunge right down to the sea. The cliff path—what little remained of Castle Grath's sea-gate stair—bore scant resemblance to the carved steps that once would've been safely ensconced within the walls of a stout stone tower.

The contours of the half arch were more than visible to her experienced eye, but its crumbling shell no longer held watchful guardsmen. Each crevice and ledge now housed seabirds who didn't appear eager for company.

There weren't any birdless handholds.

And the more she tipped back her head, the steeper the way looked. One wrong step, and she could work for Zack from the Other Side.

It was an intriguing notion, but not one she was ready to take on.

Not anytime soon, anyway.

She liked living.

And she lived to visit ancient places, so why was she letting a sheer cliff make her feel as if she'd rather be anywhere but here? Deep inside—even despite the daunting prospect of the climb and the dangers of the hurtling-rock incident—she was burning to get a look at the ruins of Castle Grath.

In fact, *burning* was an understatement.

Visiting such a site with Graeme was the chance of a lifetime. A memory she could wrap around her heart and enjoy time and again once she'd returned home to Bucks County. She could relive the day at will. Recounting the adventure the next time an assignment saw her winging it over the Atlantic—most likely back to England—in a dreaded middle seat in coach and with the passenger in front of her reclining his seat into her lap. The memories would soothe her annoyance when the little kid behind her repeatedly kicked her seat back and serenaded her with hours of wailing.

She'd cling to her moments with Graeme at the ruin when her future work stints ended and she had to make nice as she bid farewell to her British-based colleagues. It wasn't easy to paste on a smile then, pretending she didn't resent them being able to stay on what she secretly considered the right side of the Big Pond.

Braving the cliff stair would give her all those bonuses.

And it'd be a rare treat to explore such a ruin with a man whose ancestors actually walked the site when it was whole and thriving.

Her pulse leapt at the very idea.

And, she couldn't forget, Ordo would be so pleased when she scrambled over the cliff edge, believing he'd seen her safely to the top.

She could feel the spirit guide's presence, a shimmer in the air behind her.

So she took a deep breath and stepped forward, joining Graeme on the rock ledge.

"I'm ready." She put her hand in his, suddenly more exhilarated than frightened.

"That's my lass." He looked at her deeply, his gaze warming. "We'll be up there before you have a chance to be afraid."

"I'm okay, really." She didn't hesitate when he led her up the first few steps, the broadest and most intact of the old cliff stair.

But her heart beat hard in her throat as they climbed higher, the wind picking up and the crashing of the waves on the rocks seeming to increase, filling the salt air with the roar of the sea.

It *was* exciting.

But she wasn't about to look down.

Then, just when she thought the track couldn't get any steeper, Graeme vaulted easily over the edge, pulling her up with him onto solid ground. Tumbled walls and rubble were everywhere, the dark, echoing ruins of some buildings almost intact. In the spaces between, knee-high grasses blew in the wind.

Kendra's heart swelled, wonder filling her.

"Oh, man . . ." She put a hand to her breast, breathing

deep. The air smelled of sea and cloud; old stone; and dark, rich earth washed by the rains of millennia. It was an elixir, heady and intoxicating.

"See? We made it." Graeme slid his arm around her, pulling her close. He guided her away from the drop-off, using his body to shield her from the buffeting wind. "What do you think?"

"I'm speechless." She was.

They'd really reached the top, and faster than she would've believed, just like he'd promised. And now that they were here, she wouldn't have missed Grath for anything. The harrowing climb was well worth the sweeping view of the sea and, stretching behind them on the broad slope of the promontory, the secluded remains of Graeme's ancestral home.

Castle Grath in all its ruined glory.

Kendra lifted a hand, pushing the hair from her face. "I don't know what to say. It's even more spectacular than I imagined."

It was.

"I'm glad you think so." Graeme sounded distracted, his attention more on the shadows and seeming solitude of the place than on her.

His narrowed gaze warned he expected to see more than weathered stone and grass-grown rubble. That he was searching for any telltale hints of who might've been up here, lurking about the ruin.

She didn't sense a trace of badness.

Whatever evil had been in the green-black haze was gone now. The remnants of the tower stood to their left, silhouetted against the sea. Little more than a half circle of age-darkened stone, it still held a dignity that squeezed her heart. Three tall windows, set vertically, proved the tower had once commanded at least four floors, as traces of a winding stair were still visible near the top window, the narrow steps leading up into empty air.

"There's so much more than I'd expected." She slipped out of Graeme's grasp, picking her way across welts of weed-covered rubble and past mounds of tumbled and lichen-encrusted stone. "It's very much like the photograph Iain showed me at the Laughing Gull, but . . ."

She didn't have words.

Graeme followed her, his gaze still moving about, reminding her of their reason for being here. "Just have a care where you step. I don't want you turning an ankle in a rabbit hole or puffin burrow.

"It would appear our rock-pushing friends have indeed left, but the site is dangerous as is." He stopped beside a half-standing wall that held the outline of a long-disused fireplace. The wall was one of two that stretched away from either side of the gutted tower, showing—as Kendra had guessed from Iain's photograph—that Castle Grath had once been a huge and daunting stronghold.

"The well was just there." Graeme stepped beside her, pointing to a rise in the ground covered with bits of rusted iron and nettles.

"Yonder were the outbuildings." He indicated other walls, all in varying states of decay, tufts of grass springing from between the cracked stones. "Kitchens, storerooms, a doocot whose stone nesting boxes are still intact, though the seabirds have chased away the pigeons that once roosted there. And"—he frowned—"if you look close, between the fallen masonry and weeds, you'll also see the scars Ramsay and his goons left in the ground.

"They even tore into the clan graves." His gaze went to the far side of the bluff, where pillared archways adorned a length of fairly sturdy walling. "The chapel was there, though little is left except the walkway that connected it to the keep. Ramsay should've known that even if my family had hidden the Shadow Wand at Grath, they wouldn't have put such an ill-wished relic into holy ground.

"For that matter, all of Grath was sacred to us." His voice held passion, his gaze drifting over the long rows of tombstones near the pillared arches. "It still is, though I'm the only one left."

"You don't have any family?" Kendra closed her fingers around the edges of her jacket, suddenly cold.

Graeme didn't answer, his gaze still on the ruined burial site.

Kendra looked there, not wanting to press him.

Besides, she was drinking in every detail, tucking it all away to remember later. The graves were fodder for lots of future reminiscing.

The headstones were tall, though some were broken and tilting. Kendra's pulse quickened to see that many were covered with beautiful carvings. Her eyes widened as she studied the fanciful reliefs. One-masted medieval galleys in full sail appeared to dominate, but there was at least one hunting scene of horsed men, stags, and dogs. Intricate foliage and mysterious runic symbols were also well represented, competing for attention among centuries of moss and lichen. The darkness of age made it hard to discern much, but enough detail remained to set her lover-of-old-things heart to pounding.

"I can understand your pride in this place." She stepped closer to Graeme, the world around them quiet but for the roar of sea and wind, the cries of seabirds.

Enchanted, she pressed both hands to her breast. "It's just—"

"Grath is the lifeblood of my heart." He looked away from her, toward the shells of outbuildings. "I'm as much a part of this place as it is of me. My father, his before him, and every MacGrath back to the days when Scotland was young, have walked this ground, calling it our own. Every bit of earth, each stone, be it whole or crumbling, even the cold wet of the air, lives inside me, just as—"

He stopped, his brows lowering. Following his gaze, Kendra saw what caught his eye. A slight, black-jacketed youth with spiky hair was creeping along one of the higher walls. Shoulders hunched and head low, he kept to the shadows, trying to escape undetected.

"Oh, no . . ." Kendra stared at him, the dark vibes rolling off him making her breath catch.

"Shhh . . ." Graeme shot her a warning glance.

Spike Hair slunk on, nearing the end of the wall. With his gaze on the ground before him, he didn't appear aware that he'd been seen.

Kendra's chest tightened just watching him. The day turned colder, a familiar current rippling the air. Behind the fleeing youth, the sea and sky began to shimmer, subtly shifting, blending into one.

Graeme's frown deepened, unaware.

Kendra tried not to sway as the day's light altered, turning unnaturally bright, almost crystalline in its clarity. She knew the phenomena well, so she braced herself, waiting for what would follow.

"That's Ritchie Watt, one of Ramsay's followers." Graeme leaned close, speaking low. "He fancies himself a street tough, but he's only an impressionable fool. He'll no' have pushed the rock. He isn't that strong or brave. But he'll know who did." He started forward, then whirled back around to grip Kendra's arm. "You stay here while I go after him."

"Don't worry." She didn't argue. "I'm not going anywhere."

She couldn't if she wanted to.

The ghostly herring fleet was back. And this time the boats were closer, vying for position along the base of the cliffs and pouring through the narrow opening in the rocks to crowd the sheltered cove.

But the fleet wasn't what held her in place.

It was the big, weathered fisherman in rain gear and rubber boots standing in front of her.

Kendra nodded a calm greeting, the professional in her rising to take charge, giving her the composure she had to struggle so hard to keep in Graeme's presence. But Graeme was a flesh-and-blood man. Not just that; he was someone she wanted desperately.

This man was a ghost.

He looked as solid and real as she did, his large, work-toughened hands scrunching what appeared to be a thick, blue knitted cap. A heavy cable-knit sweater peeked from beneath his oilskin, and his ruddy, wind-carved face wore an expression of deep responsibility.

You can see us. His words rang clear in her mind.

"I can, yes." She didn't hesitate.

She did inhale a long breath, using the exhale to strengthen her shields. It was important to allow only good energy near her, barring any lingering negativity that might still be on the bluff. Such energies could be drawn by the brightness of her aura. They were also lured to the vulnerability of a manifested spirit, hoping to drain energy reserves.

"I can see and hear you." Kendra opened herself, letting her aura shine even brighter. So brilliant that a protective wall of white-light energy rose and curved around her and the discarnate, sealing them in a sacred circle. It was a protective field, full of glittering mist and swirling shadow that no one else saw and that ensured any glances tossed her way viewed her alone.

She appreciated giving spirits such privacy.

And—she couldn't deny—the *shielding* also saved her from answering questions she'd rather not.

Except, of course, for the once-in-a-blue-moon occasions when something went wrong and the circle of light blazed like a beacon, drawing the attention of everyone around for miles. Even those who'd normally never see anything even remotely tinged with the paranormal.

Once, someone had called the fire department, certain they'd seen a fiery conflagration erupt just outside the visitor center of Valley Forge.

Thankfully, such gaffes were seldom.

"You can talk freely to me, if you wish." Kendra mentally reached out to the ghost, showing her willingness to do what she could for him.

She also looked quickly about, scanning the space around her for Ordo or Raziel and Saami. Her guides didn't usually sit in on her encounters with ghosts, but sometimes they did. And Ordo had been around earlier, on the beach and behind her as she'd climbed the cliff stair. As a man of the sea himself, he might've been drawn to this spirit.

But the Viking was gone.

His energy imprint wasn't anywhere near. Nor did she detect any hint that Raziel or Saami hovered close by. She was alone with the fisherman.

So she cleared her throat and stood straighter, meeting his gaze full on.

As it harms none—she let the words of power whisper in her mind, ensuring that communication with the spirit would endanger no one—*by your free will, let us speak.*

I am Jock MacAllister, herring fisher and cooper. The ghost's introduction filled her mind, his rich Highland voice soft and musical.

"Jock." Kendra smiled at the name. "I'm Kendra Chase of Bucks County, Pennsylvania."

Pen-seal . . . He tried to pronounce the name and then shook his head as if it were too difficult. He did look at her with his piercing blue eyes, his curly reddish-gray hair lifting in the wind. *You'll help us?*

"That's why I'm here." Kendra flicked a glance to where Graeme stood near a large pile of weedy rocks. If she was lucky, the *shielding* would function properly and he wouldn't notice her seeming to talk to herself.

If he did, so be it.

Speaking with Pennard's ghosts was her business, after all.

And she could tell something of magnitude bothered Jock MacAllister.

But her breath snagged in the throat when the ghost bent a long look on Graeme. A slow smile spread across his face as he did, and when he turned back to Kendra, his clear blue eyes were misted.

Thon man is a good one—always has been. Something in his tone made Kendra feel as if a cube of ice had just slipped down her spine. *I like to think he named his dog after me, but I ken that wasn't the way of it. His Jock had the name first, after all.*

"I don't understand." She didn't, but she was trying. "Did you seek me out to speak about Graeme's dog?"

Stranger encounters had happened.

Dog-loving spirits sensed her sympathy and often came to her, worried about pets still on the earthly plane. Most recently, the spirit of a widow in her apartment building back home had appeared to her, upset because her dachshund's new owners, the woman's niece and nephew, weren't giving the dog his favorite treats.

So she waited, keeping herself open, prepared for anything.

Och, nae, though I am fond of his Jock. The ghost

tipped back his head and closed his eyes, as if reminiscing. *Tell him that, aye. And that I'm pleased he keeps my
salt barrels and cares for them as he does.*

"Is that all?" The icy dread in Kendra's chest—a feeling not coming from Jock MacAllister—warned that the
ghost had more on his mind than Graeme's dog and the
ancient barrels in his back garden shed.

I wish it was. We all do. The ghost was hovering
now, his feet and lower legs fading fast, the rubber
boots no longer squared firmly on the ground, but totally gone. His gaze went past her to light on the
countless fishing vessels down in the cove and crowding the shoreline.

When he looked back at her, his blue eyes shone with
earnestness. *We have one more message for the Mac-
Grath.* He drifted nearer, beginning to lose substance, so
that Kendra could now see through him.

"What is it?" She kept her tone steady.

She'd worry later how to relay the message to Graeme.

You must tell him, lass. Jock MacAllister proved how
perceptive spirits can be. *He will want to know the crack
is wider than it looks. The opening comes from within;
that is why he can't see it.*

"The crack?" Kendra blinked.

In that instant, Jock MacAllister was gone.

A quick glance at the sea showed that his fellow herring fishers and their boats had vanished with him, likely
returning to whatever fishing grounds they'd enjoyed
frequenting in their earthly lives.

And she was now bound to pass on a message from
the Otherworld to a man she wasn't just falling in love
with, but who also thought she was simply a burned-out
landscape historian enjoying a bit of R & R.

Her cover was about to be blown.

There was no way around it, even though she couldn't imagine where to begin. Wherever she started, the end result would be the same.

Graeme would distance himself from her.

It was one thing to talk about tradition, myth, and legend. Tall tales, selkies, and whatever else crossed Scots' minds in the cold of their long, dark winter nights. But to have someone say that they lived such things sent most people running for the hills.

And if Graeme looked at her as if she had the proverbial cup missing from her cupboard, she didn't think she could bear it. No, she knew she couldn't.

She also couldn't ignore Jock MacAllister's plea.

And by making it, he'd unwittingly freed her from her job's strictures of silence. Graeme was now part and parcel of her duties here.

Damn.

Chapter 15

Kendra's aura shone like the sun, and Graeme was glad that Ritchie Watt didn't seem to notice. Rays of purest white fanned out from her, lightening the grass, spilling across stone, and illuminating even the darkest corners and crannies of the ruins of Castle Grath. It was as if the sun had come down from the heavens, dropping right into the middle of his old home.

Graeme frowned, unable to stop glancing at her.

If her light grew any brighter, he'd need sunglasses.

Ritchie was almost at the far end of the wall. He still crept stealthily, unaware he'd been spotted.

Graeme shot a last look at Kendra, relieved to see she'd turned her back to him and appeared to be gazing out beyond the cliffs to the sea. It was likely the splendid view of sea and sky—admittedly breathtaking—that caused her aura to glow so beautifully.

She'd said she loved wild places.

And he loved preserving them.

Ready to do just that, he turned away from her and rolled his shoulders. Then he stretched his arms, cracking his knuckles. He also pulled the leather tie from his ponytail, letting his hair swing loose about his shoulders. Long hair, whipped by a strong sea wind, gave a warrior a distinct edge.

It also brought out a man's fierceness.

A slow smile spread across his face, cold and deadly.

His fingers began to itch, his hands craving the feel of his leather-wrapped sword hilt against his palm. For now, he took his dirk from beneath his belt, testing its edge with the pad of his thumb.

When a bead of red appeared, his smile deepened.

But it still didn't reach his eyes.

He knew they were hard and narrowed, as he watched Ritchie prepare to sprint from the end of the wall across the grass to where the moor path wound along the cliffs and then back down into the village.

It was a trek Ritchie wouldn't be making.

In a whirl of speed, Graeme put himself in the youth's path, his dirk deliberately turned so the blade caught the sun and gleamed wickedly. He needed even less time to grab Ritchie by the front of his jacket and hoist the lad a few feet off the ground.

"Was a bent knife not a good enough warning for you?" Graeme tightened his grip, letting the boy's legs dangle in the air.

"You ken what I mean to do with you now?" Graeme released him then, taking no satisfaction when the youth dropped to his knees, anger and resentment all over him, soiling the cold morning air. "Twist off your knackers is what you deserve. Wouldn't you say?"

Ritchie's eyes sparked with defiance. His barely

fuzzed chin jutted, his hands splayed on the grass as he struggled for balance.

He didn't say a word.

"Get up." Graeme made a flicking motion with his dirk. "I'll not be cutting you. Not unless you give me damned good reason. I want answers from you, not your life on my conscience."

Still looking sullen, Ritchie scrambled to his feet. "I don't have anything to say to you." He brushed at the front of his jacket, righted the sleeves. "Not one word, whatever you do to me."

"So brave, what?" Graeme leaned in, set the tip of his dirk beneath the youth's chin. "And such a fine display of loyalty to our dark-souled friend Gavin Ramsay. Is he here somewhere, hiding in the old doocot or yonder perhaps, behind one of the headstones?"

Ritchie clamped his mouth tightly. Until Graeme pressed the dirk tip deeper against the soft flesh beneath his chin. "I wouldn't know where he is."

"But you're talking now." Graeme lowered the dirk, his point made.

"I didn't tell you anything. There's a difference."

"So there is."

Graeme leaned back against the wall, taking his time to cross his legs at the ankles and casually fold his arms. Watt wasn't going anywhere, though the youth hadn't yet discovered his trap.

All Graeme had to do was wait.

Lads like Ritchie fled better than they did anything else. And when this particular misspent youth tried to run, he'd suffer a rude awakening.

Knowing the lad needed a lesson, Graeme angled his dirk so the blade once again shone in the cold morning sun. "You know Ramsay can't win against me." He kept his gaze on the dirk, his will letting the blade lengthen, its magic-hewn steel beginning to glow blue. "It's as pointless as a gnat thinking he can pester an ox to death."

"You don't scare me, seal man." Ritchie put back his shoulders. "Gavin will—"

"He isn't long for this world." Graeme shot a glance a Kendra, relieved she still had her back to him. He was happier to see the swirls of blowing mist drifting between them, a veil of haze and shadow called forth by whatever powers gave him his magic.

If she noticed, she'd be enchanted by the luminously soft Highland mist, so prized by visiting Americans. She wouldn't doubt him when he told her such mists rose out of nowhere all along Scotland's coasts, whirling and shifting, cloaking the cliffs and shoreline. She'd also believe that the mist, also called sea haar, often dissipated as swiftly as it'd appeared. That was true, after all.

This mist was different.

As if he knew, Ritchie Watt shifted uncomfortably. "You can't touch Gavin. He—"

"He sealed his fate when he pushed that rock off the cliff." Graeme lifted the glittering length of his sword, arcing it through the mist spinning around them. "He's a dead man. Be warned."

"Nae, that's you." Ritchie stood his ground, proving himself more brave than Graeme would've thought. "Gavin didn't touch the rock. He made it move. He wasn't anywhere near here, that's how powerful he is."

"Say you?" Graeme hoped his surprise didn't show.

It was bad news if Ramsay's skills had strengthened to such a degree.

"He can do more than will rocks to jump off cliffs." Ritchie's chest swelled on the boast. "He's teaching me—"

"What?" Graeme moved with lightning speed, placing his sword tip against the youth's belly. Ritchie jumped back only to hit the barrier Graeme had cast around them. "See?" Graeme stepped closer, prodding him again with the sword. "All you'll learn from Ramsay is how to ruin your life and make an arse out of yourself. He could've warned you there'd be no running from me.

"Bone Slicer hasn't tasted blood in centuries." Graeme flicked his wrist, letting the sword cut the leather of Ritchie's jacket. "She'll be thirsting for a good, long drink. Wouldn't you say?

"Your master knows that." Graeme whipped the sword tip again, making a twin gash on the other side of the jacket. "Too bad he didn't tell you."

"You were supposed to be dead." Ritchie glared at him.

"And you? What was your place in this?" Graeme already had a good idea.

"Lookout." Ritchie stood a bit taller, his voice full of pride. "He chose me to watch from the cliff and report back to him."

Graeme couldn't believe the lad's stupidity.

But he lowered Bone Slicer, thrusting it back beneath his belt when the blade once again became an ordinary-looking Scottish dirk.

"The barrier's still there," he warned when Ritchie turned to flee.

He also shot out an arm, gripping the youth's elbow. "I'll take it down when I'm done with you. You can leave then, but you'll not be going back to Pennard."

"The hell I won't be." Ritchie tried to jerk free.

"Hell is where you'll land if you don't take the chance I'm giving you."

"I don't need anything from you."

"Nae, you dinnae. And I'm no' obliged to help you.

But I like Roan Wylie and think he needs a better shot at keeping the Mermaid."

"What's a two-bit tavern to do with me?" Ritchie sounded bitter, splotches of angry red inching up his neck. "I like drinking there, nothing else."

"You'll soon be doing more there than knocking down free pints and helping yourself to Roan's cooking." Graeme lifted a hand, glanced briefly at his palm, and then reached to touch the youth's jacket.

The two cuts vanished.

Ritchie eyed him suspiciously. "What are you doing, seal man?"

Graeme took a moment to answer. "Something I should've done a long while ago. Too bad the idea only now came to me. You, lad"—he dug in his own jacket pocket, pulling out a wad of pound notes and thrusting them into Ritchie's hand—"will be hieing yourself across Scotland, down to a place I know near Oban."

"Oban?" Ritchie looked at him as if he'd said *the moon*.

"Aye, so I said." Graeme spoke with determination, the thick mist around them beginning to thin. "Oban, gateway to the Western Isles. It's fine country, full of hills, glens, and good, clean air."

"I know where Oban is." Ritchie's tone was surly. "I'm not going there."

"You'll do more than that," Graeme corrected, not bothered by the lad's resistance. "More specifically, you'll present yourself to my friend, Sir Alexander Douglas, at Ravenscraig Castle, where he'll employ you any way it serves him. I'll let him know to expect you. Ravenscraig"—he held up a hand when Ritchie started to protest—"is a hotel now, and so popular that good help is always welcome.

"They have a re-created Highland village, One Cairn

Village, with cottages and shops. Their Victorian Lodge Coach House is always full, as is their genealogy center. So there's no shortage of work. Alex might also engage you for their frequent medieval reenactment events, though" — Graeme looked the slight, spike-haired youth up and down — "perhaps that wouldn't work out very well."

"None of it will." Ritchie bristled. "I'm not going down there."

"You will, and you'll stay for a year or however long it takes for Alex to make something of you." Graeme spoke bluntly now. "He'll know when to send you back. And then you'll work another year, for room and board only, at the Mermaid. Your wages earned will repay Roan for all the free food and ale he's been giving you."

"You're a madman, MacGrath." Ritchie straightened his shoulders, sadly only looking younger and vulnerable instead of streetwise, as he'd surely intended. "I already have work. I'm Gavin's right-hand man. He used me tonight to come here and watch his stone magic and let him know if — "

"He used you, aye." Graeme resisted the urge to grab the youth and shake him. "And I'm telling you that if he has the mind power to send a boulder sailing off a cliff, he also has the means to watch what happens from afar. He didn't send you here to spy on my hoped-for death. He will have known his rock wouldn't hurt me."

Ritchie thinned his lips, saying nothing.

"I see you understand." Graeme glanced again at the whirling mist, noting it was little more than a few thin threads now.

When he looked again at Ritchie, he saw he'd assumed too much.

The lad still didn't grasp his meaning.

For that matter, Graeme himself was only guessing

Ramsay's motives. But his instinct told him he was right. And he always relied on his gut feelings.

"Ramsay sent you here to die." Graeme didn't cushion the words. "He knew I'd come up here and he also knew I'd find you. His mistake was to think I'd fall into such a blind rage that I'd kill you. He'll have hoped I would, and then the police would've taken me away, eliminating me in a way he never could do on his own.

"In other words"—Graeme watched comprehension dawn on Ritchie's face—"Ramsay set you up to be sacrificed."

The youth shook his head, still disbelieving. "He'd never do that."

"You know he would. He lives by being deceitful and manipulative. That's his greatest magic, strengthened by greed and arrogance."

"You're the one thinking you're something better." Ritchie's eyes glittered, his fists balling at his sides.

"I abhor evil, aye. And those who'd corrupt young fools like you, pulling you into the muck with them."

Graeme saw the first hint of doubt cross Ritchie's face. It was brief, a flickering only, gone in a flash. But it gave Graeme the encouragement to lower the impassable barrier he'd raised around them.

A flush stained Ritchie's face. "I don't need you telling me what to do."

Graeme shrugged. "You should've thought of that before you became involved with Ramsay. All you can do now is use that money"—Graeme glanced at the crumpled notes still clutched in the lad's hand—"and get yourself down to Oban. You'll be safe there. Alex won't let Ramsay or his goons come anywhere near Ravenscraig."

Ritchie still glowered. "And if I don't go?"

"Then you'll meet Bone Slicer in a very different way than you did today." Graeme gripped his dirk, easing it up from beneath his belt just enough for the blade to start glowing blue again.

Ritchie stared, backing away. "You wouldn't . . ."

The lad was right.

But Graeme leaned forward and met Ritchie's gaze with deadly earnest. "You have two choices. Oban and my friend, Alex, or never knowing when you'll wake in the night to find me standing beside your bed, ready to run you through. Pennard is too small for Ramsay and the vermin who flock to him. I think you're still salvageable. Choose wisely."

And Ritchie did, cramming the pound notes into his pocket and racing off along the cliff path, running in the opposite direction of Pennard.

Graeme waited until he disappeared behind a dip in the path before he shoved a hand through his hair and started back to Kendra.

The last thing he wanted was to have to explain to her how Ramsay managed to send the rock hurtling over the cliff. Too bad he had a feeling he'd have no choice but to tell her truth.

And when he did . . .

All kinds of other questions would arise.

Kendra felt Graeme's return even before she heard him striding through the high, wind-tossed grass. The air around her felt charged, turning electric on his approach. The sensation intensified as he neared, strengthening until ripples of awareness raced along her nerves and her pulse quickened, her mouth going dry.

If he'd glanced her way, noticed anything odd when she'd turned her back to him to speak with Jock MacAllister, he'd surely want to grill her.

Knowing she had to deliver Jock's message was hard enough.

She wasn't ready for a barrage of questions, especially when she had enough of her own. She hadn't forgotten that Graeme's footsteps hadn't left tracks in the sand when he'd left her at Balmedie Beach.

Nor had she missed Jock MacAllister's implied comment that he'd known Graeme during his earthly existence, impossible as that was.

He certainly was like no other man she'd ever met.

Everything about him was compelling, from his dark good looks and rich Scottish accent to the pride and devotion he had for Pennard. Now, as he closed the space between them, regardless of what she'd been doing and where he'd been, a delicious swirl of shivers washed over her and her heart beat faster.

She could tell he was almost upon her.

Unable to wait, she turned to face him as he came up to her. His gaze was fixed on her, his stride purposeful. The morning sun did wicked things to his glossy black hair. It fell loosely around his shoulders, gleaming in a way that wasn't good for her or any female with blood in her veins. As she watched, he pulled a leather band from his pocket and reached to retie his hair in a ponytail. The quivering in the air increased, the entire atmosphere seeming to shift as he neared. Kendra took a deep breath to steady herself, meeting his gaze as calmly as she could.

The village youth, Ritchie Watt, wasn't with him.

"What happened to the boy?" She was glad for something to say.

"He's a greater fool than I'd thought, that's what." Graeme stopped before her. "You won't believe what he said he was doing here."

"He got away?" Kendra looked past him, scanning the wall the youth had been creeping along. Nothing moved there except the grass, still bent by the wind, and a few wisps of curling mist, all that remained from the sea haar that had swept the bluff.

"I let him go." Graeme stepped closer and put his hands on her shoulders, squeezing lightly. "He didn't push the boulder. No one did. That's why I sent him away." He took a long breath, his gaze on a tall Celtic cross in a pocket of deep shadow near the wall with the pillared arches. "I have a good friend who runs a castle hotel near Oban, down in the southwest. Ritchie can work there. Alex will get him turned around—I'm sure of it. If the boy takes my advice and goes there, and I'm no' certain he will."

He looked back at her. "Ramsay has him in his thrall, feeding him all kinds of dangerous rot."

Kendra hardly heard a word.

Her powerful physical attraction to him made it difficult to focus on anything else. Wishing she could, she tucked her hair behind an ear and then adjusted her jacket, pretending to tighten it against the wind. Anything to keep him from guessing how strongly he affected her.

How badly she wanted to forget everything except him and how tempting it was to be alone with him in such an old, atmospheric place.

"So how did he explain the falling rock?" It was all she could think to say. She looked at him, waiting uncomfortably as the air between them thickened even more, warming with his proximity. "I have a feeling he must've said something outrageous."

She was sure of it because of Graeme's hesitation.

Her question put an almost pained expression on his face, and it was clear he didn't want to answer. Glancing away from her, he looked out at the sea, glittering now in the sun. She could tell he was searching for words.

After a moment, he turned back to her, tightened his

grip on her shoulders. "He said Ramsay used magic to make the boulder fly off the cliff. That's what Ritchie believes, anyway. I've no doubt Ramsay told him such bunk, knowing the lad would buy it. He sent Ritchie here under the guise of keeping watch. The lad was told to report back to Ramsay at the Spindrift, supposedly with word that I'd been crushed to death by a spell-driven rock."

Kendra frowned, something niggling at her. "Ramsay sent him here on a fool's errand?" And then it came to her. "He must've had a reason. The rock did fall. That means Ramsay knew it would, so how—"

"Easy." Graeme bent a long, assessing look on the nearby ruins. "Anyone familiar with this site, and Ramsay is, knows that a lot of the fallen masonry from the tower lies along the other side of those broken walls, near the cliff edge. Sending Ritchie here and telling him to hide among that rubble would've almost guaranteed one of the rocks would break away and crash to the beach below."

"I thought you said rocks don't often fall off the cliffs."

"I did, and they don't. Unless"—he stepped back, releasing her shoulders—"something disturbs them. With the exception of where Grath's sea gate once stood, where we climbed up the cliff, the edge of this bluff has been worn away over time. Rabbit holes and puffin burrows have done the rest, and now there are quite a few places where large chunks of sod and grass thrust out over the edge, with nothing but a four-hundred-foot drop to the sea beneath."

"Good Lord." Kendra felt herself blanch. "I'm glad you didn't tell me that before we came up here."

"There was no need. The old sea-gate stair is solid enough, just slippery. And"—he shot a glance at her—"I wasn't about to let you fall."

Kendra believed him, her heart warming to know he'd protect her. Again, the word *guardian* flickered across her mind, reminding her of her first impression of him on the dunes at Balmedie. She'd sensed then that he was the kind of man who'd walk through fire for someone or something he cared about. His expression now, as he stood looking at her, told her she'd been right.

"But why would Ramsay want to put a young boy in such danger?" She still didn't understand the man's motive.

"I can only guess, but I'm betting he banked on Ritchie disturbing the rocks and causing one to fall down onto the beach, perhaps striking one of us. At the least, he will have hoped such an event would send me straight for the cliff path, which it did.

"Chances are Ramsay figured I'd spot Ritchie and my temper would break." He turned toward the sea again, took a deep breath. "He would've counted on me pouncing on the lad. Slight as Watt is, I could seriously hurt him, or worse, if I struck him in a rage."

"And then the authorities would've arrested you." Kendra understood at last.

Graeme nodded, his gaze still on the water. "It'd be a tidy way for Ramsay to get rid of me. And I promise you, he wouldn't bat an eye if I had killed Ritchie. He views the lad as disposable, knowing one night of bragging and giving out rounds of ale in the harbor bars of Aberdeen would pull in enough new lackeys to serve him.

"He can charm when he wants to." His tone hardened. "You saw that on your first night at the Laughing Gull."

"His moves left me cold. He struck me as a snake-oil salesman." Kendra shuddered, remembering how he'd come on to her. "I've never cared for such men."

For one thing, she was crazy about Graeme.

And now was surely a good moment to tell him about Jock MacAllister. Unfortunately, her mind blanked each time she tried to think of a way to start. If he'd said he believed Ramsay had the skill to move a boulder from afar, she would've felt better about admitting to seeing and talking to ghosts. She could've run with his acceptance of supernatural powers and slid smoothly into such a subject.

But he'd called the notion bunk.

Through her work, she was aware how crazy that kind of power sounded to nonbelievers. There was a big difference between talking whimsically about selkie folklore and accepting that a modern-day man could sit in his home and will a boulder to hurtle off a cliff top. So she bit her tongue, letting the chance slip by.

"I'd like to see where the rock went over the edge." Graeme stepped beside her again. "If you're game, we should be able to see the spot from the tower." His glance went to the ruined shell with its three deep-cut windows. "It's solid and we can easily climb to the second embrasure. I've been up there before and know there's a fine view of the beach. The stone benches framing the alcove are intact. We can rest there before we head back down."

Kendra followed his gaze, deciding the window arch in question looked like a much more precarious perch than he'd described.

"I don't know. . . ." She didn't finish, considering.

Even if they went up there and the window seats proved as comfortable as her secondhand, overstuffed sofa back home, she'd be treading dangerous ground by putting herself in such a potentially romantic spot with him. She'd fantasized about sitting in just such a ruined tower window with Mr. Right beside her, nuzzling her neck and whispering sweet nothings in her ear as they gazed out at the sea. In her dreams, such moments didn't stop at neck nuzzles. They grew increasingly heated, indulging her deepest, darkest desires.

Graeme lifted her chin, his expression earnest. "I won't let anything happen to you."

Kendra almost laughed, nervously. What would he think if he knew she *wanted* something to happen?

"I know that." She did. He'd plainly stated why he wanted to go up there. And it hadn't been because he meant to jump her bones.

Sadly.

But she still hesitated. The wind was tugging at his hair, threatening to undo the knotted band that held his ponytail, and watching his long, black hair tossing reminded her of the crisp dusting of chest hair she'd felt when she'd slid her hand beneath his shirt down on the beach. She also recalled the hard strength of his muscles, the seductive warmth of his skin. She'd love to see his chest, run her hands freely over him, touching him everywhere.

He'd be beautiful naked.

The thought made her sex clench.

Whirls of tingly sensation swept her most intimate places, warming and melting her. And because it'd been so long since she'd experienced such intense yearning, she also felt heat shoot up her neck to stain her cheeks.

The truth was, she could almost climax just standing here *thinking* about having Graeme unclothed before her, hers to touch and enjoy.

Only problem was, after the pleasure, she'd spend a lifetime aching for him.

She frowned, wishing they'd never met.

He smiled, dazzling her in a way that made her ever so glad they had.

No matter what happened, she wouldn't have wanted

to miss a moment with him. So she straightened her shoulders and tossed back her hair, forcing a smile as she braced herself to do something she knew she shouldn't.

"Okay." She hooked her arm through his, anticipation beating inside her. "Let's go visit your ancestors' tower window. I'd love to see the view and"—she patted her jacket pocket—"maybe take a few photos, as well."

She didn't say what she really wanted.

But as Graeme led her across the grass and past the broken walls and scattered mounds of rubble, she could sense that something had shifted between them. She didn't know if it was this place or the promise of being alone together in a secluded medieval window embrasure or just the impact of having shared a moment of danger.

Whatever it was quickened her breath and made her heart pound.

And when they reached the base of the tower, stopping before a set of admittedly sturdy-looking steps, her entire body thrummed with desire, a reckless craving such as she'd never before known.

"See?" He smiled down at her, taking her hand. "It's exactly as I said. We just need to skirt these nettles"—he guided her around them—"and then we've only a short climb up this stair to the alcove. There's nothing to worry about." He leaned in, kissed her brow.

"I know," Kendra fibbed, a thousand worries weighing on her, the main one being how she'd ever live without him once she departed Scotland. Because she knew something monumental was going to happen when they reached the ruined embrasure.

"Then come." Their gazes locked for a moment, the look in his eyes underscoring her impression.

Almost light-headed, she broke eye contact first,

looking down at the broad, age-worn stones that wound up the tower's curving wall. Unfortunately, her gaze fell across his groin, and she couldn't miss the telltale ridge that indicated he'd gone hard.

She pretended she hadn't seen.

But she had, and her whole body, all her emotions, went into overdrive. Tremors spilled through her, a torrent of need that only worsened as he tightened his grip on her hand and led her up the ancient steps.

Oh yes, they'd reached a turning point.

And there would be no going back.

Not if she wanted to cast all caution to the wind and seize what pleasure she could, even if the memories haunted her forever.

Chapter 16

"There it is, right below us. A chunk of cantilevered earth broke away where the rock fell." Graeme stood looking down from the window arch, his dark hair streaming in the wind. His voice gave no indication he knew the world changed the instant they'd entered the tower's good-sized embrasure.

The spacious alcove did appear sturdy, just as he'd promised. Bathed in sunlight and shadow, the deep recess proved as romantically medieval as Kendra had imagined. Two opposite-facing stone benches framed the arched opening, their seats smooth and weatherworn. The glint of the sea winked from beyond the window gap, and she could hear the crashing of the waves echoing up from the shore. Like the wind, the sea's roar filled the alcove, adding to its magic.

And although the enclosing walls smelled of age and damp, she'd never complain. She loved the scent of old stone and ancient places. Especially at sites like Castle Grath, where, even though the ruin wore centuries of wind and rain, enough remained for the stronghold's essence to still pulse deep inside its proud, aged heart.

Kendra pressed a hand to her own heart. She could sense the life force of Grath's every stone, the well-deserved dignity of a place whose soul was, to her way of thinking, as alive and vital as in the time of the clans.

Just as she believed that the dead didn't come back to life, but rather never stopped living, so did she believe places had feelings. They certainly held the emotions of the people who'd once loved and cared for them. And, she knew as well, the energies of those who may not have been as kind. No thought or deed ever really vanished. They remained imprinted on the past. And over time, they breathed life and memory into stone. Wind, rain, and moon glow also held reminisces. At least she liked to think so.

Not everyone agreed, and many would laugh at the notion.

But to those like her who sensed such things, visiting a site like Castle Grath was a beautiful and deeply moving experience.

There was just one problem.

Nothing but emptiness filled the large, arch-topped window opening. Except, of course, the sweeping view of sea and sky. And—she swallowed—the all-too-delicious man who leaned against the arch's soaring, cold-stoned edge and was clearly expecting her to join him.

She wasn't sure she could.

One, she knew the drop-off would make her dizzy.

Two, she'd crossed a line climbing up here. Stepping any closer to Graeme right now would mean her ultimate doom. That she also knew, even as her feet started inching toward him, wholly without her consent.

She stopped at once. "I believe you. That the rock fell from here, on the other side of this tower, I mean." She pushed back her hair when wind whipped the strands into her eyes. Strong, cold wind that smelled of the sea and almost knocked her into one of the window benches. She braced herself, sure another gust would sweep past any moment. Hopefully, Graeme hadn't seen her sway.

The concern that flickered across his face said he had. "You're not afraid, are you?" He held out a hand, encouraging her. "There's a fine view of the seals from up here. You'd see old Bart basking on a rock, surrounded by his female admirers."

"It is a long drop. . . ." She put her hand in his even as she spoke, drawn to him as if by an invisible rope.

"I'll hold you tight. No worries." He gave her an easy smile, pulling her close to his side, unaware that he was sealing their fate.

"I'm okay, really." At least she would be if her heart slowed and her pulse stopped hammering in her ears. "I would like to see the view."

That was just the beginning. But she settled for leaning into him, letting him guide her a bit closer to the yawning gap that pretended to be a window. *Death trap* would've been an equally apt description. She could've thought of more, but Graeme's grip on her proved too distracting. Big, strong, and warm, his hand softened the edges of her nerves, calming her. His arm around her did other things to her. Wonderful things that made it okay for him to guide her anywhere he wanted, even a huge window opening up to a steep drop.

"Look there, a bit to our right." He nodded at the narrow ledge of grass and rock beneath the tower.

"Oh! I do see where the rock went down." She did. And her breath caught as she stared at the fresh rip in the cliff's edge. It was a semicircular gap about three feet square that exposed the black, peaty earth and a torn tangle of grass and nettle roots.

"Aye, but do you see Bart?" He closed his arm tighter about her waist, and then stroked her hair back from her face and gently turned her head in the opposite direction. "There he is near the *Sea Wyfe*. You can see what a ladies' man he is. There isn't a female seal able to resist him."

"I'm not surprised." Kendra agreed, sure no bull seal could look more proud as the huge beast lifted his thick-whiskered head, barking as ten or more females clamored around his rock, vying for his attention. "He'll be quite the hero, having saved you from certain death."

"Ach, well . . ." Graeme's face clouded over for a moment and he stepped back from the window's edge, drawing her with him. "At least we know Ramsay is taking our feud to new heights if he was willing to risk young Watt's neck to get to me.

"But the magic he thinks he has at his disposal isn't as powerful as he believes." He released her, his expression still serious.

"He really does practice magic?"

"The darkest kind, aye." He glanced over his shoulder at the sea, toward Pennard and—Kendra knew—the big house on the cliff above the harbor, where Ramsay apparently spent his time plotting Graeme's demise. "At least he thinks he does."

Looking back at her, he smiled again, his face clearing once more. "He's not your problem, lass. You'll be leaving here soon and will ne'er have to see the bastard again. As for me"—he shrugged—"I've dealt with him and his like for longer than I can remember. None of them have gotten the better of me yet, and I'm not about to let that change."

"I'm sure you won't." Kendra turned her face into the

wind, hoping its chill would dash the heat that had sprung to her cheeks when he'd reminded her of her inevitable return to the States.

The thought hollowed her, stealing the sense of completeness that filled her here, in this special corner of the world and with Graeme at her side. She took a deep breath, knowing she had no right to feel as she did. The truth was she never enjoyed boarding the flight back across the Atlantic, and always wished she could stay on in Britain.

But this was the first time the prospect of going home made her feel ill.

Of course, she also hadn't ever spent time in a cozy-quaint fishing village in northern Scotland where—her heart squeezed painfully—the most remarkable man she'd ever met just happened to live.

She *had* fallen in love with him.

She even loved his dog.

Thinking about the two of them and Pennard, sent a whirlwind of images through her mind. The loud and crowded chaos of Newark Airport, quickly followed by traffic fumes and jammed highways, then a wall of monstrously tall gray buildings that blotted the sky and stole any views of what once would've been rich and verdant land.

No less unappealing was a rush of neon signs and billboards, boxy superstores surrounded by ocean-sized parking lots, a car or SUV in every available space, empty shopping carts filling any unoccupied cranny. Kendra frowned, blinking several times to banish the unwanted reminders of just what awaited her when she left her Glasgow-to-Newark plane.

Too bad she couldn't do the same to her ears. As if determined to plague her, they rang with the ever-present buzz of a modern world as distant from Pennard

as the dark side of the moon, or maybe even Pluto. She
fisted her hands, trying not to recall the horrid roar of
leaf blowers or, much worse in recent times, the earth-
shaking drone of the dinosaurlike bucket trucks from
the year-long renovation work on her aged apartment
building.

Then there were garbage trucks, jackhammers, and
police or emergency sirens.

It was always something.

Pennard might have ghosts and Gavin Ramsay, but
there *was* peace and quiet.

The soul-balm kind she could use so badly.

Even the heavy-metal rock music she'd heard pumping out of the Mermaid hadn't been able to put more
than a slight dent in the night's tranquillity. Pennard was
a place like no other. And she doubted a place quite so
special existed anywhere else, even in Scotland.

She blinked again, for her eyes were beginning to
burn. Then she inhaled deeply, filling her lungs with the
clean, wet cold of the air. Something she shouldn't have
done, because she was instantly reminded of the stifling
heat of a US summer. How she dreaded those searing
days of glaring, fry-your-eyeballs sun that robbed one's
energy even in beautiful Bucks County, Pennsylvania.

She preferred mist and soft rain, moody gray skies
and cold air. Peat smoke on autumn wind, the lilting
tones of Scottish voices, the creaking of fishing boats in
a small stone-pier harbor, and—her heart ached—nights
of black-velvet skies with more stars than she'd ever before seen.

She wanted Scotland, and it was going to rip her in
pieces to leave.

Especially knowing Graeme and Jock would remain
behind, going on with their lives as if she'd never crossed
their path. The thought made her throat ache and she

swallowed hard, sure she'd never be the same without them.

"You needn't worry about Ramsay." Graeme was at her side, clearly misunderstanding the reason she'd gone so still. His soft voice was low, full of concern, his breath warm on her cheek. "You're safe so long as you're here with me. I'll no' let him near you."

Kendra looked him, her heart beating wildly. She could feel the brightness of her eyes, knew he'd seen the shimmer of tears.

"What is it?" He angled his head, studying her face. "If—"

"It isn't what you think." She touched two fingers to his lips, silencing him. "It's . . ."

She stepped back, letting her words trail away as she summoned courage. Then, before she could change her mind, she reached for the leather band tying his hair at his nape. She undid the knot with fingers she wished weren't quite so shaky, freeing his long, black hair to spill loosely about his shoulders.

"It was this." She lifted a handful of the thick, glossy strands, stunned by her boldness. "I wanted to see you with your hair unbound, looking fierce, wild, and so at home in this special place. Like"—she forced herself to speak true, tried hard not to shiver in the chill sea air surrounding them—"a proud Highland warrior of old.

"This place is so different from my world." She let go of his hair, embarrassed now but unable to stem the words rushing from her heart. "And you—you look so right here. As if you were meant to be of this time"—she touched the cold, damp stone of the window edge, trailing her fingers down the side of an arch crafted centuries before her own country was born—"here at Castle Grath when these walls were whole. I feel that about you so strongly."

"Kendra . . ." He just looked at her, shook his head. "You have a romantic soul."

"It's more than that." More than he'd like to hear.

Sure of it, she struggled against the emotions rising inside her, hoping he hadn't caught any bitter undertones in her words. They were there, she knew. She could taste them still, like ash on her tongue.

But she so wished . . .

"I do have a passion for this place, lass." He leaned against the window edge again, his gaze going past her to rest on the sea. Scattered clouds were beginning to show above the horizon, casting dark patches on the otherwise blue-gleaming water. "You're not far off in your thoughts, not at all. Truth is, I love this whole coast so much, there could never be anywhere else for me in all the world. I would never leave here, not for anything.

"And I shouldn't be doing this." He pushed away from the wall and took both her hands in his, lifting her fingers to his lips, kissing each one. "It's been too long since I've—" He broke off, his eyes darkening as he let go of her hands and took hold of her face, looking down at her in a way that sent heat rushing through her.

"I want you, lass." He thrust his fingers in her hair, tipping back her head so she had to meet his gaze. "You do something to me I didn't think I'd ever feel again. And perhaps I never did, no' like this." His eyes went even darker, his burr thickening. "I've wanted you since the moment I saw you at Balmedie."

"I've felt the same." Kendra could hardly speak, her heart splitting.

He lowered his head and kissed her. And it was the deepest, most scorching kiss she'd ever had. Every bit as thrilling as his other kisses, but with a searing intimacy that shook her world.

This kiss counted.

There could be no mistake that he wanted to give her this one.

And oh, how she desired him, too.

He slid his hands down to her shoulders, not breaking the kiss. She brought her own hands up to grip his face, holding him so he couldn't pull away from her. Not that there seemed any danger of that, because he still kissed her deeply, each tantalizing sweep of his tongue against hers taking her breath, almost intoxicating her. She leaned into him, reveling in his strong, hard body so close to hers, unable to get enough of him, aching for more.

"Precious lass, what have you done to me?" He pulled back to nuzzle her neck, nipping the soft skin beneath her ear, then inhaling deep, as if he wanted to fill his lungs with the scent of her.

She shivered, stroking her fingers through his unbound hair. She was half afraid she'd waken any moment to find herself in bed at the Laughing Gull. But his arms only tightened around her, much more substantial than a fantasy as he eased her back against the tower wall, his hips pressing against hers. The heat of his body warmed her through their clothes, making her tingle with awareness.

"I didn't want this." He grasped her face again, looking deep into her eyes. His own were darker than she'd ever seen, burning with passion. "I tried so hard, but the temptation was too strong. You've haunted my dreams. I've lain awake at night, aching for you."

"I know. I mean, I've felt the same." Her heart pounded in her ears and she pressed herself closer against him. "I still do."

She couldn't bring herself to say she *wanted* him. She had a strong feeling that's where they were going. And if the swell in his pants was any indication, he already knew she wouldn't say no.

"Then hear me well, lass"—he kissed the top of her head, ran his hands down her shoulders and along her arms, lacing their fingers when he reached her hands—"I'll no' be able to stop if I keep kissing you. Tell me now if—"

"Don't stop." She squeezed his hands, then let go, slipping her own inside his jacket, placing them against his hard, muscled chest. "I know what will happen."

"Kendra. You're like no woman I've known." He stroked the hair back from her face, lifted her chin so she had to look at him. "You're everything I've ever wanted, even more than that." His voice deepened, the rich, honeyed tones turning her to liquid, making her tremble with need. "I wouldn't hurt you, sweet. No' for anything in the world."

"You won't." That wasn't true. But she'd worry about the consequences later.

Right now she felt weak with desire. Too needy to care about tomorrow, and she sensed an equal urgency in him. It blazed in the dark smolder of his eyes and showed when he pulled her against him, almost crushing her as he kissed her again, even more passionately than before. She clung to him, wrapping her arms around his neck, wishing she could hold on to him that way forever.

Whatever he thought, she knew their time together was quite limited.

These moments at Castle Grath might be all the bliss they'd have.

Not wanting to think about their inevitable separation, she flashed a glance at the sea, breathed deep of the cold, tangy air. Before the stunning, oh-so-northern Scottish view drove home just how far out of her element she was, she slipped a hand around the back of Graeme's neck and returned his kisses as boldly as she dared, using her passion to show him how much this meant to her.

She needed more than kisses, wanted to be with him wholly, feeling him pressed skin to skin against and inside her, if only this once.

"Graeme." She twined her fingers in his hair, drawing him closer, their kisses now a heated tangling of tongues and soft, shared breath.

"I would lie with you, lass, taking you again and again until the light fades." He broke free from the embrace, raining kisses on her face and throat, nipping the side of her neck. "But here . . ."

Not taking his gaze off her, he pulled off his jacket and tossed it onto one of the alcove's stone benches. "This isn't the best place." His voice was muffled as he jerked his sweater over his head, letting it drop to the cold stone floor. "I'd rather have—"

"The ruin is perfect." She couldn't believe the steadiness of her voice.

"Nae, you are perfect." He took the dirk from beneath his belt, placing it on top of his jacket before he tugged his shirt from his pants, undoing the buttons with a speed that sent heat rushing through her.

He wanted her badly.

And—she couldn't take her eyes off his nakedness—she'd never seen a more beautiful man. The dusting of chest hair she'd felt earlier was just as black as she'd imagined and even sexier, spread so temptingly across his powerfully muscled chest and then arrowing down his abdomen to draw attention to the large bulge in his jeans.

Kendra swallowed. Her entire body caught fire when he bent to take off his boots. Then, before she could blink, his jeans joined the sweater on the floor.

"You see what you do to me." He reached for her

jacket, removing it with the same startling swiftness with which he'd shed his own clothes.

"I do." She touched his jaw, the rasp of his beard exciting her.

"Good." He smiled, the heat in his eyes making her tremble in anticipation. "Because I want you to know how much I desire you, Kendra." A shadow crossed his face then, his smile dimming. "I don't do this lightly. You're special." He smoothed his hands down over her breasts, cupping her through the softness of her pullover. "I can't resist you. I'm that powerfully drawn to you."

Pulling her to him again, he kissed her deeply, gently squeezing the curve of her breast. "I don't want you to leave here." He breathed the words against her cheek, their portent filling her with the sweet sensation of a rushing tide of happiness.

"I mean that, lass." He stood back, lifting her chin to look into her eyes. "If there's any way you can stay on, we'll find it."

"I'd love to." Kendra bit her lip, nodding.

She ached to stay. But his suggestion, though beyond her wildest dreams, also flooded her mind with thoughts of Zack and Ghostcatchers International, her work here, and—a ripple of dread raced along her nerves—the need to tell him Jock MacAllister's message.

And when she did...

It'd be over.

"Just kiss me, please." She pushed the worries from her mind, reaching for him.

"No' so fast, sweet." He shook his head, a slow smile spreading across his face as he removed her pullover, letting it fall on top of his own sweater and shirt. "Gods, you're beautiful." He ran his hands over her breasts, cupping and weighing them, rolling his thumbs over her chill-tightened nipples.

He leaned down to kiss her neck, nipping her skin lightly. "I'll be aye grateful to the steepness of Cliff Road for keeping you stopped there when Jock and I came along." As he spoke, he moved his hands over her hips, then along her thighs and back up again until he reached the fastening of her pants, undoing them and pulling them down her legs until she was just as naked as he was.

Kendra closed her eyes, cold air washing her even as the most sensual heat spilled through her. "I'm glad I stopped."

She was, even if she knew she'd surely regret it once she was back home and pining for him.

Opening her eyes, she met his gaze, wishing she dared stop him now—just for a moment—to tell him all the things she must. But she couldn't summon the courage, as her overwhelming need for him, for this closeness, was too powerful and urgent to risk ruining.

She wanted him so badly.

Delicious waves of pleasure spooled everywhere, gathering low by her thighs where hot tingles and driving need made her forget everything except Graeme and the wonder of feeling his gaze on her, his hands caressing her intimately.

Had any man ever looked at her with such appreciation?

She knew no one had. And seeing the hunger and desire on his handsome face was almost unbearably arousing. He'd urged her knees apart and was looking down at her, stroking her as if she were fragile, the most precious treasure he'd ever seen. She lifted her hips against his hand, his masterful touch making her burn for him.

He caressed her lightly, moving his fingers over her softly and swiftly like air, watching her face as he did so, his dark gaze locked on hers. And the intimacy of him

looking deeply into her eyes as he stroked her almost
sent her spinning over the edge. Her sex clenched as the
pleasure built, tingles and sweet, molten heat setting her
aflame.

"Oh, please ..." She could hardly breathe. "You're
killing me. Please ..."

"I mean to please you." His lips curved in a slow, dev-
astating smile as he slid his hands around her hips and
beneath her, lifting her onto a ledge in the wall. When he
raised one of her feet, opening her legs wider as he set
her foot on the alcove's stone bench, she nearly did climax. "Dinnae move, lass. Keep your legs apart and let
me just look at your beauty."

"Oh, God ..." She couldn't stand it. The pleasure
whipping through her was really too intense. He wasn't
just looking at her, but devouring her with his eyes. And
she'd never felt so decadently female, so very desired
and wanted.

But when he dropped to one knee and leaned close to
kiss her inner thigh, she jerked, embarrassment sweeping
her. "Oh, no. Please don't do that."

No one ever had.

And if he kissed her *there*, as she knew he meant to
do, she wasn't sure she could look him in the eye again.
He didn't have any such qualms, one black brow lifting
as he looked up at her questioning.

"I told you you're beautiful, especially here." Not taking his gaze off her, he lowered his head, kissing her
belly, his fingers again working their magic on the place
she was worried about.

"And you taste delicious." He kissed his way lower,
grazing her with his teeth, teasing her with his tongue.
"The sweetest nectar," he swore, licking her then, each
delicious stroke making her breath come faster. The
tingles weren't just *here* now, but everywhere. They

raced through her entire body and even along her skin, electrifying her.

"I can't bear it, Graeme. Please." She squirmed on the stone ledge, gripping its edge with one hand and digging the other into his hair. "You must stop."

"Is it no' good, then?" He flicked his tongue over her clit, not once but again and again. And the maddeningly wicked sensations were going to shatter her at any moment. "It is for me." His voice was rough, his burr thick now, the rich, buttery tones flowing through her as wondrously as the shivery pleasure he was giving her. "I'll stop if you want me to. Just say and I will."

"No." She couldn't lie. "I didn't mean it, really. I couldn't bear it if you stopped." The last words came out in a rush, heat staining her cheeks.

"So it is good, then?" He was still looking up at her, holding her gaze, and his smile almost undid her. The next movements of his tongue did undo her.

"Oh no-o-o . . ." She felt herself falling, the stone walls of the ruined tower and the sweeping view of sea and sky starting to spin around them as her heart pounded and she grew dizzy from the intense pleasure spiraling from her core. "It's too much, Graeme. I can't—"

"You can." He slipped a hand between her legs, circling one finger around the spot driving her so wild. "And"—he pushed to his feet as he stroked her, giving her a heated smile when she lifted her legs, locking them around his hips—"I'd help you there now, with me inside you."

"Oh yes . . ." She tipped back her head, levering her body against the cold stones of the tower wall as he gripped her arms to steady her. His hard length nudged her and she arched her back, lifting her hips for him as he eased himself inside her at last.

"Och, lass . . ." He stilled and then lunged deep, filling her completely, claiming her soul as she slid her arms around his neck, clinging to him as he moved slowly in and out of her. Each thrust completed her; his long, thick length felt so good, so right.

Her entire body welcomed him. The world and all her cares and restraints no longer existed. Only Graeme's strong arms holding her and his proud, masculine body making her his, branding her forever. As if from a distance, she could hear the crashing of waves and the barking of his seals. The wind seemed to increase, shrieking now as it rushed past the great open space that had once been a fine medieval window arch. All of that surrounded them, yet none of it mattered.

Nothing existed except the two of them.

Until he swept his hands up from her arms to grip her face, kissing her hungrily as he thrust deeper and faster, fiercely now. Almost as if he, too, knew this would likely be their only time together. Her heart lurched on the thought, even as her body arched, her climax ripping through her at last. And still he kissed her, rough, open-mouthed kisses, frantic and ravenous, as he finally jerked and shuddered, spilling his seed deep inside her.

And it was in that exact moment that another sound intruded on the solitude of pounding breakers and the wail of the cold, northern wind.

It was the quiet putter of a boat motor.

Drawing away from her, Graeme glanced toward the window opening and frowned at the small, dark blue boat just passing by the rock-edged entrance to the cove.

"Damn!" He stepped in front of Kendra, shielding her, although the boat looked too far away for anyone to see them up here inside the ruined tower.

"That's the *Fenris*, Ramsay's craft." Swearing beneath his breath, Graeme snatched up his clothes, throwing them on even faster than he'd torn them off. "It looks like he didn't trust Ritchie or his own far-seeing abilities enough to wait to see if his magic worked."

Kendra pushed to her feet slowly, the magic that she and Graeme had spun evaporating. She picked up her own clothes, pulling them on much more clumsily than Graeme had donned his. Unlike her, he seemed to have recovered at speed, already forgetting the passion they'd just shared. His eyes were dark and blazing again, but this time it was with anger and not desire.

"He's already gone." She saw that when she retrieved her jacket from the stone bench. "I don't even hear the boat's motor now."

"Aye, he's left." Graeme stepped closer to the window, gripping its edge to lean out and look toward Pennard. "He'll have had only to cruise by the haul-out site to see we weren't lying there, crushed by a stone."

"He'll have seen your boat, though." Kendra shrugged into her jacket, feeling sick that such beautiful moments had to end this way. "He must know we came up here."

"So he will, aye." Graeme took her hand, already leading her away from the embrasure, back down the tower's ancient, ruined stair. "And he'll no doubt head straight to the Mermaid, where he'll order a fish supper and a pint, hoping one of his lackeys will burst in with news that I've been arrested for killing Ritchie Watt."

"But you sent Ritchie away." Kendra almost stumbled on the lower steps, her legs still shaky. "There won't be any gossip until people start wondering where Ritchie went."

"That's right." Graeme looked up at the sky as they reached the bottom of the stair and stepped out of the tower's protective half circle. The sun still shone, but gray clouds were building in the distance and the air smelled faintly of rain. "So"—he turned to her—"I think we should let him wait and wonder. If we go back down to the cove now, we'll just have time to enjoy our packed lunch and then head back to Pennard before the weather breaks."

"Okay . . ." Kendra wished they could stay here forever.

But she forced a smile. "I am hungry."

She was, but it was more of him that she wanted.

How awful that he didn't seem bothered by the same need. She stole a sidelong glance at him, hurt that he could appear so cool, as if nothing at all had happened between them. Or, and this really stung, as if he wished they hadn't done what they had.

He met her glance, frowning as he reached to squeeze her arm. Her breath caught and her heart jumped, and for a moment he looked again like the guardian she always thought him to be. A man who'd walk through fire and challenge the world for someone he cared about.

He'd said he had, after all.

"When we get back to Pennard, I'll take you straight to the Laughing Gull." His words put doubt in her mind. "I want you to stay there and not leave for any reason. I need to find out what Ramsay's next move will be. I'll come for you after I've dealt with him."

"What are you going to do to him?" Kendra's mouth went dry at the thought of them fighting.

Graeme looked eager. "Only what I should have done many years ago. But dinnae you worry." He leaned in to kiss her cheek. "It won't be anything on the wrong side of the law. I'm not that daft."

"I know." Kendra nodded, her stomach tightening as they approached the edge of the bluff. The way back down to Grath's crumbling sea gate and its half arch would be worse than the climb up the cliff path.

But it wouldn't be as awful as the certainty that she'd

made a terrible mistake. And it wasn't getting naked and making love with Graeme in the ruined shell of a medieval tower. She'd wanted that and wouldn't change a moment of the pleasure they'd shared. Whether he felt the same way or not, she believed they'd made magic together.

Their souls had joined, if only for those special moments.

None of that could ever be wrong.

What did bother her was keeping quiet about her work and Jock MacAllister. She should've told him right away, taking her chances on his reaction. Now it was too late. But she still had to tell him.

She just didn't know how.

Chapter 17

Several hours later, Kendra stood outside the Laughing Gull with a whirl of conflicting emotions churning inside her. Half of her dreaded the well-meant queries she'd face upon entering the inn. Iain and Janet would want to know how she and Graeme had enjoyed the special, romantic packed lunch they'd prepared. The locals lining the bar would eye her curiously, wondering what else she and Graeme had done while at his ruined ancestral home.

It surely wasn't a secret that his seals gathered in a cove right beneath the ancient walls of his family's one-time stronghold. Everyone would put more meaning into the day's outing.

And they'd be right.

The perceptive ones would see the truth all over her.

She didn't need to be Scottish to know residents of teeny fishing villages had a knack for such things. That particular trait was international, prevalent wherever small communities were found.

There was another reason she didn't open the inn door right away.

The red phone box across the road stood empty. Yet she could feel the angry spirit energy simmering in the air around it. Her days in the village would end soon. Maybe within the next twenty-four hours, if Zack called and discovered she was changing her mind about the reasons behind Scotland's Past's problems with their Pennard Project.

Now she wasn't even sure she could help the preservation society.

Or if she should, knowing what she did.

If Graeme's theory was correct, Gavin Ramsay was the villain in this piece. Not Jock MacAllister and his fellow herring fishermen, though they had seemed determined to speak to her.

They weren't here now.

But she could feel the phone-box ghost hovering near the red call box, glaring as always at the front windows of the Laughing Gull.

She now suspected she knew why. At least she believed she knew the ghost's identity.

He was Dod Murray, Janet's deceased husband.

And maybe she could do something for him.

Helping him would also take her mind off her own problems. So she took a deep breath and looked quickly up and down the road, making sure no one else was about. Then she went through her usual psychic self-defense procedure, this time also asking her spirit guides to help make Dod Murray more receptive to her. If they were willing, of course. And as long as they did so in a way that wouldn't harm Dod or any other entities lingering nearby.

Hoping she could reach him, she waited until she felt the familiar, tingling warmth of protective white-light energy filling her. Then she silently whispered a few words of thanks before crossing the road to the spot where the phone-box ghost always appeared.

He didn't disappoint. He manifested immediately.

And he wasn't pleased to see her.

"Fool woman!" He glowered at her from beneath heavy brows. "Too thrawn to see beyond her own nose, she is. Her stubbornness was aye—"

"You don't mean me, do you?" Kendra finally understood, wondering why it'd taken her so long to grasp that the ghost wasn't staring at her, but looking through her. His fierce gaze and his rants were directed at someone inside the Laughing Gull Inn.

She had a good idea who kept him earthbound.

She decided to voice her concern. "You're not railing at me, are you?"

"You?" He blinked, seeing her at last. "I've never seen you before in my life." He peered sharply at her, speaking, as so many ghosts did, as if he still lived.

And so he did, in his own realm.

"I'm only here a short while." The words split Kendra's heart. "Even so, I thought we might speak before I leave. If it pleases you, that is." She smiled at him, reaching to touch his work-reddened hand. "You needn't say another word if I'm bothering you. I'll leave if you wish."

"Leave?" He blinked again, looking perplexed. "How is it that you're here? Speaking to me? No one ever does, no matter how long I stare, trying to get them to notice me." He sounded sorrowful, grieved. "I doubt they ken I'm about."

Kendra kept her hand on his, squeezing gently, letting her aura's warmth boost his energy. "I'm able to see and speak with you and anyone who lives where you do. It's a gift, a blessing I'm grateful to have. If there's anything troubling you, I will help if I can.

"Do you have a message for Janet?" She took a chance, hoping she was right. "Is that why you're hanging around here, watching the inn?"

"You know me?" His blue eyes rounded in surprise.

"I think so." Kendra held on to his hand, the sudden jolt in his energy encouraging her. "You're Dod Murray, aren't you?"

"That's myself, sure enough!" His voice rose, lifting as if in pleasure to have heard someone say his name. "Dod Murray, fisherman. That's me.

"And it's not just the inn I watch." He leaned toward her, his gaze flicking to a cottage two doors down from the Laughing Gull. "I keep an eye on thon house, as well."

He meant Salt Barrel Cottage, the house Kendra knew belonged to Archie Dee, the small, weather-faced man who walked about the village with his tiny, tricolored terrier, Charlie. She'd met the duo the first time Dod Murray appeared to her beside his phone box.

"Archie Dee and his wee dog, Charlie, live in the Salt Barrel." The ghost straightened, frowning again. "Archie's as big a fool as my Janet. The two of them—"

"Are you angry at them?" A terrible suspicion rose in Kendra's mind. "Is Archie interested in your wife? Is that why you're so upset?"

"Pah!" His brows flew upward. "Does it rain in Scotland? Aye, to be sure, I'm riled. But not because Archie's soft on Janet." He flashed another look at the Salt Barrel, shaking his head when he turned back to her. "Janet's keen on him, too. She has been for a while. The besotted woman thinks she'll be disloyal to me if she gives in to her feelings. That's what's annoying me.

"I've been trying to tell her I don't like seeing her alone." He straightened his shoulders, appearing a bit fierce again. "I looked after that woman right good all my days, making sure she never had a care in the world. Now she's so full of worries, I fear she'll explode from all the sorrow she keeps bottled inside her. And"—he took a deep breath, clearly wanting to speak now he had a chance—"my old mate Archie is no' better!"

"He was your friend?" Kendra wasn't surprised.

"He was, and a better man ne'er walked these parts." He leaned close, and Kendra caught a whiff of sea and brine in his energy. "We fished, laughed, and sank pints together. He'd make Janet happy again, and many are the times I've tried to tell him so.

"But whenever I corner him and that wee dog of his, they walk through me as if I weren't there. Charlie sees me right enough." His brows snapped together. "It's not like he can tell Archie."

"I've met him." Kendra recalled the little man's jaunty step and friendly eyes. "I also know Janet. If you wish, I can speak to either of them, letting them know you'd like to see them together."

"You'd do that?" Dod sounded surprised.

"Of course." Kendra smiled. "I do such things all the time. It's my work and something I'd help you with, anyway, because I like making people happy."

"I don't know what to say." Dod's eyes watered, and he looked again at the Salt Barrel. "Janet would be better off at Archie's. His cottage is a right fine place, even fitted with a new kitchen she'd love. She mopes around our old house, fussing about memories."

"Then I'll let her know your feelings. I can assure her you won't be upset if she starts a new life with Archie." Kendra wasn't sure how to approach Janet, but something would come to her.

It always did, even in the trickiest cases. She needed only some kind of toehold.

"Can you tell me something no one but you would know about Janet?" Such proof was often the only way to convince people she'd really spoken with their loved ones.

"Humph." Dod scratched his chin, thinking.

"Anything at all," Kendra encouraged. "But it must be significant enough to prove beyond doubt that my message comes from you."

"I don't know. This is so exciting, my mind's gone blank." He angled his head, still mulling. Then his eyes lit and he snapped his fingers. "I've got just the thing!" He looked so pleased, Kendra's heart swelled. "Not a soul knows about this but me."

"That should do it." She nodded, happy for him.

"She won't be pleased I told you." But he hovered closer, whispering his proof in her ear.

"That's perfect." She couldn't think of anything better. "It will work well, I'm sure."

But before she could share her hope with the ghost, Dod Murray disappeared, his wet, yellow oilskin not leaving a single drop of water on the pavement.

His energy was also gone.

The thick air and ripples of agitation around the red phone box had been wiped away, leaving only the chill salt air blowing in off Pennard Bay.

Kendra doubted Dod would make a further appearance.

As often happened, she felt a twinge of sadness to see him go, though he'd surely visit Pennard now and then. He'd pop by family celebrations or important local events, as most ghosts were wont to do.

She hoped so.

She also had work to do. And she wanted to catch Janet as soon as possible. Dod Murray was a good man, and she used the term with respect. He deserved her adherence to the promise she'd made him.

So she looked again up and down Harbour Street, relieved to see she was still alone. Then she crossed the road, leaving the red phone box behind her. Nothing waited there now except a few hungry seabirds hoping someone leaving the Laughing Gull with a takeaway fish supper might have a heart and toss them a few chips.

And if Zack called now—he always trusted her, but did check on her progress every week or so, and such a call was about due—she could truthfully say she was making headway here, helping soothe the village's disgruntled spirits.

She just wished Jock MacAllister and his friends weren't connected to Graeme.

But they were.

And that made her dread the work that yet stood before her.

As soon as Kendra stepped inside the inn, she knew something was wrong. No one was in the entry hall, so she leaned against the wall and closed her eyes, trying to pick up the source of the unpleasant energy that had hit her like a solid wall the instant she'd opened the door. Whoever—or *whatever*—was responsible, the vibes were faintly familiar.

It was definitely an atmosphere imprint she recognized.

She just couldn't place it, though she did know it wasn't Gavin Ramsay.

The Laughing Gull felt clear of his residue.

"Worn out so early in the afternoon, are you?" Janet's voice came from right beside her. "I'm not surprised."

Kendra blinked, straightening. "You startled me."

"And no wonder, dozing against the wall." The older woman sniffed, once again clutching her broom. Only this time she looked as if she'd like to sweep Kendra out on the pavement rather than attack invisible dirt on the inn's tidy, stone-flagged floor.

Kendra took a breath, wishing her manners didn't prevent her from brushing past Janet and heading up the stairs to her room.

But the woman had planted herself in front of her, barring the way. And the look she bent on Kendra made her feel like a bug pinned to a wall. Rarely had she felt so scrutinized, and so unfavorably.

Not to mention that Janet's soured mood made it difficult to talk to her about ghosts, especially the spirit of her late husband.

Even so, she had to try. She met the older woman's gaze, straightening her shoulders. "You're right. I am tired. I was just going upstairs. But something crossed my mind, running into you, and I think I should tell you."

"Is that so?" Janet arched her eyebrows, giving her a suspicious look. "I've work to do, so make it fast."

"It won't take long; don't worry," Kendra spoke softly, silently asking Raziel, Saami, and Ordo to help her find the right words. "I had a dream last night—"

"Ach, I've no time for such drivel." Janet glanced at the entry's photo-lined wall, ran her thumb along the edge of a wood-framed picture. "I've work to do and—"

Kendra cleared her throat. "I know you're busy. Iain told me about your husband, Dod. My dream was about him. In it, he came to me, telling me something he wanted you to know. I normally wouldn't mention such a thing"—she hesitated, lowering her voice—"but the dream felt so real, I feel compelled to share it with you."

Janet's face closed, her expression tightening. "I stopped believing in dreams a long while ago."

"What can it hurt to hear mine?" Kendra reached to gently touch her arm.

Janet sniffed. "I've a kettle of fish stew simmering in the kitchen. And"—she flicked her broom at the baseboard—"sweeping to do."

"I know . . ." Kendra suspected Janet worked so hard to keep her mind off everything she'd lost and the happiness she refused to allow herself now.

"The man in my dream told me you were very happy together." Kendra spoke in a rush, trusting her instinct, as she always did in such situations. "He told me to mention bog cotton."

There: she'd caught Janet's attention.

Kendra took three long breaths, readying herself to share the ghost's message with Janet. Dod had revealed that they'd made love on the cliffs in their youth. Afterward, Janet had picked some of the delicate bog cotton growing where they'd lain. He said she'd sewn the snowy white blooms into a tiny silk pouch. And that since his passing, she'd worn the bog cotton pinned inside her clothes, near to her heart.

The look on Janet's face said the tale was true.

"What about bog cotton?" She set her broom against the wall and folded her arms. "I'm thinking you better tell me."

And Kendra did, leaning close so her words wouldn't carry as she repeated Dod's account of Janet's silken pouch and its significance. When she finished, the older woman had gone white. The harshness had also left her face and her eyes were overly bright.

"I can't imagine why he'd appear to you and not me." Janet dashed a hand across her cheek.

Kendra didn't tell her Dod had been trying for years to reach her.

It wasn't necessary to cause Janet undue pain.

"I'm sensitive to such things at times." Kendra gave her the best explanation she could, thinking it better to stick with dreams rather than reveal that Dod's spirit had lingered outside the inn all this time, hoping to reach his wife or her new beau, Archie Dee.

"There is something else he wanted me to tell you." Kendra hoped Janet would be as receptive to Dod's wishes about Archie as she'd been to the bog cotton. "It has to do with a friend of yours — Archie Dee, the fisherman who — "

"I ken who Archie is." Janet flushed scarlet, snatching her broom again. She gripped the handle, leaning forward. "There be nothing between the two of us. Nary a thing."

"Dod wishes there was." Kendra said the words she must, reaching again to squeeze Janet's arm. "At least, that's what I dreamed he said." Glancing round, just to be sure they were still alone, she shared the rest of her encounter with the ghost.

When she finished, she saw that Janet's doubt had faded.

"I thank you for telling me this." The older woman looked at her, the gratitude in her eyes squeezing Kendra's heart. "I suppose I have been wearing this bog cotton long enough," she said, lifting a hand to her breast, where Kendra guessed the silken pouch was pinned inside Janet's blouse. "I'll return the bog cotton to its place inside my cupboard when I get home tonight."

"I'm glad to hear it." Kendra was, but another unspoken question hung in the air.

She took a deep breath and let it out slowly. "About Archie—"

"He's been after taking me into Banff for tea at one of the finer hotels there." Janet flushed brighter on each word. "Perhaps I'll say yes next time he asks."

Kendra smiled, her heart lightening. "I hope you will."

"Aye, well, I might just." The way Janet straightened her back and patted her hair hinted that she would. "By the way, I almost forgot . . ." She glanced at the open door to the pub restaurant. "Your other friend is in there, waiting on you. He's been here for hours and isn't too pleased."

"My other friend?" Kendra blinked.

"Aye, just." Janet flicked at her sleeve. "I would've told you right away, but . . ." She let the words trail off, looking embarrassed.

"It's okay. But there must be some mistake." Kendra lifted a hand to rub her temple, which was beginning to throb. "I don't know anyone around here. Only Graeme." She bit her tongue before blurting that even he couldn't be counted as her boyfriend. "Whoever is here can't be looking for me."

Unless Zack had flown over to surprise her, which was highly unlikely.

Janet just shrugged. "Tell that to the Highland Storyweaver. He might not have said he's your friend, but what else can he be, sitting in there all this time, his eye on the door?"

Kendra frowned. "I don't know any Highland Tale-Teller."

She didn't and was sure she didn't want to, either.

"*Highland Storyweaver.*" Janet corrected her. "Wee Hughie MacSporran is his real name. Him, that's the famous author and historian, also running Heritage Tours. Everyone in Scotland's heard of him."

"Well, I haven't." Kendra could see Janet didn't believe her.

She also had a sense of the air thickening around her, a sure sign that whoever the Highlander was, he had some kind of a connection to her. And—she glanced toward the noisy public room—whatever it was, there'd be something uncanny about it. She could feel that in the slight dizziness that hit her for a moment and also in how the wind outside was rising, bringing the sound of dried, brittle leaves rattling along the pavement. Only she knew there weren't any dead leaves lying about in the seaside village.

Glancing longingly at the darkened stair to the guest rooms, she turned instead to the door into the pub restaurant. "I'll just go see what he wants, then. What does he look like?"

"You'll know him." Janet pursed her lip and then bustled away, busily wielding her broom.

Curious, Kendra stepped into the smoke-filled pub, finding it even more crowded than she'd imagined. Locals stood three deep at the bar and every table was occupied. Haze from the hearth's peat fire hung in the air, as did tantalizing food smells. And although everyone had been talking, all conversation stopped as she moved into the room, searching for the Highland Storyweaver.

As she'd expected, she'd become an object of speculation.

Heads turned and gazes followed her progress through the tightly spaced tables. She knew just where she was heading, because Janet had been right. She did spot her visitor right away. At least she thought so, because he was the only guest with a stack of books on his table. He also looked more authorly than anyone else.

Unusually tall, the large, red-cheeked man wore loose black trousers and a white shirt, long sleeves rolled back. Even sitting, she could tell he had a paunch, and his thinning red hair gleamed in the light of a nearby sconce made from a fisherman's lantern.

He looked familiar.

And she remembered where she'd seen him as she approached his table. He was the man who'd parked his multipassenger minivan on Harbour Street a few nights ago. She'd watched as he stood near the marina's slipway, looking about the village so proprietarily.

She'd seen the word *heritage* on his minivan.

And she'd also noted the strange luminosity that had shimmered around the vehicle.

"Kendra?" He stood, offering his hand when she reached the table. "I'm Wee Hughie MacSporran, author and historian." He smiled when she put her hand in his, his grip firm. "At six-foot-four, my friends thought the byname clever when I was younger. The name stuck."

"Should I know you?" Kendra took the seat he'd saved for her. "I was told I must."

"I would've thought so." He glanced at the door, his smile fading a bit when his gaze fell on Janet, who hovered there, scrubbing the doorjamb with a cloth. It was clear she was watching their table.

Turning back to Kendra, he patted the books on the table. They were his, unmistakably so, with his name and picture gracing the covers. The top book bore the title *More Hearthside Tales: A Highlander's Look at Clan Legend and Lore.* He lifted the book, showing it to her.

"I'm doing a bit of a book tour," he said, his tone going a tad lofty. "This one"—he wriggled the book at her—"is my latest. It's selling quite well."

"I saw you the other night." Kendra ignored his boast,

simply nodding as he returned the book to the stack. "You parked across from the inn and got out in the rain, looking up and down the road."

She wasn't surprised when his brows lifted. She smiled, not too warmly. "I'm observant."

"So you are." He signaled to a server, lifting his ale glass and indicating the boy should bring two more pints to the table. "You'll join me for a pint?"

"I'd rather know why you're here, but yes. Thank you."

"I was told you'd be expecting me." He glanced at his watch. "We were to have lunch hours ago."

Kendra frowned. "That's news to me. Why we were supposed to meet?" Her nape was beginning to prickle as a sneaking suspicion made her reach for her over-sized shoulder bag and scrounge in its depths for her cell phone. "Who said that we were?"

Before he could answer, a man and a woman who'd been staring at them from a nearby table stood and headed their way. The woman was older, stout, and wore a determined look. Her companion trailed uncomfortably in her wake, his embarrassed, long-suffering expression marking him as her husband.

"Excuse me," the woman beamed when the pair reached their table. "We couldn't help but overhear that you're the Highland Storyweaver."

"I am." Wee Hughie nodded almost regally. He glanced at the camera in the woman's hand. "You're here on holiday?"

"We are, up from Berwick for a week's stay." She didn't even look at Kendra, her gaze fixed on Wee Hughie. "We're huge fans of your work. We have every one of your titles and would've brought them along for you to sign if we'd known you'd be stopping here today."

She nudged her husband, who dutifully nodded. "We

were wondering if you'd sign one of these for us?" She picked up *More Hearthside Tales: A Highlander's Look at Clan Legend and Lore* and handed Wee Hughie the book and a pen she quickly snatched from her husband. "You can sign it to Margaret and John. We'll pay for it at the till."

"I'd be happy to." Wee Hughie autographed the book with a flourish. "Did you want a picture with me?" He stood, glancing at Kendra. "My friend can take it for you."

"That would be grand," the woman gushed, thrusting her camera at Kendra.

Her husband said nothing, looking even more stricken as his wife hooked her arm through Wee Hughie's and drew him between them for the photograph. Getting to her feet, Kendra obliged, even snapping two pictures, as the woman wanted a second in case her eyes were closed in the first.

When the pair left, Wee Hughie turned an apologetic look on her. "Sorry about that." He sounded more proud than regretful. "The books are all best sellers, and such things happen wherever I go. But" — he shrugged — "it's all good for business. I also own and run Heritage Tours, taking visitors on specialized tours throughout Scotland. Many of the tour-goers are fans of my books."

"You must be a busy man." Kendra couldn't stand braggarts.

"Busier than you know." He leaned forward, lowering his voice. "I also work on the side for Scotland's Past." His words confirmed Kendra's suspicions. "It was your friend, Zack, who arranged our meeting today. He said he'd ring you."

"Oh." Kendra's heart sank. Grabbing her bag again, she fished for her cell phone, this time finding it. As she'd guessed, the battery was dead. "I didn't receive his call.

I'm not too good with technical things and"—she dropped the phone back into her bag—"it looks like I forgot to recharge my phone."

"No matter. You're here now." Wee Hughie sat back and took a sip of his ale. "Though I'm no longer sure this is a good place for us to speak." He glanced at the table where Margaret and John were still eyeing them, the woman all smiles and full of fanlike devotion. "If you don't mind leaving with me, I know just the place we can speak in privacy."

"Of course." If Zack was involved, she had little choice.

She just hoped the Highland Storyweaver hadn't been sent to inform her she'd been fired. And a short while later, as they left the Laughing Gull together, the stares of Janet, Iain, and everyone else in the pub following them, she also hoped word of her assignation with the pompous Highland author and historian didn't reach Graeme's ears.

It was a shame she knew it would.

"We'll stop here for a walk along the shore." Wee Hughie drew his Heritage Tours minivan to halt right across the road from the Keel. "There's a small cave in the cliff here where we'll be sheltered from the wind. And"—he was already opening the vehicle's door—"any curious glances."

"That's great." It was horrible.

Kendra wanted to disappear. It'd taken all of two minutes for the drive from the Laughing Gull to here, and in that short span of time, her world had tilted out of whack and was threatening to implode.

She just hoped Graeme wasn't home.

He'd said he'd be dealing with Ramsay, and the cottage did look empty.

It certainly was quiet. No lights shone in the windows although the day had turned dark, with a light drizzle falling and mist rolling in from the sea.

Even so, her legs felt rubbery as she slid out of the minivan and followed Wee Hughie the few feet to the sliver of shingled beach across from Graeme's cottage. They passed a picnic table that stood before the cave's mouth and then, much to her relief, nipped inside the nichelike opening in the rock face.

"This is better." Wee Hughie clasped his hands behind him, gazing out at the breakers rolling into Pennard Bay. "We won't be disturbed here. And"—he glanced at her—"this is more appropriate to Scotland's Past's concerns. They're troubled about goings-on at sea."

"Just how well do you know Zack?" Kendra wasn't ready to speak openly.

Not until she knew what the author wanted.

"I don't know him personally, only by phone and reputation." He turned to her, pulling a small notebook from his pocket. He wet his thumb and then flipped through the pages, finally glancing back up at her. "My work for Scotland's Past is similar to yours, although I don't see and speak to spirits. They employ me for my knowledge of Scottish folklore and myth. As you'll know, that includes a great deal of otherworldliness, including ghosts."

"I see." Kendra felt her face coloring.

"Like you, I'm sworn to secrecy and discretion. Anything we speak of will remain between us and Scotland's Past. And"—he glanced at his notebook again—"your employer, Zack, at Ghostcatchers International."

"Just what are we speaking about?" Kendra still didn't like this. "You said Scotland's Past is having trouble at sea?"

"That's right." Wee Hughie closed the little notebook

and tucked it back into his pocket. "For days they've been trying to bring heavy equipment into Pennard using barges, because access isn't possible by Cliff Road." He stepped closer to the cave's entrance and glanced toward the snaking track that wound down the bluff. "Unfortunately, none of the barges have reached the village.

"They've either had to turn back because of sudden and inexplicable mechanical difficulties, or"—he took a breath—"some crews have refused to enter the bay, claiming it's guarded by a ghostly fleet of herring boats."

"That's why you're here?" Kendra figured as much.

Wee Hughie nodded. "Scotland's Past would like to know if you've made contact with the spirits of the fishermen. I know from my research that tales of such fleets have circulated here for the past two hundred years, if not longer. The herring men might not look kindly on Project Pennard."

"And you do?" Kendra spoke before she could catch herself.

"I'm for anything that promotes Scottish culture. The refurbishment would preserve the village for posterity." He didn't bat an eye. "Heritage and tradition wouldn't be wiped out, but safeguarded against dilution from incomers. The monies brought in by the influx in tourism would benefit the entire region."

"Perhaps the locals see it differently."

"There aren't that many of them left. You wouldn't notice as an American, but nearly half of Pennard's residents are from elsewhere. Quite a few are retirees from Scotland's Central Belt and Lowlands, while others are English, having settled here to escape cities like London and Manchester." He flicked at his sleeve, not sounding at all sympathetic. "They would've snapped up the homes of impoverished fisher families when the herring industry began to flag.

"The Pennard Project would pay them well enough for their homes. And"—he looked at her—"the village would be restored to its former glory, the present residents happy in new homes on Skye or wherever else they choose to go."

"I don't think they want to go anywhere, wherever they originally came from. They're here now and they view Pennard as their own." She would, too, if she were lucky enough to live here.

"The people here are unhappy about the project." Her arguments might torpedo her career, but her tongue seemed to have taken on a life of its own. "I'm not surprised the resident discarnates are equally upset."

Wee Hughie pounced. "So you have spoken with them?"

"A few, yes." She hedged, not wanting to say too much.

"Have they been disrupting the barge traffic?" He pulled out his notebook again, once more flipping the pages. "Only two sightings of the ghost fleet have been confirmed, but not everyone will admit to having seen such a thing, even in Scotland."

"I'm sure." Kendra knew that well. "But, honestly, none of the ghosts I've communicated with have mentioned the barges. I do know they're concerned and worried about what's happening here."

"Scotland's Past won't back away from the project." Wee Hughie looked out at the sea, his expression unreadable. Dusk was starting to fall and his face was in shadow. "They might reduce their offers for the village. Your boss, Zack, is hoping you'll be able to turn things around here."

"I usually can." But Pennard was different. "The situation here is unique. I'm not sure there's much I can do. Zack knows our work isn't infallible. Sometimes the outcome isn't what we'd originally hoped. Things turn up that alter our expectations."

The author's brow furrowed. "That's happened here?"

Imagining Zack watching her from over Wee Hughie's shoulder, Kendra filled him in on everything that had gone down since her arrival in the village, leaving out only the personal bits and any mention of Graeme's tales about his family's sacred relic.

"So you see"—she met his gaze—"there's good reason to suspect Gavin Ramsay is behind much of the trouble here. Not interfering spirits."

Wee Hughie's frown deepened. "Scotland's Past won't be pleased to hear this. Gavin Ramsay's name is known to me. It would be to anyone knowledgeable about ancient myth and legend. I wouldn't be surprised if he's trying to orchestrate a situation that would land the entire village in his clutches." He shuddered visibly, ran a hand over his thinning hair. "The man's dangerous. He's rumored to practice dark magic and has had numerous run-ins with the law.

"His interest in Pennard will go deeper than carving the village into one-foot-square lots to sell to gullible Scotland-loving tourists." He took a pen from his pocket, jotted something in his notebook. "He'll be wanting the field cleared so he can search for a relic said to be hidden away somewhere in the village or up at Castle Grath, a ruined stronghold on a bluff not far from here."

"A relic?" Kendra hoped her surprise didn't sound feigned.

Wee Hughie nodded, consulting his notes. "The Shadow Wand, aye. I doubt it ever really existed, at least not with the powers attributed to it. But a man like Ramsay who believes in such things would sell his soul to get his hands on something so magical."

"Just what was it, then?" Kendra wanted to see if his explanation matched Graeme's.

Wee Hughie cleared his throat. "Ramsay claims to be the direct descendant of a dark druid named Morcant. The Shadow Wand was Morcant's most dreaded weapon. It was described in ancient parchments and early medieval texts as a highly polished relic of jet and amber, its spiraled length banded by narrow rings of clear, shining crystal. The name Shadow Wand comes from its ability to call out a man's soul if the wand is thrust into the victim's shadow."

"Good Lord." This time Kendra shuddered, even knowing Graeme's similar version. "That's terrible."

"Indeed." Wee Hughie looked at her and she could see the earnestness in his eyes. "And there's worse. Once such a soul was taken, the person was hollowed and died. The wand was said to feed off the soul's energy, thus gaining power for its wielder. In time, Morcant is believed to have fed the wand so many souls that a single victim wasn't enough to slake the wand's hunger.

"When that happened"—his words echoed in the darkness of the cave—"we're told he learned that if he stabbed the wand into the shadow of a tower or stronghold, the souls of everyone within would be consumed by the wand."

"And the Shadow Wand is around here?" Kendra knew Graeme thought so.

"So many believe." The author rubbed his temple, as if bothered by a headache. "There are numerous versions of the lore. I wrote a chapter on the wand in *More Hearthside Tales*. One of the most incredible stories is that Clan MacGrath has a branch of immortals that guard the relic. Men who were made guardians of the wand over a millennia ago and who each live seven hundred years and a day until they die, passing on the legacy to their heir."

Kendra's blood chilled. "That sounds too outlandish to be true."

"You see and speak with ghosts." The author shrugged. "Who is to say what's possible and what is not?"

"Touché." Kendra rubbed her arms against the cold. It was full dark now and the tide was coming in, the winds strengthening so the cave no longer offered shelter. "It still doesn't sound possible."

She hoped it wasn't.

But she couldn't argue with Wee Hughie's comment.

There *were* things in the world that couldn't be seen or explained. "If Scotland's Past is irritated enough by the delays and barge issues, maybe they will call off the project?" She changed the subject, afraid her face would reveal too much if they kept speaking of the MacGraths and their hidden relic.

Writers were known to be perceptive.

And Wee Hughie was already looking at her suspiciously.

"I doubt it, though they are annoyed." He rolled his shoulders and then zipped his wind jacket. "We'll hear soon enough. And"—he glanced at his watch—"I'd best get you back to your inn. I've a book signing and talk in Aberdeen tonight and need to be on my way."

Kendra wasn't about to argue.

She wanted to get back to the inn as soon as possible, go to her room, and think.

She also wanted to get away from this end of the village. A quick glance at the Keel as Wee Hughie opened the passenger's door of his minivan for her showed that the cottage was still dark and looked empty. But she couldn't shake the feeling that she was wearing a blinking red beacon on her forehead, calling attention to herself.

She knew why when the cottage door opened and

Jock bolted out, bounding across the road and shooting onto the little strand right beside the minivan.

Fortunately, the dog shot past in a blur of black-and-white fur, making for the surf line, where he ran back and forth, barking excitedly at the waves. He ignored the parked minivan, seemingly oblivious.

But Graeme stood on the Keel's threshold.

Kendra sensed him there, could see him in her peripheral vision. And she knew without turning to look at him that he'd seen her.

And—her stomach lurched—she also picked up his shock and perplexity.

Then Wee Hughie slid into the driver's seat, started the ignition, and turned the minivan. The maneuver gave Graeme an even better view of her as they swept past the Keel's open doorway.

Kendra wanted to sink to the floorboards.

Now she didn't just have to worry about delivering Jock MacAllister's message. She also had to explain what she was doing with a strange man in the cave across the road from Graeme's cottage.

Could things get any more complicated?

She didn't think so.

Chapter 18

Graeme paced the grass-grown swath of high ground that had once been Castle Grath's finest strolling gardens, an area along the cliff edge and beneath the now-ruined tower. He hoped the journey here wouldn't prove a waste of his time. He might have more hours at his disposal than he could wish to fritter away, but that wasn't the point. He still preferred to make good use of his resources.

So he welcomed the wind coming in so strongly from the sea and gave thanks for the night's cold air and full moon. The chill would keep him awake, his senses sharp-edged and alert. Moon glow bathed the ancient walls of his home, offering enough silvery light to let him see every approach to his beloved headland.

Jock was safe back at the cottage.

A promising, leather-wrapped bundle rested on the broad top of an easy-to-see boulder, waiting to attract curiosity.

His father's sword, Battle Lover, whiled patiently nearby. Graeme hoped to the gods that the blade and his other preparations would serve him well tonight.

He wouldn't think about Kendra.

Wondering why she'd ignored his warning and had left the Laughing Gull in the company of a pompous-looking clod with the words HERITAGE TOURS painted on the side of his minivan was beyond him.

He didn't want to risk the night's hoped-for triumph by fashing himself over a female he'd surely vested too much interest in already.

What mattered was that Ramsay made an appearance.

Graeme had done what he could, laying the groundwork and summoning all the craft and magic that was available to him as Guardian of the Wand.

In the end, if there was a fight, he'd use his wits and the skill of his sword arm to have done with Ramsay. And, he hoped, the bastard's foul legacy.

If Roan Wylie and his girlfriend, Maili, had kept their word at the Mermaid, Ramsay would fall into his trap, hurrying to Grath in the hope of seizing the Shadow Wand before Graeme could dispose of the dread relic.

It scarce mattered that the wand was still lodged deep in the cliff behind Graeme's cottage.

As long as Maili claimed she'd seen Graeme leave the Keel with a mysterious bundle, Ramsay would take the bait and head to Grath.

Or so he hoped.

Unfortunately, he'd been wearing a track in the grass, the night wind was getting colder by the minute, and there wasn't any sign of his foe.

Yet he was sure Roan and Maili hadn't betrayed him.

A life span of seven hundred years and a day made a man a good judge of character.

"I'll have the wand, seal man." Ramsay's smug voice proved he hadn't erred.

Turning slowly so the bastard wouldn't guess he'd startled him, Graeme bent a long, assessing look on his enemy. "You can have it, aye. Or"—he strode over to where Ramsay stood among Grath's broken gravestones—"you might be taking a jump from this world into the next. The choice is yours, depending on how well you fight."

"You'd dare?" Ramsay gave him a silky smile, strolling forward. "That wouldn't be wise. Or have you already forgotten how easily I sent a boulder crashing down onto your seal beach? Not that I'd mind besting you again."

"You can't and you know it." Graeme held his gaze, challenging him. "Before the moon disappears behind thon clouds"—he glanced at the night sky—"you'll be lying dead in a pool of your blood."

"The wand is mine and always has been." Ramsay leaned down and slid a fishing knife from his boot, the blade gleaming in the moonlight. "It's you who'll taste death this night."

"I think not." Graeme narrowed his eyes at the knife, using all his power to wrinkle the blade.

"You bastard!" Ramsay threw down the useless weapon. "Are you afraid to face me with a knife in my hand?"

"Are you man enough to fight with a real blade?" Graeme jerked his head toward Battle Lover, propped against one of the tall, Celtic crosses in Grath's burial ground. "I've brought my father's own sword for you.

"And"—he drew Bone Slicer from beneath his belt, nodding as the dirk's blade flashed brilliant blue and lengthened into a long sword—"I thought we'd fight where the playing field is leveled."

"I'll take you on anywhere." Ramsay went to grab

Battle Lover, taking a few practice swings with the sword.

"Then we'll fight behind the tower." Graeme gave his foe his best courtly nod, well aware that Ramsay knew he'd lived in the days when such mores were practiced. "You'll surely not object to facing me on the same ground where you sent Ritchie Watt to spy on me?"

Ramsay glared at him, fury blazing in his eyes. "There's nothing but rabbit holes and puffin burrows back there. The ground would break beneath our weight."

"So it could, aye." Graeme turned and walked that way, taking his time.

Behind him, Ramsay swore. "The wand, you bastard. Where is it?"

Graeme glanced over his shoulder. "It's in a leather pouch on one of the rocks near the cliff edge. Whichever one of us is still standing after we fight can have it. You have my word on that."

He just didn't say that whichever of them won would have to retrieve the relic from the cliff behind the Keel. Not that he wanted it. If he survived the fight—he knew Ramsay was a worthy swordsman—he meant to destroy the wand. After all these years of study, he believed he'd finally deciphered enough of his family's Book of Shadows to know how to accomplish the relic's demise.

But first he had to get rid of Ramsay.

"You're a dead man, MacGrath." Ramsay rushed him, swinging Battle Lover in a furious, arcing stroke as soon as they rounded the tower and reached the narrow strip of cliff behind the ruins.

Graeme drove him back with equally vicious swipes, lunging with lightning-quick moves that cut the air and pressed his foe closer to the cliff edge. "I'm no' afraid to die, even if you could kill me."

"The wand is mine!" Ramsay flashed a look at the leather-wrapped bundle, luminous in the moon glow.

"It should be no one's." Graeme's blade glanced off Ramsay's shoulder, drawing first blood. "Jump, bastard, or my next swing will take off your head."

"Like hell it will," Ramsay snarled, parrying furiously, crashing Battle Lover into Graeme's sword. But his foot slipped on the slick grass and he fell to one knee, breathing hard as he kept hold of the sword and scrambled to his feet. "It's your head that will roll. I'm not leaving here without the Shadow Wand."

Graeme whirled and snatched the leather bundle, tossing it as near to the lip of the cliff as he could. "Fetch it and it's yours."

"You're mad." Ramsay took another arcing slash at him, aiming for Graeme's middle.

"Mad enough not to kill you, that's true." Graeme launched into a savage attack, driving Ramsay farther along the cliff edge, away from the tower and toward the area where great chunks of sod and grass thrust out over empty air with nothing beneath.

"You'll end yourself on your own." Graeme swung again, letting Bone Slicer's blade whistle just a hair past Ramsay's neck.

"Snake!" Ramsay slew Battle Lover around, holding the blade point first as he ran at Graeme, screaming in rage as he tried to ram the sword into Graeme's belly.

It was in that instant that Jock bolted between them, barking madly. Kendra came running, too, following hard on the dog's heels.

"Jock, no!" Graeme yelled the command, whipping Bone Slicer into the air, away from the excited dog. "Kendra, stay back!"

She stumbled to a halt, bending over to brace her

hands on her knees, breathing hard. "What's going on here?"

Jock barked, running circles around the three of them.

"Jock, come here!" Graeme roared, tossing aside his sword to chase after his dog.

Ramsay laughed, bringing his own blade whistling down for a killing blow that would've cut Jock in two if Ramsay's foot hadn't sunk into a rabbit hole. Or—no one would ever know—perhaps landed on one of the cantilevered protrusions of sod. Either way, the ground collapsed beneath him, sending him hurtling to certain death on the stony beach four hundred feet below.

"Dear God!" Kendra sank to her knees, wrapping her arms around Jock as she stared, wide-eyed and open-mouthed at the empty space where Ramsay had stood only moments before.

His cry still echoed from the cliffs, and his discarded sword, a magic-wrought replica of the real Battle Lover, was already disintegrating, turning to dust on the grass only a few yards from where Kendra knelt with Jock.

Graeme hoped she wouldn't notice.

Unfortunately, she did.

And her eyes grew even more round as the conjured sword vanished completely. "Oh no." She looked up at Graeme, shaking her head. "What happened here? I guessed you'd be fighting Ramsay—that's why I came. But his sword—"

"It wasn't his." Graeme went over to her, kneeling beside her and taking her into his arms. "It was a replica of my father's sword, Battle Lover. Just like"—he glanced at the leather-wrapped bundle still on its rock near the cliff edge—"that pouch over there holds a busted chair leg from one of my kitchen chairs and not the Shadow Wand, as Ramsay thought was in the bag."

"But . . ." Kendra blinked, the color leaving her face. "The pouch is still visible. The sword, and I know I saw it, is gone."

"Aye, so it is." Graeme pushed to his feet, shoved a hand through his hair.

The moment he'd dreaded was here.

He hadn't actually killed Ramsay, though he'd more than skirted the strictures of law, however justifiable the man's demise.

Kendra might understand that, having learned of Ramsay's true nature.

But he could've done without her seeing the mirror sword return to the Otherworld, from whence he'd conjured it.

Now he'd have to tell her everything.

And he didn't think he'd ever faced anything more difficult in all his overlong life.

"How did you get here?"

Graeme's voice snapped Kendra's attention off the bit of moon-washed grass where, moments before, a huge medieval sword had lain on the ground.

It was gone now, vanished before her eyes.

And that only lent credence to the suspicions that had been building ever since Wee Hughie had dropped her off at the Laughing Gull and she'd headed right back down Harbour Street to the Keel as soon as she'd been sure the author had driven out of the village.

She'd heard Jock's howling from three cottages away. She'd found the front door unlocked, so she'd let herself in. The dog, apparently hungry, had led her into the kitchen, straight to his stash of dog food and his empty, waiting bowl. That's when she'd noticed the uneven floorboard.

Curiosity was one of her dominant traits, so she hadn't been able to resist examining it.

Everyone knew old houses had secret hiding places.

Graeme's contained a Grimoire.

An ancient book of magic, filled with spells and conjurations, many pages illustrated with secret signs, circles, and characters. She'd recognized some of the symbols, thanks to her work and her great-grandmother's collection of such tomes.

It'd also been obvious that Graeme studied the book—he'd left notes tucked inside some of the pages. Jottings that made clear there really was a Shadow Wand and that he was trying to learn how to destroy it. And that led her to the conclusion that Wee Hughie's tale about MacGrath guardians, men that were immortal, just might be true.

Given her career and life experience, nothing supernatural surprised her.

Still ...

"Kendra." Graeme took her by the arm, pulled her to her feet. "What are you doing here?" He smoothed back her hair, his gaze trained on her. "I didn't want you here tonight. You could've been hurt. I told you to stay at the inn. Then I saw you with a man at the cave and—"

"He's an author and"—she took a deep breath, stealing herself—"he works for Scotland's Past. He came to the Laughing Gull to speak with me because ... because I came to Pennard to work for them."

"You what?" Graeme's brows lifted. "You're part of the Pennard Project?"

"Yes, but no ..." She felt her face heating, and she started pacing along the tower wall. "I work for an organization called Ghostcatchers International and—"

"You chase ghosts?" His brows hadn't yet come down.

"No, not like you mean, not like on television." She was making a muddle of it. "I was born with an unusual ability, a gift, really. It allows me to see spirits and, if they are amenable, to speak with them. I'm also a landscape historian, as I've told you. My main employment is to visit historical sites. Along with reading archaeological remains, I deal with any discarnates that might be troubled by restoration work or similar activity."

Graeme's brows finally lowered. "Scotland's Past called you in because of the troubles in Pennard?"

"Yes." She wouldn't hide her work from him any longer.

"That's why you saw the ghostly fleet from the window at the Laughing Gull, isn't it?" Graeme reached down to rub Jock's ears when the dog leaned against his legs.

"You could say that, yes. And"—she took a breath—"one of the herring fishermen came to me here, when you ran after Ritchie Watt.

"He said his name was Jock MacAllister, and he wanted me to give you a message. He—"

"Jock MacAllister?" Graeme's brows shot up again.

Kendra nodded. "He sounded as if he knew you. Personally, although I can't imagine how that's possible. He wanted me to tell you that the crack is widening from within."

"He said that?" Graeme frowned. "Did he say anything else?"

Kendra touched a hand to her lips, trying to remember. She glanced to where Graeme and Ramsay had fought, still seeing Ramsay topple over the cliff edge. Her stomach twisted, a wave of queasiness washing through her. "It's hard to think with a dead man down on the rocks."

"Ramsay brought his death on himself, though I wish

it hadn't happened here." Graeme shoved a hand through his hair, blew out a breath. "He'll have caused the crack your ghost mentioned. His dark magic was growing more powerful by the day. It was only a matter of *when* he'd get his hands on the Shadow Wand."

"Then there is such a relic?"

"Aye. It's been hidden inside the cliff behind my cottage for centuries." He paused, watching Jock, who moved a few feet away and flopped down on the grass. "My family has the hereditary duty to safeguard the wand. Ramsay's ancestor, Morcant, a dark druid, was the man who crafted it and infused the wand with such evil."

"You've been trying to destroy it." Kendra didn't make it a question.

"It must be destroyed, lass." He set his hands on her shoulders, looking down at her much as he had that first night at Balmedie. "I would've gotten rid of it years ago if I'd known how."

"And now you do?" The notes she'd seen in his Grimoire flashed across her mind.

"I believe so." He slid his hands down her arms and grasped her hands, linking their fingers. "When Ramsay's ancestor crafted the wand, he used dark spells to conjure the evil sealed in the relic. I believe he did so by writing the spells in his own blood on magical parchment and then eating them, taking the power into himself as well as letting it flow into the wand.

"One theory is that it is Morcant's tainted blood that gives his descendants their magical strength. And that if the line is ended, the flow of that evil blood is stemmed, and then the wand can be shattered, releasing the numberless souls believed trapped inside the wand."

"But how can you shatter it if it's somewhere inside a cliff?" Kendra doubted he'd want to dynamite the bluff.

Graeme glanced aside, out toward the sea. "I've been researching—"

"In your Grimoire?" Kendra decided to come clean. "I found it when I went to the Keel tonight."

He didn't look at her, but she saw a muscle twitch in his jaw. "So that's why you came here?"

"Not really." She was going to get squeaky clean. "I went to the cottage because I knew you'd seen me with Wee Hughie MacSporran, the author. I wanted to explain. I also planned to tell you why I really came here and that"—she rushed on, hurrying the words before she lost courage—"I'd told MacSporran I couldn't support Scotland's Past's plans for Pennard and mean to do everything I can to keep the village as it is. But as I neared the Keel, I heard Jock howling, and when I got there, I tried the door.

"It wasn't locked, so I went inside." She glanced at the dog, not surprised to find him staring at them as if he knew exactly what she was saying. "Jock took me back into the kitchen, and I noticed the disturbed floorboard. I found the book of spells then. But it was Jock's howls that made me come here. I love dogs and know they only wail like that when their master is in trouble."

"You were worried about me?" He turned to face her, his expression unreadable.

"Of course I was." She shivered, remembering how sick she'd felt when she'd realized where he was and that he'd likely be fighting Ramsay. "Jock was frantic. Dogs sense such things. So I knew it was bad."

"You still haven't told me how you got here." He lifted a brow. "It's too far to walk in the dark, even on a moonlit night like this."

Kendra straightened her shoulders. "I drove."

"You drove?" He sounded incredulous.

"Yes, I did." And she'd practically sweat blood and tears doing so.

Tackling Cliff Road in the dark had been terrifying, even though driving up the horrid road wasn't as bad as driving down.

"Once we were up the cliff and out of Pennard, I followed the coastal road, watching for the signpost to Castle Grath." She smiled at Jock, warmed by how much his presence in the passenger's seat had comforted her. "Then, when we saw the turnoff and drove out here, we—"

"Jock led you up the cliff path."

"He did." Kendra blinked, her eyes beginning to sting. "But he tore away from me when we reached the top of the bluff and heard you and Ramsay—"

"Hush, lass." He pulled her close, stroking her back. "We'll speak of him tomorrow. Tonight is all about you. I took a chance fighting Ramsay on the cliff edge. Both of us could've broken through the cantilevered places. If you and Jock hadn't arrived when you did, who knows if we'd be standing here talking right now?"

"Then you aren't immortal?" She had to ask.

She'd been wondering ever since Wee Hughie told her the legend about MacGraths.

"I'll die same as everyone, when my time comes." He caught her face between his hands, leaned down to kiss her brow. "So I can't be immortal, what?"

"You're something." She was sure of it.

"Aye, I am." His eyes lit, teasing. "I'm the man who has a brilliant plan to save Pennard."

"You do?" Kendra brightened. She was also glad when he slid an arm around her and led her around the wall to the more solid side of the bluff.

He stopped before the ruined tower where they'd

made love, something that seemed like it had happened an eternity ago. Setting his hands on her shoulders, he looked down at her again, smiling now.

"I'm going to make a deal with Scotland's Past." He shook his head, touching a finger to her lips when she started to protest. "I'm going to offer them Castle Grath if they'll drop their plans for Pennard."

"Oh no!" Kendra shook her head, horrified. "You can't do that."

"Och, sure I can." He smiled, reaching to pull her back into his arms. "The place is falling down around itself. A heritage organization like Scotland's Past will take good care of the site. I've no doubt they'll jump at the chance to get the castle. Grath deserves to be visited and appreciated. I owe that much to these walls."

"But you can't stand Scotland's Past." Kendra couldn't wrap her mind around his idea.

"That's true, but I love Grath more than I dislike them. Besides" — he winked — "I have some stipulations I'll insist on."

Kendra smiled at last. "And they are?"

He returned her smile. "I'll demand that they arrange a good portion of all profits to flow into Pennard so the village can always be maintained without too much of a financial burden on the locals. And I'll ask them to match the sum they would've spent on the Pennard Project and put it in an emergency trust for village residents in need. And—"

"That's quite a lot already." Kendra loved it.

"I'll also see that they sign over Lora Finney's house so it can be turned into the lending library and tearoom you suggested." He cupped her chin, watching her face. "Lora was a good woman. She deserved better and would've loved seeing her books enjoyed."

"And her prize-winning scones." Kendra's throat

tightened with emotion. "Something tells me she'll know what you're doing and will be so glad."

"The best is to come." His smile deepened. "I'll insist they purchase Ramsay's Spindrift and turn the house over to Aberdeen University so that a seal-research outpost can be set up there. I'll make sure funds from Grath support that work. And"—he paused for a breath—"I'll arrange for part of the Spindrift property to be converted into a rescue facility for injured and ailing seabirds."

"Oh, Graeme." Kendra blinked hard, thinking of Bart and the other seals and the countless seabirds that had delighted her during their boat outing along the coast. "That's such a wonderful idea."

And oh how she'd have loved to see it all happen.

That she wouldn't be here made her eyes burn all the more. And when the first tear slipped down her cheek, she broke away from Graeme and turned aside, not wanting him to see her cry.

She never cried, didn't like getting emotional.

But right now . . .

She took a long, deep breath, hoping Graeme wouldn't notice how shaky it was.

Then, when she was sure her voice wouldn't catch, she turned back around, determined to steer the subject in a different direction.

Needy animals always got to her, so seals and injured seabirds were something she didn't want to touch on.

"You said you had an idea how to destroy the Shadow Wand?" *There!* His face turned instantly serious.

"Aye." He strolled over to her, stopping about a foot away. "If I'm reading the spells right, the Grimoire has a few I can try that should cause the cavity inside the cliff to close. If that happens, the rock will press in on the wand, crushing it. Such a possibility wouldn't have worked before. But with Ramsay dead—and just so you know, I'll tell the authorities he was up here searching about and must've fallen on his own—he was the last of his line, as far as I know.

"That means Morcant's tainted blood ended with Ramsay. If the Grimoire has it correctly, the wand's power dies when that befouled lineage runs out.

"So the wand can now be crushed, if I can cast the spell" He looked aside, rubbing the back of his neck. "I mean to try soon."

"And the trapped souls?" Kendra wondered.

"Ach, well . . ." Graeme looked back at her. "Supposedly, they'll be released, every last one of them. Of course, I won't know for sure. How can I? Unless . . ."

He stepped closer, pulling her into his arms again. "Unless you're around to watch and would see the souls leaving the cliff as they escaped. You should be able to do that." He looked at her, lifting a brow.

"I should, yes." She bit her lip, not trusting herself to say anything else.

Once Zack got word that the Pennard case was a wrap, it'd be time for her to fly home.

"When are you planning on doing this?" She had to ask.

"As soon as possible, I think." Something in his tone made her eyes blurry again. "I'm hoping you'll be able to use your skill to soothe any disgruntled spirits that might decide to hang around once they've been released. Could you do that, encourage them to move along?"

She nodded. "I could, I'm sure."

He looked pleased. "That's good." He glanced at Jock, who'd sidled over to them, tail wagging. "Jock's been with me a long time, and the Keel's just the right size for the two of us. Three wouldn't be a problem, either, but it'd be a bit tight with so many spirits about if any of them took a liking to the cottage."

Kendra only heard *three wouldn't be a problem*. She blinked furiously, dashed at the dampness on her face. "What are you saying? It sounds"—she could hardly speak—"like you're asking me to stay with you."

"And if I was?" He grinned.

Jock barked, looking equally pleased.

"Oh, dear . . ." Kendra couldn't see a thing.

"Is that your answer?" Graeme wiped her cheek with his thumb.

"I don't know what you're asking." She had an idea, but she wanted to be sure.

"Hear that, Jock?" Graeme reached down to rub his dog's ears. "She's forgotten I told her how special she is last time we were up here. That I've never met anyone like her and haven't ever felt this way about any other woman. And"—he turned back to her—"it also seems to have slipped your mind that I said I didn't want you to leave, that we'd find some way for you to stay on here."

Kendra took a long, steadying breath. "I remember all that."

"Aye, right, then. What's your answer?" He slanted a wink at Jock. "Will you make a man and his dog happy? Will you stay with us? For a while, at least? Long enough to see if you can tolerate the two of us on a permanent basis, settle in to life in a tiny Scottish fishing village?"

"I'd love to, but my work . . ."

"Have you ne'er heard how many ghosts haunt Scottish castles? Or roam our battlefields and glens?" His words made her heart pound, let her feel buoyant with hope. "I'll speak with your employer, present him with an opportunity he couldn't secure on his own.

"Your kind of work is cut out for you here." He lifted

her hand to his lips, kissing her fingers. "If you'll give it a go."

"I . . ." She bit her lip, considering.

Jock grinned at her, his tongue lolling. It was a look she couldn't refuse. As for the expression on his master's face . . .

"Oh, Graeme . . ." She threw her arms around his neck, clinging to him. "I can't think of anything I'd love more. Yes, yes—a thousand times yes!"

"Then let me kiss you, Kendra, lass." He took her face in his hands and did just that, kissing her long and deep as the night wind whistled past them, and the great North Sea breakers crashed against the shore.

Epilogue

The Keel
Pennard, Scotland
Several months later

"It's stopped raining."

Kendra jumped at Saami's familiar voice, almost dropping the dinner plate she'd been about to dip into a dishpan of steaming, soapy water. Graeme's kitchen didn't boast a dishwasher. And in the bliss-filled months since she'd moved in with him, the cottage also hadn't been visited by a single ghost.

That dry spell included the three spirits who acted as her guides.

Yet they were here now.

Saami perched on the edge of the big oak table. Raziel leaned against the counter less than a foot away from her. And Ordo had struck a manly pose near the hutch, legs spread and arms crossed. They all looked at her expectantly, as if they expected praise.

"What are you doing here?" Kendra kept her voice lowered, not wanting Graeme to hear.

He sat in the cottage's best room with Jock, poring over the strange symbols and weird texts of his Grimoire, as he did every night. The spell he'd hoped would allow him to destroy the Shadow Wand had failed. And he'd been trying to find the right one ever since.

"We came because you wouldn't have noticed how clear the night is otherwise." Saami produced an apple and took a bite, her dark eyes knowing as she flicked a glance at the door to the hallway. "How can you with a man like Graeme in the next room, waiting to ravish you?"

Raziel sent her a glacial look. "We came for more reasons than the cessation of rain."

Kendra glanced at the window, only now noting how the harbor gleamed in the moonlight, the earlier drizzle no longer spoiling her view.

She blinked for a moment, not trusting her eyes. It'd rained every day and night since the fateful evening on the cliffs at Castle Grath when Gavin Ramsay had plunged to his death.

She'd begun to think it always rained in Scotland.

And her spirit guides weren't kind enough to pop by just to remind her there was such a thing as a rainless night. Raziel had said as much.

Kendra turned to him now, not intimidated by his powerful presence. "Why are you here? I know you'll have a message. You wouldn't appear otherwise."

"Could be we wished to talk sense into that man of yours." Ordo strode forward, his blue eyes flashing. "Has he told you he loves you? Asked you to be his wife? Instead he keeps silent, grieving over seventy-five years—"

"Be still, you fool." Raziel's tone could've frozen ice. "It is not our place to reveal secrets. Kendra"—he glanced at her, his voice less severe—"will know the significance of the night's clarity, just as she will follow her heart when we tell her to watch the ground."

"The ground?" Kendra set down the plate she'd been holding. "Can't you tell me more than that?"

But she found herself speaking to air.

Her spirit guides were gone.

She saw why at once, her gaze snapping to the kitchen door, where Graeme and Jock stood watching her. Jock looked excited, as if he, too, had noticed that rain no longer spattered the roof and windows. Graeme's expression was guarded. His glance at the window hinted why the clear night mattered.

How could she have forgotten?

She'd told him it was sometimes difficult to see spirits in misting rain. Depending on how they chose to manifest, some could appear as whisper-thin as a breath. Such a soul would be even harder to spot in the kind of weather they'd had these last months.

And even if Graeme found the right spell to obliterate the Shadow Wand, he hadn't wanted to risk Kendra not being able to see the fleeing spirits.

Destroying the relic was crucial.

But so was ensuring that no long-trapped souls lingered, too confused after so many centuries of confinement to know how to seek true peace.

Kendra could help them.

But she needed a clear night to do so.

"I think I've finally found the magic we need." Graeme stepped into the kitchen, his dog right beside him. "It's a conjuration using the names of many saints and gods, a few ancient words powerful enough to control and break the darkest evil."

"Oh, Graeme!" Kendra dried her hands, hurried over to him. "Did you just come across the spell?"

He shook his head. "I stumbled upon it a while ago. The answer was encoded inside a palindrome, a word square I'd been eyeing for years." He reached for her, pulling her into his arms. "Now I believe I'd cracked its secrets. I've spent the last weeks memorizing the spell. It's too dangerous to risk speaking one wrong letter."

Kendra looked at him, the implication of his words making her heart leap.

Now she knew why he'd gone so quiet in recent times. She'd worried he'd decided they weren't good for each other and that he was just biding time to say so. She glanced past him, across the darkened hall into the best room, where the fire glow fell across the leather-tooled cover of the Book of Shadows, lying closed on the sofa.

Kendra shivered, looking back to Graeme. "You've seen that the rain's stopped."

He nodded. "I noticed at once. It's time, lass. Let's put this to rest, if we can."

Jock barked and bounded down the narrow hall that led to the front of the house. Kendra and Graeme followed the dog to the door.

"I must warn you, the spell doesn't say what happens to its caster after the magic is worked." Graeme glanced at her as he reached for the latch. "There will be a price, even if things go well."

"Yet you're going to do it." Kendra knew there was no stopping him. She touched his jaw, stroking. "You've been waiting for this moment for a long time." She hoped only she heard the tremor in her voice.

"Longer than you know." His eyes glinted in the hall's dimness. Then he opened the door, taking her hand as they stepped out into the cold, starlit night.

Chill wind blew in from the sea, and the air smelled of

wet earth swept down from the cliffs by all the recent rain. The stone pathway along the side of the house was thick with mud. A morass that didn't bother Jock as he leapt away from them, streaking toward Graeme's barrel shed and the soaring rock face behind the cottage.

"I'm sorry about the mud, sweet." Graeme glanced at her. "I'd carry you to spare your shoes, but I must begin the incantations now and will need all my concentration. I'll buy you new shoes when this is over."

"I don't care about shoes." She didn't, starting forward down the path, the mud squelching up around her feet. "What's a bit of muck, anyway?"

I love you, Kendra. More than you know.

She froze after only a few paces, not sure she'd heard him say the words she'd waited so long to hear. When she glanced over her shoulder, she couldn't tell, because he'd closed his eyes and lifted his arms in the air, chanting words in a strange language that sounded more ancient— and unsettling—than anything she'd ever heard.

She knew not to interrupt him.

She shut her own eyes for a moment, summoning the protective white-light energy that was her psychic defense. She also asked her spirit guides, and all the powers, to watch over her, Graeme, and Jock.

It was all she could do.

That, and watch for the poor souls Graeme hoped to free from his family's relic.

If they came, she'd use her gift to give them the warmth, love, and encouragement they'd need to seek the peace and rest they'd been denied so long.

Then Graeme was beside her, his face grim as he took her hand, leading her down the rest of the path to its end before the cliff.

A small space opened there, littered with mud and bits of debris that had washed down in the autumnal torrents. His coat full of muck now, Jock prowled back and forth along the foot of the cliff. The dog's hackles were lifted, his low growls proving he understood what lurked inside the dark crack visible in the rock face.

Kendra bit her lip, a surge of unease sweeping her.

She glanced at Graeme, but he didn't even seem to know she was there. He was speaking faster now, repeating the same words again and again, his eyes almost shining as he moved forward to stand only inches away from the bluff. Intent on the spell, he placed his hands on either side of the fissure, splaying his fingers against the rock.

It was then that Kendra saw his eyes weren't the only thing glowing.

An eerie blue light was beginning to stream out from beneath his hands to ripple up and down the crack in the cliff. As she watched, the light spread, slowly covering the entire bluff in a brilliant, otherworldly sapphire shade that reminded her of Raziel's eyes.

And still Graeme spoke the words of power, his voice rising, echoing in the narrow space.

Nothing else happened.

Kendra didn't move, aware only that Jock had stopped patrolling the cliff base and now stood guard before her. A sentinel who, in the weird lighting, appeared to have grown much larger and fiercer.

Then a low rumbling began deep inside the bluff, a sound that reminded Kendra of an earthquake. Only unlike any natural disasters unleashed by nature, shrill howling accompanied the grinding of stone. Thin, hollow wails that rose to fill the heavens and pierce Kendra's heart, for she recognized what they were: the cries of souls.

Her chest tightened as her pulse quickened, her heart thundering in sympathy. The earth began to tremble, and around the fissure the blue light that had spread from Graeme's hands began to spark with color. Dazzling shades that glittered, dancing along the crack and then showering upward into the air. In an eye blink, a kaleidoscope of brilliance rushed from the cliff, spinning quickly into a multicolored vortex of whirling mist.

Kendra saw more.

She saw a legion of souls—men, women, and children, even babes in arms. Their number was beyond counting. And their forms—always diverse—ranged from full-bodied to the barely there wisps she'd worried she'd not be able to see if they'd attempted the spell on a night of rain and mist. She didn't miss any soul now.

They were everywhere, so many that she couldn't even see Graeme through their number.

But she heard him, his deep voice a comfort as her own work began to drain her.

She'd never faced so many spirits at once.

Their pull on her energy dizzied her, making her light-headed.

But she ignored the discomfort, focusing harder than she'd ever done in her life. She cast her powers as strongly as she could, letting all her energy greet them, thanking them for their earthly lives and wishing them well in their new ones, as freed souls able to live and breathe again in the Otherworld, of course.

Then it was over.

The souls speeding away toward the sea, their glowing flight fading to nothingness even before they'd reached the far side of the bay.

At the rock face, Graeme lowered his hands, stepping back as the cliff's low rumbling ended on a hard, jarring *thud* as the fissure closed.

"Kendra!" He sprinted over to her. "We did it! Did you see the souls? I heard them and felt their passing, but"—he shoved back his hair, panting—"did you see them? Have they gone from here?"

"Yes . . ." She slumped to her knees, her legs too weak to hold her. "They've left. Every last one of them, and they're happy, Graeme. I felt their joy so powerfully, it took my breath."

"Thank the gods." Graeme helped her stand, pulled her fast against him. "And bless you for coming here and helping them, helping me. I couldn't have done this without you, not with such splendid results."

Kendra pulled back, remembering something he'd said earlier. "Then you're okay?" She scanned his face, looking for some sign that the spell had damaged him, claiming payment. "Nothing has happened to you?"

Beside her, Jock barked, lending his concern.

Graeme shrugged, reaching down to ruffle Jock's ears. "I cannae say, honestly. I feel no different from before. But you're right. No magic is worked without a price." His expression turned serious and he drew her close again, wrapping his arms around her. "As long as you and Jock are okay, nothing else matters."

"That's not true." Kendra leaned her head against his shoulder, relief flooding her to hear the steady beat of his heart. "To me, all that counts is knowing the two of you are safe."

"Aye, well, we are." He kissed the top of her head, smoothed his knuckles along her cheek. "Jock and I always survive. We—"

"Seventy-five years," Kendra blurted Ordo's quip, the comment that had earned him a reprimand from Raziel. "The number just came to me." She didn't mention the Viking spirit guide. "Does being a Guardian mean you aren't immortal but have a set life span of seventy-five years? Are you then visited by a replacement, taken away so he can begin his own term?"

It was the only thing she could think of.

She knew she was close when Graeme frowned.

"Och, Kendra . . ." He released her, paced a few feet, and then turned back around. "I didn't want to worry you. My life span is seven hundred years and a day. And of those years, I have seventy-five remaining.

"Now you know why I've been so quiet lately." His voice thickened, his eyes darkening with regret. "I haven't known how to tell you. It's also why I can't marry you. I've vowed to be the last MacGrath. I'll not leave an heir to suffer the overlong life I've had to live."

"But you *do* live." Kendra went to him, gripping his hands. "We can be together for all the time we have. Believe me"—she hoped he would—"I've seen and learned enough through my work not to be surprised by your specialness, or to let it come between us."

"I wouldn't call my guardianship special. And I've cursed its burden more than I've welcomed it." He looked up at the night sky, drew a long breath. "I live with it, but have despised its accompaniments. Do you recall asking me why I didn't leave footsteps at Balmedie?"

Kendra nodded, not following him.

"That's one of the benefits of being a Guardian." He made it sound anything but. "We can walk through the night and no one can trace our passing."

Kendra frowned, remembering how she'd puzzled about the trackless sand.

She also remembered Raziel's urging her to watch the ground. His meaning—if she was right—made her heart leap, hope surging through her. Breaking away from Graeme, she took a deep breath and then turned, looking back the way they'd come.

Moonlight shone down the narrow path beside the house, illuminating the muddied stone flags. And revealing three sets of footsteps: her own, Jock's, and Graeme's.

Somewhere close by, she caught Raziel's faint huff of approval as the implication slammed through her.

"Oh, Graeme!" She dashed back to him, pulling him away from the rock face and toward the path. "Look there!" She pointed, her hand trembling as she indicated the evidence. "Your footprints are in the mud, right alongside my own and Jock's."

"They can't be." He looked at her, disbelieving until he followed her outstretched arm, his jaw dropping. "Great gods!" His voice shook, his beautiful dark eyes misting. "The payment of the spell must've been my immortality. It must've been taken from me when I began the incantation. As if I'd regret the loss!"

He whipped around, grabbing her and lifting her in the air, spinning her in a circle. "Sweet lass, do you know what this means?"

"I hope so." Kendra laughed, almost dizzy as he whirled her. Jock joined in, racing madly around them. "I'm thinking it has something to do with making an honest woman of me?"

"It does, sweet. It does." Setting her down, he took her face in his hands, kissing her hard and deep.

And she returned his kiss as soundly. She tangled her fingers in his hair and held him fast, knowing she'd never let him go.

Not Graeme or his dog, whose loud and happy barking made further conversation impossible.

It didn't matter.

She had her answer already.

Graeme loved her and he'd make a proper proposal soon, maybe even that night. Her sixth sense told her it'd be perfect in every way, a moment filled with hope, wonder, and romance. And, she was sure, with Jock having a starring role in the proceedings.

She wouldn't want it any other way.

She did sigh as Graeme drew her closer into his arms.

Someday she'd also thank Zack and Scotland's Past for sending her to Pennard. But first she leaned into Graeme's embrace, her heart swelling with more joy than she would've believed possible.

Then Graeme swept her up in his arms and carried her back along the path to his cottage. Jock went with them, his step light and his tail wagging.

Life was good in Pennard.

Long may it be so.

Turn the page for a glimpse of

SOME LIKE IT KILTED

by Allie Mackay

Mindy Menlove lived in a mausoleum.

A thick-walled medieval castle full of gloom and shadows with just the right dash of Tudor and Gothic to curdle the blood of anyone bold enough to pass through its massive iron-studded door.

Once within, the adventure continued with a maze of dark passageways and rooms crammed to bursting with rich tapestries and heavy, age-blackened furniture. Dust motes thrived, often spinning eerily in the light that spilled through tall, stone-mullioned windows. Some doors squeaked delightfully, and certain floorboards were known for giving the most delicious creaks. Huge carved-stone fireplaces still held lingering traces of the atmosphere-charged scent of peat- and heather-tinged smoke. Or so it was claimed by visitors with noses sensitive to such things.

Few were the modern disfigurements.

Yet the castle did boast hot water, heat, and electricity. Not to mention cable TV and high-speed Internet. MacNeil's Folly was also within the delivery area of the nearest pizza shop. And the daily paper arrived without fail on the steps each morning.

These luxuries were made possible because the ancient pile no longer stood in its original location somewhere on a bleak and windswept Hebridean isle, but on the crest of a thickly wooded hill not far from the quaint and pleasant antiquing mecca of New Hope, Pennsylvania.

Even so, the castle was a haven for hermits.

A recluse's dream.

Only trouble was that Mindy had an entirely different idea of paradise.

White sand, palm trees, and sunshine came to mind. Soft fragrant breezes and—joy of joys—no need to ever dress warm again. A trace of cocoa butter tanning lotion and mai tais sipped at sunset.

A tropical sunset.

Almost there—in her mind, anyway—Mindy imagined the castle's drafty drawing room falling away from her. Bit by bit, everything receded. The plaid carpet and each piece of clunky, carved-oak furniture, and even the heavy, dark blue curtains.

She took a step closer to the window and drew a deep breath. Closing her eyes, she inhaled not the damp scent of cold Bucks County rain and wet, dripping pinewoods, but the heady perfume of frangipani and orchids.

And, because it was her dream, a whiff of fresh-ground Kona coffee.

"You should never have dated a passenger."

"Agggh!" Mindy jumped, almost dropping the mint chocolate wafer she'd been about to pop into her mouth. She'd forgotten she wasn't alone.

All thoughts of Hawaii vanished like a pricked balloon.

Whirling around, she returned the wafer to a delicate bone china plate on a tea tray and sent a pointed look across the room at her sister, Margo, her elder by all of one year.

"What of your watercooler romance with Mr. Computer Geek last year?" Mindy wiped her fingers on a napkin and then frowned when she only smeared the melted chocolate, making an even greater mess. "If I recall, he left you after less than six weeks."

"We parted amicably." Margo peered at her from a high wingback chair near the hearth. "Nor was it a *watercooler affair*. He only came by when the computers at Ye Olde Pagan Times went on the blink. And"—she leaned forward, her eyes narrowing in a way Mindy knew to dread—"neither did I move in with him. I didn't even love him."

Mindy bit the inside of her cheek to keep from snorting.

It wouldn't do to remind her sister that she'd sung a different tune last summer. As she did with every new Romeo that crossed her path, whether he chanced into the New Age shop where Margo worked, or she just stumbled into him on the street.

Margo Menlove was walking flypaper and men were the flies.

They just couldn't resist her.

Not that Mindy minded.

Especially not when she was supposed to be mourning an unfaithful fiancé who'd choked to death on a fish bone during an intimate dinner with a Las Vegas showgirl.

A fiancé she now knew had no intention of marrying her, had used her, and—much to her amazement—had left her his family's displaced Scottish castle and a tidy sum of money to go along with it.

Generosity born of guilt, she was sure.

The naked pole dancer from Vegas hadn't been Hunter MacNeil's only mistress. She'd spotted at least three other possibles at the funeral.

They rose before her mind's eye, each one sleazier than the other. Frowning, Mindy tried to banish them by scrubbing harder at the chocolate smears on her fingers. But even though their faces faded, her every indrawn breath suddenly felt like jagged ice shards cutting into tender places she should never have exposed.

She shuddered.

Margo noticed. "Don't tell me you still care about the bastard?" She leaned forward, bristling. "He used you as a front! His lawyers all but told us he only needed you to meet the terms of his late parents' will. That they'd worried about his *excesses* and made arrangements for him to lose everything unless he became a bulwark of the community, supporting their charities and marrying a good, decent girl!"

"Margo—"

"Don't 'Margo' me. I was there and heard it all." Margo gripped the armrests of her chair until her knuckles whitened. "What I can't believe is that you didn't see through him in the first place."

Mindy gave up trying to get rid of the chocolate. "You'd have fallen for him, too," she snapped, scrunching the napkin in her hand. "If he'd—"

"What?" Margo shot to her feet. "If I were a flight attendant working first class and he'd sat in the last row—wearing a wink and a smile—and with his kilt oh-so-conveniently snagged in his seat belt?"

"It wasn't like that. . . ." Mindy let the words trail off.

It *had* been like that and she was the greatest fool in the world for not seeing through his ploy.

But his dimpled smile had charmed her and he'd blushed, actually *blushed*, when she'd bent down to help him with the seat belt buckle and her fingers accidentally brushed a very naked part of him.

When the buckle sprang free and his kilt flipped up, revealing that nakedness, he'd appeared so embarrassed that accepting his dinner invitation seemed the least she could do to make him feel better.

He'd also been incredibly good-looking and had a way with words, even if he hadn't had a Scottish burr. He could look at a woman and make her feel as if no other female in the world existed, and topping it all, he'd had a great sense of humor. And, besides, what girl with red blood in her veins could resist a man in a kilt?

What wasn't to love?

Everything, she knew now.

Furious at herself, Mindy slid a glance at the hearth fire. A portrait of one of his ancestors hung there, claiming pride of place above the black marble mantel. An early MacNeil chieftain, or so Hunter had claimed, calling the man *Bran of Barra*, his was the only ancestral portrait in the castle that didn't give Mindy the willies.

A big brawny man in full Highland regalia and with a shock of wild, auburn hair and a gorgeous red beard, he didn't have the fierce-eyed glower worn by the other clan chieftains whose portraits lined the castle's long gallery. His portrait—the very same one—hung there, too. It was his mirth-filled face that she always sought when she was convinced that the gazes of the other chieftains followed her every move.

Bran of Barra's twinkling blue gaze looked elsewhere, somewhere inside his portrait that she couldn't

see. Yet she'd always felt that whatever held his attention, if he'd been aware of her ill ease, he'd turn her way.
His eyes would twinkle even more and he'd say something bold and outrageous, guaranteed to make her
smile. He'd been that sort of man, she just knew it.

Mindy took a breath.

She couldn't help but compare Hunter with his rough-
and-ready ancestor. Where Hunter would have chided
her for her fears, Bran of Barra would've banished them.

Silly or not, he made her feel safe. Only by keeping
her eyes on him could she flit through the endless, dark-
paneled gallery without breaking out in goose bumps.

Sadly, his roguish smile now reminded her of Hunter's.

Scowling again, she turned away from the portrait
and curled her hands into tight fists. How fitting that
Hunter had also dashed her only means of reaching the
upper floors of the castle without having a heebie-
jeebies attack.

"You can get back at him, you know." Margo stepped
in front of her, a conspiratorial glint in her eye. "Have
you thought about turning the castle into an esoteric
center? I know the customers at Ye Olde Pagan Times
would love to hold sessions here. Fussy as Hunter always was about *image*, he'd turn in his grave."

Mindy stared at her. "Didn't you hear what I said earlier? I'm selling the castle. I want nothing more than to
get as far away from here as—"

"But you can't!" Margo grabbed her arm, squeezing
tight. "The castle's haunted. I told you, I got an orb on a
photo I took in the long gallery yesterday. Three orbs if
we count the two faint ones."

"Orbs are specks of dust." Mindy tried not to roll her
eyes. "Everyone knows that."

Margo sniffed. "There are orbs and *orbs*. What I got

on film was spirit energy. I'm telling you"—she let go of Mindy's arm and tossed back her chin-length blond hair, a style and color both sisters shared—"you can put this place on the paranormal map. People will come from all around the country to ghost hunt and—"

"Oh, no, they won't." Mindy flopped down on a chair, her head beginning to pound. "There aren't any ghosts here. Hunter was sure of that and so am I. And"—she aimed her best my-decision-is-final look at her sister—"the only place I'm putting this miserable old pile is on the market."

"But that's crazy." Margo sounded scandalized. "Owning a haunted castle is the chance of a lifetime."

"Yes, it is." Mindy sat back and folded her arms. "It's my chance to go back to the airlines and move to Hawaii. I can invest the money from the sale of the castle and what Hunter left me and live off my flight attendant salary. It'd be no trouble at all to commute from Oahu or even Maui. And best of all"—she felt wonderfully free at the thought—"I doubt there are many Scotsmen in Hawaii. They can't take the heat.

"The Scots thrive on cold and rain and mist." Mindy lifted her chin, well aware her words wouldn't sit well with her Scotophile sister. "You did know that the hottest-selling clothing article in Scotland is thermal underwear?"

"You're not thinking clearly." Margo picked up her purse and moved to the door. "I'll come back in the morning after you've had a good night's sleep. We'll talk then."

"Only if you're ready to help me find the right real estate agent," Mindy called after her sister's retreating back. "I've already spoken with a few."

And each one had sounded more than eager to list MacNeil's Folly.

Mindy smiled and reached for the mint chocolate wafer she'd almost eaten earlier. Then she helped herself to another and another until the little bone china plate was empty. Chocolate was good for the soul.

And there weren't any ghostly *souls* spooking about the castle.

Not disguised as orbs or otherwise.

Her sister was crazy.

And *she* was going to Hawaii.

But first she needed some sleep. Margo was right about that. Regrettably, when she left the drawing room, she found the rest of the castle filled with a thin, drifting haze. Cold and silvery, thready wisps of it gathered in the corridors and snaked past the tall, Gothic window arches. An illusion that surely had everything to do with the night's full moon just breaking through the fast-moving rain clouds and nothing at all to do with the *orbs* that her sister claimed were darting around the long gallery.

Or so she thought until she neared that dreaded room and caught the unmistakable strains of a bagpipe. A haunting old Gaelic air that stopped the instant she neared the gallery's open door.

A door she always took care to keep closed.

Mindy's stomach dropped and her knees started to tremble. But when she heard footsteps on the long gallery's polished wood floorboards and the low murmur of many men's voices, she got mad and strode forward.

It wouldn't surprise her if Margo and her crazy New Age friends were playing a trick on her.

A notion she had to discard the minute she reached the threshold and looked into the angry faces of Hunter's Highland chieftain ancestors. There could be no doubt that it was them because with the exception of Bran of Barra's portrait at the far end of the long room, the ferocious-looking clansmen's large gold-gilt portrait frames were empty.

She also recognized them.

And this time they weren't just following her with their oil-on-canvas eyes.

They were in the room. And they were glaring at her.

Glaring, and *floating* her way.

Some even brandished swords.

"Oh my God!" Mindy's eyes rounded and she clapped a hand to her cheek.

Heart thundering, she tried to slam the door and run, but a handful of the scowling clansmen were quicker. Before she could blink, they surrounded her, their huge kilted bodies blocking her escape.

Kilted, plaid-draped bodies she could see through!

Mindy felt the floor dip beneath her feet as they swept closer, their frowns black as night and their eyes glinting furiously in the moonlight. Soon, she feared, she might be sick. She *wished* she could faint.

Her sister wasn't the crazy one.

She was.

Or else she was about to meet a gaggle of real live ghosts.

And since the latter seemed unlikely, she'd just lost her marbles. She took a deep breath and lifted her chin, peering back at them as if they weren't a pack of wild-eyed, see-through Highlanders.

Then she folded her arms and waited calmly. It was a trick she'd learned in airline training.

How to keep cool at all times.

She just hoped they couldn't tell she was faking.

She was sure she didn't want to know what would happen if they guessed.

ABOUT THE AUTHOR

Allie Mackay is the alter ego of Sue-Ellen Welfonder, a *USA Today* bestselling author who writes Scottish medieval romances. Her twenty-year airline career allowed her to see the world, but it was always to Scotland that she returned. Now a full-time writer, she admits that she much prefers wielding a pen to pushing tea and coffee. She spent fifteen years living in Europe and used that time to explore as many castle ruins, medieval abbeys, and stone circles as possible. Anything ancient, crumbling, or lichened caught her eye. She makes frequent visits to Scotland, insisting they are a necessity, as each trip gives her inspiration for new books.

Proud of her own Hebridean ancestry, she belongs to two clan societies and never misses a chance to attend Highland Games. In addition to Scotland, her greatest passions are medieval history, the paranormal, and dogs. She rarely watches television, loves haggis, and writes at a 450-year-old desk that once stood in a Bavarian castle.

Readers can visit her at: www.alliemackay.com.